From the Bottom to the Top

The Jackson Street Dreamer

By Ron Howard

This book was written with the hope that some young man or woman would be inspired to believe that they can change any negativity in their lives to something positive. This story takes the reader through the streets of violence, love, sadness, drugs, poverty, military and God. This all happens in no special order, but when it does you will feel it. This book is based on a true story; most people do not live to tell this kind of story. Ron Jackson believes that God saved his life so that he could tell this story and hopefully help troubled youth in the world to believe in positive change.

Publish by: JACKSON STREET DREAMER Publications

Author "Ron Howard"
Edited and Published by
Jackson Street Dreamer Publications

ISBN# 978-0-9795119-0-5
LCCN#2007929342

Additional copies of this book are available by mail. Send $14.95 each (include tax and postage) made payable to:

Ron Howard
P.O.Box 4322 Pittsburgh, PA 15204

Purchase on web site at
www.jacksonstreetdreamerpublications.com
Email-jacksonstreetdreamer@yahoo.com

Printed in the U.S.A. by
Morris Publishing
3212 East Highway 30
Kearney, NE 68847
1-800-650-7888

Introduction

The following story is based on a true story. All the character names are fictitious and any resemblance is entirely coincidental. This story starts with early childhood, through adolescence and into early adulthood. This story is set back in the 70's and 80's during times of violence and a lot of cocaine. This story takes the reader from a small town in Pennsylvania "Brownsville" to Miami Beach Florida, the land of cocaine and dreams. When readers are done with that trip, then they will travel through the military guarding nuclear weapons and selling military drugs as a drug dog handler for the Air Force Security Police in Hampton, Virginia for eight years. Ron Jackson made millions of dollars and not one dollar of that money made him happy. When he retired from the drug game, Ron did not take any of the money into his retirement because He felt the money was cursed. Back in the 70's and 80's, drug money was buried in the ground until he could figure out what to do with it. The money that was made is still in the ground and can still be found if you pay attention to what the book says about the money.

The reason that Ron Jackson believes this story should be written is that hopefully it will be an inspiration to others who have gone through similar hardships in their lives. Ron believes in change because that is what he did with his life. He doesn't have any regrets about his change; He just wishes that he would have done it sooner. No one told him that he could change; Ron had to find out the hard way. He hopes that after reading his story, you will not have to go through the pain that he did to realize this possibility. Most of all, it is his hope that writing this story will bring some closure within himself----a way of cleansing for him. Ron has been carrying these demons of his past for twenty years and it is time to put them behind him. He is hoping this can be done by putting his past in a book, instead of keeping it in his mind.

The individuals who lived on Jackson Street really do not like to talk about how they lived and what happened to them on Jackson Street. This street no longer exists, except in the nightmares of their minds. Everyone who lived on Jackson Street wanted to get up that hill from Jackson Street, but no one wanted it more than him. Ron is one of the few to make it "From the Bottom to the Top" where he thought his happiness would be. He has found that the truth must be told before one can be freed from the past. This book is dedicated to the memories of those who lived and survived the poverty of Jackson Street. Believe in change and you will change….

Acknowledgments

First and foremost, I would like to thank God for saving me from the streets of crime and violence. I would like to thank my wife who stood behind me at times when I doubted myself. You are my boo, my heart, my soul mate and my best friend; there would be no me without you. I realize that it is not easy dealing with a creative mind like mine---- spending hours writing down my thoughts, working and going to school, sometimes not spending enough time with you and my children. You have made dealing with these things seem effortless and I love you for that Monica. My deepest gratitude goes to all my children who helped create the man that I am today. My children stirred the fires of change for me and they are the reasons for my struggles to be a better man.

I would like to express thanks and appreciation to my immediate and extended family: A special thanks to all my children for all the love and support in writing this book. My brothers and sisters: Larry, Gerald, Diane, David, Robert, Jimmy, Armand, Sandy, Cathy, L'Shona, and Sheldon. All my nieces, nephews and the rest of my extended family. A special thanks to Harry and Joan Garrett, you have welcomed me into your family and I'm glad you did. A special thanks to Mary Shaw, who has helped me so much in preparing this story for print. I would like to thank all my professors who helped me so far through my educational career. I would like to give a special thanks to Carla Young, who helped me to organize my thoughts for writing this book. A special thanks to Mr. Canada of CCAC, your encouragement meant a lot to me. I would like to thank all the staff and kids at Holy family Institute, especially "Steve Rush" (AKA) Gene Iverson of St. Pats, who encouraged me to keep writing. A special thanks to Dave A.DiMichele, who is one of God's gifts to troubled youth in the world. I would like to thank all my classmates at the University of Pittsburgh in Developmental Psychology program "class of 2007", especially my smoking partner "Elizabeth". I would like to give a special thanks to Mrs. Delores Redding and her husband Josh, who first introduced me to God and inspired me to seek his help----you helped to create my foundation of love for God. A special thanks to all the members of the 1st Security Police Squad of Langley Air Force Base Virginia, from 1978 to 1986, we had fun. A special thanks to Clayton and Sandy Wiggins for all the good times at your house in Virginia. A special thanks to my God mom, "Louise Fleetwood" you were the mother that I never had, your memory stays in my heart and thanks for the two crazy sisters "Sandy and Cathy". A special thanks to Chucky and Denise Penn, you are an inspiration to everyone who knows you. A special thanks to Mrs. Thelma Dickinson, you are the kindest person that I know. A special thanks to the Uniontown Karate School and all the members----past and now. A special thanks to the Pa. Shotokan Karate School of Pittsburgh and all the members. A special thanks to "Helen Savage", your memory lives on. A special thanks to "Ethel Howard", you are my beginning, your memory lives on in our hearts. A special thanks to the Armand and Sandy Shackelford, you guys have made my summer vacations for the last eight years very special. A special thanks to my sister-in-law Brenda and her husband Richard Smith. A special shout out to a great singer, "Sheldon Price" you can buy his music at www.myspace.com/sheldonprice1. A special thanks to the staff at Hess Therapy, you are the greatest. A special thanks to Donald and Kena Johnson, can I be your caddy when you get to the "U.S. Open" in golf? To all my friends, family and haters, I say "Believe in change"

Chapter 1

Looking Back

My father "David Carl Jackson" was born in Dayton, Ohio and was in the military navy seals for many years. There were only two in his family; there was my aunt "Cinderella" and my father. My mother "Estelle Edwin," who was born and raised in Philadelphia, Pennsylvania, she was a city girl who moved to the small town of Brownsville, Pa. to get away from the big city to raise a family. Most of my mother's life she was in and out of orphanages and that affected the way she interacted with her children. There were 14 children in her family, 13 girls and one boy. My mother met my father in a club in Philadelphia while he was traveling in the military. They got married and had five children together, four boys and one girl, "David Carl Jackson Jr.", who was named after my father, "Gary Edward Jackson", "Robert Jackson", "Marie Jackson" and me "Ron Jackson". All of us were two years apart in age; there was an eight year difference between the oldest and the youngest child. When my parents got together, they moved to a little place called Brownsville, Pennsylvania. They did not stay together long, but they did stay together long enough to make five children.

My father was in and out of my mother's life throughout the whole relationship. I actually never met the man; I remember vaguely seeing his face, over the top of his knees when I was three years old. I was told that he was a tall man, about six feet five and about 240 pounds of muscle. He is a light skinned black man with dark brown hair and clean shaved; he looked like he could have some Indian in his blood. My mother was a small lady; she was approximately five feet two and maybe 125 pounds when they met. She had a medium brown complexion, with short brown hair that she always had curled. We moved to Jackson Street from Cemetery Road, our first house in Brownsville, Pa. There were five kids in the family to move and our father was not even there to help my mother move us. Our father never actually lived with us because he was traveling a lot in the military. He would occasionally stop by and help my mother make a child here and there until there were five of us. This did not make my mother a very happy person, and eventually she resorted to drinking alcohol, which in turn affected the way we had to live.

Jackson Street was about five blocks long and on one side of Jackson Street there was a creek we called Dunlap Creek. The good thing about this creek was that every year we were able to go swimming in it. The bad thing about the creek was that every year it would flood our house. The only good thing about our house getting flooded was the fact that the Red Cross would give us new clothes and furniture. Usually after the flood, everything in the house was destroyed; that is why we got new things. Every family on Jackson Street was fatherless, which meant about twenty families being raised by single mothers. I do not recall ever seeing anybody with a father on Jackson Street as long as I lived there.

We called my oldest brother David “Dooner” because he could not say Junior. Even at age ten, if you asked him his name, he would say “My name is Dooner”. My brother Gary was called groundhog and if you saw his teeth you would understand why they called him groundhog. When people saw his teeth, they felt that he could eat an apple through a fence if he wanted to. My nickname was “Cool Breeze” because I was quiet like a cool breeze and did not show much emotion when I was around other people. My memory of my life on Jackson Street started when I was three years old. My first memories of Jackson Street include my two brothers, David and Gary; we were sitting in a ditch across from our house. My oldest brother David said, “Two and two is six”; then my other brother Gary said, “No two and two is five". I told them both that the answer was four, and they got mad at me. Well needless to say they called me stupid, then beat me up and chased my little butt back home. They did find out later that I was right about the answer, but that did not matter to them. I must have heard it somewhere and that was just an indication of how well my memory was at age three. I could always remember almost everything that I heard, no matter whether I wanted to or not. My brothers seemed to always want to be right in spite of their lack of intelligence at times, but I got used to that from them.

None of the mothers had jobs on Jackson Street and on the weekends we always ended up over this old lady's house, "Mrs. Cassidy". She lived about ten miles from Jackson Street, in a little town called Redstone, which was more of a rural area. It was nothing like Jackson Street, thank God for that. My mother's dates would drive all of us over to Mrs. Cassidy's house. Mrs. Cassidy was like ninety years old and thinking back on it, she must have had a stroke. When she would cook our food, she would always slobber on everybody's food. My mother took us to Mrs. Cassidy's house on Friday around five in the afternoon and we spent the whole weekend there while my mother was out drinking and having fun. Eventually she would come back on Sundays around four in the afternoon to pick us up. During that time we had to endure Mrs. Cassidy; she was a strict old lady---however, she meant well for us. She was a fairly good cook and the food looked great, but she had this problem with slobbering every ten to fifteen seconds. Slobber was coming out of her mouth just as she put each plate on the table. When we saw the slobber falling on our food, it would turn our stomachs, but we were so hungry we ate around the slobber.

She always served spinach no matter what kind of meat she cooked that day. At that time in our lives spinach had to be the nastiest piece of shit in the whole wide world, but if you did not eat your spinach you were not able to get your drink. That drink was very special to us, so we ate that spinach. All of my brothers and my sister ate their spinach, but I figured out a way to get around eating my spinach. I would put the spinach in my mouth and then the first chance I had, I would spit the spinach in my hand. When no one was looking, I would slide it in my pocket until it was all gone off my plate. Well at least my siblings and Mrs. Cassidy thought it was all gone. I had a pocket full of green spinach, but I got my Kool-Aid to drink. I never told my siblings the truth about the spinach because I knew they would snitch on me and I would be in big trouble with Mrs. Cassidy. We told on each other no matter what, because it was a joy to see each other get in trouble in those days. I do not remember Mrs. Cassidy ever hitting any of us and we never did anything wrong at her house because we were all scared to death of her. We, in our minds thought she would slobber on us until we drowned.

I found it interesting how my mother would come on Sundays to pick us up and act like there was nothing in the world wrong with how she lived. She just gave Mrs. Cassidy some money and took her little rascals back down to Jackson Street. I guess when I think about it, it did give us a chance to get away from Jackson Street; I guess you could call it our little vacation. Maybe that is the way my mom thought about it; at least we were safe while she was out drinking and having fun. I cannot really make a call on that idea because I never had to walk in my mother's shoes. This is just one way of looking at our situation at Mrs. Cassidy's house on the weekends.

Our house on Jackson Street was a gray two-story house that had two medium size bedrooms. We had two sets of bunk beds in one room so that all four of the boys could sleep in one room. My sister slept in the other room with my mother. We did not have a bathroom in the house; instead, we had a thing they called a "slop jar". The slop jar was emptied every night before we went to bed to get some of the smell out of the house. All the boys took turns emptying the jar; I hated it when my turn came because it smelled so bad. That smell seemed to get in your pores and nostrils; you could not get it out. The slop jar was a metal bucket with a top on it that we use to piss and shit into. The only other alternative was to go outside to the outhouse, located in the back yard of the house. Why in the hell anyone called it the outhouse I do not know because it really was not a house. It was a little wooden shack and inside the shack there were two holes in the seats where people would sit. We could either take a shit or piss into the holes; this was a fucked up way to live.

We did not have a furnace, but we had coal stoves and the coal stoves actually heated the house. We had one stove downstairs plus one stove upstairs in the hallway right outside the bedrooms. We actually had electricity, but we did not have any electrical heat in the house. In the basement there was an opening that went into the house and once a month the coal truck would come and dump coal into the basement of the house. We would have to go in the basement and put some coal into a bucket and carry it upstairs and put it into the stoves a couple of times a day in the winter time. One could only imagine what the house smelled like considering the fumes and stuff that came from the coal stoves, but we were so used to the smell that it did not bother us anymore.

Since we did not have a bathroom, we had to take our baths in this little round metal tub in the hallway. We filled it with water and warmed the water up on the electric stove downstairs. We stood in the middle of the small tub and washed ourselves the best we could without falling on our asses. We were used to that. Until we got older we did not care much about washing our asses anyway. The tub was actually next to the slop jar. We were used to that particular style of living, and everybody on Jackson Street lived the same way so that was no big deal.

We were on welfare and we never had much of anything. We would get one pair of shoes at the beginning of a school year, and the pair of shoes had to last us all year. After a couple months, the shoes would have holes in them and that is when we developed the concept of putting cardboard in our shoes to prevent our feet from touching the ground as we were walking, running or playing. It was because of that, I promised myself that when I grew up, I would always have too many shoes to wear on my feet.

Every year the families on Jackson Street got flooded and most of the time I would pray for the flood, because every time the flood came it meant that I was getting some new clothes from the Red Cross. We learned to make the best of a bad situation when the floods came. During the rainy season or after a long winter when the snow would melt and run down from the mountains, the creek would flood. The creek, which normally was only about ten feet wide and five feet deep, would turn into a small river after a couple of days. The first flood was very scary for me; I was probably about four years old at the time. We were sitting on the front porch when we first saw the water come over the banks. This was very exciting at first for us. We went over to look closer at it; the water kept edging up closer to the street. The next thing I knew, it crossed the street into our front yard. Eventually it started to come up to the first step to the house and then up the second step, then it was on the porch. My mom said, "Move everything upstairs right now". We did not have much to move upstairs anyway, so we moved ourselves upstairs.

Of course my mom knew that we left the old couch and old beat up stove downstairs. She knew that if the flood-water would enter the house, then we would get new furniture or better stuff than what we had in the house. The water came up into the house while we were upstairs looking down at the first floor. The water only edged up maybe six inches every hour, so it did not come up all of a sudden. We went down in the living room after we got a couple feet of water downstairs. We took the tub that we used to take our baths in and took turns floating around downstairs to have some fun. We tied a rope to the tub just in case the water current came to strong and whisked us out the door into the street. When it came time for me to get in the tub, I was a little nervous because I did not trust my brothers. They put me in the tub, and then they had the rope supposedly tied until they got me close enough to the door. The damn current pulled me out of the house through an open door. They finally pulled me back in the house because I was outside the house screaming loudly for my mom. I was crying like a baby because I was terrified of drowning in the flood waters. They finally pulled me back in the house after about five minutes of hell for me.

When I got back in the house; the rope slipped out of their hands and I was floating around on the first floor scared to death. Those dumb ass brothers of mine were sitting there laughing and joking while I was screaming until finally my mom came down the steps. She walked across the room in the two or three feet of water and snatched me out of the tub and slapped me upside my damn head for being in the tub. I tried to tell her that David and Gary told me that it was alright to float around in the tub. We were not allowed to do that anymore after that incident because I almost floated down the street. I think that would have made my brothers real happy if I would have floated down the street that day. God willing, I did not go floating down the street that day because they pulled me back in time----probably because I made so much noise. We could hear up and down the streets kids laughing and having fun in their houses. You would think the kids were at an amusement park having fun on a sunny summer day. These people were in a flood and all you heard was children laughing and joking. All the other families on Jackson Street were doing the same things we were doing. They were there floating around in their washtubs too and some of them actually had made little rafts to float on the water in their houses.

If you were standing on top of the hill and looking down on Jackson Street during the floods, you would hear laughter and playing coming from the houses. This would make an outsider scratch his head and wonder what was going on down there on Jackson Street. It was not like we had anything else to do during the floods, so we tried to turn a bad situation into some fun. The mothers were upstairs or sitting on the roofs of their houses passing their drinks back and forth to each other having fun too. I remember during several floods, Ms. Margot and Ms. Irene fell off the roof into the flood waters because they were so damn drunk. You should have seen the people trying to get them out of the water. It was funny to watch. Everybody on Jackson Street could swim, if they were not too drunk to swim. What we did on Jackson Street was probably something that no one else did; we turned a flood into fun. That was what we had to do; that was tradition; drinking was a tradition; flooding was tradition; being poor as hell was tradition. But that was Jackson Street.

I do not remember anyone ever telling me that my biological father had ever been on Jackson Street, but I always heard that he was watching over us. We were big Buster Jackson's kids. Nobody would mess with us. Buster was my dad's nickname. He was known as a big bad motherfucker. You did not want to fuck with Buster Jackson if you wanted to stay alive. They called him Buster for obvious reasons. He was a big man and if he hit you, he would bust you up. My mom was a city girl from Philadelphia; every other word out of her mouth was profanity. I was not sure what my name was because I do not remember her calling me Ron at all from ages one to twelve. It was always you little motherfucker or you little bastard or you son of a bitch----those were my three names. As matter of fact, they were every child's name in the neighborhood. Shit if it was not for us telling each other what our real names were, we would have continued to think that everybody's name was motherfucker, son of a bitch, bastard, dumb, and stupid. I would say, "My name is Ron, is your name dumb bastard?" No! That is just what my mama calls me all the time.

Jackson Street was a place where you did not just have just your own mother; you had the other twenty mothers that took care of you. On different days, you could go down to the Towers family's house for dinner or you could go over to the Fitzgo's house to have dinner. Only occasionally was my mother home, and you could eat dinner at my house, maybe twice a week. It has been said, "It takes a whole village to raise a child". Well I cannot say they did a good job of raising us because there were a lot of hungry days, but they did the best they could with what they had. When it came to dinner time one piece of chicken was all you were allowed to have and we always got the bullshit pieces of chicken, like the thighs. My mother would get the chicken breast, and if she had male company, he would get the legs or wings. We always got the thighs but were happy to get that because we were always hungry. We grew up on fried chicken and fried potatoes at my house. We ate so much chicken that I dreamed that we had wings to fly off Jackson Street to live a better life.

Now as far as snacks--sweets, you would have to steal that from somebody to get that kind of stuff. Once a month, when the food stamps came, we would have a donut or some cookies as a treat. If we were lucky, we might get one donut or two cookies a piece that day. We were not going to get filled up on any snacks unless we were able to steal something sweet from someone in the neighborhood. There was a little penny candy store up the street called "Gisays", which was owned by a little Italian woman. The kids in the neighborhood would go up to Gisays with a couple pennies or maybe even a nickel to buy some candy. We would always steal some candy once we got in the store; we only had a little money and we just could not resist stealing some extra candy. That is the only way we could get some candy and that is how I learned my first words in Italian. This old woman would come out the store after she caught us stealing the candy; she would say "Bafungu". I never knew what that meant until I was older; it means "fuck you" in Italian.

Another way of getting something sweet was to rob the Goody man, who was the ice cream truck man. He came around once a day in the summer time. I do not know why he came down to Jackson Street since we never had any damn money. What we did was hide on the side of the street back in the bushes, and then one of us that had money would stop the truck to buy something. When the old white man pulled off, we would jump on the back of the truck then open the door up and start throwing the ice cream off the truck. We got maybe about a block before he noticed us and stopped the truck to chase us. We would get ten or fifteen things off the truck, but by the time we got all the stuff off the truck, the other half would melt before we got to eat it. We did not get to rob the truck often, but when we did, we had fun doing it. If we were lucky, we could rob it twice a month during the summer months. We would do anything to get something sweet because the people on Jackson Street usually did not have anything sweet to eat.

Occasionally my mother would have a man spend the night and get her groove on. I was about five years old when I first noticed that they would always come in late at night, drunk, and both of them would fall asleep on the couch. I noticed that inside of the man's pockets there would always be some money. What made me put two and two together was occasionally we would meet some of these men the next morning. The man would say, "Hey boy here's a quarter, hey boy here's a nickel, here's a dime now go get some candy, and get the hell out of the house". The man always reached into his pocket to get some money so that they could get us out of the house. I did not care who got fucked, as long as I got some money to get some candy. I started waiting for my mom to come back from the bar, which was at two o'clock in the morning. They would eventually pass out drunk on the couch. I would sneak downstairs on my little tip-toes and go into the man's pockets, but I never did take all their money because I knew that all hell would break loose the next day. I did take enough to last me a couple days at the candy store. Of course I never did tell my brothers about this plan of mine because I knew that even if I took the money, they would take it off of me.

One day I asked my two oldest brothers to go to the store with me. I told them I would get them some candy and all three of us went to the store. They were both holding my hands and we were just skipping to the store as happy as we could be. We got to the one side of the street, and these cars were flying by us. They said, "wait, wait, wait" because you might get run over by a car. My brother Gary said, "You see that car coming down the street, I bet you that I can beat everyone across the street before that car gets up here". I thought that would be my chance to beat my older brother at something and make him angry. The car got closer and closer, and then my brother said, "I'm going to count to three and we are going to race across the street". So he said one, two, and three, go". I ran into the street. I got right in the middle of the road before that motherfuckin car ran my little ass over. The car dragged me they said, about 150 feet down the street. It literally took all the skin off my chest and the front part of my body, but not my face. I don't remember any of that because I got knocked out instantly.

I woke up a month later in the hospital after I had been in a coma for a month. The first thing I saw was the white man who ran me over sitting next to my bed. He gave me a gift, and I think he said he was sorry for hitting me with his car; I'm not sure because I was still in a daze. I do not remember seeing my mother or any other family members that day. I just saw the white man. He gave me a cowboy outfit and then he left the hospital with tears in his eyes. I took the cowboy outfit out of the box, and I sat it next to my bed. I took the box and sat it at the end of my bed just to get it out of the way. I was lying there sleeping and when I woke, I heard this jingling sound like coins banging together on my bed. I looked up and saw the white people that were visiting the hospital were throwing money into the brown box that my cowboy uniform came in.

I noticed that when they saw that I was awake, they didn't throw any money in there, so I pretended to be asleep when they were around. I was pretending to be asleep whenever I saw a white woman or man at the door because I knew they would give me more money. When they seen the other coins in the box they would reach in their pockets and throw some more coins in there. After a couple weeks of this, the box was so full of coins that I could barely lift it in the air. I don't remember seeing any of that money because my mother took it from me. My mom may have given me a little change to put in my pocket, but I have no idea what happened to all that change----I'm sure my mom drank all of those coins away. Now that I think back on how big that box was and how it was filled with dimes, nickels, and pennies, I think there probably was about $100 or maybe even $200. Lord knows she drank well for many, many weeks with all that change.

I did go home in my little cowboy outfit, and I was the talk of the neighborhood. I jumped out of the taxi in my cowboy uniform and all the kids in the neighborhood ran up to me and wanted to touch my outfit. I sat on my porch in my cowboy suit and I probably wore that thing for about thirty straight days. I don't even believe I took a bath that month because I did not want to take my suit off. I loved my cowboy outfit, and that was my reward for getting run over. I am not sure it was worth getting run over by a car. I never did forgive my brothers for getting me run over by a car. I think it was pretty cold of them to send their brother out in the middle of the damn street to get hit by a damn car. I guess they thought getting hit by a car would have been funny or maybe they didn't think that I would do it. All you had to do was dare me and I would do anything without even thinking about it twice because I'm a competitor at heart. I did have my cowboy outfit and that made me a happy little five year old. Broke, poor, dirty, but I had my cowboy outfit. "***Believe in Change***"

Chapter 2

The Revenge

Well it had been about a month since that car hit me and something unusual happened; everyone was being nice to me on Jackson Street. People were bringing me little gifts, like candy, and neighbors were making me pies. Everyone in the neighborhood came to see me and to ask how I was doing. My biological father never did stop by to see how I was doing, but that did not bother me because I never saw him anyway. On Jackson Street, it was no big deal not to see your father.

Every once in a while I would hear the grownups outside talking about how they thought it was a miracle that I was alive, considering that I was hit by a big old car, then dragged for 150 feet and how none of the tires ever ran over me. I didn't have any broken bones and I only spent a six weeks in the hospital. The skin was ripped off my body, but the doctor said it would grow back without a problem. The doctors said there were no permanent injuries, and I would be good as new in a couple of months.

I just thought that the grown folks in the neighborhood were stopping by the house because they wanted to see the little black miracle boy. This was fine with me, because every time somebody came by they always came with something to give to me. It might have just been a nickel, or dime, or a candy bar or something; I think they just wanted to be near the miracle boy. It was attention that I was not used to getting, because everything up until then was negative attention.

Months later I was still wearing my cowboy suit everywhere that I went. Every once and awhile, my mom made me take it off so she could wash it. Once it was washed, I would put it back on and if it took too long to dry, I would put it on wet and go back out and sit on the front porch. That was the only thing I was allowed to do for the next couple months. The doctors told my mom that I had to take it easy for a couple of months to make sure that I was healing properly. The car accident that happened to me started getting old in the neighborhood and it wasn't really a big thing anymore. Before I knew it, life on Jackson Street was getting back to normal and I was being treated like shit again.

I was tired of sitting on the porch; it was time for fun and games again. As soon as I got the freedom to be able to stray away from the porch, I wanted to play cowboys and Indians. This was an obvious choice for me considering I had my cowboy suit on all of the time. I was the only one in the whole neighborhood that had a real cowboy suit, and I was proud of it. The other kids may have made up something in which they called a cowboy suit, some old raggedy shit hanging off their head, some old raggedy shit hanging off their waist, but I had a real holster, my toy gun and my boots. My suit was blue with a little vest, and I had a real cowboy hat. The cowboy hat was also blue and I was the shit when I had my suit on; nobody could tell me that I was not the shit.

The first thing that I wanted to organize was a cowboy and Indian fight in the neighborhood; we chose sides and I ended up with the retarded kid named "Dewey". Most of the time, he did not know what he was doing; so someone had to tell him. I had to make sure that he shot at the right team because he was dumb as hell. My brothers, David and Gary, were on the other team. I was happy about that because I really wanted to mess them up anyway. Now in order to have a cowboy and Indian fight, we had to make our bow and arrows to shoot at each other. And in order to make bows and arrows, we had to find a nice tree limb, which could bend enough to put a string on it. We cut grooves in both ends of the limb and would take a fishing string and tie it at each end. Then we bent it until it was real tight like a bow should be, so we could get a lot of power when we shot the bow. The next thing we did was to go get some more tree limbs, thinner ones, and cut the tips so that they would be real sharp. We put leaves on the back of the arrow by attaching them to grooves that we cut into the end of the arrows. If we pulled it, we could probably shoot maybe 50 to 100 feet away. It was not that great with accuracy. We thought if we got lucky we would be able to shoot someone's eye out.

What we used for guns was a stick with the bark cut off of it. We would wrap some string around it and make a little handle. We used our fingers so we could act like you were pulling the trigger. You could go without the handle and act like we were pulling the trigger by just using your finger, but either way it was better or more authentic with the bow and arrow because you could actually shoot the arrows from the bows. So even though I had a gun and the cowboy suit, I also wanted to have a bow and arrow. I was the head of the cowboys, and I thought I should have at least two weapons. I wanted to have something that would really shoot something at someone.

We picked sides. There were about ten of us altogether; there were five Indians and five cowboys. We went across the street to play in some ditches along the side of the street. There was a ditch on each side of the road, and when we got a chance, we shot over at the Indians. The problem with that was the Indians had the bows, and arrows and they had real shit flying over our heads at us. The only good thing about the cowboys, which was my side, was that I had a bow to shoot back at the Indians. I had a bow and I had a lot of arrows, because all my cowboys had made arrows for my bow. The Indians on the other side had about four or five arrows a piece, and I knew they would run out soon. I was waiting until all of their arrows were gone, so I could shoot them when they tried to make some more arrows. I was sitting there counting them and about the time I realized that all their arrows were gone they said, "We need a time out so we can make more arrows". I told them they couldn't have a time out because this was war, so they had just better stay hidden over there.

David did not listen and he tried sneaking out of the ditch, but I could see his big head moving around. I got my bow and shot at the only thing I could see, and that was his big ass head. I did not really want to shoot him in the head; I wanted to shoot him in his back or something. He kept peeking around with his big head, and I remember thinking that he was the same motherfucker that helped me get hit by that car, so if the arrow hit him in the head, then too bad for him. It was just my luck that when I shot that arrow, it stuck in the side of his head. He wiggled, shook and fell in the ditch crying in pain. He finally got out of the ditch and I could see exactly where I shot him. He tripped with the arrow still hanging out of his head. My other brother Gary (Who was also on the Indian's side) got up to help him by trying to pull the arrow out of David's head. I decided to shoot Gary too, since he also helped me get hit by that car. I knew that I was going to be in trouble with my mom anyway, so I might as well get him too. He was bent over trying to wrestle with David to get the arrow out his head, I looked at his big ass and it just looked like a perfect target. I took another big arrow out and I pulled back as hard as I could on the bow and let it go. It hit him right in his right ass cheek, and he screamed like a little bitch and quit trying to help David. He started running down the street with the arrow hanging out of his ass. It looked so funny with him running with my arrow hanging out his ass; we could hardly stop laughing at him.

David finally got up, and they were both running towards the house with arrows hanging from them. My mother looked at them and could not believe what she was looking at. My mother reached down and pulled the arrow out of David's head and snatched the arrow out of Gary's ass. We had to call the game over because these two big ass cry-babies went home and told on me. My mother was walking up the street hollering for me, screeching about how she was going to beat my ass. I took the bow that I had and threw it over towards Dewey so my mother would think he had the bow. I told her that I did not even have a bow and since I was a cowboy, all I had was this little gun here on the side, and she would see that it didn't shoot anything for real. She looked at me and looked over at Dewey. He was trying to say, "I didn't do it Miss Jackson, this is not my bow". I said "Mom, you know he's retarded and he probably does not know how he got here". She said, "Your brothers said they saw you shoot the arrow; bring your ass on down to the house anyway". I was not getting any sympathy for the car accident this time; she beat my ass all the way down the street. The funny thing about it was that I didn't mind taking that beating, because seeing the look on my brothers' faces when they got those arrows shot in their head and ass made it all worth it. They were kind of mad at me for a while, but just like soldiers, when you're from Jackson Street you learn to tough it out and get over it. They probably felt like they deserved it anyway. I am sure they felt a little guilty about my little ass getting run down by a car.

There is another little game that we used to play called "Hide the Belt". A bunch of us kids would get together and we would take a belt and hide the belt somewhere. Sometimes we would hide it underneath a porch, or in the woods, in the bushes or something like that. One time I took the belt and hid it in the bushes near the house. When somebody got close to the belt you would say "hot"; if they were not close, you would say "cold". The closer they got, the hotter they got, and that's how they knew if they were going in the right direction. This time when we were playing "Hide the Belt", it was my two older brothers, a few of the neighborhood kids and Dewey. He happened to be the one that was getting close to the belt and I was telling him you're getting hot. If you found the belt you were allowed to beat anybody that you could catch with the belt until they got back to safety, which was a post or a base. Some people that were really punks never really strayed out too far from the base. They never got the enjoyment of beating anybody with a belt either, because they were so afraid of getting beat with the belt. I guess that was our way of imitating our parents, because our parents always used to beat us with belts or sometimes worse; the game gave us a chance to beat somebody else with a belt.

The belt was hidden in the bushes and at this point in the game everybody was digging through the bushes. Dewey was the one who was the hottest, and he reached into the bushes and he grabbed what he thought was the belt. What the dumb ass grabbed was a big ass snake, but instead of him looking at what he grabbed, he just reached in and pulled the snake out. As soon as he grabbed it, he turned around and looked the other way to see who he was going to beat up on with what he thought was the belt. Dewey was running chasing all of us with a real live snake. We tried to tell him that it was a real snake in his hand, but he was still chasing us swinging the snake at us until he finally looked down at his hand. I guess he finally came to his senses and thought, "hey a belt is not supposed to move like that", and he saw that it was a real snake in his hand. He got really excited and started screaming and instead of dropping the snake, he grabbed the snake tighter.

He started running up the street with the snake wiggling in his hand all the way to his house. He still had the snake in his hand and said, "Mommy, there's a snake, there's a snake", and she slapped the shit out of him. He rolled across the porch, and the snake flew out of his hand and went into the bushes. We were all running behind him trying to see what the little retarded boy was going to do with the snake. She looked at us and she said that she was going to tell our parents on us. We said we didn't do anything; he picked up the snake on his own. She thought that we had given him the snake, but the little dumb ass had picked up the snake on his own. She picked his little ass up off the porch and made him stay inside the rest of the day. We went back home, and we continued to play the game without him.

There was also another game that we used to play; we called it "Blind Man Pluck". There would be maybe seven of us, and we put a blindfold on one person. Usually we would start with Dewey, because we felt he didn't know any better. He had a real big football head. I thought that was because he was dropped on his head about ten times when he was young and the swelling never went down. We had to get an extra long blindfold to tie around his big head. After we put the blindfold on to cover his eyes, we would spin him around until he got a little dizzy. We were allowed to sneak up and pluck him in the head with one of our fingers without getting tagged by him. If you got tagged then you had to have the blindfold placed on you.

We put so many bumps on Dewey's head that his mother had to take him to the hospital. He was alright, but he had so many bumps on his head that we told his mother that we got attacked by some bumblebees. She asked, "how come there aren't any bumps on you?" We said, "Because we ran and Dewey stayed there and tried to fight them and they stung the shit out of his big head". Of course she decided that she was going to tell our parents again, but our parents didn't care. That was what we did on Jackson Street for fun. Our parents knew we played "Blind Man Pluck" and they knew what happened to his head. Everyone knew he wasn't going to die from all those plucks; but he still did have about twenty to thirty bumps all over his head.

Another thing that we all got together to do was pick apples from the neighborhood trees. Most of the trees you could climb to get your apples, but some of them you could not climb because they were too tall. Everyone always tried to get the biggest apple from the trees. This one time it was just my two brothers and me, and we knew where this one apple tree was that had the biggest apples ever. This particular day we all spotted this big red apple in this tree. We talked about how this apple was big as Dewey's head and that was real big. We started throwing stones up in the tree trying to knock this apple down to the ground. I mean we spent hours trying to knock that damn apple down. David got tired and quit throwing at the big apple, but not me because I wanted that big apple. I knew if I got that big apple I would be the shit, and I could tease everyone else who tried and failed to get that apple. I found a brick, and then I broke it in half by smashing it against another brick, so I could throw it up high enough to hit the apple in the tree. An hour passed, and I was still throwing the brick up in the tree. The brick came down and hit me in the head and knocked me out for a couple of seconds.

David came over to where I was lying and started shaking me to see if I was dead. My head was bleeding, and he said I should go home. All I did was try to stop the bleeding from my head by pressing my shirt against my wound. Finally, my head stopped bleeding, and I got that same brick that busted my head and started throwing it up in the tree again at that apple. David was sitting on the ground watching me suffer throwing the brick up in the tree trying to knock down that damn apple. I did not want any of them little apples that fell to the ground. I said, "You can have all of them; if that big apple falls, no one better touch it or I am going to fuck someone up". I finally took one big heave and threw the brick up in the tree. The brick finally hit the branch that the apple was on and the big apple fell down to the ground. The apple rolled about two or three feet as I was standing there staring at it. I am starting to jump up and down shouting with happiness, "I got it, I got it, I finally knocked the big apple down".

Then my big dumb ass brother got up off the ground, ran over and snatched the apple off the ground. He looked over at me and started laughing as he turned his back towards me and started running toward the house. I started hollering at him, "Give me my apple, give me my apple" and I realized that I still had the big brick in front of me. I picked up the brick and when I ran close enough to him, I took one big heave and hit him in the back of the head. I hit him so hard in his head that he flipped over four or five times and the apple fell out of his hand. The whole back of his head was busted open; blood was running down his back. I picked up the apple and I said, "Now, who got the apple, now you big ass dummy?"

Gary heard all the noise and came over to see what was going on with us. He seen David on the ground bleeding, helped him up, and took him down to the house. He was bleeding all over the place; you could see a trail of blood behind him. I knew I was going to be in trouble that day, but I was not taking an ass kicking for this one. 15 minutes later Gary said, "Mom said she going to whoop your ass so you might as well come on home", but I refused to come home. An hour later he said, "You need to come home and eat something, but mom is still going to beat your ass". I thought how I still had a big apple, and I should be able to live for another couple hours off the big apple. It took me five minutes to eat that whole apple and I was still hungry. Something that I spent nine hours trying to knock out of a tree, I ate in five minutes. Anyway another hour passed and my brother came back to get me again. Gary said, "Mom said she is going to give you some food, but she still going to whoop your ass". I thought, so now I'm starving and thirsty. You would think that Gary would bring me some food or something to drink. A bug or something to eat, any damn thing to eat, but he was just dying for me to go down there so they could watch me get my little ass whooped.

So anyway the hunger pains finally got to me. There was not anything else I could do. It was almost dark, and I would not stay out in the woods in the dark. Too much shit went on out there. So Gary came up the last time and I said, "Ok I'm going to go home". Just as soon as I got up on the front porch, she took the belt out and beat my ass all the way up into the house. She beat me through the living room and sent my little ass to the bathroom to wash up. Then she fed me and sent my little ass to bed. I guess that was nice; I did finally get to eat. I really didn't care about taking that ass kicking. I didn't think I deserved it, but it was worth it to get my apple back. I would have busted him in the head two or three times to get that big red apple. Wasn't anybody getting my apple, not after I spent all that time trying to get that apple! The thing about that is I don't think David ever tried to take anything else from me. David had to go to the emergency room to get stitches in his head. My mom was there for four hours that night while the doctor put twenty five stitches in his head.

We had some strange eating habits in our neighborhood but everyone on Jackson Street pretty much ate the same way. One of our specialties was a potato sandwich. It's fried potatoes that you put on two slices of bread with some ketchup. That was one of our favorites; we loved our potato sandwiches. We'd make those big potato sandwiches and walk up and down the street like we were eating steaks. Jackson Street was where people had rice and sugar in the morning for breakfast. In my neighborhood, there was always a lot of rice, a lot of cheese, a lot of flour, but never a lot of meat. But what we would do was boil the rice till it was done and then we would take the rice and put it in a bowl and put some milk and sugar on it. Boy that was good for us. We were in heaven. As a snack we would have what we called a sugar sandwich. We would take two slices of bread, spread butter on it, take a ton of sugar, and sprinkle that on it. We would put the sandwich together, and that was our butter and sugar sandwich. It was like eating a donut. We also used to have apple butter sandwiches.

One of the things we grew up on was that government cheese. Now we would take an inch slice. Of course, it would take you all day to cut the cheese. I mean the cheese must have weighed fifteen lbs.; we needed to use a damn chainsaw to cut it because it was so thick. When it was cut, it was the best cheese in the world and we would take that cheese, put it on sandwiches and many other things. We would also put cheese in our pockets and walk around and nibble on it like it was a candy bar or something. In our neighborhood, the parents would hide the real good stuff, real cookies and real donuts. They knew that we would steal them; there was no doubt in their minds. Even if we had to stay up all night and plot. We didn't care if it was just one cookie; we were planning on getting that one cookie.

We used to go to the berry patches on the weekends, which was a couple of miles from where we lived. We'd take big brown bags and we would go pick black berries until our bags were full. Now this wasn't an easy thing to do because it was hot as hell outside. There were bulls and cows in the pastures so we had to be careful. And there were thorns in all the berry bushes so needless to say just to get one bag of blackberries, which would take us four to five hours, we would be all cut up and burned up from the sun. What happened to me the one day, I got chased by a damn bull. Anyway this day that we were picking the berries, everyone else decided to leave. I wanted to get more in my bag, so I stayed a little while longer and the best berries seemed to be where the bulls were. I looked over and saw this bush. All the berries on the bush were black and there were several bulls near the bush.

I was not worried about the bulls because I had never seen a bull chase anybody until that day it chased me. Anyway I was over there picking the berries and the bull was probably about fifteen feet away from me. For some reason, and to this day, I still don't know why, the bull looked at me. His eyes looked as if they said, "fuck you", I said "fuck you" back to him and then I turned my back. I started picking some more berries disregarding the look the bull had gave me earlier. The next thing I knew, I heard some loud footsteps coming towards me. I turned around and it was the bull trying to ram me in the ass. I dropped my bag of berries that took me four hours to fill, and I started running across the field. As I ran, my shoes came off, but I was still running and got all kinds of cuts on my feet. I was still running, running, running and the bull was getting closer and closer, I just knew that I was going to die. I was really running fast, and my feet were getting all scraped up, but I did not feel any of the pain. I finally got to a spot near the gate that I crawled under, and I kept running all the way home.

By the time I got to the house, I was tired and sweaty and could hardly breathe. My mother looked down at me and said, "Where are your damn shoes at?" Now I did not care that I didn't have any shoes on because I was so scared of that bull. I said, "I must have left them at the field because the bull was chasing me." She said "Didn't no damn bull chase you". She slapped me, beat me with the belt and said, "You better take your ass back up there and get them shoes". So I took my little ass whooping and started walking back up to the field barefooted. I was thinking----"I 'm not going to that damn field to get those shoes, mom is just going to have to whoop my ass again".

Then guess who I ran into? Little Dewey was walking my way and I said, "Hey, do you want to play a game? There are some shoes hidden out there in the field. If you go get them and bring them to me you'll be the winner". He said, "Okay", and he went under the fence. He went to get one shoe and said, "Look Ron I got one shoe". I said, "Well there's one more so keep looking". When he got the other shoe, he started jumping up and down saying "Yeah, I got the shoes, I got the shoes". Now Dewey was out there in the middle of the cow pasture and the bulls weren't too far away with his little red ass shirt on jumping up and down talking about, "I got the shoes, I got the shoes".

I guess you know what happened next; the bull started chasing his little-retarded ass. The bull chased him until Dewey got about five feet from the gate, the bull put his horns down and lifted him about twenty feet in the air over the fence. Dewey flew over the fence, still hanging onto the shoes. The shoes fell on one side and rolled about another twenty feet. I picked up my shoes and put them on my bloody feet, and I helped Dewey get back to his house. I felt kind of bad for him, but I was happy I got my shoes back. I found out later that Dewey had a broken arm from where he fell on the ground after the bull knocked him over the fence. I never told anybody why he was out there messing with the bulls because I knew I would have got in trouble again. I was just happy that Dewey didn't get killed because of what I had him do that day in the field.

As time went on, I was noticing that it seemed like everyday that a guy named "Tony Defordy" was riding by my house. I guess he was going back and forth to work. I realized that he was the same guy that had run me over about a year ago. What bothered me about that was that this white man would look at me and I would say hi, and he would never speak to me. And I thought to myself, "This is the same motherfucker that ran me over and damn near killed me, and now he can't speak to the little black boy". But he could ride everyday through my neighborhood to get to his house up in the suburbs.

In my neighborhood another thing we did for fun was---- we had apple battles. We'd get those old rotten apples that were down on the ground. We'd get on teams and chase each other around the whole damn neighborhood and bust each other in the head with these big rotten apples. As time went on, it had gotten to be too much for me to watch this white man ride by my house; without even having the common courtesy to stop by and ask how I was doing. So I thought that I would get his white ass just for the fun of getting him.

What I did was get about ten of us together and said, "Let's have some fun". I asked them if they wanted to throw some apples at some cars. At first they didn't want to do it because they thought they would get in trouble. I said, "Well you know if we hide behind some houses or behind some bushes, they aren't going to know we did it". So I figured out which time of day that this Tony Defordy comes by in his raggedy ass car. As a matter of fact, it was the same car that hit my ass.

We got about fifty apples in this big bag and we all hid behind these bushes. I said, "The first car that comes by throw the apples at it". I knew this guy's car was going to come by in a couple seconds so we were all sitting back there, about ten of us. As soon as the car was about ten feet from us we all jumped up and started throwing the apples. His windows were open and the apples were just bouncing all off of his head, and one of the apples just knocked his glasses off. All of a sudden he was fighting with the steering wheel to keep the car straight, he turned off to the right and he went through the rail into the creek.

The kids were saying, "Oh my God he wrecked his car, he wrecked his car". So we all went to the creek to see if he was okay, but the car had turned upside down and he was inside the car trying to kick the door open to get out. The water pressure must have been holding the door closed. So he was struggling and struggling; he still could not get from underneath the water. A minute or so passed and he was still under water. So the others were saying that maybe we should go and tell somebody.

One of the kids said that, “Maybe we can jump in and help him”. I said, “Hell no, we might get stuck down there to, he’ll be all right”. When two minutes passed and he was still trying to get out of the water, I remember saying, “Nobody panic he will be okay”. “He’s a grown up he’ll get out of there”, but I didn’t really care if he got out of there or not. I thought he was a mean old white man and he deserved to die in that cold creek water. When three minutes passed, all of a sudden this white man stopped moving. Every once in a while his arm would twitch, making us think he was still alive. Then everyone was saying they thought he was dead and became very quiet. I said, “No he’s down there pretending to be dead; he’s just trying to get one of us to come down there so he can drown us; remember that he is a white man and you know that you can not trust them. I bet you as soon as we leave he’ll get up out of there, so let’s go home”.

We all left and went home. Later on that day, we heard that a white man wrecked his car and crashed in the creek and drowned. So all the other kids came running to my house talking about “Did you hear about the white man, he did drown, he did drown”. I said “Well he’s probably still pretending to be dead. You can’t really believe what grownups say. He’s probably not dead. Don’t worry about it, go on home”. I knew he was dead though. I knew he was dead when we left. I could tell.

There was a little relief that was set upon me when I saw he wasn’t moving. It reminded me of when I couldn’t move, after I got hit by that car. So it felt good that he was in an accident and died. If he had been nicer to me, maybe he wouldn’t be at the bottom of that creek right now. One thing I can say is that the day he died, seemed like the day that I felt better about my accident. At the young age of six, I witnessed my first death. I was not sure how that was going to affect me and the other kids, who were all around the same age as me. The kids on

Jackson Street are very resilient; we had to be to survive. "***Believe in Change***"

Chapter 3

Tiger and the Message

At the age of ten, some of my friends and I would go to this place called Cinder Hill. There was usually about six of the neighborhood kids who went to the hill to play. This was a hillside about 30 feet high and approximately 50 feet across. It was made up of old coal cinders. We would climb to the top of the hill, and then see who could jump the furthest down the hill. We would actually measure how far we could jump down the hill. We would all line up and go one at a time. The first person would jump, and someone would go down and measure it. Then the second person would jump, and someone else would go down and measure it.

Once, when it came time for this guy named Bert to jump, I stuck my foot out and tripped him right before he was getting ready to jump off the hill. So instead of jumping down the hill he rolled down the hill and at the bottom of the hill he hit his head up against a tree. He knocked one of his front teeth out, and his mouth was bleeding badly. He cried while running all the way home. We were all worried at first. After we could not see him running anymore, we all started laughing at him. Bert never did jump off that hill again; I guess he was scared after knocking his tooth out. After jumping off the hill, we would get real dirty. We knew that if we went home like that our parents would really get upset with us. If we went home dirty, our mothers would beat us and we would be grounded for a week.

Therefore, we would go to a place called Third Arch, where we would go to swim during the summer months. It was called third Arch because it was the Third Arch underneath the railroad tracks that traveled along a bridge. All together there were four arches, but third arch was the best one to swim at. Underneath Third Arch there was a creek. This was the same creek that flooded our houses almost every year. On top of Third Arch were railroad tracks that we had become so accustomed to walking on. It was about 50 feet high from the tracks to the creek below. There was a railing on one side of the tracks and no railing on the other side. It was always dangerous to walk on the tracks because sometimes a train would come.

When we went to the Third Arch, we would jam up all the creek water that was flowing through there by gathering some big rocks and stacking them all together to stop the flow of the water. We would get all the old tin cans and glass out of there so we would not cut our feet when we swam in the creek. When we got through jamming it up, the water would be about six feet high in the deepest part of the creek. Then we would jump in the water with all our clothes on so that we could clean the cinder dirt off of our clothes. There was a six foot high wall underneath the arch that some of us would jump from into the water. After we swam for a while and we felt the clothes got somewhat cleaned, we would take them off and hang them up in the trees so that they would dry out. While our clothes were drying, we were swimming butt naked. We weren't worried about swimming butt naked because not many cars came around that road. Occasionally someone would see our little naked asses running around and swimming in the creek, but that didn't bother us.

Usually when we cleaned the creek out to make it a swimming pool, it would take a couple hours before the older kids found out it was cleaned out. The older kids (ages 15 to 18 years old), would come around there and run us out of our pool. Usually they would not let us swim after we did all that work to clean it up. All we could do was wait until they got finished swimming. Sometimes I told the other younger guys to go to the top of the arch, which was about 50 feet up and we would piss over the arch on them. Most of the time, they did not even realize we were pissing on them because they were splashing around in the water.

One time Dewey had to take a shit real bad, so I suggested to him that he should shit over the arch to see how it looked going down. Dewey pulled his pants down and hung his little ass over the railroad track, and he started shitting. The shit went down as the wind took it and hit this big guy, named "Danny" who was a big bully. The shit hit Danny on top of his head, and then it started running down his face. Danny immediately looked up and then another pile of shit hit him dead in the eye. Danny started hollering and screaming that the shit had blinded him because it burned his eyes. He hurried up and dove into the water to clean some of the shit off his face. When he looked up, little Dewey still had his ass hanging over the bridge and was still trying to shit some more. He did not realize that he had shit on Danny's head and that if he caught him, he would try to kill him.

Danny ran out of the pool butt ass naked, and ran up to the top of the arch and started beating on little Dewey. We ran to the other side of the railroad tracks because we did not want to get beat up by Danny, who was about 18 years old. There were five of us all together. I thought about all of us trying to beat up Danny, but I knew the other kids would be too scared. We told Danny to stop beating him, but Danny did not stop; he just kept beating Dewey. The poor boy's nose was bleeding from Danny constantly punching him in the face. The five of us picked up some big rocks and started hitting Danny with the stones to make him stop beating Dewey. After one of those stones hit Danny in his head, he finally stopped beating Dewey. He started chasing us over the railroad tracks while he was still butt naked. Danny was starting to get closer and closer and when he was just about to grab one of us he fell down, scratching all the skin off his dick.

The rumor was that he broke his dick when he fell down on it. After that we always called him “Broke Dick Danny” because everyone said his dick was crooked. He did not like that and ever since that day Danny was determined to get us. One by one he caught us and beat us; it took him a couple of weeks. The only reason he caught me is because I saw him walking with his five year old little sister and I thought he would not hit me with her there. I thought he wouldn’t have time to jump on me, but I was wrong. I walked by him and said, “Hey how you doing Broke Dick Danny?” He frowned up his face. It looked liked smoke was coming out his ears because he was so angry, and he hit me. He knocked me to the ground, and got on top of me and punched me about five times. Then he got up and started laughing at me, while he was walking away. I called him “Broke Dick Danny” again. He jumped on me and started beating me up again.

When he got up, he looked a little tired so when he turned his back towards me, I jumped on his back. I tried to hit him in the head. I got a few good punches in, but he got me down and beat me up again. When he got up off me, he asked if I was done yet. I said, “Yeah”, but when we got up I swung on him again; he beat me down again, he was just too big for me to handle. After the fourth time I said “Come on let’s fight some more”, he said “I got to take my sister home, I got no time for your little young ass”. I picked up some rocks and started throwing them at him.

He called me a little motherfucker and told me I better not hit his little sister. I thought about it for a minute and then I picked up a big rock and hit his sister in the head with it. I knew that would make him real angry if I hit her with a rock. I hit her so hard she started bleeding, but he did not come after me again. Instead he picked up his little sister and started running towards his house. The next time I saw Danny, which was a week later; I was with my big brother David. Danny walked up to me and threatened to kick my ass and David told him that if he touched me, he would have to beat his ass. After that day, Danny never whooped my ass again because he knew my brother would get him.

It was several months later, and during the winter when I next saw Danny again. During the winter, the creek would freeze and we would go out there and ice skate. Since we didn't have any real skates, we would slide along with our shoes on. We would form teams and play ice hockey. For hockey sticks, we would use branches from a tree and for a hockey puck we would use a piece of coal or a rock. Sometimes when we were out there running on that ice, we would find a weak spot in the ice. It was just Danny's luck that he ran into the weak spot. So that big mother fucker fell though the ice and he was holding on with his finger tips so that he wouldn't go through the ice and float down the stream. I told everyone to stand back because if we went near him, we would probably fall in the ice and drown. Everyone stood back and looked at Danny as he hollered and screamed for somebody to help him. I kept telling everyone to stay back. Danny went under the ice one time. Then he came back up and when he did, he was crying and begging for us to help him. Then Danny went under the water again and this time when he came back up it took him about thirty seconds to talk because he was spitting all this muddy water out.

He continued begging for help. He wanted us to hand him our hockey stick so he could grab it. I kept telling the guys "don't go over there because he will pull your ass in, you know how mean he is. He is a mean ass bully". The guys didn't go over there, and they kept saying, "You're going to pull us in". Finally, out of nowhere Danny's little brother "Gregory" ran between the crowd and dove over towards his brother with a stick. Danny grabbed the stick and Gregory started pulling him out. Gregory was just a little guy like us so he was having a hard time pulling his big brother out. The next thing I knew, Danny and Gregory started falling in the water.

I liked Gregory because he was one of our friends so instead of letting Gregory fall in to far; we grabbed his legs and started pulling him back out the water. All five of us were pulling Gregory; we also pulled Danny's big dumb ass out. When Danny got out he was crying like a little bitch, and he went home with his tail between his legs. He did not look so big and strong then. I never had seen older kids cry before. We started laughing at him and we taunted him "What's wrong now Broke Dick Danny?" He could not even turn to say a word because he was so tired from struggling to get out of the ice. Gregory helped his brother home; they struggled off the ice together. When Danny left, we still went on with our little hockey game. We actually had fun once his big bully ass was gone.

My siblings and I had a dog named "Tiger"; we got him when he was a little puppy. We found him on the doorstep; no one knows where he came from. He was a mixed breed dog who wasn't that big, but was real feisty. He was black and white and we really loved Tiger. We never had a dog before and for a long time we just kept him underneath the porch because we didn't know if my mother would let us keep him. Finally after a couple months of keeping him under the front porch, we finally asked my mother could we bring Tiger in the house and she said, "Yeah". She let us keep him in the basement of the house. Everywhere we went, Tiger went too. He was one of our best friends, and everybody in the house was crazy about him.

We had him for about a year when one day we let Tiger outside to go to the bathroom, and some idiot driving a car hit him so hard that he flew into the creek. The man that ran Tiger over went around knocking on doors asking whose dog it was that he hit. When he came to our door, we told him that it was our dog. The man did not even try to get Tiger out of the creek, maybe he could have saved him. Tiger was laying in the creek with his eyes wide open just staring at us, but he wasn't moving. We knew Tiger was dead. We all started crying profusely, while we were hugging each other tightly.

We were really angry at the man, but I guess it wasn't really his fault. We were trying to figure out what to do, whether we should go down into the deep part of the creek and get Tiger out of there or just leave him in the creek. We went to talk to our mother; she told us it was okay to get Tiger out of the creek. When we went back and looked down at the creek, Tiger was gone. We figured he must have floated down the creek with the current. We were really sad for a couple weeks; everyone was having trouble sleeping at night.

One night about a month later, when we were upstairs sleeping, I woke up because I heard some noises in the basement. I went down there to see what the noise was. I turned the light on and in the corner of the basement, I saw Tiger sitting there. Tiger ran to me and jumped on me, licking my face like it was a big juicy bone. He was barking and making a lot of noise, I was scared he was going to wake up my mother. When I first saw tiger, I screamed like a little girl because I thought that our dog was dead. This dog had looked dead and everyone said he was dead. I thought that this must have been a dream or something. It wasn't a dream; tiger was really back in the house. When I was down there, I played with Tiger for awhile. Then I went and got him some food. I played with him for about two hours and actually fell asleep down in the basement. When I woke up the next morning at 6:00am, Tiger was gone. I searched for a little while, and then I went upstairs to get some more sleep.

I woke up later that day and I told my brothers that I saw Tiger last night in the basement around 12:00am. They laughed at me and called me stupid and a liar. David slapped me upside the head, saying that I wasn't funny. At 12:00am that next night I heard noise in the basement again so I went downstairs. Again saw that Tiger was down there playing and I said, "Where have you been Tiger? Where did you go this morning?" Of course, I didn't expect him to say anything back; it was just something that was on my mind. I played with Tiger for about a half hour and then I said to Tiger, "You know what; I'm going to go get my brothers. I said, "You wait right here".

So I went upstairs and woke up both my older brothers. I decided not to wake up my little brother Robert because I was not sure if he could handle seeing Tiger. We all crept down the stairs because we didn't want to wake our mom up. When we got down the stairs, Tiger was sitting there. The dog was so excited to see them that he jumped up on David, making him scream like a little girl. Then Tiger jumped up on Gary, he started jumping up and down screaming for help because he was so scared. Then Tiger ran over to me and we started playing, just like we did the night before.

My brothers looked at us and they said, "He is alive, Tiger is really alive". I said, "I told you dumb asses he was alive, I don't know why you didn't believe me". All three of us played with Tiger for a couple hours that night. We all fell asleep downstairs in the basement, but when we woke up the next morning around 6:00, he was gone again. On the third night at 12:00am, I heard some noise in the basement again. This was three nights in a row that I heard the same noises in the basement. I woke my bothers and we went down there and Tiger was down there again. We were all thinking, where is this dog coming from and how is he getting into the house?

The only way to get into the house is through the front door so how was he getting into the house? He must have had a secret way of getting into the house that we do not know about. We were down in the basement playing with Tiger for about an hour, but this time we did not fall asleep down there. We got Tiger some food and went back to our beds that night. This nightly routine went on for about seven nights. On the seventh night when we went downstairs and brought Tiger some food, we played with him for a while again. I thought that Tiger might need to go outside and we had not taken him outside since he came back seven days ago. Tiger had not gone to the bathroom down in the basement and I thought it would be a good idea to let him get some fresh air.

We crept up to the front door. As soon as Tiger reached the opened door he started running. We chased Tiger all the way up to the Cemetery Road in our pajamas, which was about a mile from our house. The reason they called it "Cemetery Road" was because the local cemetery is located on this road. Tiger ran into the cemetery and disappeared into the darkness. None of us ever went into the cemetery at night because we were scared. We had to get Tiger, to get him back home so we would not get into trouble. If our mother found out that we were out of the house, she would beat our asses. So we all ran into the cemetery looking for Tiger in the darkness. Suddenly Tiger stopped running and we noticed that the gravestone that Tiger was sitting on has a name on it. The light from the street light was shining right on the grave. On the grave it read "David Carl Jackson", the same name as David. I looked at the gravestone and I said to my brother, "That gravestone has your name on it. Your name is "David Carl Jackson" to, what is going on tonight"? His eyes got big with fear and he started shaking all over, like he just seen a ghost. Then we heard some gunfire coming from across the cemetery. We turned around to look and then when we turned back around Tiger was gone again. We shouted for Tiger for about an hour, but he never responded to our pleas to come back.

We kept going back over staring at the gravestone to make sure that it said the same thing. We still couldn't find Tiger so we figured that we needed to get home before we got in trouble. We went home and tried to go back to sleep but nobody was really sleeping because David was crying all night. He kept talking about how he's going to die because his name is on the grave. I told him to be quiet; we can go back to the cemetery in the morning to look at the gravestone again. We did go back to take a look at that stone again, but this time it had a different name on it. We went all the through the graveyard. We looked at every gravestone in there and none of them said David Carl Jackson. We thought we must have just imagined it because we couldn't find a gravestone there that read "David Carl Jackson" anywhere in the graveyard.

After that night, my brothers never saw Tiger again anywhere. We waited up every night for a month, but he never showed up at our house. A year later, when I was upstairs sleeping, I heard noises in the basement again. I remember thinking, what if Tiger is back again after all this time. I went down to the basement and Tiger was there sitting in the corner again. He jumped up on me and we played for a little while. After about an hour of playing, I thought about going to get my brothers to tell them Tiger was here. I changed my mind because Tiger kept pulling at my pant leg like he needed to go outside. I kept telling Tiger to wait and let me go get my brothers, but he started barking and acting real crazy. I took Tiger outside and he started running towards Cemetery Road again. I chased him just like I did before, but I could not keep up with him. I was thinking, "Not this again" as he ran into the graveyard. I was thinking to myself, "I'm not going into this cemetery all by myself looking for this dumb dog again".

I needed to go back and get my brothers so that we could go in there together. Then I started thinking that they probably wouldn't go in there because they were chicken shit to. Then I heard Tiger barking real loud on the other side of the cemetery. It sounded like he was hurt real bad, so I thought I should go and see what's wrong. When I went in there, Tiger was looking at me with a strange facial expression. He looked like a statue sitting there with no emotion on his face. When I looked behind Tiger, I saw that damn gravestone again and it read "David Carl Jackson". I got a little closer and I read it again and it read "David Carl Jackson Sr". I remember thinking that David Carl Jackson Sr. was not my brother. That's my dad. When I turned around and looked at Tiger, he was standing behind me and I heard gunshots again. I turned back around to see where the gunshots came from. When I looked around again, Tiger was gone. I thought to myself, here we go with this hide and go seek shit again. But I didn't just hear one gunshot; it sounded like about twenty guns going off. I'm thinking "man there are a lot of mother fuckers trying to shoot at me", so I ran all the way home as fast as I could.

I ran up to the room where my brothers were, and I woke them up. I told them that Tiger took me to the grave again and they asked if I was sure. I told them that I saw the gravestone again and that I read the gravestone. I told David that his name was not on the gravestone, that the name on the gravestone was David Carl Jackson Sr. I said that it was our dad's name that was on the gravestone. They told me to go tell our mom what I saw, but it was too late to wake her up. They talked me into doing it anyway, I went to her room. I told her that I saw Tiger and how he took me up to Cemetery Road. Inside the cemetery there was a gravestone that read David Carl Jackson Sr.; it had our dad's name on it. She looked at me, looked at the clock and said, "You little crazy mother fucker I'm going to kill you". She beat me all the way back to my bedroom. I was trying to convince her that I was telling her the truth. She told me to shut the fuck up before she beat me again. I cried all night and eventually I went to sleep.

We woke up the next day and went to the gravesite where Tiger had taken me and once again there was no gravestone. I went all through that graveyard and there was no gravestone that read David Carl Jackson Sr. So David said, "I think you're lying this time". We didn't see Tiger, and we weren't with you so you're lying. So he punched me upside my head and walked away laughing, calling me a little dumb ass. The very next day around ten o'clock in the evening, my mother got a phone call and all I heard was her crying and saying no, no, no! She kept on crying and ran up to her bedroom. She stayed in there for a couple hours and all we could hear was crying. We didn't know what was wrong.

We were all down stairs sitting in the living room when she finally came out her bedroom. I remember thinking, "I hope she hurries up and comes out because I could really use some food to eat". She came out and sat down on the couch next to us and she said your father was killed today. She said "He got stabbed at the bar and your father is dead". I could hardly understand what she said because her voice was beginning to break up. We were all in shock when we heard what she said. I did not know what to say to anyone about it. I did not know the man, but I felt an emptiness come over me that I never felt before. My brothers and sister did not have anything to say either. We just all sat there looking at each other waiting for someone to say something. There was just silence and bemusement written all over our faces. None of us cried, at least not that I know of and if they did, it was where no one could see them. ***"Believe in Change"***

Chapter 4

The Tale of Two Families

I was 12 years old when my father died. After the news arrived, my mother drank the time away, crying incessantly in her room. Those around me said he was at a local bar; got into an argument with a persistent drunk, and threw this man over the bar. Then my dad got his drink and went to go sit in a booth. About five minutes later, that same man snuck up behind my father and stabbed him thirteen times in his chest. One of the knife wounds struck his heart; he died at the scene. That's how my father got murdered. Obviously that drunk didn't want to fight my father because he was a big man, so his best bet was to sneak up and stab him. My father's mistake was turning his back. After a couple days of my mother's crying, she finally told us that we, as a family, all had to go the funeral in Philadelphia.

At that time no one but me said anything. I told my mother there was no way in hell that I was going to my father's funeral, but my mother said I had no choice. She told me to shut the fuck up and that I had to go. So I shut my mouth and got quiet. The day that we were supposed to leave; everyone was packing, and I decided that I still wasn't going. I ran away that morning to the woods behind our house. My brothers all went into the woods trying to find me; I heard them calling me, but they still couldn't find me. I was hiding in a tree that was about thirty feet tall. So finally my mother came into the woods—her hollering echoing through the crossing trees. She yelled that when she got back into town she was definitely going to whoop my ass. I still didn't respond; I just stayed very still out there in the tree real quiet. My mother got in her final words and said,

"When your dumb ass comes out of the woods, go and stay with Miss Margot".

I left the woods later that night and snuck back into the house through a window I had left opened. I felt a new power climbing through that window and standing quite still in the kitchen. I was alone. I could eat and sleep when I wanted. I knew I had to be careful so the neighbors didn't see me through the windows. I didn't turn any lights on and I snuck around the house with a little flashlight that was hidden underneath my mother's bed. The house looked different through the shine of that small light as it moved through hallways and into rooms. I searched through the house to find all the goodies, all the cookies my mother had hidden, all the doughnuts, chips, and candy.

While I was consuming what had become my dinner, I discovered a full bottle of Tiger Rose wine. I figured since my mom drank all the time and seemed to travel away from her self in appealing ways that I would have a taste and see what happened. It tasted like shit, but I decided to drink some more anyway. I figured if I tasted a little more, it might taste better. That was the first time I got drunk and threw up. After I threw up, I went upstairs, lay across my mother's bed and passed out. It was probably around 11:00pm when I staggered up the stairs.

At around 3:00am I heard some noise downstairs, and I staggered to the top of the steps. I could hear someone tying to break into the window downstairs. I ran and hid in my mother's closet because I was scared. It sounded like people were falling over shit downstairs, and all of a sudden I heard some big feet coming up the stairs. I started looking around in my mother's closet to see what I could find to defend myself. I found a lighter, some lighter fluid and a butcher knife in the closet.

I was trying to be real quiet when I heard someone come into the room. I peeked out the crack of the closet, and I could see it was that old drunk "Grant Nash". This man had been a drunk ever since I was a baby, and my mother always told me to never trust that drunken ass Grant Nash. He was up in my mother's room going through her dresser drawer. Apparently he didn't find anything in there because the next thing I knew he lifted up my mother's mattress. He didn't find anything there either. Then he bent his big drunk ass down and looked underneath my mom's bed and he was feeling around. All I could see was his big black greasy ass staring at me as if inviting to stab it. While he was digging underneath the bed, I reached for the knife. I thought that if I stabbed him in his ass, maybe he would get up and run out the house.

I was trying to figure out how to hold the knife. Should I hold it overhand so I could jab him or should I grab and hold it so I could stick it in real deep? I decided to hold it overhand and hopefully stick him hard enough that he would run out the house. I opened the closet door quietly and tiptoed over to where he was looking underneath the bed; I put the knife way up in the air and came down as hard as I could, and the knife stuck him right in the ass. He hollered like a wounded animal, like he was dying. He backed out from underneath the bed and looked at me with his raging red eyes. I thought he was going to kill my ass.

Quickly, I looked to the side of me and saw my mother's table, and on it there was this big metal five-pound ashtray. I picked it up, and I busted him upside the head with it making a horrible crunching sound; he didn't holler this time. He fell back on the floor and looked liked he was dead. He wasn't moving, but I could hear him breathing and moaning loudly so I tried to bend down and pull the knife out his ass. But it was so far in I couldn't pull it out. I thought maybe I could just leave the knife in his ass and drag him downstairs. He was one heavy motherfucker, so I put one foot on his ass and pulled the knife out. He made even more noise when I tried to pull it out, than he did when I first stabbed him. Blood spilled all over the floor and furniture. I didn't know what to do. He was too big to move out of the house, and I couldn't call anyone because I was not supposed to be home. Then I remembered a game the older kids used to play called "hot foot". They stuck pieces of paper underneath someone's feet or shoes while they were asleep and lit the paper on fire.

The person with their feet on fire would start running around because his feet were aching and burning. Eventually that person would start running, trying to put the fires out by stomping and moving. So, I put lighter fluid on both his feet; I lit one foot; then I lit the other foot. Suddenly, he woke up and screamed and tried to put the fire out with his hand. It was too hot to put out with his hand, so he jumped up and started dancing around like he was doing an Indian dance. I began to back up because I knew he was going to try to kill me if he could. The fire wasn't just on his shoes but on his pants now. He jumped around even more and turned towards the window. He looked back at me and said, "You little son of bitch". Then he ran towards the window and jumped straight through the panel of glass.

The window shattered in one high pitch sound, and he hit the second story roof, rolling off and falling to the ground right in the front yard. The wind pushed and pulled at the small fires still lighting up his legs. He staggered to his feet again and started hollering, making all kinds of noises. The neighbors started to wake up—their lights turning on one by one. Finally, he ran full speed and jumped into the creek. The fire was out, but his dumb ass forgot that he couldn't swim. The neighbors started to come out of their houses; they went out to the creek and pulled his drunken ass out by a rope.

I watched from the window and suddenly my neighbor, Ms. Margot, turned back and spotted me in the window. She came over to the house and asked what happened. I told her what Grant Nash did, and she told me that I was supposed to be staying at her house. She told me I had to get my shit together and take my ass over there. After the neighbors found out what Grant Nash tried to do, they beat his ass even more when they pulled him out of the creek. They beat him so bad that they had to call an ambulance. He needed treated for his burns and his broken bones and knife wound.

I had to stay at Ms. Margot's house for three days until my mother got back home. Ms. Margot called the landlord the next day so that he could come and fix the window in the bedroom, and that was my last day of being home alone. My mother returned, and Ms Margot told her the story about Grant Nash. I think my mother felt sorry for me, so she didn't whoop my ass, but my punishment wasn't far behind. As I was standing at the door the next day, I heard my mother talking about the funeral, and she was telling Miss Margot that when she got to the funeral she found out that my father had two wives. I was standing behind the door in shock—what the hell was she talking about two wives?

Apparently my father had another family in Philadelphia and my mother found this out when she was introduced as my father's family. My mom and my brothers and sister all stood up when they heard someone introduce Mr. Jackson's family. At the same time she stood, she looked over and saw on the other side of the room, there stood another Mrs. Jackson along with her two children. My mom was really embarrassed, and she thought somebody was playing games. When she found out that he was also married to this other lady, she was wild with rage. The woman was younger than my mom, and she had two girls named "Marie", like my sister's name and "Cinderella", like my dad's sister, our aunt named "Cinderella". They were approximately ages twelve & ten, which were about the same age as my sister and me.

The whole room was damp with embarrassment. This Philadelphia family looked just as shocked as we did. The Philly family had bemused looks on their faces, especially the kids. No one knew anything about this other family, not even my aunt Cinderella. You could hear people whispering in the church, my mother knew they were talking about them. My mother told David to tell the other kids to sit down and do not say nothing to no one. My father must have been living this lie for a long time.

When he was not visiting us, he was with his other family in Philadelphia. No wonder we did not see much of him, he was too busy making other children in Philadelphia.

My father had a military funeral because he served in the military Special Forces. They did the twenty-one-gun salute. Now I understood what Tiger, who was our pet dog and would visit me from the grave, was trying to tell me because when I was at the cemetery I always heard gun fire. They buried my father at Arlington National Cemetery, which is where they buried military people. My mom and siblings went to the Arlington Cemetery where they were going to bury him, about three hours away from Philadelphia. The other family was there, too. Traditionally, after the twenty-one-gun salute, they take the flag and give it to the surviving family. In my father's case, they didn't know who to give it to, my mother or the other wife, so they decided to give it to my aunt Cinderella.

While my mother and brother were sitting at the funeral with my aunt Cinderella, my mother was crying and crying. People at the funeral thought she was crying about my father, however, in between tears, she was cursing my father out by saying, "You no good bastard, no good son of a bitch". David heard her say she should knock that other woman over in the grave when she went to put the flowers she was holding on the grave. David saw how sad my mother was and he was upset himself. When the other woman got up to put a flower in the grave, David stood up and knocked the poor woman in to the grave, and everyone started hollering and screaming in horror.

The woman bounced off the casket screaming and hollering and making all kinds of noises until finally some military men came and helped her out. When she got out, she was dirty and muddy and called my brother every name in the book. Well, you know that my mom wasn't going to put up with that. She was already looking for an excuse to beat that woman's ass. My mom jumped out of the chair; and it was on. First thing my mom did was pull her up by her hair and since it wasn't her hair, her wig fell off. They were on the ground wrestling all around the grave. Then, four titties were hanging all over the place because they ripped off each other's blouses.

Suddenly they both fell into the grave and the shit was really on now. My brothers looked inside the grave and yelled, "Beat her ass mom, beat her ass". My mom was down there beating her ass like there was no tomorrow. The lady's daughters started screaming, "Help my mom, help my mom". My brothers were telling them to shut the fuck up and that she deserved to get her ass whooped. Marie, the daughter from the other family slapped the shit out of my brother Gary, and then he fell in the grave. So my mom, brother, and the other lady were in the grave. My brother Gary figured since he was there, he might as well join in and beat on this woman too. My mother and brother were beating this woman's ass.

Finally three military men went down there and pulled them up out of the grave. My mom was dancing on top of the casket stomping and calling my dad all kinds of no good mother fuckers. The military men finally got her off it because she wasn't going to get off it until she stomped a hole in the casket. The only person from my family that was allowed to stay was my aunt Cinderella. The other woman and her kids were not allowed to stay either; they were told by the military that they had to leave. They had too physically escort the other wife away because she was making a big scene. My aunt was totally embarrassed. All she could do was watch as all hell broke loose that day. She never knew about the other family my father had, apparently he kept it a real good secret. I missed a great funeral. If I would have known all of that was going to happen, maybe I would have gone.

My mother was never the same after that. When they buried my father, they might as well have buried my mother too. She drank more. She trusted people, especially men, less and less. I don't think she ever tried to find love from another man, and she had no love to give to her kids. The thought of our father's blood being in our veins—she just couldn't get pass it. We were not allowed to ever mention our father's name in that house again or around that house or even in that town. I hated my father even before he died, but now I hated him even more for what he left behind. He left my mother a hollow woman, with no ambition. The only time I saw my mother smile or even seem to be happy was when she was drunk. I knew after my father's betrayal, there was no chance in us ever receiving love from our mother. There wasn't much love anyway, but now there would even be less.

He had no money or property, all he left us was bad memories. We thought he would have a stash somewhere that would make up for all the bullshit he put my mother through. In a couple of months, it was declared that my father married my mother first, and the second marriage really wasn't legal. My mother found out through a military investigation because they were not sure which family would get any benefits. My mother refused to except any military benefits from his death. I guess she had too much pride to take anything from him, even after his death. We were still stuck on Jackson Street with no way off and that is just fucked up. ***"Believe in Change"***

Chapter 5

Big Dog on the Block

One morning when I woke up, my dick was as hard as blue steel. I was 13 years old and my hormones were going crazy. This thing called puberty had finally arrived. I was scared and confused and did not know what to do. I thought my dick was broke. It was about twice its normal size and long. I did not want to tell my mom or my brothers about my situation. Where was a father when you needed one? My brothers were already in puberty and their voices had gotten deeper, along with body hair. I still did not have any body hair and my voice was real high. We were all playing in the woods one day when Gregory "Danny's brother" said he wanted to show us something. Gregory was the same age as us, but he reached puberty before we did. He already had facial hair, and he had a deep voice like a man.

There was just me and Dewey there when he called us over to where he was at. He pulled out his dick and started to masturbate in front of us. I thought he was crazy, because it looked like it hurt. His dick got hard and he started grinding and moaning. He closed his eyes and laid his head back. He looked like he was possessed or dying. He hollered and some white cream shot up in the air. We all jumped back so that none of that nasty looking stuff would get on us. Little Dewey started crying and ran home and told his mother that Gregory was killing himself. When Dewey's mom arrived, there was cum all over Gregory's clothes and hair. She dragged him home to his mom and he got his ass beat in front of everyone.

I was not going to do that to my dick because it looked painful. My dick would get hard all the time, even when the wind would blow. You could see it growing in my pants, because it was so big. It seemed like pussy and titties were in the air and everywhere. I just wanted to see a pussy and some titties for the first time. I remember hearing my mom telling someone they had pussy lips and everyone started laughing at them. So I thought a pussy would look like a mouth with teeth. The grownups would also talk about "Tiger-Teeth-Pussy" and I really wanted to see that. They would say that kind of pussy could bite a man's dick off, which was scary to think about.

The older boys would always fish in front of Miss Thelma's house and now I know why. Miss "Thelma" was always sitting on her front porch with no panties on underneath her dress. One day I went to fish in front of her house. I could see her big bushy black pussy as clear as day, and she did not care. I just stared looking for some teeth or to see it move. I stared so hard she finally asked me what in the hell I was looking at. I told her I was looking at that cat between her legs, so shut the fuck up. She came off the porch with a big stick and started chasing me down the street. She fell down while she was chasing me and her dress went up over her head, exposing all her ass and pussy. All the kids on the block got to see her pussy that day, I never tried to see it again. It just did not look as good as I thought it would, maybe because she is an older lady.

I started to have wet dreams every night, and I was really embarrassed because I would wake up and my underwear would be wet. Apparently in the middle of the night I was grinding on my pillow. I must have thought it was a big juicy pussy. It had gotten so bad that I was scared to go to sleep at night, for fear of having a wet dream. In the morning when I woke up I would hurry up to the bathroom to hide my wet underwear. I was really frightened because I thought if it happened too much I would die.

One day I saw one of the older boys, Danny, having sex with the retarded boy, Dewey, underneath Second Arch. They both had their pants pulled down and Danny was trying to stick his crooked dick in Dewey's ass. I don't think either one of them was gay they were just experimenting. I don't know if he ever got it in Dewey's ass because I left and told the other kids.

They all ran down to see them in action, and I think some of the other kids got some of Dewey's ass too. The next time I saw Dewey, I told him that he really shouldn't be doing that and if he did it again I would tell his mother. I know that I did some mean things to Dewey over the years, but I did not want to see that kind of stuff happening to him. I guess I was getting soft in my older age.

All the girls my age seemed to like the older boys so we were stuck with the little bony, no titties girls. The ugly girls in my neighborhood were called bats. We all thought that bats were ugly little creatures that would bite you. They were the only ones who would pay any attention to us, and they did not want to have sex yet. The older boys built a clubhouse that was underneath the ground and we were not allowed in it. We would hide and watch their clubhouse. They always had some girls down there, but we didn't know what they were doing. So, we decided to build one of our own so that we could get some girls in our clubhouse. However, we couldn't find any girls to go to the clubhouse with us.

The older boys were doing a thing called the "booty grind" to the girls in the neighborhood, so we started doing it to the younger girls. Usually the girls were both fat and ugly, but it was better than nothing. We did not have any fun doing the booty grind with the ugly girls; it just did not turn us on. Shila, one of the older girls, asked me to do the booty grind with her. We grinded so hard and so long my dick exploded and I ejaculated in my pants. When she looked down and saw my wet pants and the dumb look on my face, she ran off laughing out loud.

I had to walk home with some stiff sticky pants through the neighborhood and I was very embarrassed. It felt so good when I ejaculated; it was worth every minute of embarrassment. I finally knew what the older boys meant when they were talking about "dry fucking". I'm not sure why they called it dry fucking because my pants sure got wet when I did it. I found out later

what it meant to dry fuck. It meant having an orgasm without actually penetrating the wet juicy pussy with your dick.
I had to stop swimming naked because my dick would always get hard just from the water moving against it. So, I started swimming in my pants just to hide my hard on, because it was so big. It had gotten to the point that I just didn't go swimming anymore unless I was by myself.

As a group we would walk around playing a game called "Sneak a feel". Two of us would walk down the hallway of the school, and one person would bump a girl while the other would grab her ass or titties. We would alternate which one would get the feel and which person would do the bumping. Most of the time the girl got bumped so hard that she didn't notice, but sometimes we did get caught and we would run off laughing.

I decided to start playing sports to see if it would ease some of the stresses of my sex drive. I played baseball in the summer time and basketball in the winter. Most of the time I was so tired that I didn't think about sex. During the summer time when I played baseball, I was the pitcher. I turned out to be one of the best pitchers in the league, but I decided to quit because I had to play in a dirty uniform. My mom just would not take the time to wash my uniform, she just did not care. I did not know how to wash clothes and no one ever tried to teach me. When the coach found out that I had quit, he rode down to Jackson Street to talk to me. I told him my problem and he told me that he would make sure my uniform got cleaned before each game.

I continued to play, and we won the championship. I was glad that I stayed on the team. Winning the championship was really exciting because I never won anything like that before. We had a picnic in the park; they passed out trophies and played games. All of the other kids' parents were there to share in the celebration with their children. My mother never showed up for any of the games or the picnic. I was envious of all the other kids who had caring parents at the picnic. I always wondered what that must feel like.

We had a lot of good food: corn, ribs, potato chips, candy

and a lot of soda, all the stuff I was not used to having. One of the games that I won at the picnic was the big bubble gum blowing contest. All of the kids got a piece of gum to chew and whoever could blow the biggest bubble would win. I blew the biggest bubble that I ever blew in my life; even I was surprised at it. I won a silver dollar that I cherished for a long time. I was fourteen years old when I won the silver dollar and still had it a year later. I kept it hidden in my room underneath my bed so no one could find it.

When I wasn't playing baseball or basketball, I was going to house parties. At the house parties, we got to grind on the girls during the slow songs and sometimes we got to feel on their asses. The most embarrassing part about slow dancing was how my dick would always get hard. I decided to start wearing a jock strap to the dances but that hurt badly because it still got hard. So I had to stop doing that. It just was not worth it. It hurt too badly.

Always, no matter what party we were at, 15 minutes before the party was over someone would start a fight. The girls would always leave 15 minutes early because they knew a fight was going to break out and they did not want to get hurt. We fought for hours sometimes against rival gangs. Sometimes it got real ugly. There would probably be maybe 30 to 40 kids fighting that night, until the police would arrive. We probably fought so much because we weren't getting any pussy from the girls. All the little towns had their own gangs; our gang is called the "Jackson Street Boys". We would fight with the other gangs every time we had a chance.

Down on Jackson Street, there was a place called the White House; this was the prostitutes' home and place of work. They usually worked Monday through Saturday from 9:00pm to 6:00am... The man that owned the house was "Fred Isley". The prostitutes would walk by my house every afternoon on their way into town. If I would have had some money, I would have brought some pussy from them, which is how good they looked to me. White men from outside of the neighborhood came through in the evenings asking for directions. We would charge a dollar to give directions to the "Ho house".

One white man would bring his wife with him and pay the older boys to fuck his wife while he watched. They would fuck her in the back seat of the car while he sat and watched in the front seat. Sometimes she would fuck as many as ten boys in one night. He would pay $20.00 per person just for that, we all thought he was crazy. He showed up every Saturday like clockwork around 11:00pm. Sometimes he would pay $10.00 just to let his wife suck their dicks. This went on for a couple years. Then it stopped and no one knew why. Man, those boys really missed that easy money. I wish I could have got in on that, but I was too young.

The older boys started wearing perms with waves in their hair with a black scarf around their head. They put chemical relaxers in their hair and then put waves in it. The younger guys, we started doing it too and the next thing I knew, it seemed as if we all had them. The Jackson Street boys became known for wearing chemical relaxers and black scarves around our heads. We were the bad boys from the creek, and we did not care about getting in trouble. When people would see us, they knew there was going to be some kind of trouble. None of the working class people wanted their daughters to talk to us, but girls liked bad boys.

"Rommy" was in charge of the older boys who were sixteen to eighteen years old and I was in charge of the younger ones, who were thirteen to fifteen years old. We went to the stores in downtown Brownsville, in groups, to steal clothes every Saturday. We would take turns wearing the clothes we stole. Our mothers never asked where we got the clothes, I'm not sure why. I guess they did not want to know. The police would chase us, but they never caught us. We stole cars from the middle class neighborhoods and would burn them up back at Jackson Street for the fun of it.

One night we got a sledgehammer and went downtown to break all the parking meters to get the change out of them. Our pockets were so full of change; we could hardly run when the police came. That time the police followed the line of coins to an abandoned house on the street, and we got caught. They took all five of us to the police station and put us in the jail cell. While we were in the jail cell, we put all the coins in the toilet and tried to flush them. The police never checked our pockets when they arrested us, so we still had the coins in our pockets. However, the coins were too heavy to flush and the toilet spilled over onto the floor. The police came from the other room and found the money in the toilet. They made us clean up all that mess and get all the coins out of the toilets. We were teenagers so nothing happened to us, except getting our ass beat by our parents.

One day Miss "Margot" caught "Shila" and me on the lawn chair on my front porch underneath a blanket kissing and grinding. Miss Margot snatched the blanket off of us just as I was getting ready to suck Shila's titties. She beat Shila's ass right there and cussed me out. My mother heard the commotion and went outside and told Miss Margo that she better not be cussing me out. Miss Margot told my mom, "Keep your damn son away from my daughter". My mom told her that we were on her fucking porch and for her to keep her fast ass daughter away from her house. My mom and Miss Margot started fighting, and my mom whooped her ass. They fought for about fifteen minutes and then one of the neighbors broke it up. They both had ripped clothes and their titties were hanging out, but they did not care who saw them. Shila had run in her house when they were fighting. Maybe she was embarrassed by them. The funny thing about it is they were drinking together again the next day. Miss Margot did make sure that Shila stayed away from me. When she saw me around, she would make Shila go in the house until I was gone.

I did get to play house with the younger girls. All we did was grind and kiss and that was all I got. One thing I couldn't get was oral sex, and I really wanted to try that. Sometimes we would grind so hard we would both be bruised in the groin area. My dick would hurt so bad sometimes I could hardly walk home.

It was something I knew I couldn't do everyday. A couple times we would try to put a blanket or pillow between us to ease the pain. But, it didn't feel as good. One day I grinded so long and hard my dick started bleeding and I was very scared. I told my older brother David and he looked down and saw the blood on my pants and took me to mom and told her I fell down and hit my dick.

She made me show her my dick and she thought it was swollen and bleeding from the head, and then she took me to the emergency room at the hospital. The nurse made me get undressed and show her my dick. When the nurse touched it, it started to get hard. My mother was embarrassed and so was the nurse because, it got so big. I guess they did not expect a kid my age to have such a big dick and it showed in their face. My mom said "Holy shit, look how big my boy's dick is" and the nurse turned her head to look away. I started to cry because I didn't know what else to do. Finally the doctor came in and asked what happened to me. He told the nurse to put some ice on it, and it went down in a couple of hours. They told my mom that I must have broke some blood vessels inside, and I should be all right in a couple weeks.

I heard my mother telling Miss Margot about what happened at the hospital. She told her that I had a big dick "just like his no good ass daddy had". I figured that this would put me deeper on the shit list with Miss Margot. Soon everyone in the neighborhood found out about my big dick, and I was the shit again. Some of the kids asked to see it, but I wouldn't let them. Even my brothers wanted to see it but I said no. One morning while I was sleeping, my brother pulled my pants down and they saw it. What made me mad was that after my brother saw it, he punched me in the stomach and ran down stairs laughing. He was at the bottom of the steps laughing when I picked up a fork off the floor and threw it at him. It stuck in the side of his face and he started screaming and ran to tell mom. She beat my ass and grounded me.

Even my brothers were bragging on my big dick in the

figured he might be a little upset if he knew what his mother and I had done.

It was official; I was no longer a virgin, but I couldn't tell anybody, nobody would believe me anyway. The only other person that knew was Shila, and I knew she wasn't going to say anything. I just hoped that someday I would be able to get some of her pussy also. The next day when I saw Miss Margot she acted like nothing happened. Maybe she was to drunk to remember or she just didn't want to remember. My mother noticed she was walking a little funny that next day and Miss Margot told her that "Tonny Ball" tore that pussy up. I just laughed to myself when I heard her say that because I knew I was the big dog on the block.

A few weeks later Shila called me, and she told me she would be babysitting for her older sister that Friday night. She asked me if I wanted to come over and hang out with her and I said yes. She called me Friday evening and told me when her sister had left. She told me she would leave the basement door open. I crept through the basement door and met her at the top of the steps. She had a robe on and while I was feeling around on her I noticed she didn't have any panties on. I was surprised and really wasn't sure what to do. She bent down and started sucking my dick and it got hard as steel. She told me to come with her into the kitchen.

When we got in the kitchen she took her robe off and lay down on the floor naked and told me to get on top. I didn't even take my pants off I just jumped on top, but I couldn't find the hole to put it in, so she had to help me. Since this was the first time I actually got to get on top of someone and put it in, I really wasn't sure what to do. We had a hard time getting it in, either because she was so small or I was so big. While I was trying to put it in further she was hollering in pain. She hollered so loud I thought the kids were going to wake up so I stuck my hand over her mouth to keep her quiet. Every time I tried to stick it in deeper she made more noise so I quit trying. Finally I ejaculated. I might have made more noise than her because she reached up and covered my mouth so hard I could hardly breathe. When I pulled my dick out it had blood on it. I was scared that I had broken my dick again. After we checked we found out it was her who was bleeding. Who would have thought she was a virgin? A month later she told me that she thought she was pregnant, and I was really scared because I was only 15 years old.

"Believe in Change"

Chapter 6

The High School Dropout

I found out a month later that Shila had a false alarm about her pregnancy. I thought it would be best if I stayed away from her and I concentrated on sports instead. None of my brothers played sports. I guess they were to busy running in the streets. I played so much basketball that I didn't have time for girls. The head cheerleader "Ann Kinson" was the girl I wanted and dreamed about having all my life. She was a light skinned black girl with long black hair that hung down her back. She had a smile that would brighten up a cloudy day. She was the prettiest girl I ever saw in my life, and I had to have her.

She was from the other side of the tracks; she was one of the middle class girls. Her father used to coach the Biddy League team "The Lawyers", something he enjoyed doing for many years. This is where I first saw her; it was like looking at an angel. This was a league put together for age's six to ten to play basketball against each other. We won three championships in a row when I played on his team. She was always at the games, but I knew better than to try and talk to her. What are the chances of a person like me ever getting a girl like her? Her father, the coach for the Lawyers, always smelled like beer and was a mean man. She was from a middle class working family, and I could only dream about her.

In high school, I was a basketball star. A lot of girls would try and hit on me, but I wanted Ann Kinson. It was known around town that her father didn't like anyone from Jackson Street. He thought that they were low class and he was right. We were poor and poor people probably should stay with their own kind. He did not have to treat us like he was so much better than us. During the games when the cheerleaders would call our names, I could hear her cheering, saying "Ron, Ron he's our man if he can't do it no one can". Hearing this inspired me to play better, because I wanted to get her attention. She didn't know that I liked her. I didn't even tell my friends about how I felt. I knew they would laugh and make jokes about it. Everyone on Jackson Street knew to stay within their own class, but nothing was wrong with dreaming. We all need our dreams, without them what else do we have on Jackson Street.

I was 6'3", 168 pounds of muscle with gapped front teeth in my mouth. That is why I never smiled; I was too embarrassed to smile. I was always quiet around everyone because I didn't want anyone to see my teeth; my talent in sports talked for me. One day right before the game, I put black dye in my hair because my hair was brown. I thought black would make my hair look better, and I would do anything to try to impress Ann. But I forgot to rinse it out. It ran down my face, in my eyes, and on my uniform during the game. I was so embarrassed. I didn't even know that it had to be rinsed out real good. I was sure that people thought it was dirt, and I never used dye again. My eyes burned so bad I could hardly see the basket to make a shot; I had a real bad game that day.

In school I never took a book home or did my homework because I did not feel I needed to in order to pass into the next grade. I always passed until the ninth grade. The school failed me, but I did not care. On the last day of school, I was brought into the principal's office. The principal wanted to talk to me about a fight we were supposed to have with this rival gang. I was the leader of my gang, "The Jackson Street Boys" and they figured if they talk to me, they could stop the fight. State police were at the school because the school asked them to be there to help out.

The trouble all started in school when I knocked "Bunny Young" (leader of the rival gang) through a glass window at a dance. So Bunny and I decided to finish our fight on the last day of school. The state police were there in anticipation of a violent day among the two gangs. They made us shake hands. It really didn't mean anything because I knew I was going to get Bunny and all those motherfuckers with him. It was a quiet day at school because there just was too many police around to start a fight that day. If we would have fought that day, I'm sure someone would have died. Maybe me.

My report card came to my house a couple of weeks later, and it said that I had to repeat 9th grade. I got it out of the mailbox before my mother got to see it. I never told my mother, I knew she didn't care anyway. The next year the school put me in the boiler room, "a class for non typical students," or with the retarded kids. All the kids in this class had learning disabilities; they were the joke of the school. The room was at the bottom of the school near the boilers. That is why the kids called it the boiler room. I didn't care as long as I could play basketball, which was very important to me.

Dewey was the first one to greet me on the first day in the boiler room. I knew that I wasn't supposed to be there, because they were dumb as hell. Dewey and I started having farting battles in class because I was so bored. We drank chocolate milk because it gave us gas, to make us fart. I had gas real bad, which made me fart a lot, but I blamed it on Dewey. He would just laugh real hard when I farted so I made it seem like he was the one doing it. The teacher thought it was me, but he could not prove it. It got so bad that the teacher made me sit by his desk so he could catch me. I just quit farting, although I was really bloated. Most of the time, the class room smelled so bad that none of the other teachers ever came to our room.

One day I put thumb tacks in the teacher's chair when he left the room so that he could sit on them. He hollered loud when he sat on his chair and ended up with about fifteen tacks in his ass. He knew it was me, but he wasn't able to catch me as usual. All we did all day in that class was wood shop, welding, and some 3rd grade academics. I really had it made because I did not want to do anything academically. The retarded kids were fucking themselves up by hitting each other with hammers and wood because they did not know any better. They were dangerous but no one cared about them because they were not important enough to care. It seemed like an ambulance was up at the school everyday taking someone to the hospital. I just stood back and watched as all this craziness went on.

One day at lunch time, I went into my teacher's car, which was left open in the parking lot behind the school. I told Dewey and two of the other kids to get in the car to go for a ride. I put it in neutral, started pushing it until it started moving on its own. They were laughing when I started pushing the car, but when they went over the hillside they started screaming. I went and told the teacher that they took his car, and it went over the hill. The teacher went down the hill to see what happened to his car and the kids. The car was lying up against a tree and smoking, looking like it was ready to catch on fire. If it wasn't for the tree, it would have gone to the bottom of the hill. The car started burning and the kids were trying to get out of the car.

The teacher was trying to get the doors open but none of them would open. I went down the hill to see if I could help him get them out of the car. I was just bored and trying to have some fun; I didn't want to kill any of the kids. I took a rock and broke one side of the window then I, and the teacher, started pulling the boys out. I pulled Dewey and another boy out, and the teacher was still trying to pull the last boy out. The car was almost completely engulfed with fire and we noticed the kid in the back seat was not moving. Finally, the teacher got him out as the car exploded knocking me and everyone else on their asses. The boy and the teacher got out and were lying on the ground asking for help. I went over to the boy and dragged him up the hill where the other kids were at. I was tired because I had to drag all the boys up the hill by myself; they were heavy.

There was smoke everywhere, and the teacher was on fire. I went and rolled him with my feet because he was just too heavy to try to pick up. He rolled down the hill about fifty feet and the fire on his clothes went out. The fire truck, ambulance and police were there. I told the police what happened, how I saved the day. The boys were scared and bruised up but they were going to be okay. The teacher had minor burns and a broken leg. I found the teacher's wallet as I was walking back up the hill and took the money that I found inside of it. I kept the $157.00 that was inside the wallet. I figure that I earned it for helping him. I brought the whole class ice cream and cake the next day. That was the least I could do. There was a write up in the local paper about how I saved the day. I was a hero from Jackson Street who saved some mentally challenged kids. Even the uppity girls started speaking to me after that day. I was happy that no one got hurt real bad, especially the kids. I guess I was lucky this time. I'm not use to having good luck, but this is something I can get use to.

After a couple a months in that class, the school board made us all take an IQ test. When the results came back they said that I didn't belong in that class. I had an IQ of a 167, which was well above the intelligence in that class. They put me in the 10th grade even though I flunked the 9th grade. I wasn't happy there, because I didn't have any clothes to wear to school. All the clothes that I had were old with holes in them; I was really embarrassed to wear them.

My mother still didn't know what was going on with me and the school. After a couple of weeks in the 10th grade, the principal called me into the office and said I couldn't be there because it wasn't fair to the people who passed the ninth grade. So there I went again, off to a technical school about twenty miles away from Brownsville, (my hometown). I had to ride a bus everyday with some of the rival gang members. I didn't know if they were going to try to get me because I did not have anyone to help me if something went down. All these school changes and still not one sign of concern from my mother about what was going on in my life.

As long as I could play basketball, I was okay with that. In that school, it didn't matter how we dressed because there were not any girls there that I liked. The boys in this school were not retarded; they were just trouble makers. I was there without the support of my gang, but I wasn't scared. I had a lot of anger built up inside of me and was just waiting to release it. I knew I was going to get respect because of the reputation that I had with some of the other students that knew about me. I just had to figure out how to get more respect.

The toughest guy in the school was named, "Sugar Bear". He was short, stocky and looked like a 250 pound black bear. I knew that I needed to take him down quick, but I knew that he was too strong for me. I had to think of something, I knew that if something was to happen I wanted it to be outside at lunchtime. I found two bricks and stuck each one in my coat pockets. When I went outside the kids from some of the other gangs; about ten of them were all standing there just looking at me. It looked like they were waiting to start some trouble with me. I asked Sugar Bear, "What the fuck you looking at". Sugar Bear said, "I'm looking at you, punk nigger".

He started walking towards me and as he took his coat off and threw it on the ground. I took my coat off like he did but I didn't throw my coat like he did his. I had my coat hanging on my arm, waiting until he got close enough to me. When he got closer, I swung it as hard as I could and hit him in the head. That big nigger went down fast to the ground. When he hit the ground, I kicked him in the head with both feet. There was blood all over the place.

His boys started walking towards me, I started wiping his blood off me and sticking it in my mouth. I knew that this would make them think that I was crazy and it did. They stopped and said to each other "That motherfucker is out of his mind". So everyone went back to class, leaving Sugar Bear all crumpled up on the ground. When I left, Sugar Bear wasn't moving. I made sure I took his money and jewelry off of him. I had a change of clothes hidden in my locker just in case I got blood on me. I was glad that it was not my blood.

I washed all the blood off of me and threw my clothes in the school furnace and went to class. The ambulance and police came, but no one said anything about what happened. A week later Sugar Bear was still in a coma, in grave condition. They said even if he lived he would have brain damage. He was the type of nigger you had to hurt badly or he would keep coming back. There were a lot of stories about Sugar Bear breaking people's arms and legs if he had trouble with someone. There even was a rumor out about him killing his own brother in a fight over some shoes. I was hoping that he would die so that I wouldn't have to deal with him again and finally a week later he died while still in a coma. The police were still asking questions around the school, but everyone kept quiet. You didn't want to be known as a snitch; that would mean certain death.

Since it was a black on black crime, the police didn't stay on the case long. I felt sorry for his family, but I knew I needed to do what ever I had to, to survive and I would do it again. A lot of people asked me if I killed Sugar Bear, including my brothers, but I never answered them. I didn't feel like I killed him, I felt like I had to do whatever I had to do at the time. If you're going to be top dog you should expect someone to be gunning for you. That is why I never wanted to be top dog; it was something that was given to me. I'd rather let someone else be top dog so I could just chill in the shadows. As long as I got my respect, I was alright with anyone. Violence has always been the answer in my neighborhood. This is all I have ever seen; we are products of our environment. I felt like Sugar Bear would have killed me if I did not get to him first. You have to make your move before the other person does.

The school wanted everyone to take an IQ test, and I refused to take one. So they suspended me from school. I was scared that they would try and put me back with them so-called typical kids. They said I couldn't come back unless my mother came with me. I knew that wasn't going to happen. I never told my mother about it, and we didn't have a phone so they couldn't call. Every morning I would get up like I was going to school, but I would wait until the pool hall opened up and that's where I would stay until it was time for basketball practice. I did that all basketball season without getting caught. The coach didn't even know that I wasn't in school. I had it made. It couldn't get any better than that. I got to play a game that I loved and did not have to go to school. Everything was going great. We were on our way to a championship; the whole team was built around my game. Everyone was counting on me to help the school win the championship.

The day before we were going to play the championship game, the coach called me in his office. He told me that he was going to kick me off the team because I wasn't going to school. I didn't even say anything to him; I just turned and walked out the office. I was really hurt and depressed for a long time after that. I never played school ball again, and the team lost the championship that year. I really felt bad that I let the coach and the team down. I wish that I could go back and change what happened. I just did not think that it would ever come to this. At home, I didn't even fake like I was going to school anymore. My mother never said anything after I told her they kicked me out of school a couple of months ago. The motto on Jackson Street was "Live fast, die young and have a good looking corpse". My basketball career was too fast. I still wanted to play ball, but I could not. I didn't know what to do to fill that hole in my heart. I began to hate my life even more now. I had no one to go to for guidance. I had no father, no real mother; all I had was Jackson Street. I was the blind being lead by the blind.

Just the thought of not hearing the cheerleaders say "Ron, Ron he's our man if he can't do it, no one can", really bothered me. Who would have thought that just because of an IQ test I wouldn't have been able to do something I loved? Maybe I wasn't as smart as they thought. I was used to things not going my way and the people from Jackson Street had gained a special strength from that. The people from my street have been knocked down so many times that we get more desensitized each time it happens. I still knew that some day I would get the girl I wanted, even without basketball. Until then, I still had Jackson Street to deal with. ***"Believe in Change"***

Chapter 7

Mom's Little Secret

At age sixteen, since I was no longer in school, I spent most of my time shooting pool. I became very good at it, to the point where I was able to make a little money gambling. The first time I played pool was when I was twelve years old. A week later I was beating the guy who taught me how to play. He wasn't happy with that, because he was older and thought he was pretty good. He was in his early twenties, but he was only an average pool player. I was a natural at the game; everything about the game came easy to me. There were two pool halls in Brownsville, Loop's and Casper's. Loop's was a small pool hall with five tables and Casper's had about twenty.

It was more expensive to play at Casper's and hard to gamble there, so I spent most of my time at Loop's. "Nel Bish" was the best black pool shooter in town, and I knew that I would be as good as him one day if I kept practicing. A white boy named "Adam" was the best player in the town. He was different than Nel, because Adam was real quiet and Nel talked a lot of shit. I knew someday Nel and I would bump heads on the pool table and that wouldn't be a good day for one of us. There is an up and coming player from Jackson Street named "Sidney Prince". He is younger than me, but shows a lot of potential on the pool table. If he continues to play, maybe someday he will be the next champ from Jackson Street. Right now I am the best player from Jackson Street, and I plan on keeping it that way for a long time.

During the summer, I got a job working in the park. We did mostly painting and cutting grass. I only worked on Mondays, Thursdays, and Fridays from nine until two. I wanted to be able to buy some new clothes and it was real easy work. The job was through a special summer program for teenagers in Brownsville. I made about $150.00 every two weeks, which was a lot of money for a person from my street. My mother tried to get some of my money, but I wouldn't give her shit because I knew she would drink it all up. I always hid my money so she couldn't find it. I would get paid on Friday and my money would be gone on Monday because I spent every penny on clothes and junk food.

Some of the white boys who worked at the park chewed tobacco, and I tried it once and got real sick. I felt like I was going to die after putting that tobacco in my mouth. I never tried it again. I also tried my first cigarette, and I got sick from that too, but I thought that the older kids looked cool doing it so I kept on trying it. After about ten attempts, I finally got the hang of smoking. A group of us from Jackson Street would get up early on Sunday and go to downtown Brownsville picking up cigarette butts, but only the big ones. We would do that all summer because we were too young to buy cigarettes. We didn't care about germs. We just wanted to look cool. Some of the cigarette butts had lipstick on them, but we didn't care, because we were cool. We thought the cigarettes made us look older and more mature. I used to steal my mother's cigarettes until she started hiding them from me.

Sometimes in the evenings we would work at the bowling alley setting bowling pins. This was before they had automatic pinsetters. We would get a couple dollars for every game we set. It was determined by seniority which of us got to work on a given day. Sometimes if someone didn't show up to work, we would have to set two lanes at one time. It was very hard work, but at least it kept me out of trouble. We would usually work a few nights a week, sometimes more. One night, Gary and I were going to work at the bowling alley. It was a warm spring night in May (around 6:00pm). We got halfway across the street, and I tripped him intentionally. He fell down with an angry look on his face.

He got up just in time to get hit by a car that was coming straight for him. The car knocked him up in the air; he flew right by me as I was standing on the sidewalk across the street, where he was trying to get to. I had to duck to get out of the way from getting hit by my brother's body. He was screaming in pain as he held on to his leg. I was not sure what to do because I was stunned by the whole event. I walked right by him and ran into the bowling alley to tell the boss what happened. The ambulance came to get him, and I ran all the way home to tell my mother what happened. One of his legs was broken in two places. It was in bad shape. I never went to the hospital to see him because I felt bad about what I did. How was I to know that he was going to get hit by a car? I told my mother it was an accident when he tripped over my foot. She just rolled her eyes at me and walked away mumbling under her breath. I'm not sure if she believed me.

Gary and I had got a red bike that year for Christmas that we had to share with each other. We were excited about getting a bike; this was the best Christmas gift that we ever got from our mother. We never got much so we always had to share gifts. I got to ride it everyday while he was in the hospital for four weeks. Before then, we would alternate days for riding the bike. I figured even when he came home from the hospital, he wouldn't be able to ride the bike. He came home with a big cast on his leg, and I could tell he was still mad at me. The next day when I went to ride the bike, he wouldn't let me and said it was his turn to ride that day. I wondered how he was going to ride a bike with a broken leg. I told him he couldn't ride because of his leg and he said he didn't care, and grabbed the bike from me.

I figured this was a good time to try and beat his ass, since this is something that I have wanted to do for a long time. I knew he would not be able to beat me with a broken leg. I was getting ready to punch him, but he took his crutches and he hit me in the head. He hit me so hard that I almost passed out; I saw stars floating in the air. I looked up from the ground, where I had fallen and I asked him not to hit me again. That sure woke me up and I didn't try to get the bike on his day again. I still think he was just being mean because all he did on his bike days was sit on the porch with the bike. I would probably be acting the same way if I had a broken leg and could not ride the bike. He did exactly what I would have done.

It was time for our yearly flood again, and the creek was rising faster than usual. This time there was something different about it. Everything was moving so fast. The people seemed nervous; no one was laughing and joking this time, which was unusual for people on Jackson Street. Some people decided to leave when they noticed the water rising faster than usual and head for higher ground, but not us. We had nowhere else to go, so we were stuck in that house.

By nightfall the water had covered the first floor and didn't seem to be slowing down. It had been flooding for five hours. There was no indication that it was going to slow down. You could feel the house sway as the waves hit the house. The outhouses in the back yard started floating away; the neighborhood rats were heading for higher ground. You could see the rats scrambling up the hill; at least they had some place to go. We were a little scared, but we had no plans to go anywhere because we had no place to go.

As I looked down the steps, I could see the water was starting up the steps. That was the highest I ever saw the water come up, and I thought it was exciting to watch. It did not dawn on me that maybe we could all die in the flood. All my brothers and me knew how to swim, but my mother and sister didn't. It felt like the whole house was going to lift off its foundation and start floating away. I thought it would probably be the best thing for Jackson Street, if the whole place would just float away and we could start over somewhere else.

At this point, the only thing I saw floating away was the shit houses. No one else was paying any attention to what was going on outside. I guess because we have been through so many floods. Everyone went to sleep that night around 11:00pm. Not me, I wasn't planning on waking to find myself floating in the creek. Normally it would take about 24 hours for the water to make it up to the second floor, but this time it did that in about half the time.

When my mother woke up the next morning around 7:00am, she saw me staring out the window and she walked over to the window where I was sitting. She screamed in fear and said, "Why in the hell didn't you tell me the water was up to the roof?" She went over to the steps and the water was two steps from coming in upstairs. The water must have risen about eight feet overnight. That was a lot compare to past floods. I didn't feel the need to tell her because it wasn't like she had a boat or a phone to call someone to come save us. She woke everyone up and started hollering out of the window for the neighbors to make sure they knew how high the water was. I guess all my dumb ass neighbors were asleep or passed out drunk because it took awhile for anyone to respond to her.

The next thing I knew everyone on the street was screaming out of their windows for help, but there was no one to hear them. Finally, two hours later we heard the fire department using bullhorns telling us not to panic. They were saying that someone would be there to rescue everyone with canoes. It took them all morning to finally get us; they only had two canoes to save everyone. I think we were the sixth family to be saved that day. It was exciting watching the other families getting into the canoes from their second floor windows. All five kids, including my mother got into the canoe; I did not know if we all could fit.

The canoe was shaking and swaying, it was like being on an amusement park ride. I was scared of the canoe ride more than being in the flood. Maybe because I never been in a canoe before; this was a new experience for all of us. By the time we were all in the little canoe, the water was on the second floor and still rising. The water must have got to be thirty feet high. I had never imagined that it could get that high. We were all standing near the fire truck looking at the house being engulf in flood waters. If they hadn't come, I would have started swimming to land with or without my family. The currents were so rapid, I don't know if I could have made it across. It was probably a good thing that the fire department came to save us.

Maybe the reason I didn't wake my family is because somewhere deep down inside I wanted all of them to die. I'll never really know, because they woke up on their own. We didn't have anywhere to go and stay. So the landlord said we could stay at his house until we were able to move back in our house. I do not know where the other families went to stay, maybe at the fire station in downtown Brownsville. The landlord owned about five houses on Jackson Street, and they all looked like shit. I'm not sure why the landlord was at the flood. Maybe to make sure his fuck up houses didn't float away.

When we were in our landlord's house, I found out what it was like to have money. It was a beautiful house away from that stinking creek. The landlord was living like a king, while we were down in the ghetto on Jackson Street. The landlord would never leave us alone in his house; someone was always there to keep an eye on us. Either he or one of the other family members would be in the house at all times. I guess they didn't trust us, and they were right because I knew I was going to rob them and not feel bad about it. I heard he had a daughter about my age, and I couldn't wait to see her.

When I did finally get to see her, she was ugly as hell, plus she was fat. I never ever saw anyone so ugly before in my life, and I seen a lot of ugly people before. All the money in the world couldn't help her. I'd rather live on Jackson Street the rest of my life than to be as ugly as her. They had to look at her everyday. It hurt me to look at her for thirty seconds. All the money in the world can not change ugly. We all stayed in two rooms. My mother and sister had one room and the boys had the other room. We did eat well that week, plus we had a real bathroom with a shower in it. I wanted to stay there for the rest of my life, but I knew we had to go back to Jackson Street again. That was the first time that I really knew how much I was missing in life. This really increased my desire to get off of Jackson Street.

About a week later we were able to move back in that broke down house. The Red Cross had it all cleaned up, and my mom got vouchers for clothes and furniture. We went shopping and got some new clothes. The family going shopping was always a nightmare for my mother, but we were all excited as we rode in the jitney on the way to the store. We all acted like fools in the stores when we went, which was not that often. Mom gave us the same speech about how she was going to beat our ass if we acted up. She always wanted us to stay together so she could keep an eye on us. Whenever we went shopping, Gary, David and I would always sneak off and get in some mischief.

This time, the first place we headed for was the food section to steal some food. We would open and sample all the sweets that we could get our hands on. Then we would go to the fruit section, get some cantaloupes and play a game called "people bowling". We went to the aisles to see how many people we could bowl and hit with the cantaloupes. It was ten points for adults and five points for kids. We could get 20 points if we could knock an adult down on the floor. David was ahead on points when it was my turn to bowl.

It took me awhile to find the right person. I found a husband and a wife pushing a stroller with two little boys beside them. I rolled the cantaloupe as hard as I could. It hit the husband in his ankle and he fell into his wife, who fell and knocked the stroller over, which knocked the two kids down. The baby rolled down the aisle crying with the mother chasing behind her. We would run and hide before the store manager arrived. I was the winner and still the champ because I got the whole family.

The next game we played was called "The canned food throw", which was always exciting because you never knew who you were going to hit. We would go down the canned food aisle and throw cans over into the next aisle. The one that hit the most people out of three throws would win. Gary threw first, but he missed because we did not hear anyone scream in pain. David went next and hit an old white woman in the head. She went down screaming, and people started running to help her. One of the people that came to help her was my mom, sister and little brother, Robert.

I waited until everyone gathered around the lady. I threw all three cans at one time. I hit three people, and one of them was my mom. When I went over and saw my mom, she had a huge knot on her head. She was pissed off; she was looking for someone to fight now. She was talking to the manager of the store and cursing him out. I asked her what happened. She told me to shut the fuck up, and I did. I was happy I hit her in the head, since she has been hitting me in my head all my life. I wished I had used a bigger can; maybe it would have knocked some sense into her. The police came and put us all out of the store. I didn't even have time to steal anything. We didn't get to buy anything either. My mom went out the next day without us and brought some dumb clothes and food home. We really didn't care what the clothes looked like; as long as they were new.

That summer my aunt "Phyllis" from Philadelphia came to visit. She was my mom's older sister, and she brought her son with her. He was about five years older than my oldest brother David. His name was "Harry", and he looked a lot like us except he was short compared to me. He was about 5' 2" tall. He looked just like my mom, except he had a darker complexion. Mom told us they were coming a few weeks before they got there. She seemed really excited about seeing her sister again. I was kind of happy for her. I have not seen this kind of emotion from her in years. She was making sure the house was spotless and everything in place. I have not seen her drinking alcohol in a couple of weeks. It was like we had a new mom and that made all of us happy. We were excited also because we never met any other family before.

The day they arrived was real crazy because my mom started crying as soon as they walked through the door. She fell down on the floor, and my aunt had to drag her up to her room.

All the kids were just standing there in shock trying to figure out what in the hell is going on. My cousin, Harry, didn't even react. He just looked at us and said "Hi" and sat down on the couch. Maybe he was use to seeing people act crazy like that. I could hear my mom upstairs crying, and I really wondered what was going on. Finally after about fifteen minutes of being in my mom's room, my mom and my aunt came downstairs. They were quiet for a minute. Then they told everyone to sit down. I thought someone must have died in Philadelphia because they had such serious looks on their faces. We didn't really know anyone in Philly, so I couldn't figure out what was the big deal. My mom didn't say anything; my aunt Phyllis did all the talking.

My aunt was a big woman, weighing about 250 pounds on a five feet five frame. She looked like she could beat a grown man's ass if he said the wrong thing to her. I could tell by Harry's actions that she wasn't to be played with. He was standing there like he was scared to move or talk. My mom was a city girl. I knew she could cuss and fight, and so I figured every woman in the family was like that. My aunt said she had something important to tell us, and we should all listen carefully. Suddenly my mom started crying again and ran upstairs to her room. I hoped that she would stay there, so we could finally get out of the house.

My aunt followed after her and shut the door. This time we could hear them arguing loudly. My aunt came out and slammed the door saying, "They need to know now". My aunt started saying, "This is about your mother, and the reason we didn't tell you before is because you were too young". I thought maybe she was not my mother, and some rich lady in Philadelphia wanted us back. My aunt told us that when my mom was very young she got pregnant in Philadelphia and had a baby. She was only twelve years old and not old enough to raise a child. I remember thinking to myself that my mom had sex at a really young age. I did not get any pussy until I was fifteen damn years old. I guess they do things faster in the big city. I wish I was born in the city like my mom.

My aunt told us that since she was the oldest, she raised the child for my mother. This was 24 years ago, and this boy is sitting right there on the couch. She was pointing towards Harry when she said it. My aunt was in her early twenties when she started raising Harry for my mother. Harry stood up and said, "Yes I am your older brother; sorry we have to meet like this". I thought my aunt was playing some dumb game on us. My aunt said that she told Harry when he was twenty-one years old. My mom never saw him until today when he came through the door.

I guess that's why she broke down so bad. I started wondering what other deep dark secrets my mom was hiding from us. I asked my aunt who was Harry's dad and was Harry going to live with us now. My aunt said, "It's not important who Harry's dad is, and no he is not going to live with you". She said, "Harry is a grown man, he can do anything he wants to do". I was happy because there wasn't enough food to go around already. My aunt said, "That's enough and go outside somewhere so your mother can have some quiet time".

That was all I needed to hear. I was out the door before she could get it all out her mouth. When we got outside we, didn't say much to each other. Harry finally asked us, "How do you all have fun in this little country town?" I told him there was nothing fun about living on Jackson Street. David told him, "Don't pay him any attention. He doesn't know what's up" and they walked away. I asked them could I come and David just laughed at me. I knew he was not going to let me go, but it did not hurt to ask. I knew they were going to smoke some weed and get drunk with some girls.

David and Harry didn't come home that night, and my aunt was upset. We could feel the tension in the air. It was like the calm before a big thunder storm. I sure wouldn't want to be in their shoes today. I hope they had a good time because I don't know if they are going to have many more. My mom and aunt looked for them everywhere on Jackson Street. Finally that afternoon the police came to the house. The police said Harry and David had been arrested for stealing a car and running it into a house. They were down at the jail and someone needed to bail them out. I knew my mom didn't have any money so my aunt would end up having to go into her pocket to get them out. My aunt and my mom started arguing over who was responsible for all this trouble.

I am glad that David and Harry didn't let me go with them. The police said Harry was driving the car and there was alcohol found in the car. My mom told my aunt she didn't have any money and asked my aunt if she would loan her some to get David out. My aunt agreed only if she promised to pay her back. They went down to the police station and got them out. When they got back, my aunt got packed and left that same day. None of us got to know Harry, including my mom. When they left, my mom cried again even worse than the first time. She hugged Harry so hard my aunt had to pry her arms from around him. It was kind of nice knowing that I had another brother; I wish we would have gotten to know him sooner.

It wasn't long before mom went back to drinking and partying again. I think she drank more after my aunt and Harry left. It was pretty sad seeing her suffer with life the way she did. I was starting to understand why she was the way she was. Life has been whooping her ass for a long time. I know she has to be getting tired of all life's disappointments. David and Harry got put on probation for their night of partying. We never hear from Harry or my aunt after that day. I guess my aunt was still piss off about the whole situation with the money. I don't think my mother ever paid her back. I thought my family was fucked up before I found out about Harry. Now I can say that my family is super fucked up----What's next for the Jackson family?

"Believe in Change"

Chapter 8

Teenage Pimp

Every Sunday in the summer, there was a softball tournament down on Jackson Street. People would come from all over, (even as far away as Ohio, Washington DC and Baltimore) to play in the tournament. "Fred Isley", the pimp who owned the white house or the whorehouse, put it all together. I recall how he used to go up and down Jackson Street looking for people to work at the softball games. He would give us big buckets of white wash (a watered down paint mixture) to paint everything that wasn't moving on the field. He sold hamburgers and hot dogs along with barbeque ribs and chicken; he also sold alcohol. There was also gambling going on, but he tried to keep that quiet so the police did not come down to the field.

Hundreds of people would come down to see the game every Sunday. People would come in their best looking clothing with the hope of finding a special woman or man. If there was a tournament, they would play on Saturdays also. There were always lots of girls from all over, even the girl of my dreams, my favorite cheerleader, Ann Kinson would be there. I had been seeing this girl all my life, but I never had the nerve to say anything to her yet. She always stood out in a crowd, because she was light skinned and had good hair. She is so light skinned that if you didn't know her, you would think that she was white. She had a lot of white blood mixed up in her family. Maybe that is why her father thought that his family was better than other black people. She was 5'10" and had a great body; someday I would get the nerve to tell her how I felt about her.

The night before the softball games, Fred Isley had all his beer stands stocked for the next day. Some of the other kids and me would sneak over and steal all the beer we could carry and get drunk or sell it. He didn't bring liquor down to the field until the day of the game; I guess he did not want to take any chances of getting his watered down alcohol stolen. He made a lot of money, but we stole a lot from him. He probably knew and didn't care. He never did any inventory or had any security to watch his stuff, which made it real easy to steal. Maybe he thought no one had the nerve to rob him because of his reputation of being a tough guy.

If I could, I would have robbed him everyday of the week because I was not scared of what he would do. He was no good because of the way he used black people to make his money. People like him would be better off dead. I consider him worse than the white man. At least you knew the white man was going to fuck you over every chance they got. He had the money and the power, but I knew he couldn't keep it forever, that is just how it is. There were rumors going around that he killed a man for trying to rob him one time. I wasn't the type to worry about dying; I was more worried about living poor. I felt like I was dying everyday I woke up on Jackson Street. That how much I hated it.

Fred Isley asked me to work the hot dog stand at the softball games on Sundays. I knew he was a cheap bastard because everyone said he was. So, I had to figure out how to rob him without getting caught. He wanted to pay me $10.00 a day to work the hotdog stand all by myself. He paid me ahead of time, so I spent all of my money on hot dogs and buns and snuck them to the hot dog stand to sell along with his. So, every hot dog I sold, I would replace it with one of mine. The hot dogs were selling for $.50 cents apiece, which was a good price. I didn't want to make it to obvious, so every five of mine I would sell one of his.

If I would run out of my hot dogs, I would send my brother, Robert, to get me more. Fred only let me work that one summer, I guess he knew something wasn't right with the way I sold his hotdogs. He wasn't smart enough to figure out what I was doing that summer. I made a lot of money working the hot dog stand. I had fun. I had a special hot dog for people I didn't like; I would stick ex-lax in the hot dogs. In about an hour, they would have diarrhea all day, which made me real happy to see them running back and forth to the outhouses on the field. When Ann and her friends came, I would give them free hot dogs just to try to impress her and her friends. I sure would like to give her my special hot dog that I had in my pants.

Dewey would always come to my hot dog stand to order some food. He would give me $5.00 for one hotdog, and I would give him $.50 change. He couldn't count, so he didn't say anything. One Sunday his mother came over and asked me where his change was. I told her he ate ten hot dogs, and there was no change. I told her she shouldn't send her retarded son anywhere with money since he can not count. I told her to get off her lazy ass next time and do what a good mother would do. She walked away cursing and said she was going to tell Fred on me. I told her if she did, I would beat her son's ass every time I saw him. I really wouldn't have done that, but she didn't know that. I actually was starting to like Dewey and I think he liked me. He really does need someone to look out for him. I do not think she told Fred because he never said anything to me about it.

One Sunday at the softball game, a prostitute named, "Destiny" pulled a razor out and cut a line on the back of a man's neck. Blood was everywhere, and I thought for sure he was going to die. They were arguing earlier, and someone broke it up. An hour later, she cut his neck. After she cut him, she came over to my hot dog stand and asked me to hide the razor for her. She also asked for a hot dog to go, which surprised me more than her cutting someone's neck. I did not know what kind of person could cut someone like that and still be thinking about eating something. She must be a real cold person inside or crazy; Maybe both.

After I made sure no one was looking, I took the razor and hid it in with the hot dogs. Then I made her a hot dog with every thing on it to go. She gave me a hundred dollar bill and walked away saying, "Keep the change". The ambulance came about 20 minutes later, but it was too late because the man bled to death while everyone watched. Instead of someone trying to help the man, they just looked at him moaning in pain. I thought about helping him, but I wasn't sure how to. The police asked a lot of questions, but no one said anything about the incident. Destiny came to my house a week later to get her razor back. I gave it to her after I dug it up in my back yard where I had it hidden. She smiled and said if there was anything that she could do for me, just let her know. She walked away before I could say anything, but I could tell by her voice that she meant it. I was thinking about asking for some of that professional pussy of hers. I just didn't get it out my mouth in time.

At the end of the summer, there was a dance at a place called the "Rec Hall". At this dance I saw Ann and her friends and she was looking good as always. I finally got the nerve to ask her to dance and she said yeah. It was a slow song and halfway through the song, I moved in to kiss her; surprisingly, she turned and kissed me back. We started to slow dance harder, grinding our bodies into each other until we could hardly breathe. The song ended with both of us sweating profusely on each other shoulders. I asked her if she wanted to become a couple. She said, "Sure if that is what you want". She gave me her phone number, which was written on a napkin all balled up in her hand. It was like she knew I was going to ask for her number. I was in shock, and I told everyone we were a couple. I don't think anyone actually believed me. I didn't care because I knew it was true.

It was two weeks later before I got the nerve to give her a call. I must have picked the phone up ten times a day, but just didn't have the nerve to dial the numbers. I slept with the napkin that had her numbers on. I kept it under my pillow because it made me feel close to her. I was not sure if she was playing some kind of game with me because she said yes so fast when I asked her to be a couple. She answered the phone and I hesitated a second and then I said hello. She said, "I was wondering when you were going to call me". She said, "You know my dad does not allow me to talk to you, so we cannot let him find out about us". I told her that was fine with me as long as I could be with her. She said that her and some friends were going to the movies Saturday and asked if I wanted to meet her there. I said yes, I' am looking forward to seeing you Saturday.

I met her and we found some seats in the back and kissed until the end of the movie. I can't even remember the name of the movie. While we were kissing I started to get a cramp in my jaw, but it felt so good to be pressing my lips against hers. If I knew all I had to do was ask her to be my girl, I would have done that a long time ago. I need someone to pinch me to make sure that I'm not dreaming. Can this really be happening to a boy from Jackson Street? This kind of stuff only happens on television or in romance novels.

Things were really looking up because my mom finally got a job working at a mental institution from three to eleven. This was the first time in her life she had a job or even looked for one. I guess if they cut your welfare off, you have to do something if you want to continue to eat. She was making good money. How ironic, she gets a job after she had already made our childhood a living hell. She seemed happy about working and she deserved some happiness in her life. She did make enough money to move us out of that house to a better one, but it was still on Jackson Street.

It was far enough back that if the creek flooded, it would not reach the house. We had a bathtub, commode, and electricity with three bedrooms. My mom had a room to herself, and my sister had one also. That left one room for all four boys to sleep in, but we did not care. We were happy to be moving. We had a double bunk bed, two boys on the top and two on the bottom; it was the smallest room in the house. However, it was like a mansion to us compared to where we came from. It seems like everything that I hoped for was coming true. I had the girl of my dreams; we did not have to worry about the creek flooding the house. Life is getting so much better for me. I'm starting to expect good things to happen to me now and that's different for me.

After David and Gary graduated high school, David went to Ohio and Gary moved to Philadelphia to stay with my aunt. That left Robert, Marie, and me at the house to deal with our mother. As soon as I turned sixteen, I applied for my driver's license because I wanted to drive as soon as possible, even though I did not have a car. I failed the first time I tested, but I passed the second time. All I had to do now was get a car to drive.

The Vietnam War had started and a lot of the older boys on Jackson Street were being drafted. After living on Jackson Street who was scared of war, which will probably be a break from living on Jackson Street. My older brothers didn't get drafted because Gary had a broken leg that never healed right; one leg was shorter than the other leg. David was colorblind in both eyes so the military could not use him. I knew I would be next in line because I was the next oldest in the family. Some people coming back from Vietnam were messed up in the head and on drugs real bad.

Bert and Rommy Fitzgo had started pimping and had one prostitute each, that worked in the white house. They both got drafted and went to Vietnam almost at the same time, which was unusual because they were the only two males in the family. Rommy's prostitute waited on him, but Bert's didn't. Bert's prostitute was Destiny, the same woman who cut that man's neck a couple years ago. I saw her a month after Bert shipped out to Vietnam; she was looking real good to me. I was standing outside the bar, and she walked up to me and asked, "Would you like to be my man?" I asked her what she meant by that.

I wasn't sure if she was asking me to be her pimp or just a boyfriend. She said she wanted me to be her pimp; I was shocked to hear her say that. I told her I didn't know whether I wanted to because I heard pimps had to perform oral sex on their girls. I wasn't down with that because I was only sixteen and I thought sucking a pussy was nasty. She told me it wasn't about eating pussy. It was about companionship. I told her that I would be willing to talk about her proposal. We went for walk and talked about what she really expected from me.

She wanted me to go shopping with her, go to restaurants and make love to her. We only had to get together on Sundays, her only day off from the white house. I told her just as long as I did not have to eat pussy, I would be there. That next Sunday I went to the white house to meet her. I didn't have a car so we had to ride a cab everywhere. As soon as she saw me, she put a $1,000 in my hand and kissed me. I never thought about being a pimp because they were always beating on their women and that really wasn't for me. Maybe for that kind of money, I might have considered slapping a woman around if that is what it takes to keep getting this easy money.

My biggest fear was Ann finding out about me being a pimp. I was a 16 year old pimp and didn't know how to be a pimp. Ann and I weren't having sex, even though I had been trying so it worked out fine. I would see Ann on Saturdays and be a pimp on Sunday with Destiny. That first Sunday we went shopping and had dinner. Then after that we got a room at the hotel. I wasn't sure what to expect, but I was ready for anything. She started undressing so I did the same. I was a little nervous.

She wanted to take a shower together, so we did. She soaped her body down and then she soaped me down. This was the first time that I ever took a shower with a woman, and it felt good. Then she started giving me oral sex until I was ready to explode, and then she stopped. She walked me to the window and opened the curtain and lifted the window up. She bent over with her head hanging out the window and told me to put it in. This sounded a little crazy to me, but I did it anyway. I couldn't believe she had her head hanging out of the window for anyone to see. After I stuck it in, she asked me to pull her hair hard while I banged her pussy. She kept saying harder and harder, but I wasn't sure if she meant pull her hair or bang that pussy so I did both.

She was making so much noise I thought someone would call the police. Finally she had an orgasm after me banging that pussy for about an hour. I never did cum; I was too busy worrying about the police. That was wild, but it was kind of exciting because it was something new to me. We had sex three more times that night and each time was better than the last. She showed me all the different positions that she knew and showed me how to control my ejaculation time. I was being paid to learn how to be a great lover; I was in a dream and waiting for someone to pinch me. If this is being a pimp, maybe I should consider doing this full time.

That following Monday, I went to buy a car. This would be my first car. I found a 1960 Bonneville convertible; it was sky blue with a tan ragtop that didn't work. It was my first car, and I was proud of it. It needed a paint job, but the motor was good and that's all I needed for now. I was the only one my age with a car and that made me feel real important. Now instead of meeting Ann at the movies and staying there, we could go to the park. All we did was kiss and feel on each other, but no sex yet. After Saturdays with Ann, I was more than ready for sex on Sundays with Destiny. Every time I left Ann, I was always horny as hell and I would take it out on Destiny's pussy.

This time I picked Destiny up with my own car. I was feeling great about that. She handed me my money and kissed me, we went shopping and then had dinner. After dinner, we went to the movies to chill out and relax. She had on a short mini skirt with no panties or bra on. As soon as they turned the lights down, she started giving me oral sex. My dick got long and hard and she sat on top of it, she was grinding it like she never had sex before. We both came at the same time; it was perfect timing by us.

The whole row in the front and the back of us had stopped doing what they were doing to watch us. We just fixed our clothes and left with a big smile on our faces, acting like what we did was no big deal. When we got back to the hotel, she asked me to tie her to the bed, so I did. She said she wanted me to take my belt off and beat her. It sounded crazy, but I said what the hell. After I beat her, she begged me to make love to her. When I was done, we both fell asleep like little babies who just ate.

I was starting to feel more like a prostitute than a pimp. It was kind of like I was being used by Destiny. I guess in a way I was being paid to have sex with her; like I was a prostitute. I' am not sure how much longer I will do this pimping thing. I had to always keep my guard up because I knew she would cut someone if things weren't right, and she always had her razor on her. I would not hesitate to kill her if I had to defend myself. When I picked her up one time, she had another prostitute with her. I didn't mind; I figured the more the merrier. We went to dinner and then the movies, but at the movies is when all the trouble started. We were sitting in the back and I was sitting in the middle of two sexy women. As usual, Destiny and her friend had mini skirts on and no panties. They both bent down and started giving me oral sex. I've never even had a dream this good. I knew this was the closest I would ever come to heaven if there were one.

Then Destiny got on top of my dick and started riding me in front of her friend. Her friend got on the floor and started licking my balls; this was something new to me. After about ten minutes, Destiny got off and her friend got on top and started riding me. While she was riding my dick, Destiny was kissing me while she had her finger in the other girl's ass. I must have closed my eyes because when I opened them up the movie was over, and the lights were on. The first person I saw just standing there was Ann and her girlfriends staring at us performing all these sexual acts. She looked at me and said, "Ron, is that you?" There was nothing I could say since my dick was still buried deep in the girl's pussy.

Destiny asked me who she was, and I told her it was someone who I used to know in school. When we walked out of the movies, Ann and her girlfriends were still there waiting on their ride home. Destiny and her friend were all over me as we walked out the movie. I felt bad, but I had to play the role of a pimp and be hard. It looked like Ann was crying. That really bothered me, but I didn't know what else to do. This is not the way I planned for it to go because I really did have feelings for Ann and not for Destiny. I waited a long time to be with a girl like Ann. Now I was sure I blew it.

I tried to call her, but she wouldn't take my calls. After a couple of weeks, I quit trying to contact her; I figured it was time to let it go. Everyone in town knew I was pimping, and I didn't care. If I had a choice, I would have chosen Ann over pimping.
My mother asked me about it, and I told her I was pimping. She had never been concerned with what I was doing. Pimping was a lot of fun and the money was good, but there was a hole in my heart.

I heard that Bert, Destiny's old pimp, was coming home from Vietnam. I figured it was time to go and buy a gun in case I had to protect myself. I bought a 44-magnum because I didn't know if I would have to go to war with Bert. I went to pick up Destiny one Sunday, and she wasn't there. It was the first time in a year that she didn't show up for our meeting. I just went back home and waited for her to call me, but she didn't. The next call I got was from Bert, and he said that he needed to talk to me. I told him I would meet him at the softball field in an hour. I wasn't sure what was going on in his head, but if it was not right I would blow his head off if I had to. I put my gun in a brown bag and sat it next to me in the front seat of the car. I also stuck some beer in the bag, just in case he asked me what was in the bag. I expected one of us to die, and I wasn't planning on it being me today.

I went down to the field early to make sure he was going to be by himself and wasn't trying to set me up. I was sitting there for twenty minutes when I saw him walking towards my car. He had his military uniform on and a smile on his face as he approached the car. The closer he got, the closer I pulled the bag to me because I wanted to be ready. When he was about ten feet away, I stuck my hand in the bag on my gun. He came to the window and reached out to shake my hand. I shook his hand back and asked him how he was doing. He said, "The reason I wanted to talk to you was about Destiny and you". I said, "What about us?" He replied, "I wanted to thank you for taking care of my girl while I was away".

He explained what he meant, "Before I left to go to Vietnam, myself and Destiny talked about finding someone who she trusted to watch her back, and she mentioned your name. So, I told her to go ahead and get with you until I come back. She told me how you helped her with the razor incident on the field". We shook hands again and he walked off like he did not have a care in the world. Well, pimping wasn't for me anyway. I really felt like I was being used. I didn't have Ann or Destiny, but I still had Jackson Street and some wild memories to keep with me.

I waited all my life to get Ann and I lose her because of someone else's prostitute. This is like some cruel joke that God is playing on me. She was the best thing in my life and now she is gone. Maybe it would be better if Bert and I had a shoot out and I died. I don't know where to go from here. I feel dead inside, but I keep on breathing. I am living in hell and there does not seem to be a way out. Why am I alive? God just kill me now, please. ***"Believe in Change"***

Chapter 9

The Prom Nightmare

I saw Destiny and Bert downtown fighting one day, but I wasn't sure what they were fighting over. They were probably drunk; they always fought when they were drinking. Everyone in town knew about their drunken fights. She pulled her dress up and told him to kiss her ass right in front of everyone who was watching. There were about twenty people standing around watching them, including some young kids ages eight to fifteen. The people were laughing and joking about the way Bert and Destiny were acting. She didn't have any panties on, but I guess that wasn't a big deal to her since she was a prostitute anyway.

Bert grabbed her and slapped her across her face, and she fell on the ground. She pulled out her razor, ran up to him and cut him on his arm. He screamed in pain as he backed up away from her. While watching blood flow from his arm, he pulled out his gun to shoot her. Just as he was pointing the gun towards her, I ran over to him and knocked it out his hand. I knew he was drunk and did not know what he was doing. I figure I had to do something before they both did something that they would regret. The gun fell on the ground near Destiny's feet; I was hoping that she did not see the gun. He asked me what the fuck I was doing interfering in his business with his woman. I told him I was trying to save him from going to prison.

While Bert and I were talking, Destiny picked up the gun and fired at Bert. I grabbed him by the neck and dragged him in front of me so she couldn't hit me. The whole time I was holding him, he was saying, "Go ahead and shoot me bitch". I told him to be quiet before both of us got shot, but he still kept talking shit to her. She started firing the gun at him again; I thought that we were both going to be killed that day. The gun was a 38 revolver with six shots, and it was very loud when she fired the gun. The first bullet hit the ground right in front of us. I was really getting nervous now. The second one flew pass my head. I could hear it flying pass my ear because it made a buzzing sound. Bert was still running his mouth until the 3rd bullet hit him in his leg. He begins to drop to the ground but I wouldn't let him. I needed him for protection so I wasn't going to let go of him. He was heavy, but I held on for dear life.

I told Destiny Bert was shot, and she said, "Well he's still alive". She started shooting again, but this time she said she was going to kill both of us. She shot again and the bullet hit a passing car and busted the windshield. The car ran off the street and hit the telephone post. I looked to see who was in the car, and it was Ann and her family. Her father and mother were in the front seat together. Ann and her younger brother were in the backseat. They seemed to be knocked out and not moving. The car began to smoke. I had to do something fast so I dropped Bert and looked Destiny in the eye.

I was willing to die in order to save Ann's life. What did I really have to lose, I felt like I was dead inside anyway. She pointed the gun and fired as I walked towards her. The bullet missed but I pretended to be shot and fell down on the ground. I looked out the corner of my eye, and she started walking toward me. I expected her to turn and walk away but she didn't. So, I jumped up and she pointed the gun at me, but this time it jammed. While she was looking down at the gun, I tackled her down to the ground. The gun went off in the air, barely missing my head. I took the gun and hit her over the head until she passed out.

I looked over at Ann's father's car to see what was going on. It started to burn and I ran over to get Ann out of the backseat. When I picked her up she started moaning and opened her eyes, looking me right in the eyes. She said, "Ron you got to help my family". I really wasn't planning on doing all that, but it was the least I could do after all I put her through. I ran back after I got her away from the car and got her brother out, and then I got her mother out. I was thinking this would be a good time to get rid of her father, but she asked me to save her family and that was what I would do. The car was really burning now, but I dragged her father out anyway. When I got him about ten feet away, the car blew up and knocked me down.

When I woke up, I was lying in the hospital; apparently a piece of the car hit me in the head. I asked the nurse how everyone in the car was doing. She said that they just had some bumps and bruises on them. I had to have twenty stitches put in the back of my head. They wanted to hold me for observation, but I insisted that they let me go. When I walked out the hospital, I saw Bert and Destiny lying in beds right next to each other holding hands. Bert asked me if I was okay and I said, “Fuck you and your crazy bitch”. Those two motherfuckers could have got my dream girl killed. I’m still hoping that someday, she will be my girlfriend again.

A couple weeks later I got a phone call from Ann. I was really surprised to hear from her, in spite of me saving her family. She said she wanted to thank me for what I did. I told her she was welcome and asked her if she would she like to go to a movie or something. She said yes, but she would have to meet me there because her dad still did not want us to be together. I knew I should have let him burn in that car when I had a chance. I agreed to meet her anyway, in spite of how I felt about her dad. Now I got a second chance with Ann, I’m not going to do anything to mess this up.

She was standing outside the movie, and I hugged her tightly. After the movie I asked her if she wanted to give us another try. To my surprise she said yes, but I had to promise to never cheat on her again. I made the promise without hesitation. I was walking on cloud nine again. Being from Jackson Street, I knew that feeling this good could not last for long, so I had to enjoy it while it lasted. Everything was going good, and I was trying to stay out of trouble. I had been sticking to shooting pool and playing cards; blackjack was the game in the neighborhood.

One day while playing blackjack, my youngest brother Robert, who was four years younger than me, tried to get in the game. I told him to save his money and go find something else to do. He remained persistent about getting in the game until finally, I let him in. He lost all his money. He asked me to loan him some money so he could play some more, and I wouldn't. He got mad and hit me in the head with a 2'X4' piece of wood and ran into an abandoned house down the street. I blacked out for a second, but I stayed on my feet. I couldn't believe he had the nerve to hit me. I wasn't going to chase him because I knew I could get him later at the house. He took so long to get out of that old house, I decided to go to the house and wait outside to get him. I caught him and beat his ass, then went back to my blackjack game.

The next day when he came in the house, I jumped on him again. While I was choking him, my mother hit me in the back of my head with a large glass ashtray. If she didn't hit me, I would have choked him to death because I was so angry. I guess she saved me from going to jail for killing my brother. If it hadn't been for me trying to stay out of trouble, the outcome would have been different. I would have probably tried to kill them both that day; I really had a bad temper. I had a second chance with Ann, and I wasn't going to mess it up again.

The prom was coming up soon for Ann and everyone I used to go to school with was graduating. She told me that she wasn't allowed to go to the prom with me because of her dad. She said we could meet at the prom if we took different dates. I agreed and got "Yolanda", a girl whom I was casual friends with, to go with me. Ann got this middle class nerd to go with her. His name was "Ned". His father worked in the steel mill; he always thought that he was better than anyone from Jackson Street to. Ann and I still hadn't had sex yet, but I was waiting patiently. I thought I was going to take her to the prom and make love that night. It didn't look like that plan was going to work out for me that day.

The day of the prom I was excited because after dropping

out of school, I never thought that I would be going to the prom. I had a tuxedo and a limo on the way, which I paid for with the money I won from shooting pool. Ann called me a couple times that day to make sure that I was still going. I was supposed to pick up Yolanda around 7:00pm to take her to the prom. Yolanda was really excited about going to the prom with me; I always thought she had a crush on me. She was a nice girl, but she wasn't my type. Plus I was in love with Ann.

As the time got closer, I began to think more and more about the prom situation. The more I thought about it, the more upset I got with the whole idea. I should be able to go to the prom with my girl if I wanted to. Just because her dad didn't think I was good enough shouldn't matter to her. She should have insisted she be allowed to go with me or told her father that she was not going without me. She should have stood up for me, which leads me to believe that she didn't really love me like I loved her.

I decided at the last minute not to go to the prom at all. I knew Yolanda was going to be crushed, but I couldn't worry about that. I had to do what I thought was right for me. I didn't call Yolanda to let her know I wasn't coming, and I didn't call Ann. I did, however wait for the limo to arrive since I already paid for it. When the limo arrived, I rode pass Ann's house to see what was going on there. I got the limo to park around the corner from her house, and I got out and hid in-between two houses to watch as her and Ned took pictures.

I thought that it should have been me taking pictures with Ann, and tears started rolling down my face. I turned to run back to the limo because I could not take it anymore. I had the limo take me to the school where the prom was being held. I had the driver park the limo in the back of the parking lot so I could see everyone who went into the building. Ann pulled up in her limo. Her and her date got out laughing. The way that they were acting, it looked like they were having a good time. I crept up to one of the windows of the school and looked in so that I could see what was going on. I watched for about 15 minutes. I didn't see Yolanda anywhere. I was hoping that she would as least go and try to have a good time. Ann and her date were dancing and having a good time. I couldn't watch anymore and went back to the limo to think through the whole situation.

I never did see Yolanda come to the prom; she was probably sitting home crying. I'm sure she got over it eventually; at least I hope she did. I know I was wrong for putting her in the middle of my problems; maybe she will forgive me someday. I thought about doing something crazy like burning the building down or shooting the place up, but it would have been my luck to get caught doing that. The fact was, I still loved Ann and didn't want anything to happen to her.

Finally the prom was over, and I had my limo follow Ann's limo. I just wanted to make sure she wasn't going to have anymore fun that night with her date. The limo took her straight home without her date getting a kiss or a hug. That made me a little happier, but I was still sad about the whole prom. I had my limo drop me off on Jackson Street. When I got home my mom asked me how the prom was. She said some girl named Yolanda had been calling all evening and she sounded really upset. She said that Yolanda told her that I was supposed to take her to the prom and that I didn't show up. I told my mom I was tired, and I was going to bed. I told her if anyone called to tell them I was asleep and not to disturb me. While I was lying across the bed I was wondering if the smell of Jackson Street would ever get off me.

I talked to Ann a couple days later and she asked me what happened on prom day. I told her how I felt about her not going to the prom with me. She said that was the only way her dad would let her go. I told her if it were me, I wouldn't have gone at all if I could not go with her. She told me that I didn't have a dad like hers, and I didn't understand. I told her I didn't have a dad like hers, so I didn't understand, and if that's what it meant to have a dad, I was glad I didn't have one.

I told her that maybe someday she would feel what I felt.

She wanted to see me that night, but I told her that I would be busy for a while. I wasn't going to give up on her because I knew she would be worth the wait. I didn't hear from Yolanda after she called my house that night. I'm glad I didn't because I really didn't have an excuse for my behavior, at least any that would satisfy her disappointment. I thought that maybe someday I would be able to make it up to her somehow. I did not know how yet. The prom only comes once, how can I give that back to her. Ann will never be able to give me a prom night. I should be use to these disappointments, but I'm not.

"Believe in Change"

Chapter 10

Harry's Funeral

Gary moved to Philadelphia right after he graduated from High school to live with my aunt. He was 18 years old and happy to get away from Jackson Street and all the crime. Gary told me this story from his perspective about what happened that day in Philadelphia. He had just gotten dressed to go to work; he was a cook at a small restaurant not far from the house. A bullet flew pass Gary's head as he walked out of the kitchen of my aunt's house. Surprised, He dove to the floor and crawled behind the couch for protection. Gary was not sure where the bullet came from. He heard police sirens and looked out the window, where he saw Harry in his car slumped over the steering wheel. Harry was not moving.

Gary was thinking that maybe he was just drunk and fell asleep. His first instinct was to run out and help his brother; but the policemen had surrounded the car. The police told Harry to throw out his gun, but Harry wasn't responding to their demands. Gary could hear helicopters above the house, but could not see them. Gary decided to crawl over and turn the television on to see if anything was on the news. Gary saw the house and Harry's car on the television; he was amazed to see that. The news people were saying that Harry robbed a bank and shot two policemen. They said that they believed the suspect had been shot several times, but they didn't know how bad he was hit. Harry lifted his head up and looked towards the house briefly and then put it back down. Gary was watching it all on television. No one was sure what Harry was going to do next. This was a very tense situation for everyone that was watching. Gary was confused, not knowing what to do about this situation.

My aunt heard all the noise and got out of bed; she came downstairs and saw Gary peeking from behind the couch. She asked him what was going on outside with all that noise. He told her to look at the television, and when she looked, her mouth dropped open as she saw Harry's car with him slumped over the steering wheel. She screamed, "They're trying to kill my baby" and ran back upstairs. She came back down carrying her handgun that she always kept under her mattress. Gary hollered and told her not to go out, but she didn't listen, she opened the door and screamed hysterically Harry's name.

He lifted up his head and stared in a trance, and then he said, "Mom go back in the house before you get hurt". Gary tried to grab my aunt out of the doorway and her gun accidentally went off. The bullet hit a policeman in the leg. The policemen started firing at my aunt, and they hit her several times knocking her back through the door. Gary caught her as she fell towards the floor. She handed the gun to Gary and told him to go save his brother from the police. Gary held her head closer to hear what she was trying to say. Blood was coming from her mouth and her eyes kept rolling back in her head. She told Gary to tell his mom that she was sorry about the way things turned out with Harry. She said that she did the best she could do with Harry. She said, "Tell Harry I love him and I will always be there for him". While she was talking Gary could hear more gunfire so he laid my aunt's head down and peeked out the window.

Harry was getting out the car with two guns in his hand waving them wildly in the air. He started firing at the police, and they started firing back. He was shot about fifty times all over his body. Gary turned and went back to my aunt, he begins shaking her, but she didn't respond. He shook her harder and she opened her eyes very slowly, as if she had heavy weights on them. She said, "Don't worry I got my baby with me now" and closed her eyes as they began to roll back into her head. Gary knew she was dead and started crying and hugging her.

Gary was startled back to reality when he heard the police on a bullhorn saying, "Come out with your hands up or we're coming in". He looked down and noticed he was still holding my aunt's gun. He took a rag and wiped his prints off it, then put it back into her hand. He hollered and told the police that he was coming out so please don't shoot at him. He puts his hands up and walked out very slowly because he was not sure what was going to happen next. He was knocked to the ground by the police and handcuffed. They took him down to the police station where he stayed for several hours. After they figured out everything, he was released to go back home.

My mom was getting prepared for work when Gary called and told her what happened. She dropped the phone, started crying and throwing things all over the house. I picked the phone up and asked Gary what was going on. He told me the whole story and I was in shock. I told him that I would talk with him later and hung up the phone. I just did not know what else to say to him. There really was nothing to say, the whole thing sounded so crazy. I helped my mom up the steps to her bedroom so she could lie down. I didn't know what to say to her so I didn't say anything and just walked out of the room. I felt bad for my mom because bad shit just keeps happening to her. She hasn't been the greatest mom in the world, but she didn't deserve all of this.

I never really got to know Harry and my aunt, but I was going to drive my mom to the funeral in Philly. We packed up our little family and hit the road. When we got there, I was amazed at how many aunts, uncles, and cousins I had in Philly. We stayed at my Aunt "Patty's" house until the funeral. She had two children Marvin and Bernice. They were a little older than me, by maybe a couple of years. Bernice was tall and cute with a dark complexion. Marvin was short and fat with pimples on his face. He was an ugly dude.

The funeral was scheduled for the next day after we got into town. The family was going to have both bodies at the same funeral home. Harry's service was going to be first, and then my aunt's service would follow his. They were going to be buried side by side, the way my aunt wanted it. My deceased aunt Phyllis never was able to have any other children. Harry was her only child. My mom cried through the whole service that day, it was really sad to see. My mom tried to get in the casket with Harry; they had to drag her back to her seat. When Gary walked up to see Harry, he bent over and kissed Harry on the cheek. I just walked up and looked at him for a second and walked right out the building. I had enough and was headed to my car when I heard someone call me. I turned to look, and it was Bernice walking towards me with a big smile on her face.

She asked me where I was going and I told her I didn't know, as long as I got away from all this sadness. She said we could go to her girlfriend's house and have some fun. She said her girlfriend had some beer and weed we could take it back to the house since no one would be there. It sounded good to me especially since we were at a funeral and not having any fun at all. We went and picked up her girlfriend, "Donna" and drove to my Aunt Patty's house.

I had never smoked weed and wasn't a big drinker, but that day I was a little down and out and didn't care. I knew my cousin was fine, but her friend, Donna, was just as fine. Bernice told me her brother had a crush on her girlfriend, Donna, but she did not like him the same way. We started drinking beer and found some liquor underneath Aunt Patty's bed. We went upstairs to Bernice's bedroom; she lit the weed up and passed it to Donna to smoke. Donna took a couple puffs and smiled as she gave it to me. I took one hit and gave it to Bernice; this really was some strong stuff. I was really feeling blasted which was something I never felt before. Everything seemed to be moving in slow motion to me. The girls were starting to look like cartoon characters to me.

My mind was working overtime to determine what was real and what was not. I didn't feel like I was in control of my body and thoughts. They were laughing and joking like they weren't even affected by it. They must get high all the time. Bernice asked us if we wanted to play some strip poker to have some fun. I tried to sober up after she said that because it sounded like a lot of fun. Before I knew it, we were all naked sitting on the bed laughing and joking with each other. I was not sure if I was high as hell or if this was really happening.

I could not take it anymore so I moved over to suck Donna's titties. While I was sucking Donna's titties, Bernice started sucking her other one. I stopped sucking Donna's titties so I could kiss Donna, then Bernice started kissing Donna too. We were both kissing Donna at the same time; this was really exciting to me. I could feel Bernice's tongue touching mine as our tongues swirled around in Donna's mouth. She was moaning and grinding up against us like she was having a seizure.

Bernice asked me to hold Donna's legs so that she could suck all the juice out of Donna's pussy. I grabbed her legs gently and spread them wide open so she could get a good suck. Bernice dove into her pussy like she was starving for food. She was licking her pussy with giant tongue strokes that started at her ass and over her pussy. Her pussy would quiver with every stroke as the juices begin to form in a puddle at the bottom of her pussy. I could hear loud long sucking sounds coming from Bernice's mouth. After seeing how good a woman could feel from having her pussy sucked, made me reconsider my stand on not sucking pussy.

I could barely hold Donna's legs she was moving so much. I laid her legs on Bernice's shoulders and got behind Bernice to put my dick in her pussy. I thought she was going to stop me, but she didn't, I felt like I was in a good dream. Bernice's ass started moving in wide circular movements. I grabbed hold of her ass and pushed my dick even deeper. She screamed loudly, startling Donna momentarily. While Bernice was eating the bottom out of Donna's pussy I was knocking the bottom out of Bernice's pussy with my big dick. After about twenty minutes, Bernice looked back at me and told me to fuck Donna too with that big dick. Bernice had pussy juice all over her face from sucking on Donna's pussy. She looked like a clown with make-up on.

While I was fucking Donna, Bernice stuck her pussy over

Donna's face and she started sucking Bernice's pussy. Bernice was grinding Donna's face so hard, I wasn't sure she could get air to breathe. Bernice rolled off of Donna's face and lay beside her and started kissing her again. I pulled my dick out and jammed it into Bernice's pussy and starting fucking her real hard. I took turns fucking both of them, giving each one 100 strokes apiece. I made a game out of it by counting the strokes, plus that took my mind off of how good I was feeling. Finally, while I was inside Bernice's pussy, I ejaculated. I never cummed that hard in my life.

We must have all passed out from exhaustion, because the next thing I knew Aunt Patty was beating Bernice's ass and cussing Donna and me out. When my aunt and mom got back from the funeral, we were all lying there naked across the bed. We must have passed out from all the liquor and weed we did. Maybe we fucked ourselves into exhaustion or a combo of both. One thing for sure it was time to leave Philly because my Aunt was talking about killing someone.

David didn't go to the funeral, I'm not sure why but my mom was upset with him. I don't know why she would be upset with him because it's not like any of us really knew Harry. There was me, my mom, my sister, Brother Gary, my Brother Robert at the funeral that day. Everyone else was from Philly. Living on Jackson Street, we learned to expect bad shit to happen to us. I guess over the years we became cold inside because of that way of life. I don't think love is a natural instinct, but it is a learned instinct.

I can honestly say I never felt love for anyone in my family. At this point, I knew three people in my family who died, and I didn't feel any pain or loss for them. Maybe that was because I never got to know them. I was okay with that because it made life so much easier not to have these caring feelings. Now that I think about it, I realized I probably didn't even love Ann. I was just intrigued by the challenge of a Jackson Street boy getting something he's not allowed to have. I knew if I didn't really love her, it would eventually come to the surface. I was curious to see how my love story would end, but until then I had to deal with Jackson Street. ***"Believe in Change"***

Chapter 11

The Engagement for a New Father

One day while my mother and a female friend were driving to work early in the morning at six, a tractor-trailer truck hit them as they pulled out onto the highway. They did not see the truck coming; it was coming down the highway so fast that there was nothing they could do to avoid it. The truck flattened the whole rear of the car like it was a toy car. They were very lucky that they were not sitting in the back seat because they would have died instantly. The ambulance came and took both of them to the hospital. After doing several x-rays, they determined that my mother had a concussion and a few bruises, but would be okay in a few days.

The hospital called the house, and I picked up the phone; they said my mom was in a car accident. They said that she was at Brownsville Hospital and asked when someone could come to see her. I told my sister and brother Robert the news about our mother, and they began making arrangements to go to see her. I told them that I was not going to see her, but I did not care if they went. My mother came home in a week and things got back to normal. She never did ask me why I did not come to the hospital. I did not want to see my mom all bruised up. It was bad enough that life was giving her an emotional bruising already.

I saw "Wally Brown", a neighbor on Jackson Street, and he told me he was getting ready to go to the Job Corp in about a month. Wally lived on Jackson Street, but I only really met him after we moved to our new house. Wally was also a High school drop-out like me. We were about the same age; his birthday was one week before mine. He did not hang with the other kids on the street because he had a very strict mother. She was the biggest mother on the street. She must have weight about 400 pounds easily. No one on the street wanted to get on her bad side. She was the original “Big Mama”. This woman could slap you so hard that your out-of-town relatives could feel it. That included the grownups also; no one messed with her.

Wally informed me that individuals could get their G.E.D. and learn a trade at the Job Corp Center. He said they would also put fifty dollars a month in a savings account for you. This sounded like a good way to get off of Jackson Street and get my G.E.D. Once I got my G.E.D., I could go to college just like Ann was going to do. The college Ann was going to attend was only three miles from her house in the town called “Little California”. A friend of mine named, “Chauncey”, was going to Penn State University, which was about three hours from Brownsville. That was where I wanted to go also, because I did not want to stay around Brownsville. I knew if I got a college degree, it would be a lot easier to get Ann’s family to give me a chance to date their daughter.

Wally headed out to Job Corp about a month before I got there. The Job Corps Center was about ten miles outside of Indianapolis in Edinburgh. Ann was happy about me going to the Job Corps Center to get my G.E.D. My mother did not really have anything to say about me going, but I could tell that she was happy about me doing something with my life. I overheard her talking to my sister about me going. She told her how happy she was for me. She never was big on expressing herself to the family. I think she really loved us but just didn’t know how to express it.

I went to Uniontown, PA, which is about twelve miles from Brownsville, to catch the Greyhound bus to Indianapolis. I got on the bus at 12:00am and arrived in Indianapolis about 7:00am. There was a shuttle bus waiting for us, (which was about ten kids), to take us to the Job Corp Center. In about a half an hour we were pulling up to the entrance to the Job Corp Center. When I stepped off the shuttle, someone asked me where I was from. I told him I was from Brownsville. The person thought I meant Brownsville, New York and I didn't try to correct him because I would have felt dumb for not saying more than just Brownsville. I do not know what made me think anyone would know a small place called Brownsville, PA, with only a population of 6,000.

I realized that people were coming to the Job Corps from all over the United States. The first thing we did was get uniforms to wear. We had to wear military fatigues with boots. Everyone lived in dorm rooms with as many as three people to a room but I was used to that because of they way my family lived, so it was not a big deal to me. The next day I had to talk to a counselor about getting my G.E.D. and learning a trade. I decided to take up cooking, because I felt it would not be a bad idea to be around food all the time. At least I knew that I would not be hungry here. They allowed cooks to eat what they prepared, and I was going to eat everything I cooked. They had a lot of things to do at the Job Corp. center; they had music, karate, and boxing.

I went to find Wally. I met his roommate, who I thought seemed a little feminine for a guy. His roommate was named "Terry", and he seemed to be gay as he wanted to be. He walked like a girl and talked like one. As far as I knew, Wally was not gay, but I was not sure now since I met his roommate. They sure acted like husband and wife by the way they talked to each other. Something was shaky, but I didn't say anything to Wally. Wally said, "Don't worry about Terry, he's gay, but he's cool". This was the first gay person I had ever met, and I was really uncomfortable being around him. Wally seemed to fit right into what was going on in their room. Their room was so perfect with everything in place. I couldn't even spot a crumb on the room. I didn't know any guys that neat, hell I didn't know anybody that neat. I knew I wasn't going to be hanging around Wally too much with his gay roommate hanging around all the time.

The first chance I got to go to the boxing gym, I saw a heavyweight named, "George Foreman". George was only there a week after I got there, and then he left to fight in the Olympic games. My first inspiration to box was by watching “Cascius Clay” on television. I knew when I saw him and heard him; I wanted to be just like that. The boxing coach, whose name was “Sarge Johnson”, noticed me hanging around and asked me if I wanted to learn to box. I told him I did and started boxing the next day. I weighed 190 pounds on a 6’3” frame, but I was all muscle.

I was too big to be a light heavyweight and too small to be a real heavyweight. A light heavyweight weighed 178 pounds and starting weight for a heavyweight is a 198 pounds and I was stuck in between the two. Sarge had coached the Olympic boxing team before and knew a lot about boxing. I had a natural instinct for boxing, because I had no problem trying to knock someone’s head off. It helped that I had a lot of anger built up inside of me.

On the boxing team, we traveled a lot to New York, Ohio, Pittsburgh and even to places that didn’t have names. It was hard work, but it was fun to me, and it helped me get some of my hostilities out of my system. The coach was starting to make a lot of plans for me to do more in boxing. I was perfect for a future heavyweight champion of the world. I had the size and instincts for fighting. I fought ten fights and didn’t lose any of them; everything was going great for me. I was starting to make a name for myself in the boxing world. I was having fun boxing, but I was starting to miss my Ann. It only took me a month to get my G.E.D. and six months to get a Cook’s Helper Certificate. The boxing coach begged me to stay but I told him I couldn’t. I was just too home sick. After six months, I was on my way back to Jackson Street to start working on my college career.

My plan was to register for college, and I did as soon as I got back in town. After passing the college entry exam, I was scheduled to go to Penn State in the fall; I was really excited about going to college. Ann was excited for me to; she wasn’t too crazy about me going that far away. I heard they were hiring part-time at the steel mill for the summer, so I applied for the job and got it. Now I was working alongside Ann's dad at the steel mill, and he did not even know that I was dating his daughter. I was making real good money and started thinking twice about going to college. Ann's father never went to college and made a good living. Maybe I should follow in his foot steps.

"Chauncey", a friend from Jackson Street, was also working at the steel mill for the summer; he was definitely going back to school. His mother made sure all the boys in the family went to college. She was the only mother on the street who even mentioned college to her children. Chauncey moved to Jackson Street when I was a teenager, so I did not know him that long. We did play on the same high school basketball team together, and that is really how I got to know him.

After talking to him, I knew I wanted more education because of all the confidence he seem to have picked up by being in school. He was throwing all these words around, and I didn't know what they meant. He made me feel dumb, and I wasn't used to that feeling. The next day I went out and bought a book on terminology because I wanted to be able to talk to anyone at any level of education.

In about a month, I had added over 300 new words to my vocabulary. I was ready for anyone. When I used the new words no one really understood me. You can't really communicate if the other person doesn't understand what in the hell you are saying. The funny thing about that was I never really got to use the words to talk to anyone. I was prepared if I heard or saw the words anywhere. That was the only good thing about learning the words.

I wasn't going to be one of those people who liked to show off because they knew some big twenty-dollar words like Chauncey was. I must give him credit because he's the one who inspired me to seek more education. Once he started college most people from Jackson Street didn't really want to talk to him because he made them feel stupid. I would talk to him every chance I got just so I could use my twenty-dollar words on him.

What I found out is that those twenty dollar words don't mean anything if you're not able to communicate with another person.

It was almost the end of the summer, and the part time college help was getting ready to go back to college. The job supervisor was going around asking everyone if they wanted to work permanently. I thought about it overnight and decided that it might not be such a bad idea since Ann's dad worked at the steel mill to. I thought that maybe if he saw me working hard at the steel mill, I might impress him. He might not think that I was such a bad person and let me date his daughter. If I worked in the steel mill, Ann's dad might be more willing to accept me in his world. So instead of going to college at the end of the summer, I decided to stay at the mill. In a couple of months, I bought a brand new (1972 grey Ford Mustang Mach One) with some of the money that I was making. It was the first new car on Jackson Street, and I was proud of it because I was the one to have it.

I started boxing for the (Uniontown Boxing Club) to keep myself out of trouble. After about ten fights with the club, they took my picture and had a big article in the paper about me going to the (Golden Gloves Tournament). I had won all ten of my fights and was ready for the tournament. The Mayor of Brownsville, "Mayor Klingen", was a former professional boxer whom they called "Slugger". He was behind me all the way. I felt like a celebrity after they put my picture in the paper. Everyone wanted to ask me questions or hang around me because I had my picture in the paper. That was something special for a boy from Jackson Street.

I was working daylight in the steel mill from 7:00am to 3:00pm and going to the boxing gym in the evenings. I hardly had time to see Ann and that was not good for me. We still weren't having sex yet, but I respected that in her. I went to the Golden Gloves Tournament in downtown Pittsburgh, and it lasted for a whole week. I had to fight five fights in five days. The championship fight was on a Saturday, and I was getting tired. I was fighting as a heavyweight and all eyes were always on the heavyweights. They were considered the strongest and hardest hitting fighters in the world. My weight was 210 pounds, and I was punching hard and fast. Couldn't any other fighter keep up with my power and speed.

In my first fight, I was very nervous that night because I was not sure what to expect in this tournament. I won the fight by knocking the fighter out in the first round. In the second fight, the referee stopped the fight in the third round because the other fighter had a cut above his eye from one of my right hand punches. The third fight went the whole three rounds, and I won a unanimous decision. I won the fourth fight by a knockout in the third round. I was doing so good that I was surprising myself with the victories. I knocked this white boy out in the second round and won the Golden Gloves Tournament. This was the first time that I was a champion of anything. I was feeling real good about myself. I was beginning to have visions of being another Cascius Clay.

When I won the tournament, even my coach was surprised to see me do so well. I had not been boxing for him that long, and he was not sure about my talent yet. I got a trophy and a jacket with my name on it. I wore my jacket everywhere I went because I was proud of winning the Golden Gloves Tournament. I also carried a gun everywhere I went, because I knew most people wouldn't fight me fair, and I wanted to be ready.

Maybe someday I will be the heavyweight champion of the world. I think my coach was ready to make some big plans for me to turn pro. That's saying a lot for a boy from Jackson Street, who had nothing to start with. I also had dreams of marrying Ann someday and getting away from Brownsville and the steel mill. What were the chances of any of these dreams coming true? I guess time would tell me what is in my future.

One day my sister told me that one of her friends named, "Linda", had a crush on me. Linda was a couple years younger than me. She was a nice looking girl with a nice body, a cute face, but my mind was always on Ann. I saw Linda around but never paid any attention to her until I saw her at a party, and we started slow dancing together. The next thing I knew we were kissing and grinding on each other. She knew I was dating Ann, but she didn't care. She just wanted to be with me. I guess she figured she could take me away from Ann if I got to know her better. There was nothing that she could do to take me away from Ann, but I sure did let her try.

I would go to her house to see her while her mother was home, and her mother accepted me for who I was. This made me feel good about myself, to have someone accept me for who I was. Ann's family was so judgmental about anyone who did not live in the same neighborhood as they did. Linda lived in a middle class neighborhood, but she did not act like she was better than the people from Jackson Street. I didn't have to sneak around to see her, like I had to do to see Ann. When I would go visit Linda, her mother would go upstairs and leave us in the living room watching television. Linda always wore a dress when I came to see her so if we wanted to have sex, all she had to do was lift it up. She would tear a hole in her panties so she could sit on top of my dick without taking any clothes off. If someone would come downstairs they would not catch her naked.

We had sex almost every time I went over there, which was great because I was not getting any sex from Ann. I went to see her a few times a week. Sometimes Linda would see Ann and me together, but she never said anything to Ann about me going over to her house to see her. I felt bad for Linda, but she knew how things were when she started seeing me. She was a real nice girl but she met me at the wrong time in my life. She really helped me get through all the years of not having sex with Ann. If it weren't for Ann being my girl, it would have been Linda; she just got with me at the wrong time.

Linda and Shila were friends and did a lot of things together. One day I saw Shila downtown, and because she was drunk, I drove her home. We ended up making love on the floor of her living room. Shila had a boyfriend, but I guess she didn't care at the time, since she was drunk. We never told Linda about it, because we both knew it would crush her heart. Shila knew how much Linda loved me and if Linda found out about us, this would be the end of their friendship. We only did it that one time and then acted like it never happened because we both knew it was wrong.

One day when I was leaving Linda's house, she said she had something important to tell me. I thought she was going to say something about Shila and me having sex. She said, "I'm pregnant, Ron". I asked her if she was sure and she said, "I'm five months pregnant". My mouth dropped to the floor when she said that to me. I asked her why she didn't tell me sooner than five months. She said she was scared that she would lose me if I knew she was pregnant. I asked her if she was she going to have the baby, and she said it was too late to get rid of it. I just walked away steaming mad. I and Linda had a good thing going, why did she have to mess it up by getting pregnant.

I had to face the fact that I was going to be a father at the age of nineteen years old. After I got home and thought about it for a while, I got really pissed off at her. I figured she did it on purpose with the hope this would break Ann and I up, and she could have me all to herself. I realized that she might be right if Ann found out about her being pregnant with my baby. She had told me she was taking birth control and that was why I didn't use condoms when we had sex. I believe she set me up for the whole thing; she wanted to get pregnant. I had to figure out how to get out of this mess without losing Ann. I have come too far to lose Ann now. Why do I keep fucking up things with me and Ann?

The next week when I saw Ann at the park, I told her I had something serious to talk to her about. I gave her a long kiss and looked her in the eyes. After a brief moment I asked her "Will you marry me". She looked me in the eyes and said, "Yes" as tears rolled down her face. I was so happy that tears started coming down my face to. The next day I went out and bought her an engagement ring to wear. Now she had to tell her family about me and her because we were going to get married. I knew her dad wouldn't be happy, but hopefully it wouldn't matter now. Maybe for once in his life he will think about someone other than himself.

I was glad that I did not have to be there when Ann told her dad. I never asked Ann how he handled the news and she never mentioned anything about it. I decided that if Ann found out about Linda, I would just deny it and tell her she was just trying to break us up. Once Linda found out about the engagement, she kept her pregnancy quiet from all her friends. I don't know why. Maybe she was embarrassed to be having a baby for someone who was in love with someone else. Maybe she loved me so much that she just wanted to see me happy. I really felt bad that I could not make her happy; she really deserved to be happy to. Ann and I planned the wedding for after her college graduation, which would be in approximately two years.

Four months after I got engaged, Linda had a baby boy who she named, "Carl". I don't know where she got the name Carl from. I didn't go to the hospital to see the baby being born that day. She was very unhappy with that and decided to name the baby Carl, instead of Ron Jackson, Jr. That worked out for me since then I could really deny the baby now. Linda's friend Shila had a baby a month later, a baby boy who she named, "Rolen" after her boyfriend. I sure hope that he is not my son to. I know there is that possibility.

I went to see the baby a month later at Linda's house. While I held the baby, I thought about how beautiful he was, and how I wished things could be different between me and his mother. There is something about the innocence of a baby that goes straight to a person's heart. Maybe I'm being selfish just thinking about my happiness. The baby deserves to have a caring father in his life. Why do I have to be like my dad? I hated him for the way he was. I know this child is going to grow up hating me to. That's sad.

Just remembering how I grew up without a father made

me real sad for the baby. I knew I could only slightly get involved in his life because of my relationship with Ann. I blame it all on Linda because I felt she tried to set me up to try to mess up my relationship with Ann. I knew she thought the baby would change my mind, but I couldn't let that happen. It has taken me to long to get this far with Ann; I can not take a chance on losing her again. ***"Believe in Change"***

Chapter 12

Meeting the Family

One day we got a phone call from Columbus, Ohio; it was the hospital calling saying David was in the hospital. He got stabbed in the eye by his girlfriend during a fight they were having. They had to remove his eye and now he only had one eye to see from. My mom asked me to drive her to Ohio to see him and make sure he did not need anything. It was three days later when we got to the hospital in Columbus Ohio. I had to wait until I could get off from work for the weekend. Columbus was about a three-hour drive from Brownsville, which was not too bad of a drive. The whole trip we were talking about how messed up that was to be stabbed in the eye. My mom was talking about beating the girl's ass if she saw her anywhere near the hospital. I was pissed off also when I thought about someone making my brother lose a body part.

When we arrived at the hospital and entered David's room, he seemed surprised to see us. Sitting on the bed holding his hand was the same girl who put his eye out. He was lying back on the bed with a big patch over his left eye. He looked up with his one eye and smiled at mom. My mom said hello and asked how he was doing. He said he was fine, but the doctor had to take one of my eyes out. He said they placed a glass eye in, but he had to keep it covered for a couple weeks. I asked him who the girl was who put his eye out and he said, "This is her right here; her name is "Laverne".

He said it wasn't her fault since they were having a fight, and that she really loves him. I said, "What kind of fucking love is that when someone stabs you in the motherfuckin eye?" She said that she didn't mean to stab David in the eye and that it was an accident. I replied that maybe I should stab her in the eye so they both could be one perfect couple. Then they both could have one eye, now that would really be love, don't you think?

Laverne looked at David and said that maybe she should leave so that he could spend time with his family. I told her yeah, she should take her two good eyes and go the fuck home. David told me he didn't want me talking to his girlfriend like that and I told him, "Fuck you and that bitch". If I knew your dumb ass would be sitting here with her, I would not have come all the way down here to see you. I should fuck you both up right now".

David's girlfriend ran out of the room crying and he tried to get up off the bed to get to me, but my mother stopped him. It was lucky that she did because I was going to knock his new glass eye out of his fucking head. I told my mom that I would be out in the car waiting for her because I could not stand to look at him anymore. I went and fell asleep in the car until my mom was ready. We drove back to Jackson Street in silence all the way home, hardly even looking at each other. If this is a case of love, then I don't want to be in love with anyone.

The first time I met Ann's parents was real awkward for me, which was about two weeks after she told them the news of our engagement. They invited me to have dinner with them on a Saturday evening at 6:00pm. Ann's mom was real nice and friendly while her father was quiet at first. He talked to me about the steel mill and sports mainly; he was a big sports fan. We had a lot in common, like football, boxing and I worked in the steel mill like him. We never did talk about the wedding plans that night; I did not want to press my luck. I figured I would leave that all up to Ann and her family since I really did not care how we got married. Just as long as we did, that is what mattered to me.

While I was there, I met Ann's little brother's girlfriend. Her name was "Star". She was a beautiful young girl with a perfect body. I had to force myself not to stare at her because she looked so good to me. I would catch her staring at me and when I did she would just smile at me and turn her head. Ann's little brother, whose name was "Garland" was a 16 year old weed head. Everyone in Brownsville knew about him getting high all the time. When they said they were leaving, I knew what they were going to do. After a few hours of sitting around Ann's parents, I was ready to leave too because I was bored as hell.

About a year later, I heard Linda married "Denny Johnson", who was a few years older than her. I was shocked when I heard that because I thought she might be still in love with me. I saw her one day and asked her about it and she said the reason she got married is because she knew I was getting married. I told her she could have waited just in case I changed my mind about marrying Ann. She said that she knew I wasn't going to change my mind, and she knew how much I loved Ann. I asked her if I would still be able to see the baby and she said yes. I was really wondering if the baby was truly all mines now. I was starting to wonder if she was making love to me and Denny during the same time period.

Three months later Chauncey told me he was going to get married to his long time girlfriend. He wanted me to be his best man at his wedding, I was kind of shocked because I did not know he thought we were that close. I told him yes and he gave me all the details about the wedding. Chauncey's girlfriend, "Denise", had a baby for Chauncey and now it was time to get married. They had a nice little wedding, and I had a good time that day. Soon after the wedding, Chauncey had to go back to school to continue his education. He was majoring in Mass Communications, which was right for him since he liked to run his mouth a lot. Now that I think back on it, I guess being the best man is somewhat of an honor.

Ann and I were starting to get closer and closer to each other romantically. We still had not had sex yet, but I was waiting patiently for that day to come. One day when I was up her house, we decided to go for a walk. We were out in the alley behind her house, where it was real dark. We were kissing and hugging when I decided to ask her was she going to let me make love to her. She said we could do it now, if I had a condom.

Ever since we got engaged I had kept a pack of condoms on me, because I knew she was about ready to say yes. I hurried up and found some soft grass in the alley and we went to work. I didn't care if anyone saw us or that we were in a dark alley behind her house. After waiting for years, I was not going to give her a chance to change her mind. Now that we had sex, I feel like our relationship has been consummated. I doubt if I would have married anyone without testing the merchandise.

It wasn't the way I dreamed it would happen; I thought it would be more romantic. I thought we would be at a hotel suite, with roses all over the bed, with a bottle of expensive champagne. Maybe I should have waited a little longer and did it the way I wanted it to be. I don't know if she was a virgin and I didn't ask her. I guess I really didn't want to know. I wanted to believe that I was the first man she ever had before. After that night, I knew she was hooked on making love with me.

We were having sex every Thursday, because that was her mom and dad's bowling night. As soon as they would leave, I was tearing that ass up. We didn't do anything crazy because I didn't want to scare her with all the stuff I knew. It was just basic, normal sex like we were both rookies at least that is what I wanted her to believe. If she only knew all the sexual things I had been through, it might have scared her away from me.

We get another call from Ohio and it was about David again. This time he was shot in the head. The doctor on the phone told us David would be okay. He got shot in the mouth and the bullet hit his tooth and then exited his cheek. The doctor said David was very lucky to be alive, if the bullet would have not hit his tooth, he would probably be dead. I told my mom not to even ask me to go see that idiot so we decided not to go to Ohio. It was probably his girlfriend who shot him and I thought to myself, "I sure hope he's been beating her ass, because she's sure been fucking him up".

I found out Ann's brother Garland had been going with his girlfriend for a while. She had moved to Brownsville from Newark, New Jersey. She had four brothers and one sister in her family. All of the kids were about two years apart in age, with the oldest brother being my age. Her sister's name was "Lola", who was two years younger than Star and she was almost as fine as her. Star and Lola were very mature for their ages; they just acted a lot older than the other girls their ages. Maybe that was because they were city girls. Everyone in town was talking about how fine Star and Lola were. Their father was a preacher and made everyone in the family go to church on Sunday. I wouldn't have been able to tell they were church girls from some of the stories I heard about them.

Ann had a cousin named "Arlene" who was a good looking cheerleader. She was going with a friend of mine named, "Little Red" who I met a couple of years before. They were both short compared to Ann and me. I was six-feet-three inches tall and Ann was five-feet-ten inches tall. They were both under five-feet-two inches tall, but they made a nice looking couple together. Little Red had a lot of girlfriends but Arlene didn't know about them. I couldn't figure out why so many girls liked Red because he never used deodorant. You could always smell him, and he would always blame it on someone else. We all knew it was him smelling, but we never said anything to him.

One time Little Red and I were waiting on Ann and Arlene to meet us at the Dairy Queen. Red and I were sitting in my car when they started walking towards us and as soon as they got about ten feet away from the car, Little Red farted. It was one of them quiet ones, but it was the worst smelling fart ever. They walked up to the car with big smiles on their faces and stuck their heads in the window to say hello. Ann gagged and asked what was that smell. Arlene jumped back from the car and tripped, falling into some bushes. I jumped out of the car to tell Ann it was Little Red who farted because I didn't want her to think that I would do something like that.

Just as I was getting ready to tell her what happened, she began to throw up all over me. While Ann was throwing up, Little Red was pulling Arlene out of the bushes where she fallen. Her blouse was torn and she was pissed off about that because she just bought it that day. Little Red told her it was me who farted in the car and he apologizes for me. This fart was so bad I thought Ann was going to cancel the wedding that night.

It was almost a week before Ann would speak to me again; I was starting worry about our relationship. This fart was so bad everyone in town was talking about what happened at the Dairy Queen. This is what you could call a legendary fart, the kind that could break up marriages. It broke all known records in intensity and longevity that day. No one at the Dairy Queen was very hungry after smelling that fart. The fart surrounded the Dairy Queen like a storm cloud. The fart smelled like a combination of dead fish and rotten eggs that had been out in the desert for three days. I had to get my car detailed and throw my clothes away, that is how bad it smelled. I didn't even drive my car home that night. The odor was too strong. I had it towed the next day to the detail shop, and I never got back in any car again with Little Red. ***"Believe in Change"***

Chapter 13

The Crime I Didn't Do

I never really thought that much about religion because our family would only go to church on Easter. Our mom would dress us all up and then would drag all five of us kids to a nearby church. Every other family on Jackson Street did the same thing. It was like an annual tradition on Jackson Street. The people on Jackson Street were such fucking hypocrites; they would get drunk the Saturday before Easter and go to church on Sunday. They would all be doing the same dirt all year long and then when Easter came they would all run to get saved by God at the church. I never liked going to church because we had to sit still and be quiet. No one ever told us about God, so we really didn't know what the preacher was talking about anyway.

When the movie the "*Exorcist*" came to the theatres, Ann and I went to see it one day. I was never the same after seeing that movie because it scared me so much. I never knew anything about the devil or demons until I saw that movie. I wasn't worried about hell, since I already thought that I lived there. The movie did get me thinking about the supernatural and whether there was any truth to it. I began to wonder if I had a demon in me, because of some of the thoughts I had about killing people. Life was hard for me and after years of hard living, I became cold inside. I guessed that had nothing to do with demons.

After watching the Exorcist, I dropped Ann off at her house and went home. The first thing I saw when I walked into the house was my mom sleeping on the couch and she was snoring very loud. I heard her snore before, but now it took on a new meaning for me after watching that movie. I thought I was tough until I heard all the different noises coming out of her. I really felt like a demon was trying to come out of her. When I walked passed her, I pulled my gun out because I thought she was going to jump off the couch and try to get me. Maybe my mind was playing tricks on me. Either way, I was scared when I walked pass my mom.

I went upstairs quietly so I wouldn't wake my mother up and got into bed with all my clothes on. I had my gun lying right beside me near my hand because I felt like I was going to be attacked by something. I didn't know if I was being Paranoid or if something really was going on in my house. I sank into a deep sleep and I was awakened by what seemed like something holding me down. My eyes were open but I could not see anything and I couldn't move any other part of my body. The more I struggled the more pressure I felt holding me down. I was trying to scream but nothing would come out of my mouth. Finally I was able to get a scream out and I saw my mom at the door, she was asking what was wrong with me. I still couldn't put words together or move, but I could see everything around me. She ran over to the bed and started shaking me real hard to get my attention. Finally I was able to move again, and the first thing I did was grab my gun.

I started shooting around the room trying to hit whatever was holding me down but nothing was there. My mom reached for the gun and snatched it out of my hand. She asked me, "What in the hell is wrong with you?" I told her something was on top of me and it wouldn't let me up. She told me nothing was on top of me and that I must have been dreaming. I told her I couldn't have been dreaming because my eyes were open. Mom said that she didn't see anything, and that I must have been going crazy. I told her to give me my gun back and leave my room. She looked in the gun to see if there were anymore bullets left. She saw the gun was empty and sat the gun on the floor next to my bed.

She walked away shaking her head in frustration with the whole situation. She said, "You're going to pay for them bullet holes in the walls. You could have killed someone". Maybe I was dreaming. I don't know for sure, but it sure did seem real to me. Maybe it was time for me to find out more about God so I went to church with Ann that next Sunday. Going to church did not make me feel any better about what happened that night. I still went every once in a while with Ann. It was still good quality time together. I still didn't understand this God thing, maybe it will become clearer someday.

I was still boxing but the coach was starting to get on my nerves because he was demanding more of my time. I needed to take some time off from boxing so that I could figure out if I still wanted to do that. Instead of going to boxing practice one day, I went to a Halloween parade in (Uniontown), which is where the boxing gym is located. While I was watching the parade, I was startled by some shouting behind me. I turned to look and the noise was coming from a karate class in the building behind me. I was fascinated by the moves they were making, and I knew right then and there I had to learn how to do that.

I joined the class the next day; I was so excited about learning martial arts. I enjoyed karate a lot more than I did boxing because there was less pressure and less violence involved in it. I knew it would take a couple years to get my black belt, but I didn't care. I was learning how to control my violent behavior, and that is something I needed to learn. I tried to get Ann to join but she didn't want to, she said maybe later. I would train three days a week after work faithfully. Karate helped relax me after working in that dirty steel mill forty hours a week.

I liked the money I was making in the steel mill, but I didn't want to spend 20 years sucking up all that dust like Ann's father. After a couple of years, I was tired of it already and was wondering what else I could do. Wally started working in the steel mill too; he seemed to enjoy working in the mill because he never complained about work. I was trying to think of someone to be my best man at the wedding so I decided to ask Wally. Ann was getting ready to graduate from college and the wedding would be one year later. I had saved a lot of money for the wedding, but all I had to pay for was the tuxedos for the men. Ann's dad was paying for everything else, and I was real happy about that. Garland and Star were going to be in the wedding also.

I went to Ann's graduation from college; it was very boring for me. Ann was going to be a schoolteacher once she graduated from college. There was a big party at Ann's house after the graduation, which was when I met all of her cousins. The one who really got my attention was Renee. She was very pretty. She was even more beautiful than Ann, and she liked to drink and have a good time. She was a lot of fun to be around if you wanted to have some fun at a party. Compared to Renee, Ann was boring, but Ann would probably make a good wife for me.

After I left the graduation party, which I found kind of boring, I rode downtown to have a couple drinks at a local bar. It was only 10:00pm, still to early for me to go home on a Saturday night. When I parked the car and as I pulled the keys out of the ignition, the keys fell out of my hand onto the floor of my car. I bent down to pick them up and I heard gunfire outside my car. My window shattered and I looked up and saw someone running away. I jumped out of the car with my gun and I started to chase the person. It was hard for me to run; because I hurt my knee when I jumped up, at least that is what I thought.

So I fired off a couple rounds but didn't hit the person because they kept on running. I was kind of shook up after that so I decided to go in the bar and have a couple drinks to calm myself down. While I was sitting there, I lifted up my pant leg to see how bad my knee was hurt. I didn't see any cuts on my knee so I ordered another drink for myself. About halfway through the drink, I decided to look again because my knee was really hurting bad. I lifted my pant leg higher this time to make sure there was no cuts higher up my leg. I saw a little round hole about six inches above my knee with just a drop of blood on it. I knew that I had been shot, so I finished my drink and drove myself to the hospital.

Before I left the bar, I told Wally, who I saw sitting in the bar, to call and tell Ann that someone shot me. I would have called her myself, but I was in a hurry to get to the hospital. I expected her to come running to the hospital that night, but she didn't come. Actually no one came to see how I was doing. It was beginning to dawn on me how alone I was in this world of mine. I had to remember that this is a life that I have created for myself. I never wanted anyone to get that close to me. I did think Ann felt close enough to come running to the hospital. I was disappointed because she didn't run up to the hospital to see me. I felt that if you really loved a person, why wouldn't you be there if they are hurt? Once again, I was beginning to doubt her love of me.

At the hospital, they took an x-ray and did surgery that same night on my knee. The doctor said the bullet hit above the knee but traveled down into the knee. The reason there wasn't a lot of blood on the outside is because I was bleeding internally. The doctor cut my leg open above the knee and pulled the bullet out of it. I realized the person who shot me was trying to shoot me in the head because of where the bullet went through my window.

Ann did come to the hospital the next day while I was doped up; she came with her brother's girlfriend Star. She came that afternoon, twelve hours after I was admitted to the hospital. I was so doped up I thought I was dreaming when I saw both of those pretty women together. Ann said that she couldn't find a ride to the hospital. I didn't say anything to her comment, I just changed the subject. It sounded like a bunch of bullshit. I would have walked to the hospital to see her. She is really beginning to sound shady to me. At that time, I had an Afro and Star said she would braid my hair the next time she came up to see me. I thought that was real nice of her to offer to braid my hair.

I was in the hospital for a week and the doctor said I would have to go through about six months of physical therapy just to be able to walk again. I wouldn't be able to work, so they put me on workers compensation until I was better. I was happy that I didn't have to go to that steel mill for awhile. However, I was not able to bend my leg and that scared me. I thought I might be crippled for the rest of my life and that really bothered me.

The police came to see me while I was in the hospital to ask questions about the shooting. I told them I didn't know anything, and they quit bothering me about the shooting. It was three months before I could bend my knee halfway without terrible pain. It took a lot of work just to do that but I was determined to get my leg back the way it was. I stayed in the house for three months before I actually went somewhere other than the hospital for rehabilitation. I had to go to the hospital three days a week, for two hour sessions to work on my leg. I had to use crutches to get around, and I had to get someone to drive me to the hospital. I was supposed to do some work on my knee at home, but I did not really do what I was supposed to do.

While I was laid up with a bad leg, I was letting a couple of crooks use my car to rob some stores out of town. They came to see me one day and told me their plan on robbing the stores. I knew them from the pool hall; they used to hang around there all the time. They said that they would only need the car a couple days a week for their robberies.

The plan was they could use my car for half the money they stole. If they didn't have my car back in one hour, I would report it stolen. Each time I let them use it, they would bring me about $1,000. I felt that was pretty good for doing nothing but handing over the keys. They were junkies and would spend all their money in a couple of days. The last robbery they did, there was a shoot out because one of the cashiers followed them in his car, they had to stop and shoot him. The boy died and it was all over the news. I knew it was time to stop what I was doing.

Finally after six months, I could walk without crutches. I was happy about that. I was back on track again and ready to go back to work. There were a lot of things I needed to do before Ann and I got married, and I didn't have much time. The wedding was going to be in three months, and I needed to find a place for Ann and me to live. I didn't want to live in Brownsville so I found a place in Uniontown. It was a couple of blocks from the karate school, which was perfect for me. It was a second floor apartment already furnished with one bedroom; it was a great place to start a marriage. I was really starting to get excited about the prospect of spending the rest of my life with my dream girl.

Ann's father was spreading a lot of money around for the wedding. He was getting the biggest hall and getting the best food for the wedding. I sure hoped he could afford to do all that. I guess he wanted to go all out for his only daughter and I do not blame him for that. I personally didn't care about all that fancy stuff. I was happy to be having my dream come true. At the same time, I had never been used to things going my way and I was just waiting for something bad to happen before the wedding.

One day, a couple of detectives came to my house to talk to me. They asked me about a robbery at a dairy mart in Uniontown. At the time of the crime, I was downtown Brownsville and I had about thirteen witnesses to prove it. One of my witnesses was a Brownsville policeman named, "Randy" and that was what I told the detectives. They said who ever robbed the place had a car like mine. After answering questions for about an hour, they left my house. The detective came while no one else was at the house, so I didn't mention it to anyone.

A week later, to my surprise; they came back and placed me under arrest for that same crime. I said, "This is bullshit, you are only messing with me because I'm a Black man". They handcuffed me and walked me to their waiting car right in front of everyone in the neighborhood. They threw me in the Uniontown jail. I was very upset, but I stayed cool. I was sitting in jail next to murderers and crooks for a crime I didn't do. How ironic, especially after all the dirt I had done and never got caught.

I was really upset with the way this whole thing was going for me. I figured I would go to jail someday, but not for something I didn't do. I sat in jail for three hours before my mom came to bail me out. While I was sitting there, I was thinking about my wedding plans. I thought that if I went to jail there would definitely not be a wedding. Being from Jackson Street, we always expected bad things to happen, but I didn't see that one coming.

After I was bailed out of jail, my name was all over the news the next day. It was in the newspaper and on the radio. I was planning on trying to keep this whole situation quiet. Everyone was talking about it, especially Ann's father and family. Everyone I saw told me how Ann's dad was talking bad about me at the bars. I went to him at his house and explained my side of the story to him with the hope that he would understand. I don't think he believed me, but there was nothing else I could really do; I was starting to feel like this wedding wasn't meant to be. Is it possible that I will go to jail for a crime that I didn't do? Is God trying to punish me for trying to marry someone outside of my neighborhood? Is it just the "Jackson Street Curse"? ***"Believe in Change***"

Chapter 14

Getting Married

Two weeks later and it was time for me to go to court. I was very nervous, but not scared because I knew I was innocent. It would not be the first time a black man went to jail for a crime he did not commit. If I had to go to jail, I knew I could handle it because it couldn't be worse than living on Jackson Street. I don't think I could handle not being able to marry Ann. My lawyer wanted me to wear a suit to court, but I didn't. I wasn't trying to impress the judge or anyone else in the legal system because I did not do anything wrong. I noticed that my mom and all my witnesses were there, but I didn't see Ann. I thought she would have shown up just for moral support. I would have for her.

I wondered again if she was the right girl for me. There must be a reason that I'm having all these doubts about her. The judge came in, and we all had to get up until he sat down. The prosecution called his first witness to the stand, which was the cashier at the dairy mart. He asked him if the person who robbed the store was sitting in the courtroom. The prosecution pointed to me and the witness said, "No, he is not the one who robbed the store". The judge asked him if he was sure and he said, "Yes, he doesn't even look like the man who robbed us". The judge said, "The case against Ron Jackson is dismissed, you are free to go".

I was happy for a second and then I started getting angry for even being accused of something that I did not do. I was angry because the boy said I didn't even look like the person who robbed the place. If they would have done a line-up, this could have all been settled without a court hearing. They smeared my name all over town for some bullshit. So, I stood up and hollered at the judge, "You mean I don't even get an apology from anyone for this. If the police had done their job correctly, I would not have to go through all this bull shit".

My mom and my friends had to restrain me, because I was trying to get to the white detectives who started all this shit. By the time they got me outside, I was cool again and ready to go home. On the way home my mom asked me where Ann was. I told her I didn't know. She asked me if I was sure I wanted to marry her, a person that cannot even come to give you moral support. She said, "Something about her is not right". I was thinking the same thing at that time. When I saw Ann, I asked her why she was not at my hearing. She told me that she did not want to see me go to jail if something went wrong at the hearing. I accepted that answer and let it go for now. It was just hard for me to believe anything else. Why would this girl marry me if she really didn't love me? She must love me.

Ann and I were not planning on going on a honeymoon because Ann had to start her new job a couple days after the wedding. We figured we would have plenty of time to go on a honeymoon later. The one thing Ann's dad did not volunteer to pay for is the honeymoon. I was surprise about that because he always seemed to want to control everything that Ann did. Hopefully I would be in control after the wedding; time will tell if that is true.

The day I had been waiting for all my life was finally here after fighting to get from the bottom to the top of that hill. I would be getting married and leaving Jackson Street all in the same day. This is going to be a great day for me. Hopefully I will inspire other people from Jackson Street to believe in their dreams. Ann's father had planned a big church wedding at their family church. Wally came to pick me up to take me to the church an hour early. On the way out the door, I got a phone call. I was thinking to myself, "what now"? The phone call was from Yolanda, the girl I was supposed to take to the prom. She asked how I was doing and congratulated me on getting married to Ann. I asked her how she was doing and told her I was on my way out the door. She said, “Things would be a lot better if I would have shot you in the head that night you got shot”. Before I could say anything, she laughed and hung the phone up on me.

I told Wally to wait a minute while I ran upstairs to get my gun. He said, “What in the hell are you taking a gun to your wedding for”? While we were driving to the church, I told Wally about the phone call from Yolanda. I told him I needed to watch out for Yolanda and if he saw her to let me know right away. It is a shame that I had to worry about this fruitcake crashing the wedding and shooting me today. Now I’m having all these crazy visions of a big shoot-out at my wedding. When will this crazy shit in my life end? Will this Jackson Street curse ever get tired of fucking with me?

When I got to the church, everyone was talking about how nervous I was acting. They thought I was nervous because I was getting married, but if they only knew about that crazy phone call. When I saw Ann, it was like seeing an angel in a wedding gown. I couldn’t believe that I was going to marry someone as pretty as her. This just was too good to be true. I was just waiting for something terrible to happen. Maybe this is a dream and I’m going to wake up right before she says “I Do”. My mind is really racing as the preacher asks Ann will she take this man to be her lawfully wedded husband. The best words that I ever heard in my life were, “I now pronounce you man and wife, and you may kiss the bride”. I thought about putting one of them (Big, Juicy, Wet, I Hate Your Dad Kisses On Her). I decided to be nice and just briefly press my lips against her. I did grab a handful of ass while I was kissing her, just to let her dad know who’s in control now. Surprisingly the wedding went smoothly without anyone acting crazy.

When we were on our way to the reception hall in the limo and I thought to myself; I had married the girl of my dreams. I did not know if life could get any better for me, considering this was my dream come true. There were 300 people at the reception, there was a full house. The last time I saw that many people together was at the softball games on

Jackson Street. An up and coming Jackson Street boy named, "Sidney Prince" sang at the reception. Sidney was an excellent pool shooter and an even better singer. He was a lot younger than me, but he always tried to hang with me. He was the new generation of Jackson Street boys and I did not have time to school him on life. He is like a younger brother, who is always trying to be like his older brother.

He had plenty of potential and I could have brought it out of him, but he needed to learn on his own. Maybe he will be the next "Jackson Street Dreamer". The one thing that I did do for him was to tell everyone in Brownsville that I would hurt them if they messed with him. He did not know I did that, but if I didn't, he probably would have got his ass beat a lot of times. I knew sometimes he had a way of rubbing people the wrong way, especially the older guys. The song he sang was "*Ain't No Sunshine When Your Gone*" by Lou Rawls. He did a great job on the song. He has plenty of talent. Sidney will make a lot of money someday with his voice if he never gives up on his dreams.

The food was good and everyone was having a good time. The alcohol was flowing, and there were a lot of drunken people at the reception. After we ate, Ann and I did an apron dance to a slow song. That's a dance where each of us took turns putting on a carpenter's apron with big pockets on it. All the women would pay money to slow dance with me, and all of the men would pay to slow dance with Ann. The first one in line to slow dance with me was Star. She walked up to me and smiled while she stuck some money in the apron, I could not tell how much money.

She squeezed up to me as tight as she could get, then looked me in the eyes and asked me if I was happy. I told her I was and she said that was good. I was trying to be cool but my dick started to get hard. She is just so sexy. She could feel my dick getting hard and she squeezed even harder up against it. She felt so good; there was nothing I could do to control the hard-on I was getting. It was scary how good her body felt up against mine. I didn't know how in the hell I was going to be able to explain this to Ann if she saw this hard-on. We were only dancing for a few minutes, but in my mind we were naked and making wild animal love.

Ann was on the other side of the dance floor and couldn't really see what I was doing. Finally someone hollered and told Star to let someone else get a dance with me. It was Star's boyfriend Garland with an untrusting look on his face. I tried to hide my hard dick so nobody could see it, but I know Garland saw it sticking out in front of me. While Star was walking away, she asked me if I was sure I was really happy. I did not respond to that question because my hard-on says it all. There was something special about Star that made me feel good just to look at her. I didn't even feel that way about Ann and we were getting ready to spend the rest of our lives together. When I thought about it, I realized I should feel that way about the person I marry. Something did not seem right about this feeling that I had for Star.

At the end of the night we counted the money from the wedding, there was $6,500 in addition to all the gifts we received. We were going to have a good financial start to our marriage. After a couple days laying around in our new apartment and making love all day, it was time for me to go back to work. I was going to ride the bus to work so Ann could use the car for her new job as a teacher.

I came home from work one day, about week into the marriage and Ann said her father stopped by to see her. She said he was running low on money since he spent all that money putting the wedding together. She told me that she loaned him some money and that he would pay us back in a couple weeks. I told her that was fine, but asked how much she loaned him. She told me that she loaned him $5,000 of our money.

My mouth dropped to the floor as I heard that come from her mouth. I asked her was she out of her fucking mind doing something like that without talking to me about that. Ann said that she didn't think that I would mind since her father said he would pay us back. I said for that kind of money I do mind, you should have talked to me first. I knew for sure I could not trust this girl anymore. This was only the second week of marriage and what would be next with her. I needed to break this control her father has on her now. I'm not sure if I can, but I will keep on trying.

Six months later, we decided to try and have a baby, so Ann stopped taking her birth control pills. Every weekend Ann dragged me to Brownsville to visit her father and mother to have dinner with them. Her mother always treated me good. I could tell that the father has to force himself to be nice because it just did not seem to come natural. When we were at Ann's parents' house, she always seemed cold towards me. She would not even sit on the same couch that I sat on in front of her dad. It was like she was scared to show affection in front of her dad.

After a couple of months of that, I started dropping her off on Fridays around 6:00pm. I would go out to the club and have a good time drinking and dancing then go back home, leaving Ann in Brownsville. She would spend the night on Fridays and I would go to get her on Saturdays around 5:00pm. Ann was okay with that as long as we spent Saturdays together doing something. On Saturdays, Ann and I would do something together like a movie or dinner. Ann just could not go one week without seeing her parents. I guess you could call her a "daddy's girl".

Ann's cousin, "Renee", lived a couple blocks from us and would often stop by; especially on the Saturdays that Ann did not go to her parents' house. We would sit around and drink plenty of beer and alcohol. Renee and I started going to the clubs together because Ann didn't like going out. Renee and I went to the clubs together more than Ann and me. Ann would actually encourage us to go to the clubs together so that I would have someone to go out with. I thought that she did that so her cousin could keep an eye on me at the clubs. The next thing I knew Renee and I were fucking like rabbits every chance we got.

When you put alcohol, a pretty girl and a man together what can you expect to happen? ------Sex and more sex.

A year later Ann had a baby girl, we named her "Ronnay Jackson". She came out with light skin and dark black curly hair. I didn't want to see the baby being born. I did not know if my stomach could take it. Her mother went in the operating room with her while Ann's father and I sat in the lobby. I thought the baby was going to bring me and Ann closer, but it didn't. Ann was at her mother's house even more now with the baby. Renee and I were still fucking like rabbits with no shame. I really believe Ann knew and just didn't care since there were rumors all over town about Renee and me fucking.

An entire year had passed since Ann gave her father the $5,000, and we still had not gotten one dime back from him. I finally confronted Ann again about the money to see what was going on. She told me that the truth was that she gave her dad the money because all he did for the wedding. I was pissed. I told her, "Since you and your father are so close, maybe you should go back home to live". Ann packed some of her clothes and left with the baby that same day. I didn't expect her to actually leave, but she didn't even hesitate about leaving. I figured she would be back in a couple of days and everything will be okay. Now her father would have plenty of time to finish brain washing her about me. It was a mistake for me to let her leave without trying to work it out. I had no control over her again, and now her father was getting just what he wanted. This is not the way it is supposed to be. This was not in my dream ever.

It had been five months since Ann had left, and I'm really missing her. I found out that Star and Garland were having problems too. Star and I started talking for hours at a time on the phone about our problems. The phone conversations really helped me get through the hard times that I was having. She was very mature for her age and that helped a lot in our conversations. I wasn't really sure how old she was, and I didn't care at the time. I was helping her ease her pain, and she was helping me get through mine. I received divorce papers, which took me by surprise. The papers came through the mail. We had only been apart for five months, and she wanted a divorce. I knew her father had something to do with this quick divorce.

All I had to do was sign the paper and it would be done. It would not cost me a cent. I thought about it for a day or two and decided to sign it. A month later, we were divorced. Star told me that Ann had been seeing this drug dealer named, "Shady", who sold weed and cocaine in town. Shady had recently got out of prison after serving ten years for drug trafficking. Shady is the same age as Ann's dad. I wonder how her dad is going to react to that relationship when he finds out about that. Star said that Ann had been seeing him since before we even separated.

So, all that time she had been cheating on me, just like I was cheating on her. The reason Star knew was because she and Garland went to the Sheraton hotel with them to party one time. Shady had gotten suites for everyone and they had plenty of drugs to go around. This story was hard for me to swallow so I asked Ann was it true. She asked me, "Who told you about Shady"? I told her that is was Star. Ann said, "That bitch needs to know how to mind her business". I hung the phone up; I really needed to sit down somewhere quiet. I couldn't believe this shit was all true.

It wasn't long before Star and I decided to go out together and have a couple drinks at a club outside of Brownsville. She was looking real good that night with a short dress on and her titties showing through a low cut blouse. After we had a couple drinks, we went to a hotel room to make love. She had the sexiest body I had ever seen, and she knew how to use it. She started sucking my dick like she was a professional, well beyond her age. We fucked for hours before we took a break to talk. I was getting ready to go to sleep when she told me she had to go home. I asked her why and she told me she was only sixteen years old.

I was shocked because I thought she was at least eighteen years old because of how mature she acted. I hurried up to put my clothes on to get out of that hotel before we got caught. If I would have known she was only sixteen years old, I might not have made love to her since I was twenty-five years old. She was more mature than any woman I had ever met before. She sure had me fooled. After that night we didn't see each other for a long time. I'm not sure why, maybe she went back to her old boyfriend.

A year later, a friend of mine named, "Sly" had moved to Florida after high school, and he was in town visiting. We went out and had a couple of drinks, and he told me he sold drugs down in Florida and he was making a lot of money. They had a five-bedroom condo on the beach and he asked me if I wanted to go back with him the next time he was up this way. I told him yes and I started making plans to go back with him. One thing I had to do was take my black belt test in karate. I took my black belt test and passed it with no problem. Sly told me that in his business, he would need a bodyguard and an enforcer. I told him I could do both if I needed to. I was excited about getting away from Brownsville after all the bullshit that was going in my life.

Star heard I might be going to Florida and asked if she could go with me. I told her I would let her know. If only I would have been able to get Ann to leave town, maybe we would have had a chance. The more I thought about the bullshit I went through trying to get that girl the angrier I became. I still was seeing Star every once and a while, but we would talk on the phone almost everyday. She and Garland were still seeing each other on and off. She told me she didn't like having sex with him anymore because he didn't have the size like me. I like Star a lot, but I was not sure about taking her to Florida with me.

She sure would be nice to wake up to everyday. She does make me feel good about myself. I don't know if being with her is always going to remind me of that bullshit with Ann. Over the last couple months I had been having trouble sleeping at night. There was so much anger built up inside me that it was getting harder and harder to control sometimes. I felt like killing myself to get rid of my misery. I wondered if I would feel better

if Ann was dead, and I thought about killing her to find out. Death might have been the only way we could be together forever, and her father could use $5,000 he owed me for her funeral. How can I get rid of these hostile feeling about Ann?
Maybe getting away is the best answer for me.
"Believe in Change"

CHAPTER 15

TO KILL OR NOT TO KILL

One day I took a ride down to Cinder Hill, where I used to play on Jackson Street when I was a kid. I had decided I'd rather kill Ann than live without her, and Cinder Hill was a good spot to dig a grave. By the time anyone finds her body I'll be in Florida on the beach. After I dug the grave, I went back home and called Ann on the phone. When she answered the phone, I told her I had something important to talk to her about, but I needed to see her in person. I asked her to meet me at my old house on Jackson Street in one hour. She said that if it was that important she'd be there, but that she couldn't stay very long.

I put my gun in my pants and headed to Jackson Street; everything was falling into place. While I was sitting in my car waiting for her, there was no doubt in my mind I could go through with it. When she drove up, I got into her car and told her to drive down to Cinder Hill so we could talk in private. I asked her did she tell anyone that she was coming to see me. She said, "No, my father doesn't even want me to talk to you on the phone". I said, "Good, I would hate to see you get in trouble for talking to the father of your baby". When we got there, I tried to pick a fight by slapping her in the face, but she started crying and didn't say anything at all. She just held her face and put her head down; this is not what I expected her to do.

I saw blood coming from the corner of her mouth and I didn't like the way it made me feel. I felt sad inside to see her hurt. I did not anticipate feeling that way. I expected to feel happiness to see her in pain. It was supposed to feel good to slap her, but it just didn't. Why am I feeling sorrow for Ann? Why should I care about her? Is it because I still think I love her? Can

I finish this plan of mine?

That was the first time I ever hit a woman in anger, and I did not like this feeling. I didn't want her to suffer, so I pulled my gun out and put it to her head. She looked up at me and said, "Please don't do this Ron, we have a child together". Tears started to come to my eyes as I cocked the trigger back to shoot her. She put her head back down as tears poured from her eyes; she just sat there waiting for me to shoot. I was wondering why my finger would not pull the trigger. Why is this so hard? Maybe it is just not in me to do this to her. I knew then that I still loved her and love would not let me kill her. Maybe I should put myself out of my misery.

I took the gun away from her head and began to hug her. I just wanted to let her know that everything was going to be okay. We must have hugged each other for fifteen minutes before we let go. I looked her in the eyes and told her how much I loved her. I told her how sorry I was that things ended up this way. Then I put the gun to my head and pulled the trigger, but the gun did not fire for some unknown reason. Before I could pull the trigger again, she screamed and asked me not to do this. She said, "We have a child to think about". She reached her hand out to get the gun, but I just stared at her like I was in another world. This whole thing was beginning to feel like a bad dream to me.

Finally, after a few minutes, I said that maybe this was not our day to die, but we need to figure out how to live together. There must be a reason that my gun didn't go off. Maybe it was God, maybe I just had a fucked up gun, who knows. I have another chance and I'm going to take it. I put my gun back in my pants and asked her to drive me to my car. I knew after that we would never be together again, so I hugged her and said goodbye. When she pulled off I pulled the trigger on my gun, just to see if it would shoot. I shot five straight bullets in the ground without any misfires. Now I'm really confused why the gun didn't go off when I put it to my head. I guess it just was not my time yet.

It was time for me to stop feeling sorry for myself and start making some money. I figured if an old ass drug dealer like Shady could get a girl like Ann, then I knew I could do almost anything after I got the drug money. My plan was to become a big time drug dealer or die trying to be one.

Star and I started seeing each other again, casually at first. I was still working at the steel mill and going to karate practice almost every day during the last several months to stay out of trouble. Karate practice and work were the only things that help me keep my sanity until Star became my friend again. Her parents were not very happy with that scenario, but we did not care if they were happy or not. I knew I was happy every time we were together, and that was what was important to me.

The void in my heart from losing Ann seemed to be filled when I was with her. Star's parents threatened to send her to Los Angeles if she continued seeing me since her brother "Tonny" lived in Los Angeles, California. He made a living as a singer and was doing very well. She would stop seeing me for a while, but she would be back with me a few weeks later. We seemed to be drawn to each other. We were like an addictive drug to each other. Life always seemed so much better when we are together. We were junkies for each other's companionship.

I finally saw Sly again, and he asked me if I still wanted to go to Florida with him. I told him yes. He told me he would be leaving in about one week so I better be ready. I told him I would definitely be ready; I needed to get out of town. I was ready to get away from Brownsville before I ended up killing someone. A few days later while I was packing my bags, Star showed up at my house. She said that she heard I was going to Florida with Sly in a couple of days. She said, "You know I still want to go with you. You know I'm in love with you. I have to be where you are, no matter where you go". I asked if her parents were going to have a problem with that. She said that she was eighteen years old now, and there was nothing they could do about it. I told her if she wanted to go, it was all right with me as long as she knew what she was doing.

I talked to Sly the next day about Star going to Florida with me. I wanted to make sure it was okay with him if I took someone with me. He told me he didn't advise it because there was going to be a lot of pretty women in Florida, but Sly said that if I really wanted to, it was alright with him. I figured I would not have to look for any pussy; it would be lying right next to me; plus I really did like Star. I figured I could spend more time taking care of making money than chasing pretty women.

Hopefully I would be getting out of this town for good. I was excited because this was the first time I ever went to Florida, and I was leaving with a pretty young lady on my side. I didn't even tell the steel mill that was quitting; I just quit going to work. I emptied my savings account out, which was only $2,000. I was ready to start my new adventure. Everything about this felt right to me.

A couple days later we headed to Pensacola, Florida to live in a condo on Navarre beach. We left on a Saturday at 6:00pm, driving my 1978 grey thunderbird that was filled with our clothes. We were following behind Sly's car, heading down I-95 towards Florida full of excitement and adventure. There were no big goodbyes from either my family or Star's family. Star's family was angry with her for going to Florida with me, and I just did not care to say goodbye to mine.

We drove for eighteen hours, making only four bathroom and gas stops along the way. Star didn't do any driving because she didn't have a driver's license yet. She did give me oral sex while I was driving, every couple hours, and that was good enough for me. We were traveling at speeds up to 110-miles-per-hour at times, and we were lucky that we did not get stopped by the police. A few times, her oral sex was so good I could hardly keep the car on the road. Sly saw me driving crazy a couple of times through his rear view mirror. He asked me if I was tired when we seen each other at the rest stop. I just laughed at him. If he only knew how good her oral sex was, he would have understood why I took Star with me.

We finally arrived at the condo and I could not believe my eyes, it was like I died and went to heaven. The condo was right on the beach surrounded by the ocean; it looked just like a postcard from the beach. The condo had five bedrooms, a big living room next to a huge kitchen. From the living room, you could look right at the white sandy beach. On the beach there was nothing but bikinis and ass walking around. Now I knew what Sly was trying to tell me when he said there would be a lot of pretty women in Florida. I was still glad I took Star with me, because she still was the prettiest girl that I knew. Looking for some pussy would be distracting, especially when you were involved in the drug game. That is how people got killed, and I knew that I needed to stay focused at all times. I had the pretty girl, I had the pussy with me, and now all I need to do is make the money. This is a great plan.

The first couple weeks were just fun and games on the beach with Star. We spent most of our time on the beach and at the clubs partying all night. I took Star everywhere with me because she was always a lot of fun to have around. After knowing the place better, it was time to make some money. Sly had a partner named, "Devon", who I also went to school with while I was in school. Devon went into the military right after high school instead of going to college or the steel mill.

After he got out of the army, he stayed in Florida and started running drugs from Florida to Pennsylvania. Sly, who had a football scholarship to go to college, met up with him after he flunked out of college. They were both on the high school football team and became very close to each other during that time. When Devon got out of the army, he asked Sly to come down to Florida to help him run his drug business. They have been living together in Florida for the last three years and making a lot of money selling weed and cocaine.

I remember the first time I tried to snort cocaine; Sly put

a big plate full of cocaine on the table in the living room for anyone to try. I looked at it and told him I didn't want any of that stuff, and that I did not need any drug to make me feel good. He said that just means that there would be more for him, and he snorted a long line up his nose. Surprisingly, to me, Star said yes and snorted a couple lines up her nose. I didn't notice anything happening to her, so I decided to try some because I did not want to seem like a wimp. I didn't feel anything at first, but then it hit me ten minutes later. My mouth stayed dry and it was hard for me to sit still.

After about an hour of snorting cocaine, we all decided to go to the club to have a few drinks. Star and I drank alcohol and danced till early in the morning, and then we went home. We fucked until that afternoon like we were rabbits. I was determined that would be the last time I was going to snort cocaine. I did not want to get hooked on any drugs, especially the drugs that I was going to sell. I didn't want anything to distract me from what I came to do, and that was to make a lot of money in Florida. I could almost smell the money in the air.

My first job in Florida was to collect money from people who had drug debts with us. Most of the time things went smoothly, but sometimes people just did not do what they were supposed to do. You could not let anyone get away with not paying because then it encouraged others to try to get away with the same thing. Since I had a black belt in Shotokan Karate, I knew how to damage a person in many different ways very easily.

I remember the first time I had to hurt someone for the business; it was not hard for me to do. It took me three weeks to find this person, but when I did he sure did pay for it. I hid in a tree for five hours before he showed up at his house. As he walked down under the tree, I jumped down and kicked him in the head. He fell down to the ground holding his head in a daze, not sure what happened to him. He tried to get up and I kicked him again in the head, knocking him unconscious this time. I looked around making sure no one was watching because I did not want any witnesses. I sat down on top of him and used my thumb to pop one of his eyeballs out, a technique that I learned in martial arts classes. He moaned as it popped out and hung down the side of his face.

It looked like it was hanging from three strings coming from the inside of his head. Blood was starting to run down his face so I pulled the eyeball from the strings that it was hanging from. I stood up with the eyeball in my hand and walked over to his house very fast. I laid it on the doormat and rang the doorbell. As I was running away I could see his mother looking down screaming in shock. I hoped this got his attention; if not I knew what I would do next. If he was dead, we would never get our money, so I really did not want to kill anyone. I realized that if he didn't understand after this, then he would never pay us and should be dead. I wanted to make a statement for everyone who had dealings with us. I wanted everyone to know that we are not to be fucked with.

When I was fucking this person up, it felt like I was in some kind of trance. I knew what I was doing, but it felt like someone else had taking over my body. I didn't feel bad because I knew that it was the nature of the drug business. I knew that I had to commit 100% or not at all. This is my life now. I burned the clothes that I had on so that there would not be any blood evidence on me. I took the clothes to a part of the beach that was near my house and burned them there. I had another set of clothes in the trunk of my car just for that situation. I changed my clothes and headed back to the condo and I jumped into the bed with Star and we fucked the rest of the night.

There was a story on television about the incident that occurred last night about a man getting his eye knocked out when he was mugged. Sly and Devon looked at me and started laughing because they knew that I had something to do with it. Star looked at me and asked what was so funny. She did not see anything funny about what happened to that man. I told her it was nothing; it was just something that happened earlier between

Sly and Devon.

I had no sympathy for anyone who tried to steal money from us, because they were crooks. A couple weeks later, after the man got out of the hospital he came to see us at the beach house. The doorbells rang and I looked through the peep hole to see who it was. The guy that I messed up was standing there with a bemused look on his face. He had a patch over his eye and a brown bag in his hand nervously waiting to get in the house. I opened the door and asked him how I could help him today; he asked if he could talk to Sly for a minute. I asked him if I could I see what was in the brown bag. I snatched it from his hand before he could answer me. I wanted to make sure that there was no weapon in the bag. I looked in it and it was full of money, which I was happy to see.

I walked him back to Sly's room; I knocked on the door and I told Sly someone was there to see him. I padded the man down to make sure he did not have a gun on him and I let him in the room while I waited outside the door. I listened at the door and I heard the man crying like a little baby, begging Sly for forgiveness for not giving him the money sooner. Ten minutes later, the man walked out empty handed, with his head hanging down, wiping tears from his one good eye. I showed him to the door and told him to take care of himself and his family.

A couple days later we had a meeting to discuss our next move in the drug business. We met a Cuban man named; "Suarez" and he told us he had a serious connection in Miami, which would take us to the next level of the drug game. We made plans to go make a purchase from his connection. We were going to go from two kilos of cocaine a month to fifteen kilos a month. This was the move that was going to make all of us millionaires by the next year. After the meeting, Sly told me that Star had been calling her old boyfriend Garland back in Brownsville. He showed me the phone bill to prove it. I was pissed off, but I didn't want Sly to know that.

I told him that I knew she was calling. I told him that I told her it would be okay. He said, "I just wanted to make sure that you knew. He laid the bill down and walked out of the room. I took the phone bill to Star and asked her about it. She said that they were just friends keeping in contact with each other. I slapped her across her face and told her not to call him again while she is here with me. I told her if she felt the need to talk to him then I would pay her way back home and I walked out the bedroom. I thought she was being disrespectful to me by calling her old boyfriend when she was there with me. That lead me to believe that she still had feelings for him and I felt that I needed to be cautious with her. I did not know if I could handle another heart break so soon after Ann.

A week later me, Sly, Devon, and Suarez was heading down to Miami Beach. Suarez decided to bring his five-year-old son on the trip. He thought it would look good if we had a child with us. He wanted it to make it look like we were going to the beach for a little vacation time. We had tennis racquets and scuba diving gear with us. We also had $150,000 in cash hidden in the trunk of the car to buy some cocaine. When we were passing through Tallahassee, Florida, the police pulled us over for a random vehicle stop. We were not worried because we agreed there would be no drugs in the car during the trip down. We also cleared all the drugs out of the condo. We didn't want any drugs near us until after we made this deal. This is the most important deal we ever made; we didn't want to take any chances.

The police asked all of us to get out of the car so they could search us. We figured that this was just another case of black profiling and we were used to that. Everyone was smiling and being friendly when all of a sudden Suarez started running down the highway. We looked at each other and asked, "What in the hell is wrong with him". We did not understand why he was running from the police, especially since none of us had any drugs on us. The police caught up to him on the other side of the highway, knocked him to the ground and put handcuffs on him. They started searching him and pulled out a whole Kilo of cocaine, which was hidden inside his pants. We were shocked.

Why does this fool have drugs on him? Is he fucking crazy?

The policeman called for backup and next thing I knew there were three police cars surrounding us with guns drawn. They told us to lie on the ground with our faces buried in the dirt. One cop came over to get the little boy, who was in shock after seeing his dad tackled by the police. The boy started screaming hysterically for his dad, and he broke free from the police and ran across the highway towards his dad. He was running down the middle of a six-lane highway with cars and trucks speeding by him blowing their horns. A semi trailer truck ran over him and we could hear a crushing sound coming from the little boy's body. After he got ran over by the front tires, the back tire hits him and threw his body in the air. His body went flying right over our heads while we are lying on the ground. Suarez was screaming to the policemen, "My son, please help my son!"

We were all handcuffed and taken to jail while the little boy was still lying along the side of the highway. During this whole time, we did not say anything to each other. We were all in shock from seeing that poor little boy dead on the side of the highway. I really felt bad about the little boy getting killed like that because he did not have to be there. This brought back memories when I got run over by a car on Jackson Street. I felt a sadness run through my body that I never felt before. I start thinking to myself; "Why does a child have to die for me to make some money? Are these signals from God that I'm not supposed to be in this business? Is this still part of the Jackson Street curse? It was his father's idea to bring him along on the trip; I wish he had not brought the little boy". This is sad….

We were all locked up for about a month before our lawyer got the police to make a deal with us. I talked to Star everyday on the jail house phone. I told her not to come visit me because I didn't want her to see me locked up like an animal. After being locked up for thirty days, I knew prison life was not for me. Considering what happened to the little boy, our lawyer got them to drop all the charges provided we left Florida in the next couple of weeks.

I don't know what kind of deal the police made with Suarez, but no matter what kind of deal was made, it still would not bring back his poor son. I would hate to have to live with his guilt for bringing his son into a hostile environment like the drug business. We all agreed to the deal and started making plans to leave town. We did not get to make the millions like we thought, but at least we were free. The good thing about what happened is I did not get put in prison and nothing would be on my record. The bad news is that the police got the $150,000 that we had hidden in the car, and a little boy is dead.

During the next couple of weeks, the police were video taping our every move. Several neighbors stopped by to tell us that the police were hiding in between houses taping us. We were worried the house was bugged so we had to leave the house to talk any business. We needed to collect as much money as we could from the people who still owed us money. We needed to build up our money so that we could continue our business in Brownsville.

We decided to leave town in small groups so we wouldn't attract too much attention from the police. I explained to Star that we had to leave town for business reasons. I told her that it would be best if she left without me because I did not want anything to happen to her. Star left ahead of me with Sly and Devon's girlfriend, early in the morning, about 4:00am. We still had sixty pounds of marijuana we needed to figure out how to get to Brownsville without getting caught. We decided to hide the weed in my car inside the tires for the trip home.

We hired a private company to deliver my car to Brownsville. They charged us $1,000 to deliver the car to an abandoned house in Brownsville. We paid the company the cash in advance and it was all set to be there in a week. Since I didn't have my car, I decided to fly home, rather then ride on a bus for twenty hours. Devon was the last to leave the house; he left about a month after I left. My flight was a three-hour non-stop flight to Pittsburgh. I knew if the plane stopped anywhere I might not get back on it. This was the first time that I ever flew in a plane. I was scared, but I needed to get out of town fast so I had to do it.

I was happy when we finally landed at the airport because I did not like flying. My sister picked me up at the airport and we were on the way back to my mom's house. My mom had moved in another house in Brownsville, off of Jackson Street. She said I could live there with her until I got my own place. My sister lived there with my mother, but not my little brother Robert. I didn't know where he was living, all I knew was he was living with some girl somewhere. It was like old times except we didn't have to worry about the floods of the creek.

The next day I saw Star in a car with her old boyfriend riding around in town. It bothered me to see her with him, but I wasn't worried because I knew she would come back to me. I did not try to contact her, even though I wanted to, because I just did not have anything to say. Star's sister, "Lola" and I started hanging together a couple weeks later. Even hanging with her didn't take my mind off Star, but it sure did help.

I was starting to make a lot of money selling that sixty pounds of weed we got from Florida. When the weed got in town, we hide it until Devon came in town. We all agreed to split the weed up three ways, getting twenty pounds apiece to sell. The gang did not break up; we just relocated to do our business. The money that we brought back from Florida was to be reinvested in the business. We were back on track again.

I had not seen or heard from Ann since I got back in Brownsville, I'm sure she knew I was back in town. I figured her brother mentioned it to her when I got back, since he was with Star the next day. I knew she was still with Shady, as (The woman on the side). The truth is that Shady already had a wife and would only see Ann when he could get away from home. In my opinion Ann was too pretty to be (The woman on the side), but maybe after dealing with me she suffered from low self-esteem. Maybe she was happy with all the money he gave her. Maybe she was hooked on his drugs. I don't know and really don't give a fuck anymore. I need to focus on what I need to do in order to make this money. This money is going to buy my happiness. Some people say that money can't buy you happiness, but I would like to find out on my own if that is true.

"Believe in Change"

Chapter 16

A NEW BEGINNING

Our drug business was booming, and everything was going my way. Star came to the house a couple days a week to get some free weed and make love. We were not going together, but she liked weed as much as she liked making love to me. I guess you could say that we were friends with benefits. I was making so much money; I bought a new Cadillac that was white with a leopard interior. I got a remote starter put on the car with big white gangster tires. I had so much money that I didn't know what to do with it, so I kept it buried in the basement of my mother's house. I didn't smoke weed, so it was all profit for me. That is the way it was supposed to be.

I had my mother selling weed for me when I was not at the house. I also got Star's brother, "Ernest", to work for me selling weed. Ernest was Star's oldest brother, and he was about my age. He was not very happy with me seeing his sister, but there was nothing he could do to stop it. I had about ten people working for me at one time. I had the drug market locked down in Brownsville, because we still had the Florida connections. I did not sell cocaine, only weed because more people could afford it.

Star and I started dating again after about three months and was just seeing each other exclusively. Her parents were not happy with that, but who cared what they thought? I knew one of their daughters was going to be mine, either Star or Lola. Star started spending a lot of nights at my house after a couple of weeks into the relationship. We were together almost all the time and I did not care what the people in town were saying. The people in Brownsville were saying that I stole Star from Garland.

One morning when I went to take Star home, I noticed that there was something unusual on my car. There was paint remover on the hood of my beautiful car, melting away all my paint. I figured it was Garland, and I was pissed off. I told Star I was going to kill him when I saw him again. She asked me not to do that because she didn't want me to get in trouble, so I told her I wouldn't.

The very next week I found sugar on the metal rim where the gas goes. I didn't even tell Star about that, but I knew who did it. The sugar did not make it down to the motor so the car did not get damaged by it. The reason I knew who did it is because Ann's man, Shady, called me a few days later. He said that he heard I was going to mess his car up because I thought he was messing my car up. I told him I didn't mess with people's cars; that was for bitches and faggots.

Shady told me that Garland told him I said that I was going to mess with his car. I told Shady that Garland was lying, and everything between him and me was cool. Shady sounded real nervous on the phone when he was talking to me. He stuttered a lot, so it was hard for me to keep up with what he was saying. I don't think he really wanted to fuck with me. I could hear it in his voice. He said he was sorry for calling; but he wanted to make sure we were cool. I told him I was cool with everyone unless they fucked with me first. That was a strange call because I never talk to Shady before. I never knew he stuttered that much. I never met a stuttering ass drug dealer before.

Star's parents finally got fed up with her seeing me and made plans to send her to Los Angeles. Star told me she was going to Los Angeles for a week, but I knew she was lying to me. I didn't expect to ever see her again if she left town, especially if she went all the way to California. It bothered me a lot to think about not ever seeing her ever again. I thought about trying to change her mind, but I figured she had to find herself. If our relationship is meant to be, then she will come back. I'll just wait and see. A week later she was gone to Los Angeles, and I was alone again. I had a lot of money to comfort me, and that helped a lot, but I felt as if a part myself left with her. The same night Star left town, I went to kill Garland at his house. I got my gun and walked up to Ann's parents' house where he was still living.

The first thing I did was shoot a couple bullets into his car to get him to come out of the house. Then I hid on the side of their house and waited for him to come out. His mother came to the door and walked out on the porch to see what was going on. I started to pull the trigger, but when I saw who it was, I put the gun down. I waited to see if anyone else was going to come out. No one else came out, so I put my gun away and ran home in the darkness. I don't know where Ann's dad was at. It would have been hard for me not to shoot him if I would have seen him. As soon as I got home, I received a phone call. No one said anything over the phone, so finally I just hung the phone up. I decided to sleep in my car that night hoping someone would come and try to do something to it. I spent the whole night hiding in my car, but no one showed up. It would have been my pleasure to kill Garland for fucking with my car.

Star had been gone for a month, but she called me at least once a week to see how I was doing. Ever since Star had left, her sister, Lola, had been with me everyday. At first it was just as friends and then we were starting to have sex, but it wasn't like with Star. Lola had a lot to learn, and I didn't feel like teaching her all about sex. That didn't stop me from fucking her every chance I got. Several times her father came down to my house late at night looking for her. She would be back in my bed hiding while I was at the front door lying about where she was. When he left, she would sneak out the back door and run all the way home trying to get back before her father did.

One day Star called me and told me she was ready to come back home. Her parents wouldn't give her the money to do it. I told her I would pay her way home if she really wanted to come home. The next day I went to the airport to get her ticket sent to the airport in Los Angeles. Her flight would be coming in two days, and I planned on being there waiting for her. I really missed being with her. She made me feel really special in so many ways. Her flight arrived at 3:00pm; I was very excited about seeing her again. I did not want to let her know how much I missed her, so I knew I had to act cool. When I saw her walking through the airport, I realized how beautiful she really was and how much I missed her. We walked to each other and kissed briefly, hugged, and then we were on our way back to Brownsville. I drove her straight home so she could spend some time with her family. We agreed to see each other the next day after she got settled in at her parent's house.

The next day I saw her riding through town in Garland's bullet riddled car. I was happy to see the bullet holes in his car. I was not happy to see Star with that ass hole. I decided not to say much to her for a couple of weeks, just to show her that I did not care what she did. When she called, I would tell her I couldn't talk and hang up the phone. Finally, she came to the house to see me face to face. When I saw her, I couldn't resist her any longer and we made love right there on the floor. After we made love, we wiped the sweat from each other's faces in a loving way. She told me I was the only one for her and asked me to please forgive her for being so childish. After that day, we got closer and closer; we were inseparable.

We did everything together. I never thought that I could feel that way about anyone again. The feeling for her was so strong that it was scary. I never felt this way about Ann. I think that it was more of a challenge with Ann rather than love. I think that getting Ann, (a girl who I was not allowed to have), had been the victory I was looking for. I do not believe love had anything to do with me wanting to have Ann. I just wanted her because I was not allowed to have her because of my social status. It certainly was not what I was feeling for Star. We were like Bonnie and Clyde, and we would hurt anyone that tried to mess with us. This thing called love had made its way back into my life.

A few weeks later, Star and I went to Ohio to start a weed distribution in that area. A friend of mine named, "Little Red", who lived in Cleveland, was going to help me start a business there. I took some weed to Cleveland and was selling it from the hotel where we were staying at to give the people in Cleveland a taste of what I had to offer. After a week, everything I had was gone, all five pounds of weed. Star and I spent a couple days at the hotel just spending money and making love. The last night we were there Star told me how much she loved me and asked me if I wanted to get married. I was a little shocked to hear that from her, because I did not realize she was that serious about me. She also said she wanted to have my baby, which sounded like a lot of fun to me. I didn't have to think about it long. I knew I was in love with her so why fight it. I explained to her that we had to change the way we lived if we wanted a marriage to really work. That meant not selling drugs and getting a job like normal people. I told her that we would have a better chance in another town or state. She agreed and showed me her container of birth control pills and emptied them in the toilet. She said with a smile on her face, "Now it's time to start making a baby". She didn't have to ask me twice, I was ready to start.

A month later Star was pregnant and everything was falling in place. She got pregnant so easily that I figured that it had to be our destiny to get married. I went to see the Air Force recruiter and then took the Air Force entry test. I passed the test, and the recruiter told me they would take me in a couple of months. That left plenty of time to tie up loose ends in my life. I bought Star a big engagement ring, and we planned the wedding a week before I was to go to the military. Her parents were not very excited about the whole situation, but decided to give us a chance.

I decided the first change in my life would be to quit selling drugs. That was a hard decision, but I felt a necessary one if we were going to make the marriage work. I gave my drug business to my mom and didn't ask for a penny from it. All I wanted was to get married and have a happy quiet life; start over new and put the past behind me. I knew that I was going to miss the money and the excitement, but I felt Star was worth it. The plan was coming together perfectly. It was like it was already written and we were just following the story.

I finally sat down and had a long talk with Star's mom, "Angel" before the marriage. She was a very nice, intelligent lady, who was as pretty as she was wise. She had a very extensive religious background, and she could sing like a sparrow. Mrs. Angel told me if I expected my marriage to work, or even have a chance, I would have to accept God in my life. I really wanted this marriage to work, so I was willing to try anything to give us the best chance. Star's mom told me that she knew I was going to get one of her daughters; she just wasn't sure which one it would be, Star or Lola. I knew I would get one of them to, but I was hoping that it would be Star. Mrs. Angel told me to think about what we talked about and let her know if I was willing to give my life to God. I was not sure what giving my life to God meant exactly, but I'm sure I'll find out.

A month before the wedding I got a call from Ann, which was a shock to me. She was the last person I expected to hear from before my wedding. I was completely taken by surprise to hear her voice. I asked her how she was doing and how the baby was doing. She said her and the baby was fine. I hadn't seen the baby for months because it was just too hard for me personally to see her. When I saw the baby, it brought back such bad memories. I thought it was best I just stayed away until I got myself together mentally.

Ann said that she heard I was getting married to Star and that she was pregnant with my child. I told her that Star and I were getting married in a month at her mom's house and that a week after we get married I would be going into the Air Force to start a new life. Ann started telling me how much she still loved me and how she wanted me back in her life. She asked if she could meet me and talk about it some more. I thought about it for a while and then I said why not, and we set up a place to meet.

We decided to meet at the park to talk because it was quiet there at night. When I saw Ann she had on a short, sexy red dress with some red boots on. That was the sexiest I had ever seen her look since I known her. She always wore plain clothes and was very conservative to look at. Tonight she was looking like someone from a sexy magazine; I was very impressed with the way she looked. I wasn't sure that I would be able to resist her because of the way she looked. I got out of my car and sat in hers. She reached over and kissed me on my cheek. She started off by saying that she still loved me and that she and Ronnay needed me back in their lives again. She said that she would do anything to prove how much she loved me. Tears were coming from her eyes as she was talking to me. She sounded very sincere about what she was saying, but I had no reason to trust Ann or believe a word she was saying. I thought that she was just upset that I was with Star, especially since Star was the one who told me about her cheating on me.

I needed to find out if I still had any feelings hidden inside of me for Ann so we went to a hotel and made crazy love for hours. The sex was great, but there were no feelings to go with it. It was just sex. The only feeling that I had was guilt for cheating on Star. When we were done neither of us said anything to each other; we just put on our clothes and said goodbye. I started to call her the next day, but I decided not to because I didn't have anything good to tell her so why say anything.

The truth is there was no love left for her. I knew that after we made love that night. She was probably trying to break Star and me up, and I wasn't going to let that happen. I had to find out if I had any feelings left for her. Star did not know Ann called me, and I never called Ann again. I was concerned that Ann was going to tell Star about the night we spent together. Maybe I was just being paranoid or feeling guilty. Either way we were done for good.

One day Star's mom invited me to a church revival on a Wednesday night. I told her that I would be there. Star and I drove to the revival together. We arrived at the revival and there were a lot of people there. That was the first time I had ever been to something like that. Everyone was so friendly. Star and I sat next to her parents as the services started. The music started and everyone was jumping up and down praising God. At one point the preacher asked if there was anyone there who wanted to be saved by God. I felt like everyone in the place was looking at me to see if I was going to get up. It felt like the question was directed right to me. I watched as people walked up to get saved. Everyone was standing and cheering as one by one someone walked to the front.

In front of me was a lady who must have weighed 400 pounds. She was shouting and jumping for joy, when all of the sudden she landed on my foot. She hit my foot and tripped, falling backwards towards me. This woman was 400 pounds, but she must have a vertical leap of two feet. She hit my foot with such force that I screamed out loud, saying, "Oh my God". Everyone turned to look as I was trying to stop the lady from crushing me with her enormous body weight. With the help of everyone in our row, we were able to stop the lady from falling. I thought that my foot might be broke. It was ten minutes before I could put any pressure on it. Even if I did walk to the front; there would be a noticeable limp. If I ever go to church again, I will make sure there is no fat ass, biscuit eating woman sitting in front of me.

Finally, I got the courage to walk up to the preacher. When I got up there, he asked me if I wanted God to take away my sins, which I knew were a lot. I told him yes, and he started praying over me. Tears rushed to my eyes and a feeling of cleanliness came over me. My legs got numb and I fell to my knees. I became very dizzy, like I was going to pass out. The preacher told me that God had forgiven all my sins, and that he would always forgive me. When I staggered and limped back to my seat, Star and her parents were crying for me. The whole church was shouting with joy. After the service, I drove Star home. We really didn't say anything to each other. I had so many things going through my mind, but I couldn't say anything. I had never felt like that before, and I didn't know what to make of it. I knew that I wanted to change the way I thought and acted.

The next day I was counting the drug money that was hidden in the basement. The money added up to $200,000, which was more than I thought was there. I didn't feel that just quitting the drug business would be enough if I really wanted to live right. I had to think about what to do with the dirty drug money. I heard it said that if you just put your life in God's hands he will take care of you. So if I really believed in God, then I knew I should get rid of all the sinful material things from my drug activities. I knew that would leave me with nothing, but I had to believe God would take care of me.

I wanted to give the money to someone that would do some good with it. I felt the church people would do the most good with the money. I was tempted to keep some of it, but I really needed to make a 100% commitment in my belief. I put the money in two pillowcases and snuck into the church at night. It was on a Saturday night when no one was there to see me. I climbed up and stacked the money on two large ceiling fans above the seats in the church. My plan was to have the money blow into the crowd when the fans were turned on the next day. Maybe this would inspire some people to think miracles do happened if you just believe in God. Hopefully more people would try God in their lives because of what was going to happen at the church. I don't know what made me come up with this idea. I don't know why I do a lot of things anymore. Maybe I'm being lead by God and don't know it.

I made sure Star and I arrived at church early that Sunday so that I could sit next to the ceiling fan switch. At a certain time in the service, I was going to turn the fans on and watch the money blow down. Star asked me why I was acting so strange. I told her that something very special was going to happen today. She asked me what, but I told her to wait and see. About halfway through the services, the preacher announced the most recent born again Christians. He had us all stand up one at a time to be acknowledged by the church. When he called my name, I stood up slowly and raised my hands in the air. While I was raising my hands I hit the switch to turn on the fans and said "thank you Jesus".

The money started blowing all over the church causing chaos. The people in the church were going crazy trying to grab some money. Everyone was jumping up and down praising God, including my future wife. Star started grabbing some of the money and I told her to put it back because it was the church's money. I grabbed her arm and pulled her through the crowd trying to get her to safety. After about ten minutes we finally made it to my car. We went down to Star's parents' house where we were going to eat lunch and discuss the wedding plans. All her parents could talk about was what happened at the church. Mrs. Angel looked at me and said, "Do you see how good God is"? I said, "Yes, God sure can make some changes in a person's life". She said, "God can make you give away all your riches and you will do it without looking back". That last comment started me to thinking. Was it God who gave me the idea on how to get rid of the money? Is God working through me already or has he been doing it all the time?

The wedding was going to be a small ceremony; the only people who were going to attend would be my sister and Star's family. The wedding was going to be at Star's parents' house, which was a small modest house. The preacher of the church was going to do the ceremony for us. I didn't want to have anything real big like my last one. I wasn't sure I was doing the right thing getting married again so soon after the last one, but I knew I loved Star, and that was at least a good start. I knew if there were love and God in our lives, we would always have a chance.

My only hope was that Star was as devoted to making this work as I was. I knew that I could never go by what people say, only by their actions, because I believe love is an action. After the wedding, I planned on giving my Cadillac to my brother, Gary, in Philly. He had been keeping my other car for me, and I was going to ride that back home. Going to Philly was going to be our little honeymoon because now I was broke again. We were planning on being there for a week, and then I would be on my way to basic training for six weeks in San Antonio, Texas.

The day I went to see the Air Force recruiter I also went and filled out an application to become a State Policeman. I had not heard from them yet, so I guess I was meant to go into the Air force. I thought that if the State Police called, I would probably do that instead of going into the military. The military must be my destiny.

Finally the day of the wedding arrived, and I was very nervous because I just was not sure of myself. Something inside of me was telling me I was making a mistake to get married so soon. I did not know if it was wedding jitters or if it was something I should be really concerned with. I was committed so I just had to play it out and trust in God. Star did not seem nervous at all. She was very relaxed when I saw her. Never once did she ask, "Are you sure that we were doing the right thing?" To be so young, she was very confident for her age.

The wedding went as planned, and that evening we headed to Philly for our honeymoon. We had a nice quiet week in Philly and headed back to Brownsville with my other car. We got back on a Saturday afternoon; we had a nice time together in Philly. That Monday I would be catching a flight to San Antonio, Texas for the beginning of my new life. The plan was for Star to come to Texas after basic training was over for me. It would be the first time in years I went six weeks without any pussy; that might be harder than the training camp. It would be like when I was going through puberty all over again. That Monday morning Star drove me to the airport; we both were in tears as we arrived at the airport. I told her I would call her the first chance I got. I gave Star a long hard kiss and then watched as she walked away.

I boarded the plane for a three hour flight to Texas; I was a little nervous thinking about what I was doing. My mind was really buzzing because I didn't know what to expect when I got there. I was broke and all I had was the clothes on my back. I knew that I did have God in my heart, and that was supposed to be enough to get you through. If someone had told me several years earlier that I would be on a plane to Texas for basic training, I would have thought they were crazy. I am sure a lot of people thought I was crazy when I told them what I was going to do. Who would have thought a person like me would find God and would try to do the right thing? I was still trying to convince myself that this was not a dream.

I wondered what was going through Ann's head after she assimilated all this information about me. I wondered what was going through my drug buddies' heads that were still in the game. I wondered how long my mother would continue to sell drugs after I was gone. I wondered if I was strong enough to live this new life and put all my trust in God. I wondered if the people that I had hurt in my past would be able to forgive me someday.

Since I was from Jackson Street, I didn't expect life to be too quiet for me no matter where I went. That wasn't the way I was raised and that is the only life that I have known. I had sex, murder, and drugs in my past. What were the chances that none of my past would not come back to haunt me someday? There has to be a God for me to really be doing this. It must be God who saved me from prison or murder. He must have a great plan for me. There is something he wants me to do; I just wish I knew what it was. I will just follow this path and see what the next chapter has to say. ***"Believe in Change"***

Chapter 17

Boot Camp

While I settled in for a three-hour flight to San Antonio, Texas, my fear of flying, once again raised its ugly head. Once I got over this uncomfortable feeling and began to relax, I began to reflect back on my past: What were the odds that a person who lived the way I did would be on his way to join the military to help defend our country? I felt there was a better chance of me being murdered or sent to prison. This is why I knew there was a God. How else could this happen to a person like me?

Murderers and drug dealers go to prison but not me; I was going to join the military. Maybe God felt sorry for me because I was raised on Jackson Street. Whatever the reason, fear and apprehension consumed my thoughts of my future. I had so many questions and no one to direct them to. I didn't believe that boot camp could be any harder than living on Jackson Street. I didn't know what it was like to have a full stomach until I was fifteen years old. That food was stolen from the neighborhood grocery store. The plane was starting to make its descent and my new life was about to begin. It was time to get my mind ready, because I knew the military was going to be a mind game.

We were greeted by "Sergeant Green", a black man, maybe forty years old with a southern accent. After he confirmed who we were, he hustled us onto a bus that headed towards Lackland Air Force Base. There was complete silence on the bus; no one dared say anything because no one knew if they were allowed to talk on the bus. Once we arrived on base all hell broke loose. It seemed like we were being fed to hungry sharks.

There were three Drill Sergeants waiting for the bus to stop moving. They didn't look happy to see us. We grabbed our bags and rushed to get off the bus, we lined up outside the bus within a few seconds. I was thinking to myself, "What in the fuck did I get myself into?" Once we were lined up outside, Sergeant Green introduced the other Drill Sergeants. He started by saying, "The people you see here will be your mother and father for the next six weeks". There names were "Staff Sgt. Morris", "Staff Sgt. Johnson", and "Staff Sgt. Wilson". Staff Sgt. Wilson was a woman, which wasn't hard to notice because of her big titties. Her nickname was the "Black Widow" because she would eat you up and spit you out for later. I know it's going to be interesting dealing with her for six weeks.

We had to run over to the gymnasium after the drill sergeants showed us where it was located. We had to take all our things with us and if we dropped anything, we had to leave it on the ground. It only took a few minutes to run over to the gym and if you were last, they made you do pushups. Everyone was bumping into each other while they were running. We looked like a herd of cattle that was just startled by some wild creature. After we got there, they gave us our uniforms to wear for the next six weeks.

We were instructed to take our uniforms to our barracks, which would be where we would spend our next six weeks. Each dorm had about thirty small beds, about three feet apart, fifteen on each side of the room. We were only given two minutes to change our clothes and once we got our uniforms on we had to run over to the base barber shop for haircuts. For years I had been trying to get the perfect afro and now thirty seconds later it was all gone. That's fucked up.

I was really starting to think I made a big mistake by joining the military. Looking around the barracks, I saw all these young white faces, the whitest people that I have been around in a long time. Their average age must have been about 18 years old, which is at least five years younger than me. I'm thinking that maybe this is too much of a change in life for me at this age.

Is this something that I really need to do in order to make myself right with God? Do I have what it takes to handle this kind of living? Will God reward me for making such a big difference in my life? These are questions that I hope will be answered in the next six weeks. We spent the rest of the day learning how to make beds, clean toilets, and how to talk to the drill sergeants. The beds had to be perfect, toilets had to be cleaned with toothbrushes, and you had to address the drill sergeants by saying, "Yes sir" or "Yes ma'am".

The only break we had was at 7:00pm and that was to take a shower and get ready to go to bed. At 8:00pm it was lights out; everyone had to be in their beds, which were randomly given out to us. No one really cared where they slept because were just happy to lie down after a long day. I hadn't been to bed at 8:00pm since I was five years old, but I was tired and happy to lie down.

During the night I could hear some of the younger kids crying, and I was wondering how they were going to make it six weeks, if they were crying after just one night? This whole first day seemed like a nightmare because just that morning I was kissing my wife goodbye and now I had people in uniforms shouting at me and telling me what to do. On the streets if anyone would talk to me like that, I would fuck them up. I knew I couldn't think like that now and that I must keep my head together if wanted to make it through this.

Just as soon as I closed my eyes, it was time to get up. The lights came on and all I heard was someone shouting "get the fuck up ass holes". We were told that we had five minutes to shit, shower, and shave; or we would have to do fifty pushups. All I had time to do was to piss and get my clothes on. Some of the other airmen were stupid enough to try to do it all. They ended up doing a lot of pushups. It was only 5:00am and they were taking us to the field to do calisthenics for one hour.

The field was an old baseball field that no one used anymore. It was about a mile away and we had to run all the way to it, which was hard for some of the airmen. The drill sergeants expected us to run two miles, in 15 minutes at the end of our six week boot camp. If we were not able to do it, we would be sent home. I was in good shape, but not that kind of shape yet. This was going to be hard for me; it was kind of like training for a boxing match. I'm just going to act like I'm training for the heavy weight championship of the world. The hardest part for me would be going six weeks without sex. I hadn't gone that long without sex since puberty, and back then, that wasn't my choice. I just couldn't get any pussy.

The schedule for us was very challenging and we had to be in bed at 8:00pm and up by 5:00am. From 5:00am to 6:00am we ran and did calisthenics. They only gave us ten minutes for breakfast and our plates had to be empty. After our ten minute breakfast, we had to march around the outside of the barracks until 7:00am. We had academics from 7:00am until 11:00am, and then we would go to lunch. They gave us only ten minutes for lunch, and then we were marched to the barracks, where they would let us rest until 12:30pm. We marched from12:30pm until 1:00pm around the barracks, the drill sergeants did not want us to sit to long. At 1:00pm we marched back to class and stayed there until 3:00pm and then we had to go on a ten mile march, which took two hours.

At 5:00pm we marched to the mess hall for dinner and we were given fifteen minutes for dinner. After fifteen minutes, they would come and check our plates to make sure they were empty. If they weren't empty, we would have to do fifty pushups right there inside the mess hall. Everyone made sure all their food was gone. I had no problem eating all my food. I was use to cleaning my plate. We ate an assortment of food and none of it was good to me. I'm sure that prison food could have tasted better than this military food. The Drill Sergeants made us eat the food so fast, we did not really have time to enjoy the nasty taste of the food.

After dinner we were allowed to call our families on some pay phones that were outside of the barracks. Sometimes I had to wait in line for an hour just to get to use the phone. I probably called Star every night because that is how much I missed her. When I called her, I put the bill on my old phone number because I didn't have that kind of money to call her everyday. I knew the phone bill was going to be high, but I was not going to use that phone number anymore in Brownsville anyway. If I did not talk to Star everyday, I do not know if I could get through this boot camp. She reminded me why I was going through all this bullshit.

There was a white boy in boot camp we called "Smiley", because he always had a smile on his face. The drill sergeants got tired of that smile, so they made him walk around the dorm laughing out loud for eight hours straight. After that day, he never smiled again in boot camp. Every night I could hear him crying underneath his sheets like a little baby. I didn't feel sorry for him, but I sure got tired of all that damn crying. One night about 2:00am, finally I did something about it. I crept over to his bunk while he was under his sheets and started beating on him until he was quiet.

I ran back to my bunk and put the sheets over my head. I guess this boot camp had got the best of me. I needed to let my frustrations out on someone. No sex and all this bullshit would drive anyone crazy. The Drill Sergeant turned on the lights and asked what all that noise was. I told him I thought something was wrong with Smiley because he was crying underneath his sheets. When the drill sergeant pulled the sheets back there was blood all over the place. Smiley wasn't moving, so they called the medics and took him to the hospital.

The next day we found out he had a broken nose and a broken arm from the punches that I hit him with. They asked us questions about what happened to Smiley, but no one knew anything. They finally dropped it and finally we were able to get some sleep at night. I felt bad for doing that to Smiley, but he was driving me crazy with all that crying at night. I needed to get some rest at night in order for me to get through this madness, called boot camp.

After Smiley got out of the hospital, he got his discharge

papers a few days later. I guess I did him a favor by beating on him; at least he will be home with his family now. The Drill Sergeants and the other airmen thought I might have done it, but wasn't sure enough to say anything to me. After that night, all the other airmen in the dorm started coming to me for everything. They were crying to me about everything from missing their girlfriends to missing their mothers. Every night at different times someone would wake me up with some dumb ass problem, so I still wasn't getting any sleep, how ironic was that.

One of the sergeants called me into the office. It was the black widow, and she asked me if I wanted to be a flight Chief. A Flight Chief is a person that would be in charge of all the other airmen to make sure they did everything that they were supposed to do. She said I would have to meet with her everyday to let her know what was going on with the other airmen. I told her yes, I thought it would be worth it just to look at her big titties everyday. I would have done almost anything to be near any woman at this point. Just the word woman made my dick hard.

The other airmen were already coming to me for everything already, so I thought to myself; why not give it a try. Now I was the person waking them up in the morning and putting them to bed at night. This made me feel like I was the airman's father or mother. I was not sure if I wanted this added responsibility; I just wanted to do what I needed to do and move on to my next assignment. The other airmen accepted my position very naturally; there was no animosity from anyone. I was older than any of the other airmen and they had already begun looking to me for advice anyway. It was a perfect fit.

Going into the third week, all I could think about was getting some pussy. I was going to bed with a hard on and waking up with one. Every time the wind would blow, my dick would get hard; it was starting to get embarrassing. The only woman I saw was the black widow, and she was my drill sergeant. When I would go to her office, I had to stand in front of her desk and salute her until she said, "At ease airman".

While I was standing in front of her, I could look down her blouse and see the tops of her titties. My dick started getting hard as I stood in front of her. She looked at it and started smiling. She was smiling, but I was embarrassed because my dick was hanging halfway down my leg. She saluted me and came from behind her desk. She was a short lady, only about five feet, two inches tall, but she had one of the sexiest bodies I had ever seen. She had a brown complexion with short black hair. She wasn't very attractive in the face, but after three weeks of no pussy, I thought she was beautiful.

She walked up to me and asked me to report the day's activities to her. She had a short military skirt on that came a little above her knees that day. She stood about a foot in front of me; I could almost smell her pussy through her clothes. I told her there was nothing to report today and she asked if I was sure because it looked like something was on my mind. She said this as she was staring down at my dick, which was beginning to get hard. She asked me if I was married and I told her yes. I had the dumbest look on my face. She said it looked like you really miss her; and she indicated that maybe she could help me with something.

Before I could say anything she reached out towards my dick, then started rubbing on it through my pants. She walked behind me and locked the door and she pulled my dick out and started sucking it. It was so big she could hardly get it in her little mouth. I couldn't take anymore; I lifted her up and threw her on the desk. I reached under her skirt and tore her panties off with one pull. I had never sucked pussy before, but when I saw how good her pussy looked, I just had to taste it.

I learned how to suck pussy from watching two women eat each other. I started sucking her pussy like a thirsty animal in the desert. I felt like I was in the mess hall and only had ten minutes to clean my plate. It was like someone had hit fast forward on a movie, I was sucking so fast. I was so involved in sucking her pussy that I was forgetting to breathe. I must have held my breath for two minutes before I came up for air. Then I dived back in. The sound of me sucking her pussy was like the sound of a dog lapping up water in a bowl. That is how juicy her pussy was.

After sucking her pussy for about 15 minutes, she was so wet her cum was dripping down her leg. I buried my dick deep into her pussy and started pounding it wildly. I put my hand over her mouth to keep her quiet because she was moaning loudly. I did not want anyone to hear us or think I was hurting her in a bad way. I was just about to cum when the phone rang; she had the audacity to reach over and picked it up. It was her husband on the phone, and I started to pull my dick out, but it felt too good. I kept on banging that pussy. She was trying to act normal, but I kept banging it harder and harder. Finally it was too much for her and she told her husband that she had to call him back.

She hung up the phone and hugged me so tight I could hardly breathe. It looked like her eyes were rolling back into her head; I was hoping that she did not have some kind of medical condition. She started screaming so loud I had to put both hands over her mouth and she started shaking like she was having a seizure. I was starting to get worried, so I figured I needed to hurry up before she died or something. I was starting to make so much noise she had to cover my mouth with her hands. Once we were finished, we fixed our clothes and it was all military again. I saluted and went back to the barracks to make sure my people were doing what they were supposed to be doing. The next couple of weeks we were having sex every way imaginable in her office. I was just as tired from sex, as I was from calisthenics and marching.

Star was planning to join me in Texas after boot camp was over. I just hoped God would forgive me for having sex with the black widow. When I talked to Star, I was beginning to feel guilty about what I was doing with the Black Widow. She asked me when she could come to be with me in Texas. I told her there were two more weeks of boot camp left, so it wouldn't be long now. After I got off the phone, I felt bad. I decided that I had to stop having sex with the Black Widow, so I quit my job as a flight chief so I wouldn't have to be alone her anymore. She wasn't very happy with that and gave me a hard time, but it wasn't anything I couldn't handle. I knew I would rather put up with the bullshit than feel the guilt I had to carry around for cheating on my pregnant wife.

I had been thinking so much about sex, I forgot all about the money the military was paying me. After four weeks the hard part of our training was over and the drill sergeants were going to give us a Saturdays off. We were paid on that Friday for four weeks of hard work in boot camp. When I looked at the check, I thought I was going to faint the check was so small. The check was for $700; I used to spend that much at the bar in one night.

I didn't know how they expected me to support a wife and family on this kind of money. I gave a couple hundred thousand to the church before I left for the military because I didn't want to start my life with that dirty drug money. Now after looking at this paycheck, I was starting to think I had made a huge mistake. The church said, "Once you give your life to God, he will take care of you". I certainly hope so, because I'm going to need some help.

That Saturday I cashed my check and went to the recreation center where they had pinball machines, a bowling alley, and pool tables. They also had a dance hall where there were girls, something I have not seen for awhile. I thought I was in heaven, after four weeks of basic training. A lot of the guys were getting drunk, but not me, I wanted to enjoy every minute of my freedom with a clear head. I played pool and ate all the junk food I could find at the snack bar. We had to be back in the barracks before 10:00pm that day. Some people did not make it back in time and lost all their privileges for the next two weeks. They were stuck in the kitchen peeling potatoes for the next two weeks. I got back at 8:00pm and talked on the phone with my wife for two hours.

The only difference in the next two weeks is the drill sergeants taught us how to shoot an M-16 rifle. I had to qualify with the rifle or I wouldn't get out of boot camp. I had to get a certain amount of bullets in the target on the shooting range to certify. I had never shot a rifle before, but I have always been a fast learner. I earned my marksman ribbon, an academic achievement award and passed the physical endurance test. There were only about half of us that made it through boot camp out of about thirty airmen. Those who did make it got their orders to be shipped to their next base.

Their next base was where they would learn their trade. Some would be cooks, nurses, mechanics, and like me, some would be Security Specialists. This was just a fancy name for Military Police. Some were going to different parts of the United States, but not me, because Police School was right there in Texas. Police School was for four weeks on the other side of base.

The ceremony for boot camp graduation took all day, because there were a lot of other airmen graduating also. We all had to march pass the Base Commander and salute at a precise time in our marching. There must have been a couple hundred airmen marching that day on base. I didn't realize there were that many people on the base at the same time that I was training. We were given another paycheck, and I had about a $1,000. We were allowed to live off base after boot camp and I wanted to find a place for us to live, so we could be a family. I also had to pay for a plane ticket to get Star to Texas, and I only had two days to do all of this before police school started. I knew that when I got done doing that, I would be broke again. I was not used to being without money, but I realized it was time to get more acquainted with it. I grew up in poverty and I had hoped I would never see it again. I made it through the first time and was sure that I'd make it again, if I just would hang in there. ***"Believe in Change***"

Chapter 18

The Security Specialist

I found a small one bedroom apartment for me and my wife near the base; it was about a mile from base. I could walk that distance to the base every morning in about twenty minutes. I did not have to worry about walking in the snow because Texas very rarely got any snowfall. In a few days, Star was flying to be with me. It seemed like I had been gone for years. I was very excited about seeing her again, because I knew she would help me get through all this stuff that I had to do in the military.

Security Police training was more like a regular job, because you got to go home at night to see your family. What made the job so arduous was that I had to wear about thirty pounds of equipment everyday for work. You had to wear a flax vest, ammunition belt, and a helmet—all in addition to carrying a weapon, which weighed six pounds. We also had to wear green fatigues with a black beret on our heads. After about eight hours of training, walking home was a task by itself.

Being a Military Policeman was a lot like being a civilian policeman, except the laws differed slightly. Even though we were policemen, we could not arrest anyone off the Air Force base. Even if they did the crime on base and the military police chased the criminal off base. We had to stop chasing the criminal at the base gate and notify the civilian police. On base, we were authorized to employ the use of deadly force, if determined necessary at that time. When I was a drug dealer, I carried a gun everyday, so I was used to carrying a gun regularly. Now I would be able to carry a gun and not worry about hiding it or being arrested for carrying it. I guess it was a natural transition for me to carry a gun again.

Every morning we would load our weapons with blank bullets to play war games. This was a lot more fun than what we had to do during boot camp. Everyday we shot guns and arrested people; and surprisingly, that was fun for me. I never wanted to be a policeman, never even dreamed about being one. Now I would be carrying a badge and arresting people for the government. Sometimes while playing war games, we would get shot and have to pretend to be dead. We would have to lie on the ground, sometimes for an hour at a time. There would be bugs and snakes crawling on us, but we were not allowed to move. If we got caught moving, the trainers would make us run two miles, after we did fifty pushups. I was so tired most of the time. If I got shot; I would just fall asleep after ten minutes. I didn't even care what crawled on me.

We got paid again on Friday, and I went to rent a car for the weekend because Star was coming to Texas that night on the 7:00pm flight. I would be there waiting for her with open arms. I knew I couldn't afford to rent a car, but I didn't know what else to do. When she got off the plane, she ran to me and gave me a big hug. Once I saw her again, all the doubts about whether I made the right choice about marrying her were gone. Her stomach had got a little bigger from the baby, but she still looked good to me. There was something about her that always made me feel good when I was with her. We made love all weekend, and before I knew it, the weekend was over. The next thing I knew, I was walking back the base to play some more police games.

Texas was a beautiful place, but since it was January the average temperature was 70 degrees everyday. When I arrived in Texas, I weighed 225 pounds, and now my weight was 210 pounds. I had not noticed my weight loss until my wife mentioned it to me when she saw me. At 6'3" tall, I guess I was looking a little thin, but I was in great shape. This was the best shape I had been in since I received my black belt in karate.

My wife and I went out to a restaurant on the weekend to celebrate us being back together. While we were at the restaurant, an old friend of mine showed up. It was the black widow and her husband. The stories that I heard around base and among the other airman gave me more insight on the relationship of the Black Widow and her husband. Her husband had been in the military for a long time and had met the black widow in training. He had been married to a white woman before, but that ended when she cheated on him. That broke his heart because she was his childhood sweetheart and his first love. They got married right after high school, he joined the Air Force and they only stayed together for about two years before she left him for another man.

When he met the black widow, she was very naïve and young and fed up with black men because they had treated her so bad in the past. The only thing that she missed about black men was their big dicks. This is something she told me one time after we made love in her office. They sat right across from us at a separate table and she said hello to us as they sat down. Star smiled saying to them "Hello, how are you doing?", But I just looked over and nodded my head at them. I hadn't known the rumors were true, she really did have a white husband; if I would have known that, I would have kept banging her pussy. I guess I just don't like white people for all the bullshit they put me through as a kid.

I tried not to look her way, but it was hard because she had a short mini skirt on. Her husband was a short, half bald white man, but he looked familiar to me. I was not happy seeing a black woman with this white man. I guess after being called so many niggers by white men when I was young made me feel that way. It seemed like the white man had everything, so I didn't want him to have our black women also.

I kept catching the black widow staring at us, so I thought I would have a little fun. Every time she would look over, I would kiss Star until the black widow turned away. I over heard the black widow and her husband talking very softly. He was asking her why she kept staring at me and she said she was not staring. He caught her staring again, and this time he slapped her across her face in front of everyone in the restaurant. There must have been at least thirty people in the restaurant, with almost all of them being white. I could feel the tension in the air. Everyone got real quiet and just stared at them. Star looked at me and said, "Did you see him slap that poor lady?" I said, "Yeah, that's a bunch of bullshit. Someone should slap his punk ass". I had never seen a white man hit a black woman before. This was hard for me to handle.

She got up and threw her drink in his face and called him a white motherfucker. He raised his hand to hit her again and I stopped him this time by grabbing his arm before he could land the hit. He said, "Look nigger, I'm a Master Sergeant in the military, and I will kill you if I have to". I had to restrain myself from breaking his neck right there in front of all these white people. I threw him down to the floor and held him there, hoping he would calm down. The Black Widow got up and kicked him in the head and told him to "Why don't you go fuck yourself with his own little dick". I was hoping she would kick him some more, but she turned and ran out the door.

Blood was gushing out his nose as I got up off him. When he got up, he looked at me and said, "You're going to be sorry about this nigger" and he walked out of the restaurant. I was going to follow him outside and beat his ass, but I didn't want to upset my wife anymore. We stayed and finished our dinner and started walking home about an hour later. We didn't say much about the incident.

Our apartment was about a mile away, but it was a lovely night for a walk so we didn't mind. We were holding hands and walking down the street when I saw a car coming towards us. I didn't think much of it because we were safely on the sidewalk. As the car got closer, it came onto the sidewalk heading towards us at a high-rate of speed. I could see sparks coming from underneath the car from the muffler scraping the cement sidewalk.

I was waiting for the car to turn away, but it did not; it

kept moving straight towards us. I grabbed my wife, and we dove off the sidewalk into the soft grass on the side. I could not see who was driving the car; it all happened so fast. We were a little bruised, but we were alive and that's what was important. Star asked me if we should call the police and tell them what happened. I told her no, because we could not really see who did it. I had an idea who it was, but I did not want to upset her. I think it was the Black Widow's husband, but it could have been her for all knew.

Whoever it was is going to wish they had killed me, because I would get my revenge as soon I find out who it was. When that Monday came, Star did not want me to go to work because she was still upset from almost getting run over during the weekend. What kind of person would try to run down a pregnant woman? This has to be someone with some serious mental health issues. Now I have to watch my back everywhere I go. This is just like my drug dealing days all over again. When am I going to be able to just relax and enjoy life?

The third week of training was basically the same, except they taught us how to use the rifles with the night vision on them. The night vision on the rifles helped a person see their target better at night. Our last week of training was going to be at night in the woods surrounding the base. We were also asked if we wanted to be a k-nine dog handler earlier during that week. It sounded exciting, so I decided to sign up for it and see what it was all about. I was told that if I got accepted, I would be notified at the end of police training. If I got picked I would have to stay in Texas for another ten weeks learning how to train dogs.

We were told that we would learn how to train dogs to sniff drugs, to sniff bombs and to attack people on command. I was more curious about being a drug dog handler than anything else because I had dealt with a lot of drugs in the past. I always wondered how they were able to do that so efficiently, no matter what the drug dealer did to hide the drugs. This might be some good stuff to know if I ever decided to get back into the drug game. God willing, I will not have to go back to my old ways.

The last week of police training finally came and we all had to work from 11:00pm to 7:00am. Star was not happy with that, but I had to do whatever they needed me to do. The military always said if they wanted you to have a wife, they would have issued you one with your uniform. I was not crazy about walking to base at night, but that was the only way I could get there. I would have felt a lot better if I had a gun to carry to work just in case someone tried to run me over again. Our guns were always left on base at the Base Armory. The Armory is a place where all the base weapons are stored. We had to sign them out every time we came to base and turn them in before we left. I wondered if someone was going to try and kill me again since the person failed the first time. I was used to living like that, but I was more concerned because I wanted to take care of my wife. That's hard to do when you have to go to work everyday and leave your wife at home.

I remember the first night of night training and we meet our new drill sergeant. The drill sergeants lined us all up and said, "This is your new Drill Sergeant for night training". It was "Master Sergeant Wilson", the Black Widow's husband. He was the same person who I got into a fight with at the restaurant. My mouth almost dropped to the ground when I seen who he was. He started walking the line so he could inspect us; I was hoping he would not remember me. Well that did not happen; he smile and looked me in the face and said, "Your shoes were not shiny enough Airman Jackson". He made me do fifty pushups, and I knew I was going to catch hell from him this week. This fucking Jackson Street curse just will not leave me alone.

That night we did not do much, except go over the rules of night training. The drill sergeant kept finding reasons for making me do pushups every chance he got. I must have done over 500 pushups that night, but I was not going to let him get to me. I did not tell Star who my new drill sergeant was because I did not want her to worry about me. After three nights of taking abuse from him, he called me into his office and the first words out his mouth were, "Didn't I tell you I was going to make you pay for fucking with me? You might as well quit now, because I'm going to break you nigger".

I told him if anything was going to break, it would be his wife's good pussy from me banging it. He came from behind his desk and started towards me, but he changed his mind when he saw how big I was. He said "I wish I would have run your ass over with my car that night when you and your wife were walking down the street". He told me to get the fuck out of his office before he killed me. I just saluted, stared him in the eyes and walked out the door without saying anything. I did not see him anymore that night, and I was very happy about that; maybe he went home early. I know God must be working in my life because I felt like killing him. But I didn't and that is a miracle to me.

While I was walking home that morning, a car pulled up beside me and slowed down. It was the Black Widow and she said, "I need to talk to you, it is very important". So I got in her car and we drove to the park to talk where no one would see us. She asked if I told her husband about me and her having sex. "No I said, but I think he knows something, because he sure is fucking with me". I said "Why are you asking about it now; did he say something to you"? She said "He came home early last night and asked all kind of questions about me and you". I asked her, "What did you tell him about us?" and she said, "Nothing at all, do you think I'm crazy? He said you told him we made love before, and you were bragging about it". I told her he was not telling the truth because I would not say anything like that about her. She said, "He had been acting very irrational lately, every since the problem at the restaurant".

I leaned over and kissed the Black Widow on the cheek, then told her not to worry. I said "He doesn't know anything about you and me; he's just messing with you". She started to kiss me and before I knew it I was pulling her panties off without even thinking about it. I put her panties into my pant's pocket, and we started to make passionate love. She told me how much she missed my big dick. We made love for hours, in and outside of the car, even on the hood of the car. When we got off the hood of the car there was a large dent on it. I did not tell her because I did not want to worry her about it. When we were done, she dropped me off a couple blocks from my apartment and I went home. Here I go again, fucking up and feeling guilty about it. I have to learn to control myself.

I told my wife I had to work late, that's why I was late getting home. I felt guilty about what I did, but it was not sex, it was revenge. I really did try to break her pussy this time when we were fucking. I think I did this time because she could hardly walk when we were done. I knew he would not be getting any of that pussy for a long time because she has to be sore down there. I slept well that morning because I felt like I got some revenge for all the bullshit I had to put up with the Black Widow's husband. I still felt like I needed more from him. I wanted to see pain in his face.

While I was walking to work the next night, I noticed something in the pocket of my uniform. It was the Black Widow's red panties still in my pocket from that morning; I had forgotten they were there. I was lucky my wife did not find them in my pocket; there is no way that I could explain that. When I got on the base, I noticed the Black Widow's car sitting in the parking lot. I figured her husband drove it to work that night at least that is what I hope. I really didn't want to see the Black Widow again after this morning.

I had an idea on a way to mess with Master Sergeant Wilson's mind one more time before I leave Texas. I took his wife's panties and jammed them into the gas tank of the car. Then I wrote a note and put it on the windshield so he could see it. I wrote please fill your tank up like I filled your wife's pussy up. I also wrote, "Fix the dent on your hood because it looks like a big dick was on top of it". I smiled all the way to work; I just could not get that smile on my face all night. I know everyone noticed it, but I just told people I was happy because we only had one more night of training to go.

That night was quiet, except for the Drill Sergeant making me do all those damn push ups again. I took it all in stride because I knew I would get the last laugh when he got to his car in the morning. He would stand there and laugh while I did my push ups, I did not see anything funny. That morning when training was over, I walked over to him and said, "I hope you don't run out of gas on your way home". He said, "What you are talking about airman?" I said "nothing" and walked away with that same smile on my face that I had all night.

I wanted to hide somewhere so I could see his face when he read the letter on his car. But I didn't think that was a good idea so I went straight home. I didn't know how he was going to react, but I was sure I would find out later that night. Finally, I only had one more night of training and he had not broken me. It was tough, but I did it.

When I woke up that afternoon, I wondered what happened with the note I left on Sergeant Wilson's car. I did not feel bad, because he should not have been messing with me. I had a bad feeling about going to work, but it was my last night and I had to finish the training. I had to go in if I wanted to graduate with everyone else I started with. My wife and I spent a quiet day at home before it was time for me to go to work. She asked me to stay home that night because she had a strange feeling about me going to work. She was still acting strange every since we almost got hit by a car. I told her that I had to go and I gave her a big hug as I was walking out the door. She was acting like I was going to my own funeral. I have came this far, I know I can get through one more night with this ass hole.

As soon as I got to base, I started looking for Sergeant Wilson's car, but I did not see it anywhere and that was strange. He was not at guard mount for our nightly inspection, so someone else had to do it. I was happy because it looked like I was going to have a good night because I did not have to deal with him. Since this was the last night, they were going to have a competition and the winner got to go home early. They broke us down into squads of fours and sent us out in the woods. They made me the squad leader and I took my squad to go find a good position in the woods. I made sure everyone had their gear on and was ready to go. I wanted to go home early tonight.

I found a place beside a little creek that looked good because everyone had to cross the creek to get to the other side. On the other side of the creek were some trees, so we each climbed a tree and waited. After about an hour, the first squad crossed the creek and we jumped out the trees and killed them all. All we had to do is kill a couple more squads, and we could go home early that night. We killed another squad and we only had to kill one more before we were done for the night.

Once the people were killed, they had to report back to camp for reevaluation of what they did wrong. It was awhile before we heard someone else coming across the creek. We could hear a voice and it sounded like they were calling my name, which was strange. They were saying, "Airman Jackson come out and play, I got something for you". All we saw was one person, but his voice sounded familiar to me. It was like they were trying to trick us into moving and giving up our location. When the voice got closer, all we saw was one person coming towards us. I told the other squad members to jump down and kill him when he got under their trees. I heard a lot of gunfire and I figured my people got him. I looked down and saw that my people were lying on the ground.

One of my people was moaning like he was really shot, I was thinking to myself, boy is he a good actor. The man standing above him was asking him where Airman Jackson was hiding. Then I recognized whose voice it was, it was Sergeant Wilson and he was looking for me. The Airman told him that I was up in the trees, and he started firing at them randomly. I kept hearing noises like bees flying pass my head, when all of a sudden something hit me in my chest.

It hit me so hard it almost knocked me out of the tree. My chest was starting to burn and I did not understand why it felt that way, unless I was really being shot by real bullets. Two more bullets hit me and that time I did get knocked out of the tree. As I come crashing down towards the ground, I was wondering why my bullet proof vest was not working. I dropped my rifle on the way down. It only had fake bullets in it anyway. I fell about fifteen feet, landing on my back. When I looked up from the ground, Sergeant Wilson was standing over me pointing his rifle at my head with a demonic look on his face.

I thought about just playing dead, but I figured he was going to shoot me some more no matter what. There was nothing I could do; I figured my time had come for me to die. So I made sure I stared him straight in his eyes before he pulled the trigger because I wanted him to see my bravery in my eyes. I wasn't going to go out like a punk. He asked, "Are you ready to die nigger? What do you have to say now"? I said, "Don't shoot me in my dick because your wife might need it again someday". I saw red in his eyes.

I was watching his finger as he started pulling the trigger back; I forced my eyes to focus directly into his eyes. I was thinking to myself: "This would be a good time for God to jump in here. I certainly would not have predicted that I was going to die like this. I guess I was on borrowed time anyway. I should be dead or in prison for all the shit I did. I don't know why I thought I was going to get away from my past. I can't say I didn't have an interesting life because I did". I told Sergeant Wilson, "Hurry up because I had to take a piss".

Right before he could shoot, one of my squad members tackled him down to the ground. I guess he should have made sure they all were dead. The rifle went off and the bullet landed next to my head. The bullet was so close to my head that dirt went into my eyes from where the bullet hit the ground. While he was wrestling with him, I grabbed the Sergeant's rifle and hit him in the head with the butt of the gun. I hit him in the head so hard, he passed out and I put him in handcuffs. I use our radio to call for help. Twenty minutes later they took him away. They took me and my squad to the hospital that night, but only two of us survived.

I only thought the bullets were going through my vest because of the way the bullets were burning my skin. The burning I was feeling, were the hot bullets wedged in the vest next to my skin. They let me out the hospital the next day. The two that died were shot in the head at close range. The airman who saved my life was expected to make a full recovery from his injuries. Ironically his name was "Jesus", a Mexican from San Antonio Texas. My vest had three bullets lodged in the chest portion of it; thank God I had that vest on. I wanted to keep the vest, but they had to keep it for evidence. I also found out that Sergeant Wilson killed his wife before he came to base to kill me. The other Airmen said that he strangled her to death. I was sorry to hear that, because I really didn't want that to happen to her.

She was a very sweet person who got mixed up in the wrong thing. If I could have changed anything about that whole situation, it would have been her death. I would have preferred it was me who died instead of her. I'm sure in some way; a part of me did die that night when that gun was pointed at my head. I felt surrounded by death when that gun was pointed at me. She was just a person looking for happiness and found more pain in her life. I knew there would be many sleepless nights because of what happened and I hoped that she can find happiness where she is at now. If I would had known, I would have shot that motherfucker in his head that night after I got his gun.

I made it to my graduation that Monday and got my certificate and a badge. Now it was official, I'm a (Security Specialist) in the military, so watch out world. Now I just need to figure out how to accomplish my goals without leaving death and destruction behind. I'm happy to still be alive. I know God had something to do with it. ***"Believe in Change"***

Chapter 19

Living with the Dogs

I found out that I qualified for K-nine training and would be starting in a few days. There were only a few people picked to be K-nine Handlers. Out of the fifteen people in my group that tried out for it, only three of us made it. The first thing we did after we were accepted was to go visit the dogs at the kennels to see what kind of dogs we were going to have to work with. Before we went inside to see the dogs, the instructor told us which dog we would be training with for the next ten weeks. He told me my dog's name was "Rembrandt", like the famous painter. I asked him why the dog's name was Rembrandt; he said I would find out soon enough. Inside the kennels, there were twenty stalls with an assortment of dogs in them, big and small. They were all some type of German shepherd, some were mixed breeds and others were full blooded. Some of the dogs were already trained and some still needed to be trained just like us.

The instructor told us to go inside the fenced in area and find our dog's stall, which had the dogs' names on top of each kennel. When I got to my dog's kennel, I noticed there was shit all over the place. It was on the walls, the floor and even the bars of the kennels. Then I knew why they called him Rembrandt, because he took his paws and painted the kennel with his shit. He did this a few times a day and I realized I was going to have to clean it up. My job was to feed my dog and make sure the kennels were cleaned everyday that I was there. My work schedule was going to be Monday through Friday, 6:00am until 2:00pm.

My dog Rembrandt was a black, mixed shepherd, weighing 120 pounds, standing about three feet high. He was about five years old and had already been trained as an attack dog in the military. I guess you could say he was a veteran. He had been around for awhile and was use to getting new handlers. When I came to his kennel, he did not bark and jump around like the younger dogs did when I walked by them. He just slowly walked to the bars of the kennel and started smelling me to get my scent. Since he had already been trained, I thought he should be easy to work with. Although I knew he might be easy to work with, I would still have to clean all the shit out of his kennel everyday. There always seems to be some shit in life. At least this shit I can clean up.

The instructor explained what we were going to be doing for the first week of training. The first week was going to be spent getting to know our dogs and them getting to know us. So for eight hours a day we would be feeding our dogs and cleaning their kennels. We were not permitted to go inside the stalls for that whole week. The only time we were away from our dogs was one hour for lunch. We were around the dogs so much we started smelling just like a dog at the end of the day. We could tell by the expression on people's faces as we walked by that we smelled like dogs. I could hear people whispering and making faces when I walked near them. Even my wife could not wait for me to get in the shower after work. By the end of the week, I did not even notice the smell anymore; I guess I was getting use to it. It was like the smell of Jackson Street, you get use to it after awhile.

That second week we cleaned the dog's kennels and fed them every morning at 6:00am. Then we went to class from 8:00am-11:00am, studying about the proper way to train a dog. In class we learned all about how to train dogs and how the dog would become part of the handler. We were expected to become an inseparable team no matter what the conditions were. We still had not taken our dogs outside of their kennels yet, but we were allowed to go inside the stalls.

They wanted to be sure our dog was going to be comfortable with us before we took the dogs outside of their stalls. My dog was very comfortable with me after two weeks; he would run and jump every time he saw me. I was around him for almost eight hours a day for the last two weeks and I felt that I was growing on him. I still was not confident the dog would not try to attack me when I went in the kennel; I guess I needed more time.

The first time we took our dogs out one of the kennels for our first training, one of the Airmen was bitten by his dog. At the time we were learning how to march with our dogs. The dog bit a large hole in the Airmen's thigh as he was trying to give the dog a command. I could see the pain on the airman's face. There was nothing I could do to help him. The Airman was kicking the dog trying to get the dog off of his thigh. That just made the dog bite harder until the instructor told him to use the choke chain around the dog's neck. Once the Airman used the choke chain, the dog released his bite. The dog had to release his bite because the dog could not breathe from being choked. I had a new found respect for dogs after watching that dog bite the airman.

Because the Airman did not use the proper technique to get the dog off of him, he was terminated from k-nine training. Our trainers were very strict on how we treated the dogs, because each dog after training was estimated to be worth $40,000. That was how much money the military figured they put into the training each dog. Depending on the dog's reaction to certain training, some dogs qualified to be drug or bomb dogs. Those that did not make it as drug or bomb dogs were trained to be attack dogs.

The way the military determined which dogs qualified to be what, was a very simple procedure. They would take a small rubber ball and show it to the dog first, and then we would throw the ball. After we threw the ball, we would say "Seek" and if the dog chased the ball, we knew the dog would be a good drug or bomb dog. Most people think the dogs are looking for drugs or bombs, but actually they are looking for a little rubber ball to play with. The ball has a scent of drugs or bombs depending on what they were trained to look for. The most aggressive dogs were just trained to be attack dogs for obvious reasons. Once it was determined which dog would do what, the real training got started.

After a couple of weeks of learning how to train the dogs to march, sit, and lay down, we were ready to train them to attack. All the dogs were not taught attack training. Some were just trained to be bomb or drug dogs. We knew by the end of our basic dog training whether or not the dog was going to be an attack dog. The first thing we learned was how to receive a dog bite on ourselves. They showed us how to put a padded arm guard on to protect us from the dog's bite puncturing the skin.

We had to be able to relax while the dog was jerking our arm around so we wouldn't have a muscle pulled. It was hard to relax when you have a 150 pound dog chewing on your arm. One of the airmen was so tense his shoulder was dislocated by the force of the jerking. The way we were told to make the dog stop biting was to say "Out" while the dog was biting. If the dog did not stop biting, we had to grab the dog's neck and choke him until the dog let go. This was very dangerous because sometimes the dog would try to bite our hand while it was on the dog's neck.

Every day after training we had to check our dog for ticks, which was no fun for me. If we found any ticks we had to remove them from the dog in a certain way. The way we did that was by lighting a match and blowing it out and taking the hot end of the match and sticking it on the tick's ass. This would make the tick retract his head and then we could pull it out in one piece. If we tried it without burning the tick's ass, we might leave the head in the skin and that would cause an infection. We also had to check ourselves daily for ticks. Some of ticks in Texas could kill you if you didn't get them out in time. I had my wife check me everyday from head to toe before I took my shower after work. Everyday she would find as many as five ticks somewhere on my body. The same procedure we used on the dogs to get the ticks off was the same one that was used on us.

We all took turns letting the dogs attack us during our training. We had to hide in the woods and run across an open field when we saw the handler and his dog coming. The handler would release the dog and say "Get him" and the dog would chase us down. Normally the dog would clamp down his teeth and stay in that one spot on your arm. The dog always attacked the arm first because that is what we stuck out for the dog to bite. Once the dog got close to us, we made sure to turn and give the dog our arm to bite. The one time the dog that attacked me did not do that, he started biting on the bottom of my arm and kept working his way up. Without me knowing it, the arm pad had slipped down exposing my forearm to the dog's teeth. I did not know it at the time, but the dog had ripped a five inch gash in my arm. I was so caught up in the moment that I did not even know the dog was ripping my flesh. The dog must have been chewing on my arm for at least three to four minutes before the handler called him off me. I didn't notice until after the handler told his dog to stop biting me that there was so much blood coming from my arm. The trainers had to apply a tourniquet to stop the bleeding. Blood was all over my uniform.

On my way to the hospital, I thought I was going to faint, but I fought that feeling. I was in a lot of pain, but I didn't show it to anyone because I did not want anyone to think that I was a punk. It only took about five minutes to get to the base hospital because it was only about a mile away. The trainers, all three of them didn't wait for an ambulance; we drove in a military police truck. We drove all the way with our lights and sirens on to get there quicker.

When we got to the hospital, they rushed me into the emergency room. I expected the doctors to give me twenty-five stitches or more in my arm, but they didn't. All they did was to take a large Q-tip and clean out the wound. They said the wound had to stay open to make sure it did not get infected. They did not want to stitch it up and then have to open it up again because of an infection. I was told that without the stitches, the bite would leave a large scar on my arm. I did not care about there being a scar on me. I was just happy there was no muscle or ligament damage.

I thought I would get a couple of days off, but they didn't do that. The trainers told me I had to come back to work the next day and be ready to work. I told them I would not be able to use my arm. The trainer said there was nothing wrong with the other arm. I think they were afraid that if I stayed away too long from the training, I would not want to work with dogs again. I was an investment to the military and they did not want to lose their investment so soon.

The very next day the dogs were biting on my good arm and that did not make me very happy. I was a little apprehensive at first, but I was able to get thorough the day in one piece. I thought the whole situation was very insensitive of the military to make me continue to work, especially since I had an open wound on my other arm. I knew then, that this was not the organization I would give my life for in a war. My plan was to get all I could out of the military and then move on to the next chapter of my life. This was not quite what I expected when I joined the K-nine unit. I thought that I was going to have fun, but not yet. Hopefully things will get better for me.

I found out that there was just as much racism in the military as there was on the streets where I come from. Even though we wore the same green uniforms, this still did not make us the same skin color. With the mixture of people in the military, it was not unusual to find some people who had never met a black person before. One day while I was standing in line during training waiting to release my dog on an attacker, I heard the word (nigger) again.

The white boy in front of me was calling one of the other black airmen a black nigger. It had been a long time since I heard that word and it took me by surprise to hear it again. He turned around and looked at me and said, "Oh I' am not talking about you, I'm talking about him over there". He was pointing at one of the other black airmen out in the middle of the field with his dog. I told him to keep his comments to himself before he got fucked up. He smiled and turned around.

He was quiet for about five minutes and then he called the airman a nigger again. It took everything in my power not to punch him in the back of his head. He did not look back at me this time and I kept my mouth shut, but I knew I was going to fuck him up the first chance I got. I was hoping I would not have to confront racism in the military, but I guess I was in some kind of fantasy world. I thought if I put on that government uniform I would be immune from such ignorance. I decided I was going to have to show this white boy how we handled racism on Jackson Street. I knew I was going to have to figure out how to do it without getting in trouble with the military.

That evening while I was home, I thought of a way to get the white boy and make it look like an accident. I decided to loosen one of the hoops on my choke chain, so that it would come apart with only a minimum amount of pressure from my dog. In order for the plan to work, I had to make sure I was behind the white boy again in line. The next day he was still calling one of the other black airmen a nigger every chance he got. He probably did not like my dog either because; he was black as coal. A black man with a black dog and carrying a gun; I must have been the white boy's worst nightmare.

It was almost time for the white boy to go out and release his dog on an attacker. He walked out to the middle of the field to prepare his dog for release on an attacker. While he was walking out, I was telling my dog to watch him to get my dog hyped up. I always did that before I sent my dog to attack someone. I was whispering in a very soft voice, so no one else could hear me. Now all I had to do is wait for the right time to say the words "Get Him" and my dog would attack. Just as soon as the white boy released his dog and starting running after him, I told my dog to get him. My dog jumped up and started running towards the white boy and that's when my choke chain broke.

I acted as if my dog had pulled me to the ground, so it would take me awhile to get to him. I had to make sure I put on a good act, just in case anyone was paying attention to me. The white boy only ran a few feet before my dog caught him and clamped down on the boy's ass. He started screaming, "Get your dog off me, you fucking dumb ass nigger". As soon as I heard that I made sure that I fell down again so it would take me even longer to get there. I really felt good watching my dog chew a new hole in the boy's ass.

By the time I got to the airman, Rembrandt was chewing on his upper leg and working his way down to the ankles. The more blood the dog tasted, the harder he would bite. No one else was running to help him, they was just standing there in shock watching. I don't think anyone else cared enough to try and help him. When I got to the white boy I asked, "How does it felt to have this nigger's black dog ripping the white meat off your ass?" While I pretended to try and get my dog off of him, out of the corner of my eye I saw the trainer running across the field. My dog was on the white boy's arm when I was finally able to choke him off the boy. I wish I could have let him bite the boy longer.

When I pulled my dog off, the dog tried to bite me because he was so excited about biting someone. I clipped my leash to my dog's leather collar, because the choker was broke. The dogs always had a leather collar on; we put the choke chain on right before training everyday. I took my dog about ten feet away as they started working on the white boy to stop the bleeding. The trainer asked me what happened and how my dog got loose.

Before I could respond the white boy told him, "That nigger let his dog loose on purpose". That was all he got to say before he passed out from blood loss. The trainer asked me to help him get the boy to the truck, but I told I couldn't because of my bad arm. They had to drag the boy across the field leaving a trail of blood all the way to the truck. Before he drove away, the trainer told me to take my dog to the kennels and to meet him at his office in an hour. I had an explanation for what happened, so

I really wasn't worried.

When I got to the instructor's office, there were two people waiting for me. My trainer was there with his supervisor, and they were not looking very happy. The first thing he said was, "The Airman that your dog attacked has a broken leg and a broken arm. We don't even know if he will recover enough to be able to remain in the military. He told us that you released your dog intentionally, because you did not like him. I told them it was true about me not liking him; however, I would not release my dog on anyone unless it was in the line of duty.

I explained to them how my choke chain had broken and that it was not my fault. They wanted to see the chain so I went out to my car to get it. I handed it to them and watched as they went over the chain checking every link. They saw where it had pulled apart and they said they would have to keep it for evidence. They told me there would be an investigation and they would let me know if they needed to talk to me again. They said they only had one more question, "Why did it take you so long to get your dog off the Airman?" I told them I did the best I could, considering I still had an open wound on my arm. I wasn't sure if they believed me, but I knew they could not prove any wrong doing on my part. They dismissed me and as soon as I got outside their office I laughed out loud. It is nice when a plan comes together.

The airman had lost so much blood, the military was asking people to volunteer their blood for him. No one from my unit went to the hospital to give blood for that racist pig, especially none of the other black Airmen. A couple of weeks later, we heard he was getting discharged for medical reasons. I don't even think the military was upset for losing a racist dog like that. I figured that now maybe he really did have a reason to hate black people in his life. Training was hard enough without putting up with a racist white boy.

We spent the next few weeks learning how to train drug and bomb dogs. I had a lot more fun doing that than I did with the attack dogs. The most interesting part about training the drug dogs was learning how they got the dogs to look for the drugs and bombs. They had a safe inside the office of the kennels where they stored narcotics and materials used to make bombs. Inside the safe they had a pound of 97% pure cocaine and a pound 97% pure heroin. They also had a pound of top grade marijuana they used to saturate these little rubber balls that the dogs learned to look for.

The dogs really weren't looking for drugs, they were looking for those little rubber balls, so they could play with them. I had not seen that many drugs since my drug dealing days in Florida and Brownsville. On the streets, those drugs would have been worth over a half a million dollars. I decided I was going to make it my goal to find out how the military got their hands on those kinds of drugs. If I could have found a connection like that when I was dealing drugs, who knows were I would have ended up. I guess my mind is always going to think about making more money. It is just in my blood I guess.

The next couple of weeks went by fast and before I knew it I was graduating from K-nine School. They gave everyone their orders and I found out they were sending me to Montana for four years. I was not very happy with that because Montana was not any of my four choices the military had given me to choose from. While I was in boot camp, the military gave me a paper to fill out, asking me to pick four bases that I would like to be stationed at. They gave me a brochure on living in Montana which said, if you like hunting or fishing this is the place to be. Well I did not like either so I knew it would not be the place for me. I needed to come up with a plan.

I was informed if I could find an Airman with the same rank; I could trade orders with that person. I found a black Airman from Philadelphia who wanted to get further away from home than Virginia, which was the first choice on my list. He was the same black Airman who was letting the white boy call him a nigger. He said I heard what your dog did to that white boy and I really appreciate it.

He told me he would be happy to trade orders with me

after that entire mess that white boy put him through. He indicated that he wished my dog would have killed the white boy for everyone's sake and that the world would be a better place without him. We both went to the Commander and they did not have any problems changing the orders. Now I was a happy man because Virginia sounds like a lot more fun than Montana. Look out beaches because here I come. ***"Believe in Change"***

Chapter 20

New Base and Old Problems

After K-nine training, my wife and I flew back to Brownsville to visit her family for awhile. The Air Force gave me a week to get to my next duty assignment. I decided to pick up a car her dad was fixing up for us since I gave all my cars away. I was not looking forward to going back to Brownsville so soon, but I needed that car so we could get around. We were going to stay at Star's parents' house long enough to get the car and leave. I was only gone for a year and a lot of the bad memories that happened in Brownsville were still in my mind. The only good memory was when I got saved by God and married my wife, then left town.

Star's mom picked us up at the airport and drove us to Brownsville that afternoon. She greeted both of us with a smile and a big hug. There was a little tension in the air, because her daughter had married one of the biggest drug dealers in Brownsville. I am sure that was not what she had planned for her daughter's future, considering her religious background. But because Star and I were in love, there was nothing anyone could do to change the way we felt about each other. All I wanted from "Mrs. Angel" was to just give us a chance.

Before we got married, I promised Star's mom that I would give my life to God and I have been trying. Maybe I could try harder. She asked me about whether we had found a good church in Texas and I told her no, but I planned on finding a good one when we got to Virginia. The truth is no one in town wanted to see me and Star together, not even my mother. My mother even thought Star was not the right one for me, which is what she told me one day when Star and I first started seeing each other exclusively. Star was there when I needed a friend, and that meant a lot to me. She made me happy and now I want to try and make her happy.

No one really gave us much of a chance, but I know if we keep God in our lives we would always have a chance. Both of us had not been to church since we got married, and that was not good for a man with my background. Deep down in my heart I really did want to live a positive life and do the right thing for my family. While I was in Brownsville, I found out my mom was still selling drugs at her house. The drug business she had was the same one I gave her when I quit. All the money she was making was supposed to be mine, but I was not upset with that. Even when I was making all that money, I still was not happy. I was hoping that void would be filled by God and a new life. The only people who knew we were coming into town were Star's parents and that was how we wanted it.

After walking for six months, I was happy to be getting any car that ran. Star's father, "Joseph" was a preacher and a part time mechanic, so I knew the car would run well. The car was about ten years old and had rust holes all over the body of the car. The interior was almost just as bad, but it drove well and that's what counted. It seemed to be in good enough shape to get us to Virginia. I knew safety was important factor for Star's father because he knew his daughter was six months pregnant.

After we had a good home cooked meal, we all went to church that evening for a sermon. Star and I devoted our lives to God again, just to please her parents and ourselves. The whole church got together and had a long prayer for us just too confirm our faith. Everyone seemed happy to see we still felt the same way about God and the church. After church that night, I was confident we would be able to make it in our new life as "Born-again-Christians". I also knew that it was not going to be easy for either one of us. It is a lot easier for me to go back to being a criminal. So far being a Born-Again-Christian has been an adventure for me.

The week in town went fast and before long it was time to get out of town again. Early the next morning we decided to head to Virginia before anyone else found out we were in town. I thought about going to see my mom but I decided it would not have been in my best interest to do that. I knew I really should not associate myself with known drug dealers, especially since I had God in my life.

We arrived at (Langley Air force Base) without any mechanical problems with the car. I made arrangements to live in Temporary Living Quarters (TLQ) until we could find an apartment off base. It only cost me twenty a day to live in temporary living quarters, but we could only stay there for thirty days. When I got on base, they gave me a listing of rental properties to go and look at. We really could not afford to spend too much on a place to stay with the little bit of money the military was giving me. So we had to settle for a place that made us pay according to our income.

A month later, we found a place called "Briar Patch Apartments" which was low-income housing for poor people. It was located in (Newport News), about five miles from base, but at least I did not have to walk to work. I thought I was done with living in the ghetto but here I was again right back in the ghetto. Briar Patch was a series of row houses in the worst part of Newport News. I grew up on Jackson Street, so I was not worried about living in the ghetto again. Jackson Street was the epitome of the ghetto in my hometown or any other town. I still wasn't happy going back to the ghetto. Will I ever get away from this shit?

The only thing I'm worried about was if my wife could handle this style of living, because she came from a middle class family. I knew it was going to be arduous trying to live right, but not this hard. We did not have any furniture, so we had to rent a bed, a living room set and a television from a rental center. My wife was six months pregnant, so I decided it would be best that she did not work at that time. The church told me that no matter how tough things became, God would get us through it. Star and

I prayed about it every night and planned on waiting patiently until things improved. I did not know that in order to be a good Christian, I would have to suffer like this.

After a week orientation on base, I was assigned to the (1st Security Police Squadron). I spent a week at the kennels getting to know my new dog, whose name was "Zuma". He was a full blood German shepherd weighing about 125 pounds, with a brown coat of hair on him. He was only about two years old and still a little hyper, as most young dogs are. I spent most of each day just going through basic drills with him, to make sure he knew what he was doing. I did not want to get in a real situation and find out he was not ready. After about a month, I thought he was ready to start riding with me around the base in my police truck.

On base there were two sections of Base Security. They were "Security and Law Enforcement". I was a Security Policeman and was in charge of protecting the military's million dollar resources, such as the F-16 jets and nuclear weapons. Just one F-16 jet was worth 16 million dollars and I could not even guess how much the nuclear weapons were worth. The nuclear weapons were kept on base at a place called the "Weapons Storage Area" (W. S. A.).

Only the security police with top clearances knew about the W.S.A. We had to sign a contract not to mention anything about it for seven years after we were discharged from the military. The military did not want anyone in the (City of Hampton) to know that they were living near nuclear weapons. I don't think they would be to happy living that close to something that dangerous.

Law Enforcement's main job was to protect the entrances to the base to make sure only authorized people came through the gates. Some of their other jobs were giving traffic tickets and going to domestic disputes on base. Security Police wore green fatigues and black berets on their heads and they also carried M-16 rifles and drove blue trucks on base. Law Enforcement wore dress blues with black berets on their heads. They did not carry

M-16's; their weapon was the 38-revolver on their sides. They drove around in white and blue sedans, while we had to drive them big ugly trucks. Security and Law Enforcement really did not like each other. Law Enforcement always gave us the impression they thought they were better than us. We were supposed to work as a team, but that was not always the case on base.

Security worked three shifts on base, 7:00am-3:00pm, 3:00pm-11:00pm, and 11:00pm to 7:00am. I had to work the night shift 11:00pm-7:00am because I was only an airman basic and that is the lowest rank on base. I was supposed to get a promotion soon to be airman 1st class, and then I'd make a little more money. My wife was supposed to have the baby in late June, and I realized I could hardly feed us with the money I made. I must have dropped about ten pounds from living on hot dogs and baked beans in my house. I forgot what a good steak tasted like; I couldn't even remember what one smelled like. I knew if I was patient, things would get better for me and Star.

On base, the Security Police had its own police gas station; we had a key to unlock the pumps to fill up the trucks everyday. There was not anybody at the pumps to monitor how much gas we took. Considering how little money I was getting paid, I figured there would be no harm done if I took some of the gas. So I bought a five gallon gas can to fill up every night and put the gas in my car. I figured it would be okay since I was using the gas to go to work. I know this is not what a good Christian is supposed to do, but I had no choice because I was broke. I figured God would understand.

Virginia was a very beautiful place to live with all the beaches and great weather. It was surrounded by the ocean, with some great beaches everywhere you drove. It seemed like the perfect place to start a family. In contrast to Pennsylvania, the land was flat. You could see for miles down the road. In the brochure they gave us, it said the average yearly snowfall was three inches over a twenty year period. In Pennsylvania, the average snowfall was about forty-five inches yearly; that was a huge difference. Even though I lived in the ghetto, it still did not take me long to get to the beach from my house if I wanted to go. Right now, I didn't even have extra gas money to even ride to the beach.

On base, there was the regular Security Police and there was K-nine Security Police. I was K-nine and we were treated differently than the other police. We would go to guard mount, which where the sergeant would inspect you to make sure that we were dressed properly for duty. The K-nine trucks had cages that separated the back seat from the front seat. Most of the time, I just rode around base with my dog in the back barking at people. There really was no designated area we had to be in. Basically we were able to go anywhere on the base and no one bothered us. We had walkie talkies, so if "Central Control" needed us they could call at any time. Most of the time I would take my truck to the park and me and Zuma would sleep until morning. Some of the other K-nine units would go fishing off the shore during their shift. This was a pretty easy job so far.

One night while I was sleeping in the park, I heard a car pull up and park. There were two people in the car, and it looked like they were kissing. I watched them from my truck as they started to remove their clothing. I waited until I was sure they had all their clothes off and walked to their car. I saw it was a boy and a girl making love in their car. I thought about not bothering them, but I changed my mind. I decided to have some fun with them. I was bored as hell anyway, so why not. There is nothing wrong with having a little fun. It has been awhile since I had some fun.

I went back to the truck and got my dog Zuma, and then we crept back to the car. It was a warm night so all their windows were down in the car. I still had my leash on Zuma to make sure he did not get away from me. I told him to "Get Him," and he put his head in the back car window. He was barking and scratching on side of the car door. When he did that, the kids starting screaming and ran out the car on the other side. They were naked running towards the water. Before I could say anything, they had jumped into the water without looking back. I was in shock because I did not expect this reaction to my dog; I thought that the kids were just going to scream. My dog wanted to chase them, but I had to calm him down.

While they were splashing around in the water, I used the opportunity to see if they had any money in their clothes. I only found a $150, and I needed every penny of it. I made sure no one was looking and hid the money inside my ammo belt. I heard the girl screaming for help, so I put my dog back in the truck and ran down to see what was wrong. When I got there, the girl was standing there, naked and crying, saying “please help my boyfriend.” I asked her what was wrong, and she said that he was still in the water, but he couldn’t swim. I pointed my flashlight out towards the sound of splashing water and saw the boy’s head bobbing up and down.

I really did not want to go into that water, but I also did not want anyone to drown because I was playing around. I had been swimming almost all my life because I grew up next to a creek, so I was not worried about going into the water. What I was worried about was that I could not see anything in the dark out in the water. I sure could not swim with my flashlight in my mouth. The girl started screaming again. She asked me to please hurry because he was drowning. She said, “I tried to save him but he is just too heavy for me”. I told her to calm down; I’ll see what I can do.

I took my gun to the truck and dove into the water with all my clothes on. I started swimming towards the sound of the water splashing until I saw him. Right before I reached him he went under and did not come back up. When I got to the spot where he went under, I dove down to pull him out. I could not find him. I desperately dove under again. This time when I opened my eyes to see I could not keep them open long because the salt water made them burn. How am I going to find someone if I can’t open my eyes underwater? I don’t know how I’ am going to save this young kid.

I started swimming back towards the surface when I felt

something hit my boot. I did not know what it was, but I reached down and grabbed it anyway. It was the boy's arm and I pulled him to the surface and then to the shore. I could not tell if the boy was breathing or not, I just was worried about both of us getting to shore. I was tired but we finally did get to the shore, and the boy was not breathing. The girl could see he was not breathing as she stood over him and she became frantic.

I used my walkie-talkie and called for assistance and then I started mouth to mouth resuscitation. I told the girl to go put her clothes on before the other police got here. She ran to the car to get her clothes. She got dress and ran back over to where we were. After a couple of minutes, the boy started breathing again. I breathe a sigh of relief along with him. The girl started hugging and thanking me. The boy started talking to the girl. He asked her, "What happened and where are we at?" She told him, "You were not breathing and the policeman saved your life".

I told the girl to take his clothes to the water and get them wet so we could put them back on him. I told them, that I was not going to tell the other police what they were doing in the car. I told them that I would just tell them they were down here skinny dipping and got pulled in by the waves. They both agreed and soon the boy had his clothes on.

Law Enforcement arrived, along with the ambulance and I explained what happened to the kids. I told them that as I was riding by I heard the girl screaming and drove down to see what was wrong. Then she told me that her boyfriend was in the water and could not swim and needed some help. I pulled him out the water. He was not breathing, so I did mouth to mouth on him.

The Law Enforcement Sergeant told me the boy that I saved was the base commander's son, and he was going to want to talk to me about it. This made me nervous. If I knew the boy was the Base Commander's son, I would not have bothered them. I was just trying to have some fun, now look at the mess I got myself into. Can anything just be simple for me?

The sergeant told me once I wrote my report I could go home, but I wasn't sure the boy and girl were going to stick to the same story after I left. I was hoping they would since it would be a lot easier to explain to their parents. No one wants to know their 14 year old children are having sex in the back seat of a car.

When I went home that night, I wasn't sure what was going to happen when the Base Commander heard about the incident. At least I had some extra money in my pockets, and I sure did need it. I was happy that no one died from my little joke. That would have been hard for me to handle. If I didn't need the money that I stole so badly, I would have put it back. The next time I see somebody in a car, I going to drive the other way. ***"Believe in Change"***

Chapter 21

A New Stripe and a New Mouth to Feed

That next afternoon my supervisor called me at home and told me the Base Commander wanted to meet with me in his office at 2:00pm. I was apprehensive because my supervisor did not tell me exactly what the Commander wanted to talk about. I was not sure if the boy and the girl had changed their stories or if it was about the stolen money. My supervisor told me to wear my dress blues, because it was a formal meeting. Security Police only wear dress blues for formal occasions. I made sure my suit was pressed and my shoes were shined, so I could make a good impression. I had no reason to expect anything good to happen at this meeting.

The Base Commander was a (Three Star General) and a white man. I did not want to take any chances. I arrived at the Base Commander's office about twenty minutes early, just to get a look around. I told his secretary my name, and she told me to have a seat and that he would not be long. She smiled at me and said I heard you did a wonderful thing last night; you made the General very happy. I was surprised to hear her say that, but I did not show it in my actions. I just said, "Thank you" and put my head down as if I was reading the magazine in front of me. I was too nervous to read anything.

Hearing her say that put my mind at ease, but I still was not sure what was going on. The anticipation was driving me crazy; I wished he would hurry up and get this over with. The palms of my hands are starting to sweat. The secretary had a special affability about her that made me feel at ease while I was sitting there. Every once and awhile she would look over and smile at me.

Her phone rang and finally the secretary told me I could go in. When I walked pass she said, "Good luck Senior Airman Jackson". I didn't know why she called me that because I was only an Airman Basic. In order to be a Senior Airman, I had to be in the military for at least two years. The last time I had checked I was only in for eight months. I figured that maybe she just made a mistake. I knocked on the general's door. After he said come in; I walked to the front of his desk and saluted him. He saluted and then told me, "At ease Airman, just relax". He told me to have a seat and then said, "I wanted to talk to you about last night to confirm my son's story".

He then asked me, "Airman Jackson, can you give me your story on what happened last night?" I unabashedly told him the same thing I told my supervisor. He told me the reason he called me in was to thank me for saving his son's life. He started honoring me with accolades, and I told him that I was just doing my job. I said, "Anyone would have done the same thing if given the same situation". The commander said, "Well it was not anyone else, it was you and I would like to do something for you".

I know you've only been in the military for eight months, but I'm going to promote you to the rank of Senior Airman. You will receive your paper work in a couple of days and you can start wearing your three stripes. If there is anything else I can do for you, don't hesitate to ask me. You will also be getting a medal of valor for what you did. I thanked him and went home to tell my wife the good news. I knew Star would be happy for me. She knows how badly we need more money. I guess God is going to come through for us.

My wife was elated for me and we decided to go out to dinner to celebrate that night. I used the $150 I stole to buy dinner at the restaurant that night. We went to (Fisherman's Wharf), a seafood restaurant with a large seafood buffet. This was the first time our stomachs were satisfied in months, and it made me very happy to be able to see my wife having such a great time. With my promotion, I assumed we would be able to do this more often. Maybe we would be able to move out of the ghetto into a nicer place with the extra money. I kept hearing that if you put your life in God's hands, he will take care of you if you just are patient. Well we are being patience.

I had to take my uniforms to the cleaners to get two more stripes put on them. Things were finally starting to look a lot better for me since my promotion. We had finally found a good church to attend in Virginia after being there for months. We really were not looking as hard as we could have for a church. That is probably why it took us so long to find a church to go to. I asked God to forgive me for stealing that $150 from the Commander's son. We started going to church three days a week, Wednesdays, Fridays and Sundays.

I started reading my Bible a couple hours a day so I could learn more about the Bible. Both of us had quit smoking cigarettes and drinking alcohol since we became Born-Again-Christians. It was hard, but we were trying to do everything according to how good Christians should live and abstinence is part of being a good Christian. In reading the Bible, I learned that the more I put into being a Christian, the more I will get out of it. I need to work harder at being a good Christian.

Star and I started looking for a better place to live a couple of weeks after I got my promotion. We found a place in (Hampton) called, "Queens Terrace"; this was a vast improvement, compared to where we were living. We were moving at an auspicious time, because we did not want our child to begin his new life in the ghetto. Star's mom was coming to stay with us for a few months, so she could help out after the baby was born. I was glad we were moving before Star's mother came to visit us. I did not want her to see how we were living in the ghetto. I was ashamed by the way we were living. I was sure that Star was also. I hated being broke, but the situation was finally starting to abate. Hopefully better days are on the way now.

With only a month left in the pregnancy, Star's mom

came in town to help out. She was a health addict so we had to make sure we were not doing anything bad to our health. I did not want to hear any negative comments about anything we were doing in Virginia. Most of the time her conversations were quite informative to me, and I liked that. She was very easy to talk to, but she could be very hard to understand at times.

After she was in town, she did help us out financially with the bills. That really took a lot of financial pressure off of me and that was a blessing. No matter how many times I read my Bible, it still seemed hard to understand for me. Star's mom tried to help me with my understanding of the Bible, but that did not improve it. Some of the time what she explained was the opposite of what my understanding was about the Bible. Most people think she is the epitome of what a good Christian should be and I do also. The more I started to comprehend through the advice of others and time, the more I begun to appreciate the words in the Bible. Who would have thought that I would be reading a Bible?

We were not sure if we were having a boy or girl, and that's the way I wanted it. My wife wanted to find out, but I cajoled her into not finding out because I wanted it to be a surprise. Although Star must have gained about twenty-five pounds, but I was still sexually attracted to her. Star's mom was always at the house, so I did not know when we would be able to make love again. I did not care if her mom heard us making love, but Star was adamant about her not hearing us.

All I could do was pray about it and hope that would take care of the problem soon. We have the rest of our lives to make love. I can wait until her mother leaves. I was happy Star's mom was there because I had to work nights. I would have been worried every night while I was at work, worrying about my wife's well-being. Star and her mom knew to contact my Security Police unit if there were any problems at home, and I would be right there. I left the car with Star and took a bus, just in case they needed it while I was at work.

I was so excited about Star having a baby. This is going

to be our love child. This is a child that we planned on having because we were in love with each other. It's going to be a beautiful day when our child is born. Star is healthy, what could possibly go wrong? Having a baby is a gift from God. While out on patrol a few weeks later, my dog and I were sleeping in the truck at the base park, when I was startled by my walkie-talkie. I heard, "K-nine Patrol One; you need to take your dog to the kennels and get over to hospital". I answered back, "What for, what's wrong?" and they said with laughter in their voice, "You are going to be a daddy soon".

They told me they had just stopped my mother-in-law for speeding on base, and she explained everything to them. They then said they were giving them a police escort to the hospital, so I better hurry. I turned my red lights and sirens on and hurried over to the kennels to put my dog away. There was a police car waiting to take me to the hospital when I got to the kennels. I was really excited. It seemed like my Squadron was excited for me. I was breathing hard on the way to the hospital. It felt like I was having a baby because I had a large knot in my stomach.

When I arrived at the hospital, my wife was already in a room being examined by a doctor. My supervisor gave me a couple of days off from work. Star's mom seemed very nervous, but Star was very calm when I got there. Once I saw how calm she was, I took a deep breath and settled down myself. She was not quite ready to deliver the baby, so the doctor gave her something to induce the labor. It was only 1:00am and it looked like it was going to be a long night. Hopefully the baby would come soon with no health problems. My bubble was busted a little because I was ready to see my baby. Now I have to wait a little longer.

Eight hours of labor, there was still no baby and we are all a little anxious now. My wife had been pushing so hard, the blood vessels in her face had broken. Now she looked like she has a case of the measles or something even worse. I could see the anguish in her eyes, and that's when I decided to question her doctor's thinking. I asked him how much longer before they do a cesarean on my wife. He said it would be better if she had a natural child birthing, we should wait a little longer.

It was 16 hours later and my wife was still trying to push the baby out after resting for a few hours. I went home and showered, changed clothes and still no baby. Now I'm ready to bust someone up side the head. My next conversation with the doctor turned bitter because I did not understand what he was waiting for to do the cesarean. The blood vessels in Star's face were looking even worse. I felt bad because she was trying so hard to push the baby out and nothing was happening. I was concerned the doctor was not addressing my wife's problem properly. I shared a few harsh words with the doctor and stormed out of the room.

24 hours of labor and it was becoming very hard for me to figure out what the doctor wanted my wife to do. My job only gave me three days off and it looked like I might spend them all in the hospital waiting for the baby to be born. I confronted the doctor again and told him I wanted to get a second opinion on the way he wanted my wife to have this baby. He told me, "That is your prerogative, but I still think we should wait a little longer". I wasn't very certain about the chances of her having a natural child birth since it has already been twenty-four hours of labor. I don't think he was very concerned about what my wife was going through in her struggles to have the baby. I was being very patience with this asshole doctor.

After 36 hours of labor, I decided to call the Base Commander to see if he could help me resolve this situation. He told me to call him if I ever needed something. He was shocked to hear my story and asked me the doctor's name. I told him and he told me, "Don't worry about a thing; I will take care of it right now". A half-hour later, my wife was in the operating room being prepared for her cesarean birth. I do not know what the Commander said to the doctor, but it worked. It was 2:00pm and finally my wife was going to have our baby after 36 hours of pure hell. I was permitted to go in the operating room, even though I was not crazy about it. I really didn't want to see all that blood and guts, but I knew she wanted me to be there when the baby was born. That the least I could do after she went through 36 hours of hell.

It only took 15 minutes for them to do the surgery (Cesarean Style) on Star. They gave her a lower epidural for the pain so she was conscious, but she felt no pain of the birth. The doctor gave me some scissors and let me cut the umbilical cord of my son. I felt like taking the scissors and putting them in the doctor's ass so he could feel the pain my wife felt. Everyone was amazed to see how huge the baby was. It was a boy and he weighed almost twelve pounds. His eyes were wide open after a few minutes. He looked like he was already six months old at birth because he was so big. I left the room while they cleaned my wife up and gave her stitches. The doctor gave Star what they call a bikini cut, which is an incision along the pubic hair line so it would not be that noticeable.

The doctor came out while I was sitting in the hallway, and he looked at me and said, "Congratulations; he sure is a big one". I looked at him and said, "Fuck you; I should put my big foot up your ass for thirty-six hours and see how you like it". I stood up and he ran down the hallway in fear without looking back. The nurses told me I could go and see my son now if I wanted to. I walked down the hall and he was in the room with about ten other babies in cribs. The nurses gave all the babies nicknames, showing their sense of humor and wrote them on the side of their cribs. On the side of my son's crib they had "Jumbo Jackson", because he was so big. When I saw that, I smiled for the first time in thirty-six hours.

The first time I got to hold my son, which was two hours after he was born, I noticed something was obviously wrong with his head. His head was shaped like a long football and neither one of us had a head shaped like that. I demanded to talk to a doctor because I needed to know if this was some kind of birth defect. I would not have been so concerned if his head was just big, but it was big and shaped like a football. I know you're supposed to love your children no matter what, but it sure is a lot easier when they don't look like a space alien.

When the doctor arrived, he explained why his head was shaped like that. He told me because the baby's head was being pushed so long down the birth canal, it took the shape of it. He told me that if we just massaged his head it should restore back to its normal shape in time. Just as the doctor was leaving, the Base Commander, who just arrived said, "I do know at that age, a child's head is very soft so it should work". He said "There still is no excuse for them waiting thirty-six hours to do the Cesarean procedure. I will make sure someone is reprimanded for this conduct, this is something I promise to you". I thanked him for everything and he left.

Three days later we took our son home. We named him after me, "Ron Jackson Junior". We didn't have a crib for him, so he slept in his bassinette next to our bed. Star's face had returned back to normal, and she no longer looked like she had the measles on her face. Star's mom was going to stay with us another month until she was sure that Star was okay.

I heard the doctor who gave me all the problems at the hospital, received orders to go to (Alaska) a week later. I heard this story from my Sergeant, who was also pissed off about what my wife had to go through at that hospital. I think the commander gave him those orders because of the way he handled my son's birth. I was excited about having a child I could actually watch grow and hopefully this would be the beginning of great things to come for us. I never had a father, but my son will. I'm not going to leave him in this world all alone to figure things out like my father did me. I'm going to tell him about the mistakes I made so he doesn't make the same ones. I'll do everything in my power to stay in his life. This is my promise to him and God….. ***"Believe in Change"***

Chapter 22

My Sister Gets Married

I decided to call my sister Maria and tell her about our new addition to the Jackson family. Maria and I have never been that close, but I wanted to tell someone about my good news. My mother had six children, and Maria was the only girl in the family; she also was the only one my mother ever got along with. I'm sure it was because she was a girl. This was something that I felt because of the way she acted towards the boys when I was growing up. I would understand my mother for abhorring men, because of the way my father treated her.

He really treated her bad, and I do not believe she will ever get over that. That still was no excuse for not loving your children. I guess it bothered me that my mother could never show us love. Now I'm starting to believe that she just didn't have the capability to do that. I don't think she was ever shown love. If a person is never shown love, how can that person really give love? I' am sure this had something to do with how she treats her kids. She is just empty inside from living a rough life. I know that feeling well.

Maria also had some good news to tell me; her news was that she was going to get married in six weeks. She asked me if I would be able to come to her wedding and bring the baby. I told her that I could not guarantee that I would be able to get time off so soon but I would try. I was happy for Maria. She deserved some happiness in her life also. I didn't think the Air force would let me do it. Plus, the baby would only be six weeks old. She really seemed excited about me being there so I figured I would at least ask my supervisor if I could get the time off from work. I did not know if any of my other brothers were going. My sister did not say if they were going to be there. I was happy to hear she found someone that could take her away from Brownsville.

She told me that her fiancée was from (Pittsburgh Pa.), and that is where they are planning on living after they get married. The place was called (Homewood); it was a tough part of the city. My sister was tough so I knew she could handle it. When my sister was 18 years old, she started dating some asshole and had a baby boy a year later. It was the same person that I had tried to kill back in high school when he was in a rival gang. If I would have killed him, I would not have had to worry about her ever dating him.

At least I got a nephew from the asshole, which was the only good thing he ever did. I was happy because I knew she has found a nice guy, and they were going to move to Pittsburgh to live. Just the few things Maria said about him made me think he would make a great husband for her. Now the only one in the family still in Brownsville will be my drug dealing mother. I'm just going to put her situation in God's hands. I need to stay focused on me.

I wanted to continue studying my martial arts, but I could not find a Shotokan karate Club in Virginia that was near me. I did not want to start learning a new style of karate so I decided to join the "Base Boxing Team". I thought about trying out for the "Air Force Boxing Team", but they wanted me to live in Texas without my wife and family for six months out of every year. I knew my wife would not be very happy with that idea, so I did not even consider that option. I knew I needed something to release my frustrations in a healthy way so I had to figure out a way to drain the stress from my body. It is stressful for me, trying to be a good Christian.

I did start feeling good when I started boxing again because I was able to punch someone in the head without getting in trouble. Boxing was not something new to me; I used to be a

"Golden Gloves Champion" when I lived in Brownsville. That was before I received my "Black Belt" in karate, which was five years after I quit boxing. Karate calmed me down and helped me walk away from a lot of bullshit that I would have normally hurt someone about before. My wife was happy about me boxing again, because she knew that it would help keep me out of trouble. I was not sure how involved I was going to get with boxing; I was just going to play it by ear for now. I would have to see how astute the coach was when it came to teaching boxing. Hopefully, I would be able to adapt to his style of teaching with no problems. This was a good healthy outlet for stress.

When my son "Little Ron" was first born, I was apprehensive about taking him to Brownsville with his head shaped like a football. The doctors were correct when they said his head should resume its normal shape in time. After three weeks, his head began to start to look normal, other than him having a big head like his dad. He could not help having a big head because big heads ran in the Jackson family. His big head did not really stand out, because he was big all over. I was ready to take my big, strong, little man back home to show off my new family. I was a proud father and I wanted everyone to see how good I was doing, especially the non-believers who said I could not change.

I remember when I told my mother I was going to change my life, the only thing she wanted to know was what I was going to do with my drug business. Before I could respond to the question, she asked me if I could give her my drug business. I am not sure why I said yes, but I did and that's how she got started. Maybe deep down inside I wanted to see her dead or put in prison. I did not care which one came first. It could be I was just scared I would not have anything to come back to if I was not able change to my life like I planned. I guess I still was not convinced even God could help me change my life. When I gave my life to God, I thought life was going to be a lot easier, but it had not been that way yet.

Four weeks after the baby was born, my mother-in-law finally went back home. It was nice having her here to help out, but I was ready for her to go back home. Star asked her to stay longer, but she declined her invitation, stating that she had a family back home that needed her also. It seemed like everyday her husband was calling her, asking when she was coming back home. I think she used us as an excuse to stay away even longer, because he was a very demanding person from what I seen. He was one of them old school Christians who believed a woman's place was to listen and to obey her husband's every wish. I did not want that kind of relationship with Star. I don't think being the way Mr. Joseph is, has anything to do with God.

Star's father was the type of man who would beat his children if they did not go to church. The reason Star wanted to change her life was because she wanted her father's approval. Her father's tough leadership style was probably what made the children rebel when they got older. Star and her father got into many physical confrontations when she was growing up. She had a lot of spirit and that's what I liked about her. If she wanted something, nothing was going to stop her from reaching her goal. Star was always ready to listen to her heart before her mind. That is probably why we got married. Whatever the reason, I'm glad we did.

Now that I look back on meeting Star, I guess no matter what I said, she was going to get me anyway. Everyone thought since I was the older one in our relationship, I was the one who made a move on her. Actually it was the opposite of that; she was the one who made the move on me. She had beauty and brains, which would be hard for any man to resist in a woman. Everyday I was with her was like a dream to me. I would pinch myself to make sure I was not asleep. I knew if I wanted this dream to last, we would have to change our life style. That is what we did.

I knew I had to stop dealing drugs and she had to stop using them. The reward I received from dealing drugs was a lot of money, but that did not bring me my happiness. I did not find that until I met Star and then I knew I did not need to sell drugs and make money to find happiness. Star had been using drugs since she was 15 years old; I just hoped she could find the same happiness without them. I didn't know how hard that was going to be for her because I never used drugs like that. I believe if we keep God in our lives, neither one of us would revert back to our old ways. Everyday that I was with her gave me more reason to fight my demons. I'm still fighting them everyday.

My sister's wedding was coming up soon, so I asked my supervisor if I could have a couple of days off for it. He told me someone else already asked for that weekend off and there was no way he could do it. I really wasn't expecting him to say no, so I had to figure out a way to get them days off. I still had two weeks before the wedding, which left me plenty of time to figure out something. We were not concerned with the baby being so young because he was the size of a six month old baby and healthy. While I was as work I went into my supervisor's office and found out who was taking vacation on the weekend I needed off. It was someone named "Carlos Santana", who also was Security Policeman, but he worked the three to eleven shifts. All I had to do was to get him to change his vacation days and I would be on my way.

I noticed in his records that he lived in the same housing complex as I did. He was not married, but he lived with his girlfriend "Carla", and they also had a baby boy. That was something we had in common that I could use to help me get what I needed from him. I also found out he was from (West Palm Beach Florida) and I used to live in Florida briefly when I sold drugs. I made it my business for my family and me to meet them by strolling the baby thorough the housing complex until we bumped into them.

One day, as we were strolled the baby through the neighborhood, I saw Carlos outside washing his car. His girlfriend was sitting on the porch with their baby just chilling talking on the phone. I knew as soon as Star saw his girlfriend with the baby, she would start talking to her about the baby. She was more outgoing than me. I was more of an introvert, but if I had to be more outward I would do it. Just as I anticipated, Star walked over and introduced herself to his girlfriend. They started talking like they knew each other for years. I walked over and introduced myself to Carlos, and we started talking about the military. Carlos and I walked over to where the girls were and sat down next to them.

Their baby was six months old, but Little Ron was just as big as theirs was. They were amazed to hear that he was only five weeks old and so big already. After 20 minutes, Star and Carla exchanged phone numbers promising to call each other the next day. Before I knew it, my wife and Carla were doing everything together. I was happy Star had found someone her age, who she could relate to. Carlos was part Cuban and part black and Carla was all black; they seemed to make a nice couple. They appeared to get along well and that was nice to see in a couple. Carlos met Carla when he got stationed here about a year ago and before they knew it she was pregnant. Carlos was a couple of years older than her, just like I was a couple years older than Star. We had quite a few things in common with them. I don't know if they had any serious religious beliefs. They didn't mention God so we didn't. Their religious backgrounds weren't important to me right now.

We invited them over to our house for a cook out a couple of days after we met them and they said yes. I went out and bought a small grill so we could barbeque some hamburgers and hot dogs that day. This would be the first time I was at a cookout and not drinking any alcohol since I left Brownsville. The cookout went well; everyone appeared to have a good time that day. While at the cookout, I had to find a way to broach the conversation about going to my sister's wedding. I asked Carlos if he and Carla were planning on getting married anytime soon. He said, they were thinking about it, but he was not sure when.

I told him that my only sister was getting married, but I could not get any time off to go to the wedding. He asked me what days I was trying to get off. I told him my sister's wedding was next weekend, but someone already had those days off. He said, "What a coincidence those are the same days I have off from work". He said Carla and he were going to ride home so his mother could meet Carla and see their baby. He said that he could go see his mother anytime, but that this was my only sister's wedding, so he would tell the supervisor that he was going to give his days to me. I thanked him and told him I owed him one for being so considerate. I love it when a plan comes together. Now it was time to make some plans to go back home for my sister's wedding. I called my sister and told her the good news; she seemed very excited to hear it.

We arrived in town a day before the wedding and Star wanted us to stay at her parents' house, so we did. I felt uncomfortable being in Brownsville again because of what I was attempting to do with my new life, which was to change it. When I left town, I felt clean and just visiting Brownsville made me feel dirty again. Maybe it was just the guilt of all the sins I committed here when I sold drugs. There were many girls in town with broken hearts because of me. That chasm that was left in their hearts would hopefully someday be filled with God's love also. I have to stop these negative thoughts from permeating through my mind.

That evening my family and I went to visit my sister and mother just to see how they were doing. When I left town, I was hoping the next time I saw my mother she would not be dealing drugs. That was wishful thinking, because she had not changed. She was still smoking marijuana and selling it, but she did quit drinking alcohol. That was good because her drinking was the bane of my childhood. It's great that she has quit drinking, but the damage has already been done to my childhood. I got a chance to speak to my mother alone. I thought I could persuade her to change her life.

Star and the baby were sitting in the other room talking to my sister while I was talking to my mom. I asked my mom how long was she planning on staying in this drug business. She said in a satiric way, "What gives you the audacity to ask me about what I do". I told her I would feel responsible if something happened to her while she was selling drugs. She told me that she could take care of herself, so don't worry about her. I could tell that no matter what I said, it was not going to change her mind about how she was living.

I knew it was time for me to take my family away from her house, so we went back to Star's mother's house. There was something ungodly about being in my mom's presence. I have never felt that uncomfortable around her before. There was a feeling of death and destruction all around her. I guess that feeling is always around anyone who sells drugs. You just don't notice it when in the drug game.

Star could tell I was troubled when we left my mother's house by the way I was acting. I believe God wants me to help my mother, so I have to figure out a way to do that. I had a couple of days before I left town. I was sure I'd think of something before I leave town. The first thing I needed to do was to go to my sister's wedding, since that was what I came in town for. Of my siblings, only my brother Gary came in town from Philly for my sister's wedding. I had not seen him in a couple of years. He gave my sister away at the wedding.

Gary lived in Philly ever since he graduated from High School. The wedding went very well. I was happy when it was over because it was very boring. They had a small reception with about thirty people attending. I did not get to meet my sister's new husband. I talked to Gary for a short time and then we left the reception. I saw my mother, but we did not say anything to each other at the reception. I did figure out a plan to help her, so I knew I would be hearing something about her soon.

Before I left town, I found out who my mother's drug connection was. It was an old friend of mine "Sly", who came up in the drug game with me. I told him I didn't want him doing business with my mother anymore since I was no longer in town. I also told him to put the word out that I would be very unhappy if anyone did business with her. Everyone in town knew what I was capable of doing if someone crossed me because of my reputation here. I figure once my mother lost all her connections, her business would dry up and she would quit selling drugs.

I felt good about trying to help her because I was the one who got her started in this dirty business. Whatever I did, I did for God. Maybe this would help encourage her to do the right thing; time would give me the answer. It feels good trying to help someone else. I feel good about myself again. I feel like I have earned the right to call myself a Christian for the first time. I wonder if this is the feeling that Mrs. Angel got when she helped me find God. Is this a feeling that is sent personally from God himself? If I feel this good when I help a person, than why don't more (So called Christians do it)? ***"Believe in Change"***

Chapter 23

All alone Again, Making Money

I had been in the military a little over a year and half and financially we were still struggling. One time while we were at the grocery store, we put some expensive steaks underneath the baby's stroller. The closest thing we ate to a steak was hamburger, and we were getting tired of eating that. The plan was to take the steaks without paying for them and hope that we did not get caught doing it. This was the first time we ever thought about stealing anything, especially food. We figured God would forgive us since it was only food to eat and who was it really hurting.

I knew it was not the Christian thing to do, but those steaks sure did taste good that night. Every time went shopping at the grocery store, we would steal food that we could not afford to purchase with our little bit of money. I would have really been embarrassed if we got arrested for stealing food. Once we got a taste of the good food again, we just couldn't stop ourselves. I guess there are worse things we could be doing.

One time we had just put some lobster and shrimp underneath the baby's stroller when this lady and two young girls stopped us. She said, "That's a pretty little girl you have there" but because she was talking about my son; I told her he was a boy. She said, "He is so pretty I thought he was a girl with them big brown eyes". She was an older lady with two girls "Robin and Cathy", she told me the ages of her daughters, one was 13 and the other was 12 years old. The oldest one, Cathy was real quiet and Robin didn't know how to shut up.

Her daughters both wore thick glasses that looked like the bottom of pop bottles. She gave us her phone number and told us if we ever needed a babysitter her youngest daughter Robin would be happy to do it. She seemed like a very nice lady, with two cute daughters, but their cuteness was being hidden by them big ass glasses. I was wondering where their (Seeing Eye Dog) was at.

The next time we were in the store we met the lady again, and she invited us over for dinner. I fell in love with her cooking the first time I tasted it, she cooked that good (Down-South-Food). She was from (South Carolina) and took a lot of pride in her cooking. Star never was that great of a cook so it was nice to have a real home cooked meal. It was not long before we were eating at her house at least once a week. I was looking forward to eating at her house because she was like the mother that I never had. She did not want me to call her by her name, which was "Mrs. Woods". She wanted me to call her mom.

She said I was like the son she never had, so she always called me son. Star also called her mom when she addressed her. She had a husband named "Kendell" and he was just as nice as her. He liked to drink a lot of beer and alcohol, especially when I was around. I am sure he drank a lot when I was not around also. Meeting them was the best thing that happened to me since I went to Virginia, except when Little Ron was born. Robin and Cathy were lucky to have a mother like her. Good mothers are hard to find, especially where I come from. When I was a young child, I use to dream about having a mother like Mrs. Woods.

Star started looking for a job and she found one at a nearby Seven-Eleven-Store, which is a convenience store. I wanted her to stay home with the baby, but we really did need some additional income. The only shift she could get was the 4:00pm-12:00am for a couple days a week. The military had me working 3:00pm-11:00pm shift at this time, so we had to find a babysitter a couple days a week. We got Robin to baby sit for us on the days Star had to work. Robin was excited about baby sitting for us. Star would take the baby over to Mrs. Wood's house on her way to work. We were both comfortable with that because we knew the baby was in good hands there. Everyone there loved the baby like he was their own.

One day after Star had been working for a couple of months at the Seven-Eleven, I was looking in her purse for some loose change. I did find some change, but I also found a pack of cigarettes in her purse, which was unusual because we both agreed not to smoke anymore. We had decided together, to put stuff like that behind us. This was our way of trying to be better Christians. I got very angry. I was disappointed in her because she had been lying to me about cigarettes. I wonder what else she has been lying about to me.

We got into a verbal argument that day. I couldn't believe my wife was sneaking and smoking cigarettes at her new job. She was starting to revert back to her old ways of smoking cigarettes again. My biggest fear was she would start doing the things she used to do, like drinking and using drugs again. I really did not feel I could trust her and you need trust in a marriage if you want it to work. Out of anger, I told her if she was going to be sneaking around and doing things like that, she could just go back home. I really didn't mean it, but it came out my mouth like I did. I was just so angry. When I'm angry anything might come out my mouth.

When I came home from work that night, she was gone back home with my baby boy. She left a letter telling me that she thought it would be best if she went home for a little while. I was surprised when I found out she was gone because I really did not expect her to leave so easily. It was like she had been waiting for a reason to leave me and jumped at the very first one. This was the first argument that we had since we got married.

I guess she just wanted to go home and get back to her old ways. Maybe I should not have given her that choice to go home. I should have tried to talk it out, instead of losing my cool. I just didn't see this one coming. I guess all we had been going through had finally gotten to be too much for her. I am not sure what was going through her mind when she left with the baby. It had to be more than an argument over a pack of cigarettes.

I decided I was not going to be the first to call, so I just waited to hear from Star. I had too much pride to ask her to come back home. I was starting to feel sorry for myself. I spent most of my time at work, hardly talking to anyone. I didn't even tell Mrs. Woods and the girls about Star leaving me. I couldn't even explain why Star left because it didn't make any sense.

A month passed and she still did not call me, I was starting to become very anxious and sad, so finally I called her one night. I tried to reason with Star, but she just kept talking shit. The conversation did not go well and it ended with me telling her I was going to kill her. When I told her that, she hung the phone up. I knew I was not really going to do it, but she didn't know that considering my past history.

I heard she was running around with her old boyfriend and that upset me a lot. I heard this from my sister in a phone conversation one day with her. I was not going to let her know how bad what she was doing made me feel inside. I really felt betrayed after all the sacrifices I made trying to change my life. I gave up my lucrative drug business, joined the fucking Air Force, gave all my money away and this is my reward. This is fucking bull shit!!! Is this the plan God had for me? If so then I don't like it.

I decided to give up the apartment we lived in and move on base in the barracks. It did not cost anything for me to live there and that was all I could afford right then. When I moved in the barracks, which took a lot of the financial pressure off of me, I was determined to make the best of my situation. I did not want Star to know how depressed I was becoming, so I planned to keep myself busy. I still went to visit Miss Woods and the girls, but not as often as I used to.

In the barracks I had a room to myself, while most people there had roommates to deal with. The room had two small beds in it so I pushed them together to make one bed. I had a big television in my room that was hooked up to cable so I could watch anything I wanted. I did not have a phone in my room; I had to use the phone that was in the hallway of the barracks. I was fortunate to get a room to myself because most people had to share a room. I was real happy about that. Sometimes just the little things can make a person happy.

I was hardly eating anything because I did not have much of an appetite since Star left me. All I did everyday was go to the gym on base in the morning, eat lunch and go to work from 3:00pm to 11:00pm. The gym was not that far away; I could walk to the gym in 15 minutes. That's all I did for the next couple of months, other than sleeping at night. I lost twenty five pounds. I was down to 185 pounds, but I was all muscle. After six months in the barracks and still no word from Star, I noticed the other Airmen were always broke a week before pay day. They were always coming to me asking to borrow some money until pay day.

One day an Airman came to me and wanted to borrow $20.00 until payday and he said he would give me $30.00 for the $20.00 that he borrowed. I could not turn down that offer and that's how I got started in the (Loan Shark Business) in the military. Before I knew it, I was loaning out about $1,000 a month and getting back $2,000. Even though the money was flowing in, I still was not happy, but at least I was not broke anymore. I realized a long time ago that money was not going to bring me happiness. However money was nice to have if you are feeling depressed.

The other Airmen liked to drink a lot of beer and liquor so I decided to put a fully stocked bar into my barrack's room. I sold shots of liquor to the other airmen. I also sold beer, potato chips, and candy and ham sandwiches from the bar. If they did not have money, I would let them get up to $50.00 on credit at my bar. With all the money I was making on the side, I never had to cash my military checks anymore. My checks were just going into the bank and sitting there.

I decided to buy a white Lincoln Continental with white gangster tires on it with some of the money. The first day I drove it, I rode over to Mrs. Wood's house to show it to Robin and Cathy. They thought it was the sharpest car that they ever seen and so did Mrs. Woods. I did not here from Star so I assumed that she did not need any money for the baby. I knew she was living with her parents and they would make sure she did not need anything. I guess I really didn't care if she needed anything. Her parents had money so their grandson would be alright with them.

A year later, I started going to the night clubs to do some socializing because I had not been with a woman for a year now. That is how long Star has been gone; that year seemed to go fast for me. I guess I really was in love with Star because I didn't even think about being with another woman since she was gone. I have not even considered going to church or reading my Bible since Star left me either. It was not because I quit believing in God.

I knew there was a God, but I had lost what little faith I had. I wanted God to help me find a way to change my life. I was not able to do that, so I was doing what I did best, making money. I was not very good at being a good Christian, but I have always been good at making money. Without Star and my son, where was the incentive in being a good Christian anymore? Right now, I'm just trying to make as much money as I can.

One night I met a girl at the Non-Commissioned-Officers-Club (N.C.O.C) and went to her apartment to have a few drinks. One thing leads to the other and we ended up making love. I was on top up her tearing that pussy up when we heard a knock at her door. She told me earlier that she didn't have a boyfriend. That was the only reason that I agreed to go to her apartment. I asked her who would be knocking at the door this time of night---it was 3:00am. She said, "Oh it's no one, don't worry they will quit knocking and go away".

I started banging that pussy again and the knocking started to get louder. Ten minutes pass and then I heard the front door begin to open. I roll off of her and ask her who in the hell is coming in the door? She looks at me and says, "I think it's my old boyfriend, he must still have a key". I hurried up to get my clothes back on as she goes to the living room where he is hollering for her. I hear them arguing about why he is here. I finally get all my clothes on and walk to the living room and sits down on the couch.

The only person in the living room is her old boyfriend. He asks me did I know about him. I tell him hell no. There is a lot of tension in the air now. Before we could say anything else; I hear gunfire coming from the kitchen. Two bullets land right in front of his feet, missing by a few inches. I instinctively start reaching in my pants for my gun and realize that I don't have one. Now I'm thinking to myself; what in the fuck have I got myself into this time. Am I going to get killed in the middle of a lover's quarrel?

He says to her, "You are not the only one who has a gun". He pulls his gun out and points it towards the kitchen. I'm ready to leave, but I don't want to get hit by a stray bullet. I tell him, "This is your problem, not mine. If you don't mind, I'll leave right now". He says, "You don't have to leave, I'll leave" and storms out the door. When he closes the door, she runs from the kitchen to make sure that it is locked. I told her that she didn't need to lock it because I'm leaving also.

She still had a gun in her hand so I made sure I was being nice as I said my goodbyes to her. She apologized for the confusion and told me to give her a call tomorrow. I smiled and said, "No problem, I would be happy to give you a call as I eased my way thorough the door. She must be out of her fucking mind! Once I got to my car the first thing I did was thank God. I just was looking for some quiet companionship, not all this drama. This was a night that I certainly will remember for a long time. Maybe I don't need to go out and meet anyone. I sure will think twice before I go to another woman's apartment.

One day out of nowhere I got a phone call from Star, which caught me by surprise. A whole year had passed. When she called me I wondered what was on her mind now. I really did not know what to say to her, so we just talked about the baby. She told me he was doing well and he was walking now. She said she was going to send me some pictures of the baby so I could see how big he was. Before I knew it, we were talking a couple of times a week on the phone.

At first it was just her calling me and then I started calling her just as much. It was like when I first met her, we were always talking on the phone. It has been over a year since I have seen them, but I really was not missing her anymore. I was wondering what my son was doing and how big he was now. I was curious to see him.

Since I had started going to the clubs, there was a lot of girls who were interested in me. Star and I had been talking back and forth for a couple of months now; by now I had a lot of female friends, but there was not any I was serious about. I went over to see how Mrs. Woods and the girls were doing. We sat down and had some of her good food that day and she asked me what was on my mind. She always could tell when something was bothering me by the way I would act around her.

I told her Star had started calling me again and I'm a little confused. I asked her what she thought about Star calling. She asked me if I thought she was trying to get back together. I told her that we had not talked about it. We just talked about the baby and what he was doing. I told her that I sure was not going to ask her to come back because I was having too good of a time being by myself and dating. I do not think she believed a word that I said about not wanting to see Star again. She just looked at me, smiled and said, "It's going to be okay son because God still loves you". I think she knew what was really in my heart. She could tell that I still was in love with Star. She is a very wise lady.

Star called me a couple of weeks later and asked me if I would like to see the baby. She said she wanted to bring the baby to Virginia for a weekend if that was okay with me. I told her sure, that would be fine, and that I would get a hotel room for them. When I went to the bus station around 3:00pm on a Saturday to pick them up a few days later, I was apprehensive. I did not know what type of feelings I would have when I saw her again. Much to my chagrin, my heart began to melt when I saw her standing there with our baby next to her. I guess my love for her was dormant, waiting to strike at my heart again. I don't understand why I love this woman so much. It has been over a year and the feelings are just as strong as when I first married her. She must be the one for me. That's the only answer.

When she saw me, she smiled and ran towards me with arms wide open to give me a big hug. The baby ran behind her laughing as he ran, as if he thought his mother was playing a chasing game with him. The baby was not sure who I was because he had not seen me in such a long time. I knew then that she still had a grip on my heart and that could be good or bad for me. I was just going to have to be strong and use my mind, not my heart this time around with her. I must protect my heart better this time.

We went to the hotel room so they could freshen up after their eight hour bus trip from Brownsville. I asked her if she wanted to go to the mall, and do some shopping for the baby. When we arrived at the mall we sat and ate something at one of the restaurants that was inside the mall. We started shopping in the mall, and after fifteen minutes of walking in the mall Star started telling me how much she missed me. I told her I missed her too and that I had a rough time dealing with the separation. All of sudden she started crying right in the middle of the mall with about 100 people staring at us.

When she started crying, the baby started crying and everyone in the mall was wondering what in the hell was going on with us. I found an exit and we went outside for some privacy. There were still some people outside in front of the mall, so we walked to the rear of the mall. She had buckets of tears coming from her eyes and the baby was crying even louder than she was. I was carrying the baby while I was trying to appease Star. Before I knew it, we were all crying and hugging each other. She just kept repeating how much she loved me and she could not live without me anymore. This must have lasted for at least an hour or more and then I took them back to the hotel.

At the hotel we were finally able to calm the baby down and put him to sleep. While he was asleep, we made passionate love for hours until the baby woke up again. After making love, we decided our relationship was worth giving another chance. I told her that I would let her know when I found a place to live, and I would send for her and the baby. The next day around 7:00pm, I drove them back to the bus station to catch the bus back home.

I went back to the barracks to think; I was seriously concerned whether this plan was the right thing to do. Everything was going great for me, so why would I change anything right now? I guess it's because I still dreamed about having a good wife and family to come home to after work everyday. In spite of all the money I was making, loneliness still consumed my life daily. I still believed Star was the missing element in my life and I owed it to myself to give my marriage a second chance. If it didn't work, at least I would know we tried to make it work again. If I don't give it another chance, I would never know and I need to know in order to move forward with my life.

I had to close down my bar in my Barrack's room because I was getting ready to move out. I was going to lose money from that, but I just did not care about that right now. I was not going to give up my Loan Shark Business because I was making too much money from that. I did not have to live on base to keep this business; I could do that from anywhere.

It took me about a month to find a place for Star and me to live. I found a nice place to live in a little community called (Phoebus), which was right outside of Hampton. It was not too far from base, about three miles, so that was good for me. I moved out of the barracks and filled the apartment with new furniture. I told Star that she could come anytime. She came that following weekend. We were excited about starting over again.

It was kind of like getting married again and starting our honeymoon over again.

A couple of months later, Star found a job working as a hair stylist in a barber shop right outside the gate of the base. We got our old babysitter back; Robin was more than happy to start babysitting again for us. When Star was gone, she went to cosmetology school for about six months, but she didn't get her degree. She dropped out after six months. She only had another year to finish. She still knew how to do hair so the owner did not have a problem with that. Besides that, she was a good looking girl and that alone would bring men in the doors to get their hair cut.

With the money I was making and the money Star made, we were doing well financially. Maybe we would have a better chance to make our marriage work, if we do not have to be concerned with paying bills all the time. This is our second chance; I hope nothing happens to mess this up.

"Believe in Change"

Chapter 24

The Military Drug Empire

After three years in the air force, I was now Sergeant Jackson and with that rank I got to work the daylight hours. The daylight hours were 7:00am to 3:00pm, with six days on and three days off. This worked out fine for me because I could spend more time with my family. Star was still working at the barber shop as a stylist and a barber. My son was being watched by Robin a few days a week. Robin was now fifteen years old with a sexy body and a cute face. I was amazed watching her grow into a sexy young teenager. Thank God Mrs. Woods got her some contact lenses, and got rid of them big eye glasses.

There was a rumor on base that the airmen were using a lot of drugs in the barracks. It was determined by the base commander that K-nine needed to take the drug dogs into the barracks. The first time I took my dog through the barracks I did not find anything inside the rooms. It was like they knew I was coming. When I finished my search and went back outside, I found an assortment of drugs on the lawn. My dog was going crazy smelling all the drugs on the lawn. He was running from one end of the lawn to the other.

I found cocaine and marijuana just lying there for anyone to pick up. I had to go back to the truck and get a large trash bag to put it all into. I thought about how much money I could make reselling the drugs. So instead of turning the drugs in, I decided to put them in the trunk of my car. I know what I was thinking of doing was wrong, but sometimes I just can't help myself. I guess it's in my blood.

This seemed like a good opportunity for me to make some extra money selling the drugs back to the Airmen. Maybe I'm just being greedy because I'm already making extra money doing the loan sharking. I guess God is just going to have to forgive me again. I just can't seem to resist the temptation of selling drugs. Maybe I just need the excitement of the drug game.

Since the Airmen had to throw all their drugs away, they would probably be looking to purchase more drugs. My assumption was correct. A few days later I started reselling their drugs back to them; it was great. They did not know they were buying the same drugs twice when they purchased them from me. I guess they would have been a little angry, if they knew that was what I was doing. At least I sold the drugs back to them at a very low price.

In order to train the drug dogs, the military used their own drugs that they kept in a safe at the kennels and I had the combination to the safe. I decided to exchange some of my cocaine with the 97% pure cocaine in the safe at the kennels. I took two ounces of the pure cocaine and two ounces of the good marijuana. I mixed my low quality drugs with the good stuff and they did not even know. I got to the point where I did not have to enter the barracks, all I had to do was say loudly at the door, drug dog in the building and they started throwing the drugs out the windows. All I had to do was walk around and put the drugs in trash bags and take it off base.

Star did not know about my new drug activities, and that's the way I wanted to keep it. I rented another apartment just to keep the money and drugs there because I did not want it in my house. After a few months, I rented another apartment just to keep the money in it. In case somehow they found the drugs, I did not want to lose both the money and the drugs at the same time. I needed to recruit some people I could trust to help me out, because I realized I could not do it all myself. I concentrated mainly on the cocaine business because it was less bulky to move around and there was more money to make. I was making so much money that I quit loan sharking.

There was a new product on the market called (Crack

Cocaine), which showed a lot of promise. It was more addictive than powder cocaine and was half the price. The best place to purchase it was (New York) the Bronx. I was traveling to New York once a week to make purchases to send back to Pittsburgh, where I had a connection to sell it for me. I was buying the crack for five dollars a capsule and reselling it to my people in Pittsburgh for twenty dollars a piece.

I was the first person to bring crack cocaine into Pittsburgh and it was selling like hot cakes. I also was the first to sell crack cocaine in Virginia and it sold just as fast as it did in Pittsburgh. Every week they were sending me money through "Western Union" and every week I was sending them more crack. I did not know how deep I wanted to get in this business again, but every thing was moving so fast, it was very hard for me to stop.

The time was getting close for me to get out the military since my four years were almost done, so the military offered me $5,000 to re-enlist for another four years. I did re-enlist, but I did not do it because of the money. I did it because it was safer for me to stay in the military if I was still going to sell drugs because I was the police on the base. There were only five ways to enter the base and I had security police selling drugs from every entrance. Almost everyone in the 1st Security Police Squadron was selling drugs for me.

In the military, since I was the police, what could be safer for me than being in military while I sold drugs? I wanted to find out where the military got its drugs from and where they stored them. My feeling was that what they kept inside at the kennels was only the tip of the iceberg. I followed my supervisor one day to the weapons storage area where they stored nuclear weapons. I found out that was not the only thing they stored with the nuclear weapons.

When the supervisor opened one of the stalls, I noticed sitting next to the nuclear weapons was what looked like stacks of cocaine and marijuana. There had to be hundreds of pounds of drugs and that were just in one of the stalls. In order for my supervisor to get into where the drugs and nuclear weapons were stored, he had to know the combination to unlock the door. All I had to do is find out what the combination was.

One day when he was off from work, I decided to look into my supervisor's locker. I did not expect to find anything, because he always kept it unlocked; none of us really kept our lockers locked because we trusted each other. Inside his locker I found a notebook, and in back of the notebook there was combination numbers. I was not sure what the numbers were for. I figured I would try them on the door to where the drugs and nuclear weapons were stored. Surprisingly, the numbers worked, but I did go inside the area to make sure there were drugs. I was not going to take anything until I had some other drugs to switch for the good stuff.

That next week I purchased five pounds of cocaine from New York, and then I took the cocaine to the weapons storage area. I exchanged it for five pounds of the pure cocaine; the cocaine was so pure; I was able to put a pound of cut on each pound. Cut is a way of diluting the cocaine with a powder that is similar in density to the cocaine itself. That turned my five pounds into ten pounds at 50 % purity. That was good considering the average street ounce was only 30% pure. This gave me a lot of room to make plenty of money on sales.

Making my product ready for sale would take me many hours of preparation because I had to put the cut on it and then I had to bag it up in ounces. I would have a hundred or more ounces bagged up when I was done. I decided to sell the ounces for $1,000 a piece, which was the lowest price in Virginia at that time. I rented a storage place to keep the bulk of the drugs there because I certainly did not want it at my house. It was a (24-hour storage place) and I had a key, so I knew could get into it anytime I wanted to get some to sale.

I decided to stop selling the crack cocaine, because I thought it would be better to just concentrate on one drug. I was never sure what they mixed with the crack, but whatever it was made it highly addictive. The people who used it would do just about anything for it. The cocaine I sold could be snorted or cooked to smoke in a pipe and was not as addictive as crack cocaine. The people who snorted or smoked my cocaine were easier to deal with. The "Crack Heads" always seemed out of control, to the point that they would steal and even sell their bodies to get some crack cocaine. This created too much uncertainty for me to keep on selling crack in Virginia.

My biggest dilemma was what to do with the money I made selling drugs. I bought some water proof metal boxes and dug some four feet deep holes in the ground out in the Virginia woods. I started burying $25,000 once a month in each hole as I made the money selling drugs. The only money I lived off was the money I made from my military paycheck. Star had an idea what I was doing, as far as me selling drugs, but she was not sure about it. She had no idea how deep I was into it, because all she saw me do is sell some grams or maybe an eight ball of cocaine to some friends when they came to visit. I kept about an ounce at the house in a small safe; just to sell to friends if they needed some.

It seemed like every time I weighed my cocaine that was in the home safe, it would always come up short. Star would always say, "You must have weighted it wrong the first time". I knew she must have been stealing it while I was at work. That was the only thing that made sense to me. There is no way that I could be weighing the cocaine wrong every time. At first I was very upset, but I calmed down once I remembered her drug history. So instead of letting her steal it, I decided we would do a little on my days off, which were Fridays, Saturdays and Sundays every week. I thought that if I did some with her then I could help her control the use of the drug. She was excited about my plan. I was only planning on doing a certain amount then stopping when it was all gone.

When we would do some cocaine on the weekends, it was hard to get her to quit getting high. All we did was snort the cocaine, until one night she asked to see if she could cook up some cocaine to smoke it in a pipe. I never seen anyone cook up cocaine before and I was curious to see how it was done. We were having fun so I did not care; I just wanted to make her happy at the time.

Once she cooked the cocaine up, she took an empty beer can and put some pin holes in the top of it. She put some cigarette ashes on top of the holes, then she put a piece of the cooked up cocaine on top of the ashes and lit it with a lighter. She put the beer can opening up to her mouth and inhaled the smoke out of the can into her mouth. She held the smoke for a while in her lungs and waved me towards her, then blew the rest of the smoke in my mouth. She was like a (Professional Chemist) the way she cooked the cocaine up. She must have been doing this for a long time.

This was the first time I smoked some cooked up cocaine, and I did not like it so I blew it out right away. This was a very intense high and it was not one to play around with. I needed to think of some way to distract myself from this high I was feeling. So I started sucking and licking all over Star's body until she begged me to stop. I got up and took a couple big snorts of cocaine to take the rest of that high from the cooked up cocaine away from me.

I told Star I did not want to cook anymore cocaine up, but if she wanted to she would have to do something crazy for me every time she smoked it. She said okay, so I let her cook some more up a few minutes later, I only let her cook up about a half a gram at a time. I did not want to have a lot of cocaine cooked up at one time because I knew that I could not get her to think about anything else until it was all smoked up.

Every time we took a hit of cooked up cocaine Star would do whatever I asked her. She would take all her clothes off and dance around like a stripper, grinding and feeling on herself. Just watching her act crazy turned me on so much my dick stayed hard all the time. She made it so exciting for me; I never wanted to stop getting high with her. I did not care about getting high; I just liked watching Star act freaky in front of me.

After a couple of weeks of that, it has just got to the point where I was looking forward to partying with Star every weekend. I just wished she would act freaky without us using drugs, but I still was having fun getting high with her. I guess I was hooked on the freakiness of getting high with Star. All I thought about all week was getting high and freaking with Star.

Getting high with Star was fun at first because we played around and acted crazy. After a few months of getting high, she didn't act crazy anymore; she just wanted to get high. Apparently the high was more important than us having fun together and that started to bother me. She always promised we would have fun, but after that first hit all she could think about was her next hit. I was not going to sit around like some drug addict getting high and acting like a zombie waiting on the next hit. I had too much pride in myself to go out like that. I had to think of something to bring some excitement back into getting high.

The next time we got high, she did not want to have fun again. I told her I was going to stop getting high with her if she did not call one of her girlfriends to party with us. So she said she would call her friend, "Zena" and ask her to come over for a couple drinks. She said yes and we went to pick her up at her apartment, which was about ten minutes away from where we lived. Zena was younger than Star and had a sexy innocence about her that really turned me on. She was five feet, two inches tall with long brown hair and a brown complexion. She had a sexy body to go along with her pretty dark brown eyes. She was truly a beautiful young girl, only eighteen years old.

Star must have really loved the high to bring such a pretty girl into our marriage without worrying about her trying to steal me from her or me falling for Zena. I was surprised Star agreed to it, because I did not expect her to do it for me. After we had a couple of drinks, I put some cocaine on the table and we all snorted a couple of lines.

I told Star she could cook up some cocaine if everyone took off all their clothes first. So she persuaded Zena into taking her clothes off as I stood back watched her beautiful body. Seeing Star and Zena totally naked made me wonder if I was dreaming because if I was dreaming I did not want to ever wake up that night. Having cocaine was like having magical powers to make people do whatever I wanted them to do. I loved having this power.

After they got a couple of hits of the cooked up cocaine, I told Star if she wanted to keep getting high she had to suck Zena's pussy. I was shocked how easily she agreed to it and just as shocked how good she was a sucking another woman's pussy in front of me. She threw her down on the floor and stuck her tongue deep inside Zena's pussy as if searching for a hit of cocaine with her tongue. I was so turned on; I had to take a big drink of alcohol just to calm me down. After a few minutes, you could see the juices flowing from Zena's pussy onto the carpet. I didn't know that much juice could come from a pussy.

After twenty minutes of sucking, they both were ready for another big hit of cocaine to regain their energy level again. For the rest of that night they kept on acting crazy and I kept putting the cocaine out for them to cook. They were hooked on the drugs and I was hooked on the wild crazy sex shows that they were putting on for me. So now every weekend Zena was our personal (Sex freak), and I did not mind getting high with them. I was living every man's fantasy thanks to a little drug called cocaine, plus I was making a ton of money. I needed to be careful that I did not get hooked on my own drugs or the fun I was having getting the girls high with the drugs. No one was getting hurt so I didn't see any harm in what we were doing.

I thought that would keep her content for a while, but I was wrong because she was still stealing cocaine every chance she got. Now she was stealing it and putting more cut on it, so the weight would stay the same. I would have never noticed it, except I started receiving complaints from my customers about the quality of my stuff. I had never received any complaints about my cocaine before.

I always took pride in putting out the best product. I

guess having drugs in the house was too much temptation for her. I quit keeping drugs in the house. I needed to have total control over when and where Star got high. I would just grab a package to party with on the way home from work. If we ran out, then I would ride and get some more. This seemed to work pretty good for me. I was just worried about traveling while I was high. Especially, since I had drugs with me. I was having so much fun that I didn't even care. These drugs had me doing some dumb things. ***"Believe in Change"***

Chapter 25

Caught in the Act

One day, several months after we have started using cocaine on the weekends, I came home from work and Star was talking on the phone. I asked her who she was talking to and she said that her girlfriend "Sophie" so I asked to speak to her. I grabbed the phone, but she held on to it real tight and would not let it go. She was not saying anything to me about why she would not let me have the phone. We ended up wrestling for the phone so hard that I just let go and the phone hit her in the head.

Her head started bleeding down the side of face. The force of the hit had caused a gash to open up. I asked her why she didn't just let me talk to her friend. The only thing she said was that she did not know why she did not let me talk to Sophie. This whole situation was strange to me. I was beginning to wonder who she really was talking to. Whoever it was, she sure was determined to hold on to that phone.

We could not stop the bleeding, so I had to take her to the hospital on base. It only took ten minutes to get there because we lived so close. Before we arrived at the hospital, we agreed to tell the doctor same story. When we arrived at the emergency room, we told the nurse at the desk that she tripped and hit her head on the side of the table in the kitchen. The military is very strict on domestic violence, and I did not want them to think we were fighting. I did not need any unnecessary attention on myself because of the life I was living---selling drugs. While she was in with the nurse, I reflected back on the whole scenario; it really did not make any sense for her to have acted that way about handing me the phone. While she was in the room waiting to be seen by the doctor, I decided to call Sophie.

I asked Sophie, "Was Star talking to you on the phone today?" She seemed startled by the question. She hesitated for a second and then she began to tell me everything. She began by saying; "It was not my fault she started going to bed with him. I just introduced her to him, but I did not tell her to start fucking him". I was shocked hearing all this information about Star. I asked her would it be alright if I came over so we could talk about it some more. She said yeah and I left Star at the emergency room still waiting to be seen by the doctor.

I met Sophie in the hallway of her apartment complex and we began to talk again. Sophie was from the Philippines, but she spoke very good English when she had to. Star had met her about a year ago while she was out buying some groceries. Over the last few months they started going more places together.

Sophie was not very attractive looking, but she had a special innocence about her that made her seem interesting to a man. She was only about four-feet-eight inches tall with short black hair and brown eyes. I really was not sure of her age, but if I had to guess, I would say she was about 32 years old. She started crying while she was telling me the story. She told me how sorry she was for how things turned out. She told me that Star had been seeing this Airman on base for a couple of months. She said that she had just recently found out that they were making love together. She said that she thought that they were just smoking weed together.

I was overwhelmed with this information. I couldn't believe Star was cheating on me. I wasn't sure why Sophie told me all this shit. Maybe she had feelings for the Airman that Star was sleeping with. Whatever the reason, the truth is out there now. How do I deal with this crazy information? It seems like no matter what I do, some shit comes up.

I hugged her and told it was not her fault I married a whore like Star. She explained to me how she told her not to sleep with the man anymore because she did not want to be put in the middle of this deceit. She told me the Airman was stationed on the same base with me. She told me his name and where he worked, plus what kind of car he drove. I had to stop her from talking. I had heard enough to know that I did not want to be with Star anymore. I did not want Sophie to see me break down in from of her, so I thanked her and left so she could not see me cry.

I sat in my car as tears flow from my eyes. I asked God, "Why was this happening to me? Is this my punishment for selling drugs"? I have learned to expect the unexpected, but the shit that happens to me is hard to anticipate. I wiped the tears from my face and pulled myself back together. Momentarily the thought to kill Star lingered on my mind. I brushed that aside because I knew that I could never go through with it.

I was not sure if I was going to go back to the hospital to get Star. But there was always that possibility that Sophie was lying to me. I needed to find out for sure. So I decided to go back to the hospital. The sooner I got Star back home; the sooner I could find out the truth. When I got to the hospital, the doctor was just finishing putting stitches in her head. I did not tell her I went to see Sophie. We did not say anything to each other on the way home. She seemed very nervous as we pulled up to the apartment. I guess she could sense the tension in me.

When we got in the house I went to the living room and sat down. She went into the bedroom and lay across the bed. I still did not say anything to her for about twenty minutes. Then I finally I asked her to come to the living room and sit down. I told her that I wanted to talk to her about what happened tonight. She said that she would be right out. She sat across the room, about ten feet away from me; maybe she thought I might attack her or something. I asked her "What was the deal with the phone today, why wouldn't you let me talk on the phone?"

She said, "I was just playing around". I said, "Really because I talked to Sophie and she told me everything about what you been doing with that Airman on base". I told her,

"Don't even try and deny it because I know everything". She said, "Ron, I didn't mean to hurt you, I just needed someone to talk to". Star started crying. She said, "I was confused about everything that was going between me and you". Out of anger, I called her all kind of whores and bitches. I was hoping she would say something smart so I could slap the shit out of her. She just kept on crying.

We went back and forth shouting at each other across the room. She was trying to blame her actions on me. I told her if she was unhappy then why didn't she come and talk to me about it. This went on for about thirty minutes. I heard knocking at the door. I went to the door to see who it was. I could hear someone saying, "This is the police open the door right now". Someone must have called the police because of all the noise we were making. I opened the door, told him to come in. I sat back down on the chair as the policeman walked into the house.

He said that one of the neighbors complained about loud shouting coming from this apartment. I told him everything was okay; we were just having a misunderstanding about something. The policeman asked about the bandage on Star's head. We told him the same thing that we told the doctor. I promised the policeman that we would keep the noise down. He looked at Star and said, "You sure everything is okay Miss?" Star forced a smile on her face and said, "Yes officer, we can handle this". Once he left, I told Star it would probably be a good idea for her to go back home. I told her that I was not sure what I would do if she stayed in Virginia. She agreed and walked back to the bedroom.

We picked up Little Ron at Mrs. Wood's house that next morning on the way to the airport. He had spent the night because Robin was going to take him to amusement park with their church. I was glad that my son was not home to see us acting like fools that day. We just told him that he and his mother were going to see grandma for a vacation. I told Mrs. Woods and Robin that I would explain everything to them later. I did not know if I could ever be with Star again as man and wife. I had mixed feelings about her leaving. There was a (hate/love) thing going on in my heart.

I drove them to the airport around 10:00am. I was happy my son did not get to see me and his mother act like fools. After we got to the airport, I hugged my son and said goodbye again for the second time in his young life. I just looked at Star and turned my head because I could not stand to look at her anymore. I felt that she really did me wrong. I did not know if I would ever be able to forgive her again.

The evening after everything got quiet, it dawned on me that I was all alone again in that house. Tears started to fill my eyes until finally I could not hold them back anymore. I cried like a big baby for the couple of hours until I finally fell asleep on the couch. When I woke up the next day, I promised myself that I would never let anyone get that close to my heart again. It seemed like I said that before, but sometimes you follow your heart instead of your mind. Love is unpredictable….

Maybe Star is always going to be my weakness. I know I was wrong for bringing all those fucking drugs into me and Star's lives. I thought I was doing it to make her happy, but really it made her sad. I believe this sadness made her go to another man. I helped feed the monster inside of Star with all the drugs. I created the monster that she eventually became. I have to be a man and except the blame. I thought I was doing the right thing. I just wanted to share some happiness with the person that I loved. I hope what I did doesn't ruin her life forever.

After a few weeks of feeling sorry for myself, I went out to the club and met a nice girl, whose name was "Lauren". She was a college student at Hampton Institute majoring in journalism. She was a very pretty girl, much younger than I was, but I did not care. She was tall with long pretty brown hair, which hung halfway down her back. She had medium brown complexion with light brown eyes, and a beautiful smile. She was just what I needed to take my mind off of Star and all our problems. The next day I took her to dinner at the N.C.O. Club and then back to my place to chill out for awhile. We talked for a while and then I made my move on her to see if she wanted to make love.

We made love all night long and then I took her to breakfast the next morning at around 10:00am. I had a great time being with someone other than Star, but there was still something missing. The problem was that I could not stop thinking about my wife in spite of how wrong she had been to me. Maybe because I knew that I was part of the problem. I hoped that in time my love for her would fade away. Then I could move on with my life. Maybe God was making me pay for selling drugs. I knew I would have to pay for my sins, but I was not sure how. Sometimes I think how easy it would be for me if God just killed me. He certainly has enough reasons to get rid of me. I'm convinced now that I'm supposed to suffer before I leave this earth. Maybe there is some truth to the saying, "We create our own Heaven and Hell right here on earth". Right now what I have been creating a living hell…

Several months had passed and I still had not heard anything from Star. I really did not care because I was not ready to talk to her anyway. I was still dating Lauren, but it was mostly a sexual thing and I did not want to make it anything more right then. She was trying to get serious, but I promised myself that I was not going to let anyone get that close to me again. I realized that maybe I should be honest and let her know that we could not get any closer. If I told her that, maybe she would not keep giving me some of her good pussy. Maybe I will just keep my mouth closed for the time being.

No matter what I did with her, it did not seem to make me satisfied. I needed some time to determine my next move in life. The thrill of selling drugs had begun to abate and the thought of having wild sex parties was not going to make me happy. The money I was making selling drugs did not excite me either. I needed to do something totally different and then see how I felt. I went to see my Commander about getting an assignment to (Holland) that I had heard about. The assignment was for a whole year. He told me that I could have it if I really wanted it. I told him I would let him know in a couple of days if I really wanted to do it.

If I agreed to the assignment, he told me I would have to leave in thirty days and there would be no exceptions. All my instincts told me to stop everything I was doing and get out of town. I have always listened to my instinct, that's why I lasted so long in the drug game. The money I was making was not being used for anything, and I really was not sure what I was going to do with it anyway. My plan was to save it until I got out of the military. The only money I lived off was my military check. All the drug money was just sitting in the ground spread throughout the Virginia woods.

There was no one that I trusted enough to watch over what I was doing in the drug business. It was time to get out while I was ahead. So I told my Commander a couple of days later that I would take the assignment. I had to tie up some lose ends before I would be ready to leave town. I had to decide what to do with the money I made from selling drugs and where to store my vehicles. The only person I thought I could trust was Mrs. Woods, but I did not want her to get into any trouble for trying to help me. She and the two girls are the only bright spots in life now. I wouldn't do anything to fuck that up.

I told my Commander I needed to take some leave time, so I requested two weeks of my vacation. I had plenty of time saved, so he had no problem agreeing to my request. That gave me enough time to figure out what I needed to do before I left town. I went over and told Mrs. Woods and the girls that I would be leaving for a year. Mom started crying and then all of us starting crying together. I certainly was not going to tell her that I had volunteered for the assignment because she would have been upset with me for doing that.

I still had five kilos of cocaine that I did not sell in storage, and I had to find someplace to hide them. I did not trust leaving them in storage for that long without me checking on them once a week. I decided to hide both the money and the drugs in (Bethel Park), which is a military park located on "Langley Air Force Base". I started to count all the money, but I get tired because it was so much there. I purchased two fire and waterproof metal safes and put the money in one, and then I put the drugs into the other safe. I waited until 2:00am and I loaded everything into my car and I drove to base hoping I did not get stopped for anything.

When I arrived at the park I went to the lake and set up my fishing pole as if I were fishing. There was no one else around so I left my fishing gear there and drove to the other side of the lake. Back in the wooded area of the park, I dug a hole four feet deep and one foot wide. I buried the safe with the money in it. Then I buried the safe with the drugs in it about ten feet away. I checked the area one last time to make sure no one was watching me. I got done just in time because the sun was starting to come up after four hours of digging. I gathered all my fishing gear and went home to get some rest so I could finish the rest of my plan.

My next plan was to get my revenge on the man who was fucking my wife behind my back. That next night, early in the morning around 4:00am, I broke into his vehicle. I hid two ounces of cocaine, with $1,000 cash underneath his back seat. I also put a small hand gun in the glove box next to his military identification card. I made sure that all the serial numbers were taken off the gun. I made sure my finger prints were no where to be found on anything. Then I made an anonymous phone call to Law Enforcement from a pay phone off base. I informed them of the drugs and the gun that was in the Airman's vehicle. Then I drove back to where his vehicle was parked to watch the action. The police found his vehicle and waited until he got off from work to question him about the call.

When the Airman got into his vehicle, they surrounded his car. They asked him to show them his Identification and without looking, he reached in the glove box. He just started grabbing stuff. He pulled the small 32-caliber handgun out to see what it was. One of the policemen shouted gun and they all started shooting into the vehicle. I was parked across the street so I could see the whole thing unfolding. It was like watching a movie and I was the Director…

The shooting only lasted for a few seconds and it was over just like that. They pulled his limp body out the vehicle and threw him onto the ground. He looked like he was hurt very bad, but I did not care. I hoped he was dead. I found out later that he was going to survive his wounds. However he would be spending about 15 years in a military prison for attempted homicide and drug distribution. The police report said that he was trying to shoot them with that gun. If all my other plans worked as smoothly as this one, I probably would still be married now.

Well everything seemed to be falling in place and then out of nowhere I received a call from Star. She said that she heard I was going over seas and she wanted my son to see me before I left. I told her yes and asked her how did she find out that I was leaving. She told me it was Robin. She asked me not to say anything to Robin about it. I guess Robin and Star had been keeping in touch all this time and I did not even know it. I agreed to see my son, but that did not change the way I felt about Star. I still have not forgiven her for what she did. I guess as long as we have a child together, we will always be drawn to each other. One of us is going to have to be strong and quit trying to make this relationship work. Hopefully I will be the one that will step up and stop this craziness before someone gets killed. ***"Believe in Change"***

Chapter 26

The Getaway

The day before my flight to Holland, Star and Little Ron arrived in town to see me. They were staying at Miss Wood's house, so I went over to visit them that afternoon. I was very happy to see my son, but not so happy to see Star. However, I was very cordial in meeting her again. I did not want her to know that I was still hurting from what she did to me. I took Star and little Ron out to dinner that evening so I could spend some time with my son. I knew Little Ron would be more comfortable if his mother was around. It felt like old times again, and that worried me because I still had feelings for her.

I had not been around her for almost a year, and she still had some kind of hold on me. I was happy to be leaving town, because I am sure I would have said yes if she tried to get back together with me again. She asked me if it was okay if she wrote me while I was gone, and I told her yes. Since we had a child together, I knew we should at least try to be friendly towards each other. We had a nice quiet dinner together, and then I took them back to Mrs. Wood's house.

My flight overseas was leaving at 6:00pm the next day; uncertainty filled my thoughts. I was very apprehensive about whether I was doing the right thing, but I knew I had to get away. All my instincts told me to stop what I was doing and get out of town before something bad happened to me. The commander told me that it would be an 18 hour flight without stopping. The pilot was going to refuel while the plane was still in the air. That sounded very dangerous to me, but that was not going to change my mind about leaving Virginia.

I only packed a few civilian clothes to take with me, because I really was not planning on doing much overseas other than working. Star and little Ron walked me down to the flight line where the airplane was going to take me to Holland. Once we got to the restricted area, they had to say goodbye to me. I hugged both of them and walked away carrying my duffle bag.

She looked very sad as I walked away, with tears forming in her eyes. It bothered me to see her so unhappy because I was leaving. There was still that soft spot in my heart that I could not get rid of. The only thing I could do was to stay away from her until I got my head together. I knew if I was not leaving right then, I would have turned around and asked her to start over again. Fortunately I did not have that choice because I was already committed to leaving.

As I walked up the steps into the aircraft, I felt the fear of the unknown coming over me. I had never been in the air for eighteen hours before and really didn't know how my body was going to handle it. When I got on the plane, we had to sit in these little seats against the sides of the aircraft, which was very uncomfortable. There were about 300 other airmen on the aircraft with me, but no one I knew. In the middle of the plane were armored tanks and peacekeepers. The inside of the plane was the size of a basketball court. I never knew anything this big could actually get off the ground.

As the aircraft rumbled down the runway, I wasn't sure it was going to pick up enough speed to get in the air. The plane seemed to be going to slow and it was so big. Surprisingly it did finally lift off and I was on my way to Holland. I took a sigh of relief once I was in the air. I had visions of the plane crashing as it was taking off. Once we were in the air, we were allowed to walk around and socialize with each other. I had to find something to do for 18 hours, so I played cards with some of the other airmen and slept a lot.

I slept more than I was awake; I guess it was the motion of flying that made me feel so tired. I was glad that I was able to sleep so much. If not, the flight would even be more boring.

Each minute in the air brought an inner peace to me. I felt as if I was leaving all my troubles behind. I felt like I succeeded in running away from my old life. It has been said, "You can run, but you cannot hide". Am I really just hiding? Maybe.

About halfway there, the pilot announced that he was going to attempt to refuel in the air. He knew this was a dangerous maneuver, and he did not want us to worry if we saw another plane close to our plane. I was very worried because it felt like we were being knocked around in the air. Our aircraft was shaking and vibrating like it was ready to break. Everyone had concerned looks on their faces. One wrong move and the plane could be falling out of the sky.

We did not have parachutes on, so we would certainly die if something went wrong. This was not a good feeling for me. A parachute would not have helped me anyway because I did not know how to use one. That was one thing that was never taught to me in the Air Force. This was the first time that I ever thought about a parachute before.

After about three attempts to refuel, the pilot was finally able to get the refueling completed, and we continued on our journey. I finally heard the words everyone had been waiting to hear for hours. The pilot announced that we were preparing to land, and we had to return to our seats. That was the best news I heard in eighteen hours. Now I had a whole year to get ready for the next flight back home. At least the next time I'll be on my way back home. I was sure that would be a flight I would be happy to make when that day came.

When I first put my feet on the ground, it felt like the ground was constantly moving. The feeling was similar to smoking marijuana or some of kind of hallucinating drugs that I tried in the past. That was the effect of being in the air for eighteen hours on a plane. I did not know how long the feeling was going to last, but I hoped not very long. I was not the only one staggering around on the ground. Everyone who got off the plane was doing the same thing. After we got our gear, the

Security Police bus drove us to the barracks, where we would live for the next year.

That afternoon, we were briefed on our work assignments and the fact that we would be working with the (Dutch military). The Commander said that we would be working three shifts, and with my rank I would have my choice. I told the Commander that I wanted to work daylight instead of the other shifts. Our main duty was to guard the F-15 aircraft that would be flying over to Holland later this week. The reason the planes would come over after us was so that we could set up a secure area for them.

The problem with working with the Dutch military was they only spoke a little English. The United States government agreed to teach the soldiers some of our fighting techniques. In Holland, when you turn eighteen years old, the government makes every man spend at least two years in the military. I thought that was a good idea because if they had to go to war, the military would at least be ready to fight.

It was not that the Dutch soldiers did not know how to speak English. If they had to, they could speak a little English. It was mandatory that they study three hours of it every week, while they were in high school. The reason they did not use English that much was that they were not confident enough to use it around Americans. I had no idea what they were saying, when they spoke Dutch, but they at least could understand some of what we were saying to them. They could have been calling us idiots or worse, I wouldn't know. The soldiers seemed very nice and friendly in spite of the language barriers.

After a couple of weeks of just going to work, I decided to go downtown to see what it was like. Everyone was telling me about the (Red Light District) and the naked women that you could see in the windows. This is a place where naked women showed off their bodies in the windows of storefronts. It was completely legal. If you liked what you seen in the windows, you could go into the place and buy some pussy. You could buy some pussy for only ten American dollars. I thought that was a great price.

I was horny, but I did not have the nerve to buy some pussy. I was told that the prostitutes made everyone use condoms even when they were just receiving blowjobs. I just had too much pride to spend money on sex after getting it free for all these years. I was used to fucking all the time, so it was not a big thing to me to see all those pretty asses in the windows. I don't think I will be coming down here very often because I might get weak and buy some pussy. After a couple of months of no pussy, anybody might get weak. I wanted to relax and stay focused and get my tour of duty over and go back home.

There was also a place called the (Houseboats) where you could also go buy some pussy. You had to go inside to see the girls. There were no windows with the girls sitting in them. The prices were the same as the Red Light District; the only difference was that the girls were on houseboats. The airmen were spending a lot of their money on pussy and alcohol while they were in Holland. I was trying to figure out how I could get some of that money. It did not take me long to come up with a plan. The plan was to get them to gamble on their time off from work. I set it up by running card games at the barracks.

The main game we played was poker, and I took 10% off every pot we played. Sometimes there would be as much as $1,000 in one pot, and my cut would be $100. I also supplied them with beer at no cost to them. I knew the drunker they got, the more money they would spend on gambling. I ran the game six days a week, in the evenings. I took Sundays off just to rest. I not only ran the games, I also was a player at times. I stayed so busy that I lost track of the time that I had been in Holland. I did not know if it had been six months or eight months; it all seemed like a dream to me. I guess being so busy, I just lost track of time.

Star was sending me letters at least once a week. I could tell that she was hoping to get back together with me by her writings. I was not going to make any promises to her, even though I knew that I was still in love with her. I did tell her that if we got back together that I wanted to have another baby with her. She wrote and said that she wanted to have another baby with me also. I knew that deep down in my heart if I saw her, I would probably say yes to anything she asked me to do. I'm not sure why I felt the way I did about making this marriage work. Maybe I just wanted to be a father to a child because I never had a father of my own. It might have been more about that, than it was about loving someone so much. Maybe it is just as simple as being in love with a person.

The first restaurant in Holland that I went to was a strange experience for me. When I ordered a hamburger and some potato chips, they gave me a burger on a plate with two pieces of bread sitting next to it. Instead of receiving potato chips, they gave me an order of French fries. The food really wasn't that good; I was missing that good old American cooking. I did find a McDonalds in downtown (Amsterdam). That food was not good, plus it cost twice as much as it did in the U.S. I didn't realize how much I missed home cooking. Boy could I go for some of Mrs. Woods Southern cooking now. Even Star's cooking sounded good right now.

Over in Holland, we had to convert our American money into Dutch money, which was called guilders. I was not sure of the conversion rate, because I was not really paying attention when they explained it to us. I did know the U.S. money was worth more than the (Dutch Guilders). Some of the businesses accepted the American money, but most of them did not. As long as it was considered money, I was happy to have it in my pocket.

One day I was downtown walking around, and I saw some people walking around with some wooden shoes on. When the people walked, it sounded like horses were walking down the streets. The shoes looked very uncomfortable, but they were very colorful to look at. The shoes had flowers printed on the sides of them, which made them look very pretty. I purchased a couple of pairs so I could take them back home as souvenirs. I figured that I should have something other than a lot of money to remember my experiences over here.

Before I knew it, eight months had passed, and it was almost time to go back to the United States. I was ready to go back, but I was not sure I was ready to deal with my personal demons. I was not sure what to do about the drug business and Star. I also had to decide whether or not I was going to stay in the military; all these decisions were not going to be easy ones. I still had a little time to figure them out. Star was still writing me on a regular basis, but I did not tell her exactly when I was coming home. The only person who knew exactly when I was coming home was Mrs. Woods and Robin. I really did not want Star to know because I did not want her waiting there when I got off the airplane. I knew if I saw that pretty face and my son, it would be extremely hard for me to walk away again.

It has been so long since I had some pussy that when the wind blew my dick got hard. I tried to keep myself busy so I would not think about it so much, but it was almost impossible now. Even when I took a shower and washed my dick, it would get hard. I had to make sure no one else was in the shower when I got in so I would not get embarrassed if it got hard. I still refused to buy some pussy. I would rather masturbate to relieve the tension. It hasn't got to that point yet, but it's getting close.

The next couple of months went by fast and now it was time to get ready to go back to the United States. I can't say I had a good time, but I did need this time away to get my head together. I was not absolutely sure about what I wanted to do when I got back in the U.S., but what I was positive about was that I needed some pussy. My mind was clouded with the thought of getting some pussy almost every minute of the day. I didn't know that I could go a whole year without some pussy. It's a miracle…

I would have never thought that I could go that long without being with a woman. This is the first time I went this long since I lost my virginity. I was fifteen years old then. Soon I would be flying back to my country, the land of pussy and cream. I also must remember that it was the same place where my heart was torn apart. I have to do a better job of protecting my heart. I don't know how many more times I could take it being broken. I had a lot of time to think about all the mistakes that I made in the past. I not sure if I'm capable of making the necessary changes to avoid similar disasters. I still am waiting for God to give me the strength to fight my demons. There seems to be a battle between the Devil and God over who is going to get my soul. Neither one wants to give up on me. I guess both of them see the potential in me. While this battle is going on, I'm being torn apart inside. ***"Believe in Change"***

CHAPTER 27

The End of a Military Career

The flight back home seemed to take forever; after 18 hours, I finally landed at Langley Air Force Base. It was a great feeling to be back in the U.S. again. I had a new found appreciation for living in America after being overseas. I walked off the plane looking to see if anyone was waiting for me to arrive. Thank God no one was there. I traded flights with another Airman, with the hopes of sneaking in town without anyone knowing it. I wanted to have some time to get my thoughts together before I saw Star or anyone else. The only ones who knew I was taking an earlier flight were Mrs. Woods and Robin. I told them that I would call them once I got settled in. I had to pay a Airman extra money to get the earlier flight, but I didn't mind. I had plenty of money…

It took about an hour to gather all my things off the aircraft. There was a shuttle bus that drove us right to our barracks. I had not even got my stuff unpacked before I heard a knock on my barracks' room door. I figured it was one of the other airmen who was over in Holland with me, but it wasn't. Instead of asking who it was, I just opened the door. My mouth dropped to the floor when I saw who it was. Standing there, looking like an angel was Star and my son. They both said with big smiles, "Surprise". Before I could say anything, she ran in the room and kissed me. Little Ron was hugging on my leg, doing a little happy dance.

I felt like a starving man who just received a piece of food. I just couldn't get enough of her tender kisses. I had to control myself because I did not want her to know how much that I missed those lips. I reached down to pick up my son, and he started smiling at me. I asked her how she knew I was coming home that day. She told me that Robin called and told her when I was coming home. She told me that she and Little Ron had been staying at Miss Wood's house for the last three weeks waiting on me to come back.

She really wanted to make sure that she was the first person to see me. She probably assumed that she would be the first woman that I was near in a year. That was a good assumption by her because I needed some pussy real bad. After I unpacked my clothes, we went out to have some dinner and rode over to mom's house to say hello. Mom was really happy and Robin had a thousand and one questions to ask me. We stayed there a couple of hours, and then we went back to the barracks.

Star and I spent most of the night talking and making love after little Ron went to sleep. I knew after that night that I wanted to spend the rest of my life with her again. We spent the next two weeks finding an apartment. Once we moved in, we decided to get started on having another baby, so Star got rid of her birth control pills. For the next six months we fucked like rabbits; it was great. Things were moving fast between me and Star. Maybe too fast. She is like a drug and I'm the addict and when she is near me, I start using all over again. I hope I don't end up like most junkies. Dead, from an overdose….

I decided not to return to the drug game. I wanted to give our marriage the best chance possible. Six months later, when I was looking in Star's purse for some change, I found some birth control pills and asked her about them. She told me that she lied to me. She said, "I was scared I would lose you if I didn't agree to have a baby". I was wondering what was taking her so long to get pregnant. I was pissed off because she told me another lie. She begged me to give her another chance to make it right. I told her that this was her last chance.

A month later she was pregnant. I didn't know if she did it because she wanted to have a baby or if she was scared of losing me again. It was my hope that this baby would bring us even closer so I was happy. The nine months went by fast, and we decided not to have the baby at a military hospital. We had not forgotten all the trouble we had with little Ron. Star didn't want to deal with those dumb ass military doctors.

Two weeks before her due date, I took vacation leave for thirty days. Star wanted to have the baby in Brownsville. Her mom was really happy about that. I was also because I did not have to worry about Star's mom staying too long at our house. While we were in town, we stayed at Star's mom's house until she had the baby. We were only in town for a week before Star had a baby girl; we decided to name her "Ronella" because it had some of my name in it. She was only 7.5 pounds when she was born, almost five pounds lighter than her big brother.

While I was in town, I asked about Ann and what she was doing with her life. My sister told me that she moved to Washington, DC with my other daughter, whom I had not seen in almost eight years. My sister told me that she had a job working for the government making good money. When I first went into the military and got stationed in Virginia. I tried to get Ann to let my daughter Ronay spend the summers with me. She always had some kind of excuse as to why my daughter could not come, so I quit trying.

I knew it was because I was married to Star, and she had never gotten over that. Ann never did anything to try to bring Ronay and me closer. I can't remember one time when Ann asked me to come to see Ronay after we were separated. At least I knew I tried to see my daughter, and that is more that I can say about Ann trying to keep us closer. I can only imagine what Ann told my daughter about me—maybe things like "Your dad does not want to see you" or "He just does not care about you".

I did not attempt to visit any of my family members, other than to talk to my sister on the phone when I was in town. We have never been close, and I felt there was no reason to change that now. Mrs. Angel was always something special to me because I always wanted to have a mother like her. I did not think Star knew how blessed she was because she was always complaining about her. At least she had a mother who cared and was not ashamed to show love for her children. Some people just do not appreciate what they have.

We only stayed in town a few days after the baby was born, and then we headed back to Virginia. Star's mom wanted us to stay longer, but I was ready to go back to Virginia. I still was not comfortable being in that town where I had nothing but bad memories. I remember thinking that life is funny; all the bad things that I have done, it is just amazing that I am not dead or in prison. This is simply a miracle of God!!! I have a beautiful wife and two lovely kids. I'm truly blessed and I'm going to try to do everything I can to make this work. I owe that to myself and to my children.

A few months after the baby was born, my second tour of duty with the Air Force was over. My Commander asked me to reenlist for another four years. I thought about it for a few days, and I told him I would if they let me cross train into computers. He said okay, but it would take six months. I extended my contract for six more months until my new orders came in. After six months, I still did not have the new orders; I was starting to get pissed off. I made an appointment to see the Commander. When I got there, he told me that my orders were never put in the system. He could not find them anywhere. He told me that I should go talk to the person who I gave my new application to, which was my supervisor.

The next day I went to see my supervisor and I asked him, "What happened to my application for cross training into computers?" He looked at me with this dumb grin on his face and said, "I must have forgotten to send it in". Then he proceeded to tell me how bad the Air Force needed Security Policemen with my experience. He continued to blow smoke up my ass about how all I had to do was another 12 years and I could retire on (Easy Street). He said, "You already got close to nine years in the Air Force and it would be foolish to quit now". He said, "I hope you're not upset, but I just wanted to do what was best for the military". Then he said, "The military needs always comes first, and that's how it has always been Sergeant Jackson". I couldn't believe this asshole was telling me all this bullshit. I was starting to see red. I wanted to knock that smug look off of his fucking face. Why can't people just do what they say they are going to do? Why does life have to be so difficult?

I stood up very slowly and looked him in the eyes; then I held my hand out to shake his hand. He reached his hand out and we begin shaking hands. I told him that I understand that the military's needs come first. I told him, "Since the military's needs have been met, maybe I can get what I need now". He asked me what I needed. I told him, "I could show you better then I could tell you". I pulled him towards me and used my free hand to punch him in the face. He tried to swing back, and I started beating on him like he was a punching bag. He crumbled to the floor. Just as I was getting ready to smash his face in with my boot, I heard the door to his office open. I turned to look to see who it was. It was two Law Enforcement policemen with their 38- revolvers pointing at me. Oh shit, How in the hell am I going to get myself out of this now?

They were standing there looking like they were shaking in their boots. The policemen told me, "Stop, we are authorized to use deadly force on you if we have to". They looked like new recruits; they must have been about 18 or 19 years old. I had on my uniform, so they knew that I was a Security Policeman. I was hoping they would give me some slack on this situation.

I wanted to get back home so I could talk to my wife before I got put in jail. I told them that it was not my fault, and I started walking towards the door. They shouted for me to stop, but I just did not feel like going to jail before I could speak to my wife. I kept on walking towards the police officers with my hands up in the air. While I was walking, I was trying to explain to them that I just wanted to go home and talk to my wife. I was hoping that they would understand.

They begin to back up slowly as I walked towards them.

They still had their guns pointed towards me. I was making slow cautious steps. I didn't want to make any sudden movements. I still had my hands up in the air. They could see that I wasn't carrying a weapon. This was all taking place in a matter of seconds, but it seemed like forever to me. Everything was going fine until my supervisor woke up. He ran across the room and jumped on my back. He was trying to choke me. I threw him down and raised my hand to punch him. That is when I heard a gunshot.

After I heard the gunshot it seemed to get real quiet in the room. My mind seemed to be floating in a dream world. I felt pain burning through my body. Then numbness can over me. All of the sudden I could see myself lying on the floor in the office as if I was outside my body. I could not do anything to help myself off the floor. I could only look at myself lying there bleeding. I felt like a feather being lifted slowly by a light summer breeze.

A bullet had stroke me in the right arm and traveled up my arm along the bone until it exploded out the back of my neck. The blood from the neck wound was causing me to choke until I felt like I could not breathe anymore. Blood was coming out of my mouth and ears. I thought this was death finally coming to get me. I didn't feel any fear or pain anymore. I have been expecting this for a long time. I have always encouraged death to come visit me….

In my mind: it was like I was drifting through the times of my life until I found myself walking down Jackson Street again. I was happy walking down Jackson Street. I grew up on Jackson Street, I'm use to being here. It was dark and the only light I could see was on some porch down the street. I knew if I made it to that light, everything would be alright. I thought the light would be my safety. It was taking so long to get to the light that I started to get scared. I started running towards it, but it was almost like I was running in mud. It was taking forever, but I was getting closer. I could hear some voices coming from the front porch. The voices were saying something, but I could not understand what they were saying to me. I started running faster toward the voices. I was getting very tired. I was thinking about how nice it would be to sit down on that porch.

All of a sudden I felt a sharp pain in the back of my leg and I fell to the ground. I reach down to grab my leg to see what happened. I was shocked to see my dog, "Tiger" holding my leg with his teeth. This was confusing to me because my dog had been dead for a long time. Cautiously I started petting Tiger, and he started jumping around with happiness. Now I could see who was on the porch; it was my dead father and brother, "Harry". They also had been dead for quite some time.

This was really turning into some fucked up nightmare. Who in the hell am I going to see next? I started walking towards them and Tiger bit me in my other leg. He would not let go of it no matter how hard I attempted to get him off. He was just too strong for me. Before I knew it, he was dragging me away from the porch. I could not figure out why. I was begging Tiger to stop, but he just wouldn't listen. I was really scared now because I thought he was pulling me away from safety. I could hear my father and brother encouraging me to come to the porch, but I could not fight him off my leg. I felt isolated and alone. I felt like I would surely die if I did not get to that porch....

The porch light and the voices were getting further and further away. Then there was silent and complete darkness surrounding me. I couldn't feel Tiger on my leg anymore. Then I felt him lick my face and I tried to find him, but he was gone. I thought I was finally dead. Is this what it's like when you die? I was tired and just wanted to sleep for a while. I felt like I had just fought for the heavyweight championship and lost. While I was lying there unable to move, I heard a noise. It sounded like someone was crying. I opened my eyes and saw Star sitting next to me crying and holding my hand. She had her head down reading a Bible out loud.

I never saw her read a Bible before, so I knew I had to be dead. I did not see my son or daughter with her, and I tried to say something to her, but no words would come out my mouth.

Finally I squeezed her hand, and she looked up at me with a surprised look on her face. She reached over to kiss me and ran out the room screaming for the doctor. The doctor looked at me and welcomed me back. He told me that I had everyone worried for a while. He said that I was very lucky to be alive.

Star told me that I had been in a coma for a month after I got shot, and the doctors did not think I was going to survive. She told me that Mrs. Woods and Robin had been by to see me almost everyday. I guess it just was not my time to die yet; God must have had another plan for me. After going through many weeks of therapy for my arm and my neck, I was able to go home. The military decided to drop the charges against me. The Base Commander owed me a favor for saving his son's life when I first came to the base. Thank God the Commander owed me a favor. The military gave me a general discharge. This was a lot better than going to jail with a dishonorable discharge.

I had been in the military so long, almost ten years, and I felt uncomfortable being a civilian again. I had gotten used to wearing a uniform and keeping my hair short. I felt different not having my dog and rifle with me. I had to figure out what my next move was going to be for my family. Some military people get out and work for the post office. I thought that's what I would try, since the post office has a preference for prior military people. The post office paid good money, and that's what I needed if I was going to support a wife and two children legally.

I did not want to use any of the drug money that I had buried to survive because it was dirty money. If you play in dirt, then you will get dirty. I just had to see what was in God's plan for me. I learned a lot from being in the military and I know it saved my life in many ways. If not for the military, I would have probably been murdered or put in prison by now. This is so ironic because the same thing almost happened at the end of my military time. I guess life is funny like that. I'm not sure why God keeps saving my life, but I know there is something he wants me to do. I have a feeling that it is going to be revealed very soon…. ***“Believe in Change”***

Chapter 28

Trying to do the Right Thing

A year later in (1987) and with no response from the post office, I was starting to get a little worried. My unemployment was running out and most of my savings was gone. Star was not working either; it was not because we were not looking for jobs. No one seemed to be hiring, and things were getting real tight on money. I did not want to use that drug money to survive, but I did not know what else to do. I certainly was not going to sit back and watch my family suffer if they did not have to. No matter how hard I tried to stay out of the drug game, I always seemed to be drawn back into it. I figured if I was not supposed to get back in the game, God would have helped me find a job. Enough is enough; it is time to go back to what I know best…

My plan was to sale all the drugs that I had left and get out of the business for good. It shouldn't take me too long to sale the drugs. I could just take the money and live off of that until I found a job. But I want to make enough money so that I will never have to worry about working again. I'll take all the money I make and put it into legitimate businesses someday. I went back to the Air Force Base, dug up my drugs and put all my drug money together. I rented a storage place to hide the money and the drugs. Since I had been out of the business for a while, I took my time getting started. I had to see who my competition was, so I could make a plan to handle them. Selling drugs is about making money, not making war, although sometimes you have to do both.

After being in the drug game for a couple of months and making money again, I met two guys that were deep into the drug game. I was looking for a better drug connection, and they had one. I met them through a girlfriend of Star, and things started to take off. They were getting their cocaine straight from (Miami Beach, Florida), and it did not get much better than that. The guy named, "Brew" is from (New Orleans), and "Ricardo" is from (Virginia). Ricardo was dating one of Star's girlfriends, and her name was "Blake". Ricardo is the one who had the Florida connection, and it was a good one.

We were able to get a kilo of cocaine for $10,000 each if we went to Miami to pick it up. If we wanted the cocaine delivered, it would cost $15,000 a piece. For the $15,000 a kilo we had to drive the money down to Miami first. We figured that it was safer to have the cocaine delivered because we only had to worry about getting caught driving with a lot of money in the car. People do not normally get put in jail for carrying a lot of money in their car. The police just steal the money...

The plan was to purchase an old car to drive the money down to Miami Beach. We did not only give the money to the connection, but we also left the car there so he could bring the cocaine back in the same car. The connection's name is "Lewis"; he was a Cuban living in (Coconut Grove). Lewis was a friend of Ricardo's brother, who was currently doing prison time for drug trafficking. He recruited Ricardo to continue what his older brother had started in the drug business. Ricardo liked to smoke weed everyday, and I considered that a weakness and probably the reason he had not tried to expand his business to a larger level. Ricardo has been in the business for three years and was still only selling one kilo a month. I believe that it was the weed that stole his ambitions, or maybe he was just too scared to get any bigger.

My other partner, Brew was an honorably discharged army sergeant. He got out to work in the shipyards as an electrician. He worked a few years there and then he hurt his back. Brew received a monetary settlement from the shipyard company and decided to invest his money into the drug business. Brew was the only one in his family who had not been to prison so far. Brew's weakness was that he liked to snort cocaine and would fuck anything that lay there long enough. I had heard that Brew would wake up in the morning and instead of having a cup of coffee, he would snort a couple lines of cocaine to get him started. He still was able to handle his business, so it did not bother me that he got high off cocaine everyday. I know eventually that will be his downfall. I guess we all have our flaws.

We all got together for a meeting at Brew's condo and decided to put $50,000 a piece into the first investment. That meant we could get ten kilos of cocaine for $15,000 each if our connection delivered the drugs to Virginia. In 1987, this was the beginning of the "Kilo Club" in Virginia. The name was my idea because I thought our organization needed a street name. When we make enough money to purchase a building, then we will use the name "Key Club" in place of Kilo Club. We did not want to just let everyone know what we were doing. The only way that a person could become a member of the Kilo Club was that the person must sell at least one kilo of cocaine a month.

The best part of the membership for us was the fact that the kilo had to come from us. The reason it was beneficial to join the Kilo Club was the fact that no one could beat our prices in Virginia. After one year, the business had twenty members who all worked for us. The only reason we did not have more is because we did not accept just anyone who wanted to join. We investigated everyone who wanted to be a member to make sure they were right for the Club. We would not accept anyone who had been convicted of any drug violation, no matter how long ago it had happened. Potential members were only allowed to contact us once. If we decided to give them a membership, we contacted them. Anyone who did not abide by that rule would be considered disrespectful and a possible undercover policemen.

At the meetings with potential club members, it was explained how important it was to not try to contact the club again. I decided that only an enemy would do that, and all of our enemies should be destroyed. I never met with anyone other than Ricardo and Brew because I figured the more people who knew me, the more opportunity for the police finding out about me. I did not need the fame and the glory; all I wanted was the money. Brew and Ricardo respected my wishes about not wanting to meet anyone new. My leadership role with the club just happened naturally. I guess I had more of a vision then they did. Maybe it had something to do with them getting high all the time. If someone found out about me, I knew exactly who to kill, and that would be Ricardo or Brew.

If you did become a member of the Club we would give them their first kilo of cocaine. They would have thirty days to pay us $30,000 or we went looking for them. Our profit was $15,000 dollars on each kilo. We were grossing $600,000 a month. We had twenty kilos being sold every month. We had to put half our income back into the business just to supply our club members with more cocaine. That left us with about $300,000 to split three ways. This gave us $100,000 a piece to do anything we wanted to do with it. I preferred to keep a low profile, but not Brew and Ricardo; they both had brand new cars and spent money all over town. I convinced Brew to invest some of his money into a carpet store in (Newport News). By doing that, it would at least look like he should have that kind of money to spend around town. The sooner we put the money into legitimate businesses, the less likely the police will be looking at us.

I explained to Brew that he could keep buying the same rug inventory every month, and it would look like he was running a legitimate business. Once Brew filled the store with new rugs, he then could use his own drug money to keep purchasing the same rugs over and over again. He could have someone come to his store and buy some rugs and Brew could keep them in storage until the end of the month. He then could put the rugs back in the store for sale again, plus it was a good way to launder that dirty drug money. This worked so well that he opened up two more stores a couple of months later, one in (Hampton) and (Norfolk).

I encourage Ricardo to go into the used car business. He basically did the same thing as Brew did with his inventory. The cars Ricardo bought were the same cars we used to deliver the money to Miami. The cars that we were sending down to Miami only cost us about $2,000, but inside the trunk in a secret compartment was $300,000 in cash. That was a very expensive car if something went wrong. Ricardo had three car lots, mostly used cars on the lots. He would just buy a car from one lot and put it on one of the other lots so no one would see the same car sitting on the same lot all the time. Once our man in Miami delivered the cocaine, we would put the car back on the car lot again to sell. Our man from Miami would get on a plane and fly back to Miami to wait to hear from us again.

Lewis first language was Spanish, so I decided to learn a little Spanish. I did not let anyone know that I was learning to speak Spanish because I thought knowing how to speak Spanish could be an advantage for me. I knew that I would be dealing with a lot of Spanish speaking people in the drug game, and I needed every edge that I could get. This was a life or death business, and I did not want to be killed because I misunderstood some important details of a business conversation. I decided to go to college and study business management. I wanted to learn more about legitimate businesses. Drugs are easy to sell, but managing money is a different story. I knew that the more I knew about business, the more my chances of succeeding would be. After a year of business management classes, it was time for me to create more ways of laundering my drug money.

I started looking for a building so we could open up a club to sell liquor and food. I found a building in Hampton that used to be a bar, and I talked to the owner about leasing it. The owner was a retired businessman who ran a bar there for 20 years. The bar has been closed for the last two years because of the owner's health problems. It was a nice sized building with a bar and a dance floor already in place. The owner of the bar agreed to lease the building to me for $1500 a month for two years. I talked to my partners, and they agreed that the plan was a good idea. The business was going to be called the "Key Club", (A.K.A. The Kilo Club). We would be taking memberships fees at $500 a year; at least that is what we told people that we did not know. Having a Club that sold liquor would be a great way to launder money.

The best thing about having a Club instead of just a bar is that we could stay open all night long because we were a "Private Club". We had to do some renovations, like a new dance floor and some painting inside the building. We also needed to purchase an alcohol license because one did not come with the building. I put Brew in charge of getting the license because he said that he knew someone who wanted to sell theirs. Brew said that man wanted $50,000 for the license, and we agreed that was a reasonable price so we gave Brew the money. The liquor license only allowed us to sell liquor, but not any wine or champagne in the club. I figured we could get a winery license later as business got better for us. I was beginning to have visions of Key Clubs all over Virginia. I can see my way out of the drug business now. This is going to take me to the next level. I'm going to make all this money and move my family to the beach to retire. I' am also going to buy Mrs. Woods and the girls a big house on the beach.

The building also had a nice kitchen in it to cook and sell food. None of my other partners wanted to deal with selling food. I decided to fix up the kitchen and make it my own personal project. I told Brew and Ricardo if I got the kitchen open that all the profits from the selling of food would be all mine. I had to pay the health inspector $2,000 to give me a license to sell food from the club. I was only planning on selling some fried fish and chicken dinners from the club. I thought about asking Mrs. Woods to cook for me, but I wanted to keep her as far away from this life as possible. I decided to keep it simple because drunken people just want to eat something.

We decided to start interviewing for some waitresses and bouncers to work at the club. We wanted some young girls with looks and nice big asses to keep the men coming back. We purchased little skimpy outfits for the women to wear to help attract the men. When the women put the outfits on, they looked like black playboy bunnies. I even gave Robin a job at the Club because she had a nice big ass on her. Robin was out of school and over eighteen years old. I wasn't going to give her the job at first, but I didn't want her to be mad at me. I wasn't sure how Robin would act in a Club full of drinking men. If Mrs. Woods knew what she had to wear, I knew she would have not let her work there for me. I knew Robin liked showing off her body because she always wore some short and tight clothes. I knew that I could count on her to be there for me if I needed her to watch my back.

I remember when Robin was sixteen years old, me and Star decided to take her to the N.C.O. Club to celebrate her birthday. We knew she was too young to get in the club, but Star put a lot of makeup on her to make her look older. Star bought her a sexy grownup dress, ear rings, and high heels. I told Robin not to say anything when we go to the door of the Club. I knew if she opened her mouth then everyone would know she was sixteen years old. She still had baby teeth in her mouth and she talked dumb like a teenager. When we got to there, I slipped the man at the door a hundred dollars. He walked us all the way to our table. I order some champagne to celebrate. While waiting for it to come, I told Robin what I expected of her.

I said Robin, "You can fast dance all you want, but there will be no slow dancing at all". Robin smiled at me with her little baby teeth and said, "Okay big brother, you can count on me". The champagne came to the table and I gave a toast to Robin. She swallowed the whole glass in ten seconds. I told her that she better take it easy before she gets drunk. She just smiled and asked for another glass full. I figured why not, this is her birthday.

A guy came to the table and asked Robin to dance. She

looked at me as to get approval. I nodded my head yes and watched her as she walked to the dance floor. This was the first time that I took a good look at her since Star put all that makeup on her. Robin looked like a grown lady. No one could tell that she was only 16 years old. I couldn't even tell from looking at her. I looked at Star and said, "I think we might have creative a monster tonight". Star laughed and said, "She going to be alright".

Just I soon as I turned my back, Robin was out on the dance floor slow dancing with some 25 year old nigger. I jumped up out of my seat and walked out to where they were dancing. I walk around them about five times until I got Robin attention. I leaned over and whisper in Robin ear and said, "You don't want to see me act a fool do you?" I said, "If I see you slow dancing again, I'm going to kill you and whoever you are dancing with".

That was the last time she slowed danced that night. That's my little sister, no one going to be grinding up on her like a whore. Robin had a lot of fun that night, but I never took her to the N.C.O. Club again. It felt good watching her have a good time. I hope Mrs. Woods never finds out about me taking her out. Robin wasn't ready for the club, I probably should have taking her to "Bush Gardens" (the amusement park) like other sixteen year olds. I love her; she will always be my weakness. There isn't much I wouldn't do for Mrs. Woods and the girls.

We planned on opening the club up on just Thursdays through Sundays from 10:00pm to 6:00am. Thursday through Sundays was the main days that people felt like going out and drinking in Hampton, Virginia. We hired a DJ from Philly, who was the brother-in-law of Ricardo. He brought that "Philly Swing" to the club, which made the club different from the rest of the clubs in Virginia. The (Fire Code) listed a 300-person capacity, but that would not be a problem because we did not expect that many people to show up at the Club on any given night.

It did not take Brew long to get the liquor license, only a couple of weeks. He put the liquor license on the wall behind the bar and everything was working out the way we planned it. In the next couple weeks, we should be able to officially open up (The New Key Club). Hopefully, this will be one of many in Virginia. The goal is to become a legitimate businessman and eventually get out of the drug business. It looks like the plan is working. Maybe I have finally got rid of that fucking Jackson Street curse. Milk and honey, here I come….

"Believe in Change"

Chapter 29

Grand Opening, the Key Club

One day I went to Mrs. Woods and asked her would she make me a white silk suit for the grand opening of the Key Club. She said yes, and all I had to do was buy the material for the suit. She had my suit ready in a couple of days, and I gave her $500, even though she did not want any money. I was planning on being the best dressed person on the night of the grand opening. I grew up in poverty and never had many clothes to wear, so I promised myself at a young age that I would never have that problem again.

My partners went into the car and rug business, and I went into the clothing business. I opened up three stores and called them "Ron's Closet One, Two, and Three". The stores were located in Hampton, Newport News and Norfolk. There was a good reason for the names of the stores; all the stores had my personal clothes hanging on the racks. Everything in the stores was my size only and nothing else. Even all the shoes were a size 13 to fit my feet.

I had fulfilled another one of my Jackson Street dreams. I remember being in one of the stores and watching some potential customers go through all the clothes trying to find something in their sizes. One of the customers came to me and asked me why everything was the same size; I told him that we sold out all the other sizes. I told him to check back next week when we received another shipment from New York City. I had so many clothes that it made sense for me to open up clothing stores to store them. It was a great way for me to launder that dirty drug money that I was making. Some people might think that I'm a little obsessed with clothes. Buying clothes is therapy for me, it makes me feel good. Unless you have walked in my raggedy, cardboard sole shoes before, then you would never understand me. Everyone on Jackson Street understood because they lived it….

It was a warm night in Hampton, on the night of the grand opening; it had to be about 95-degrees. We decided to have our grand opening on a Saturday night at 9:00pm, instead of having it on a Thursday night. We were going to be open from 9:00pm until 6:00am. By law only Club members can be in the Club after 2:00am. Just in case the police came in the club to check, we issued temporary memberships to all our customers at the door. We charged everyone ten dollars at the door to get in the club. If we were able to fill the Club to its capacity, we would make $3,000 just at the door. That is why I decided to work at the door, to keep my eye on the money the door made. I did not trust anyone else to hold our money. Business isn't about trust, it's about business. Money is one of the biggest temptations in the world. I believe it will turn a preacher into a thief if he is around it long enough….

Star and I went to Club together after taking the kids over to Mrs. Wood's house for the night. We opened up at 9:00pm, and nobody was waiting to come into the Club. I started to get a little worried. At 11:00pm we had twenty people in the club and things were moving real slow. 12:00am comes around and there were about seventy-five people drinking and dancing in the club. People just kept on coming and by 2:00am we were filled to capacity, I had to start turning people away. People came from Norfolk, Virginia Beach, Suffolk, Newport News and Hampton. Everyone was dress to kill, especially me.

Instead of the people that I had to turn away going home, they just stayed out in the parking lot. They were still going to wait to get in. I decided to let another 100 people in. Now we had 400 people in a 300 capacity club. I remember hoping that the "Fire Marshall" would not show up to check us for fire code violations. We got through our first night without any problems. I was very happy about that because there was a bunch of drunken people leaving the club that morning.

We made a lot of money that night; we made $4,000 at the door, I made $3,000 at the kitchen and we made $6,000 at the bar. That Monday we opened up a business account at the bank to deposit the money into. We put the money in all three of our names because the money was legitimate. We had nothing to hide from the police. It felt good to make money that we did not have to hide from the police. This was a great Grand Opening for the Key Club. I hope there are more great days to come….

That next week we opened up on a Thursday night at 9:00pm. From now on Thursdays will be our first night of business. We did not have as many people come out that night, but we did have 150 people drinking and dancing. I thought that was pretty good for a Thursday night, considering the weekend did not really start until Friday. We made $1,500 at the door, $1,200 at the kitchen and $4,000 selling alcohol. If the Key Club continued to do this good, I could begin to see my way out of the drug business. I planned on continuing what I was doing in the drug business for at least one more year and hopefully I would be going completely legitimate. I'm not sure what Brew and Ricardo plans are for the future. I can't worry about them.

Although we did not have winery license, we decided to start selling champagne at the club. We could buy a case of good champagne for $75.00 a bottle and sell it for $150.00 each. We were able to double our money. That deal was hard to turn down even if it was illegal for us to sell. Besides we needed to have something special for the "Big Ballers" to show off. We wanted to have something to make them feel special. We only sold the champagne at the V.I.P. tables at first and eventually we started selling champagne to anyone who could afford to pay $150.00 a bottle. We sold about ten bottles a week and sometimes more.

Everything was going great until one night after the club closed; the money from the alcohol sales was missing. No one seemed to know anything about it. I had an idea who might have stolen the money, but I could not prove it. I knew that the bartender named, "Troy" had a drug problem. I could tell just by the way he acted. He always seemed to be sweaty and edgy all the time. That night I would not let anyone who worked at the club leave. I wanted to question everyone about the stolen money. I was very calm about the whole situation. At least that is what my employees saw on my face. Deep down inside I was very pissed off. I couldn't believe someone had the nerve to steal our money.

If it was just a couple of hundred dollars, I would not have been so upset, but I knew there had to be at least $7,000 to $10,000 in the cash register bag. I questioned Robin first because I didn't want her to worry. I didn't want her to think that I thought she had something to do with the stolen money. She told me that Troy had the money last. She said, "After that I did not see the money anymore". Robin said, "His girlfriend left the bar before he was done working and she usually waited for him".

The only reason Troy even got his job was because he was a cousin of one of our members. He was a low-level street dealer, who did not qualify to be a legitimate member of the Key Club on his own. I didn't want the word to get out that anyone could rip the Key Club off , so I had to do something fast. When I questioned Troy, he was very evasive with his answers and could not sit still in his chair. I told him that I did not think he had anything to do with the stolen money. I did not want him to think that I was on to him and his fucking girlfriend. I wanted him to think that he had nothing to worry about. I was so sure that he had something to do with the stolen money that I felt like shooting in the head right there in the office. I knew that would be a dumb thing to do, especially considering how good the Key Club was doing. There is a time and a place for everything….

That following day, when Troy came to work, Brew and I went to his house. We didn't go until after his girlfriend showed up at the Club. We sat outside the house for about an hour to see if anyone was at home. We did not see any movement, so we went to the rear of the house. We heard a dog barking in the house, so we looked through the back window but we could not see anything. We knew there was a dog, but we did not know what kind or how big the dog was. I told Brew to get his gun ready because I was going to break the window so I could reach inside to open it up. I put some tape on the window, so that when I broke the glass it would not make to much noise. I knew if I put my hand into the window, that I would probably get it bitten off by the dog. I grabbed a tree branch that was on the ground and put it into the window first. Nothing happened so reached my hand in and unlocked it.

Once I unlocked the window I saw the dog running towards the window. I opened the window just enough for the dog's head to fit outside of it. The dog stuck his head out the window, trying to bite me. I wrapped a rope around the dog's neck and choked the dog until I was sure that it was dead. The dog was a Doberman pincher, weighing about ninety pounds and full of fire, so it took about two minutes to get the dog incapacitated. I took the rope from around the dog's neck and let the dog drop to the floor of the house. When the dog hit the floor, that's when I realized I was still hearing barking in the house.

The next thing I knew another dog reached his head out the window and bit into my arm. I was surprised, but I did not want to make any noise while the dog was biting into my flesh. I didn't want to do anything to wake the neighbors up. These fucking dogs were already making enough fucking noise. I'm sure the neighbors must be use to hearing them barking. We had to do something fast because the dog was biting my arm. I was trying to stay calm as possible. This was hard because I had a ninety pound dog biting the fuck out of my arm….

Brew pointed his gun at the dog, but I told him not to shoot. I didn't want to take a chance on how well he could shoot his gun. He might miss the dog and hit me with the fucking bullet. Plus a gunshot would definitely wake up the whole neighborhood. I told Brew to use the rope to choke the dog. Once Brew started choking the dog, the dog stopped biting my arm. After a couple of minutes the dog was dead. We could finally do what we came to do. There was a little blood dripping from my arm, but I was not worried about that.

We had wasted enough time dealing with these dogs. Luckily no one heard all that noise. I let Brew climb through the window first to make sure there were no more unexpected surprises in the house. Brew came back to the window and said the house was empty. I climbed through the window very cautiously. We started going through the house room by room looking for our money. Finally, I looked underneath the mattress and there it was, all $8,000 just laying there. I grabbed a pillow case and stuffed the money inside of it, and we took the money out to the car. I told Brew that I needed to go back inside to make sure I did not leave anything behind in the house. I told Brew to stay in the car with the money and make sure no one came to the house. Brew didn't know it, but had a plan.

When I returned back to the house I unhooked the gas line to the dryer and the stove. I blew out all the pilot lights and turned the gas on. I made sure all the windows were closed in the house. I didn't want any of the gas to leak outside the house. I did not tell Brew about my plan because I knew that someone would probably die if the house blew up. I did not want anyone to be able to say that they knew for sure I had something to do with a murder. I knew Troy and his girlfriend smoked a lot of cigarettes. I figured there would be a good chance they would be smoking when they opened the door of their house.

When I got into the car Brew asked what took so long. He was getting ready to come back to the house to make sure I was alright. I was glad he did not come to house looking for me, because he was also a cigarette smoker. It would have been a dumb way to die if he would have come back into the house with a cigarette hanging out his mouth. Brew wanted to go straight back to the club and blow Troy's head off, but I told him to calm down. We needed to wait and do it the right way so no one would know it was us. I told him that we did not want any fingers pointing at the Key Club or us. I told him that Troy deserved to die, but he was not worth us doing 20 years in prison. I told Brew to act normal when we got back to the club so no one would think we knew anything.

When we got to the club I decided that we had better sneak in the back entrance, so no one would know that we were out of the club that night. Hopefully they would think that we were just back in the office taking care of some business. We both went out into the Club and mingled with the crowd, being sociable as we normally do. After about an hour, Brew and Ricardo and I sat down in the office and discussed how we found the money in Troy's house. Ricardo was not surprised because we all knew that Troy had something to do with the robbery. We could not prove it, so we had to do something about it. I told Ricardo that we were not going to do anything about it right now, but we will take care of it later. I was thinking that hopefully his house will blow up and we can close the case on that asshole Troy….

When the Club closed that night, I got all the employees together and apologized to them for accusing them of stealing money. I gave each one of the employees an extra fifty dollars in cash before they went home that night. I wanted to let them know that I was sincere. When I offered that money to Troy, he said that he did not want the money. He said, "I' am just happy that it's all over with". I handed the fifty dollars to his girlfriend and she did not hesitate to take it out of my hand. That greedy bitch still was taking money out of my pocket.

It was probably her idea to steal from the Key Club in the first place. A smile came to my face. I noticed they both had cigarettes in their mouths as they walked out the door of the club. I wanted to follow them to their house, just to see their house blow up around them. But I thought it would be smarter to go straight home that night. I got home around 1:00am and put a bandage on my arm. After that I went straight to bed because I was mentally and physically tired.

I was still asleep at 12:00pm that afternoon when Star came running into the bedroom shouting at me to turn the news on. She asked me what happened to my arm and I told her that I cut my arm on some broken glass at the club. She said that a family of four's home had blown up and caught four other houses on fire. The news said the explosion occurred at 6:30am and the whole family was believed to be dead. The news was saying that Troy's girlfriend and their two children lived in the house. Star asked me was that the same one who is a bartender at the club. I told her that I think it is the same person from the club.

Troy was 27 years old and his girlfriend was 30 years old. Their little boy was seven-years old, and the little girl was five years old. The other four families whose houses caught on fire were able to get out of their houses in time. They had no injuries. The news was saying that there must have been a gas leak in the house that blew up. However the Fire Department had to investigate why there was a leak in the first place. The explosion was so powerful that there was hardly anything to investigate; everything was in little pieces including the bodies of the family in the house.

I went to the funeral that next week with Star to show my respect for one of my employees. It was a closed casket funeral for all four family members, I really doubt if anything was in any of the caskets because the explosion was so powerful. I saw the club member named, "Steady", who was Troy's cousin. He was the one who got Troy a job. Because he was a legitimate member, I hired Troy. He saw me and suspiciously walked in another direction. I thought that was a little strange because he would normally say hello to me. I wondered if he thought I had something to do with his cousin's death. Maybe he had something to do with Troy stealing our money. I need to reconsider dealing with him….

I told Brew and Ricardo to watch their backs because I did not trust Steady anymore. He may try to retaliate for his cousin's death because he might think we have something to do with it. A few weeks later the word on the streets was that the

Key Club had something to do with Troy's death. No one had any proof because only God and I knew what really happened that night. I did not feel bad because of what happened to Troy and his girlfriend. It wasn't personal, it was business. I did feel bad about the children getting hurt. Children were not supposed to get hurt in this business. I hope God can forgive me for that. If I knew there would be kids in the house, I wouldn't have done it. I knew sooner or later the police would come around to ask question's about Troy's death. I wasn't worried about getting caught. I was worrying more about what God was thinking….

The police had already started questioning my employees, but they did not really know anything. I was sure that if they did know something, they would be too scared to talk anyway. The police came to me at my house a few weeks later to ask me questions about money being stolen at the club. I told them that it was all a big mistake and that we found the money. I do not think the police believed me, but I knew they could not prove any wrong doing. I was not happy with all this negative attention that the Key Club was receiving from the police and the newspapers. I knew it was time to be very careful about everything we did in the Club and the drug business. I did not know if I could count on my partners being as careful. I was not comfortable with the fact that if my partners messed up, I could end up dead or in prison. If this feeling doesn't go away soon, then maybe I will have to go away. I always went with my instincts and if something doesn't feel right, then it probably is not right. Things have changed and I have to adapt to these changes…. ***"Believe in Change"***

Chapter 30

Putting it all in the ground

Final Chapter

A few days later after seeing Steady at the funeral, I decided to have a meeting with Brew and Ricardo about whether to continue doing business with Steady. We decided that it would be in our best interest to stop dealing with him. I just didn't believe he could be trusted anymore. Brew met with Steady and told him that his services were no longer needed. He was not very happy with that and stormed out of the meeting. After the meeting he began making threats against the Key Club on the streets. He was telling everyone how he was going to take the Key Club down and how he would be running Virginia. The Club was so powerful; there was no real chance of that happening. In this business we had to take every threat seriously. If we continued to take care of business and not make any mistakes, we would be fine.

Several months passed and we were making a lot of money. We were thinking about opening up another Club in Virginia Beach. One night at the club, it was almost time to close; Robin came to me with watery eyes. She said she had something important to tell me. I had no idea what she was going to tell me. I just knew she was going to tell me someone had died. After she regains her composure she begins to tell me the news. She told me that Star had moved out of the house that night while I was at the club. She also said that Ricardo and his girlfriend helped her move. Star had told Robin all about it a few days ago, but begged her not to say anything to me. Robin kept it in as long as she could. She just couldn't see her brother going home to an empty house. That would have been a fucked up surprise for me.

I was shocked because I did not know things had gotten that bad between me and Star. I had been spending a lot of time running the club and my drug business and I figured she understood. What bothered me even more is the fact that my partner's girlfriend get him mixed up in my family business. I guess he did not expect me to find out that he had anything to do with it. That motherfucker shouldn't have done that. After all I have done to help him make more money. Where is the loyalty? I won't be able to forgive him for this. I was wondering why Ricardo and his girlfriend were not at the Club tonight. I thanked Robin and told her not to worry about it because I was going to be alright.

When I got home that morning at 7:00am, the only thing Star had left in the house was a bed and one television. I had $25,000 in cash and ten ounces of cocaine hidden in a safe. Both were missing even though the safe was still locked. Star must have somehow found out the combination to the safe. I found out the next day after I woke up, that she had moved into Ricardo's and his girlfriend's apartment. Their apartment was only four houses away. I was not happy being that close to Star. This would make too easy for her to come over to my apartment and fuck with me. I needed to do something about that.

After further investigation, I found out the reason they helped her move into their apartment. So they could get out of their lease. They wanted to move into their new house. That cheap bastard could have kept his apartment and still moved into his new house. I'm starting to realize how dumb this motherfucker is now. A few days later I walked over to Star's apartment to talk to her. It took me that long to calm down. I also wanted to see my two children and make sure they were alright. She explained to me that she just was not happy with the way things were going between us. She said that she knew I would not let her leave. I told her that I would have moved out if she needed to be by herself. She said, "I know if I would have talked to you about it, I would have changed my mind". I felt sorry for her; she really seemed sincere in what she was saying. I'm starting to wonder now, will I ever be able to change. Should I continue to believe in change? Doubts are beginning to cloud my thoughts again…

I told her that I understood, then I asked her what happened to the money and drugs in the safe. She told me that she did not know who took anything from the safe. She said that she didn't even know the combination to the safe. I knew she was lying, but I did not tell her that, I just walked out the house quietly. I guess my desire to make money overshadowed my wife and children's happiness. If I knew my marriage was going to end up like this, then I would have done something about it. All that money did not mean anything to me if I did not have my wife and children to enjoy it with.

It is hard to win in this business because it seems if you do what you have to do to make the money; you have to pay with some kind of loss in your life. Like my family. It seemed to me that you can never have both and I finally understood that. I would have given all the money back if I thought that would help me get my family back. I was sure that there was a hole in Star's heart that I could never repair. I knew in my mind that the best thing I could do for Star and the kids was to leave them alone. Drugs and a family do not mix and I'm finding that out the hard way….

A few weeks later I moved out of my apartment to live with Brew. He had a big three bedroom condo and he was living there all by himself. This seemed like a smart thing to do until I found another place of my own. I did not want to stay in my apartment because of all the memories of my wife and children. Plus I did not want to live that close to Star. The problem living with Brew was the fact that he liked to party all the time. Brew would wake up in the morning and snort cocaine like he was having a cup of coffee. He had wild parties almost everyday in the condo and before I knew it, I was right there partying with him. We had so many girls coming in and out the condo that I could not even remember their names.

One night at the Club a couple of months later, I looked through the peak hole of the front door and saw this beautiful girl standing there. I opened the door and before I knew it, I had the barrel of a gun in my mouth. The girl was nowhere to be found. The man who had the gun in my mouth said, "I am "D.E.A." and you're under arrest for selling alcohol illegally". Ten other agents rushed in behind him. All hell broke lose in the club. All the people in the club started getting rid of all the personal cocaine and weapons they had on them. They were throwing the cocaine across the club. Some of their bags of cocaine were busting on impact on the walls and floor. Causing the inside of the Club to look like it was snowing. You could hardly see because there was so much cocaine in the air. Even the ones who did not get high were getting high from the cocaine filled air. What a fucking nightmare this was turning into....

The Agents turned all the lights on and announced to the club that anyone who did not work at the club should leave right now. The Agents had a list of the employees at the door. They were making sure no one who worked at the club got pass them. It only took ten minutes to get all the customers out of the club. They were moving fast to get to the exit. All this time the D.E.A. Agent still had his gun in my mouth. I could not even ask this ass hole what in the fuck was he looking for. Finally he took the gun out of my mouth and took me to a table. He sat me down with everyone else. The more that I looked at the Agent, the more familiar he looked to me. After a few more minutes it finally came to me how I knew that face. He was the same motherfucker who came to the club and ordered bottles of champagne. That sneaky bitch....

The Agent walked over to the bar and grabbed the liquor license off the wall and threw it down, shattering the frame on the floor in front of me. I kept my cool and just sat in my chair looking across at Brew, hoping he stayed calm too. Brew looked back at me for a second and then put his head down to look at the broken liquor license. The Agent said, “The only thing legit about that license was that it was written on real paper”. I told him that can’t be true because I had a receipt showing the Key Club paid $50,000 for that license. The Agent looked at me with a smile on his face and said, “I don’t care if you had five receipts, the license is a fake”. The Agent said the main reason that we raided your club, is the fact the club was selling champagne without having a winery license. We just recently found out about that fake license.

He said, “Everyone who is an owner is under arrest for selling alcohol and wine without a liquor license. The employees are under arrest for working in an illegal establishment that sells alcohol and wine to its customers”. The employees started saying that they did not know anything about the license being illegal. The Agent told them, “You will have your day in court so shut the fuck up”. I told all the employees not to worry about a thing because this was a big mistake. Of course I didn’t believe a word I just said to them. The police must have something or why would they be here. They can’t be that fucking dumb….

The Agents took the names of all the employees and wrote them citations and then let them go home. Since Brew, Ricardo and I were the owners; we were arrested and taken to jail that night. The Agents did searched the Club with the hopes of finding drugs. We never kept any drugs at our place of business. The drugs that they did find came from the patrons who threw them. The Agents questioned us for about eight hours. They asked us questions about drug activities and Troy’s death. They also questioned us on every other crime that occurred in Virginia in the last twelve months. They even went at far as saying they had witnesses to most of the crimes.

I knew they were lying because we did not leave witnesses. Finally they let me make a phone call and Star came to the jail and bailed us out. We were all on a $50,000 bail, but we only had to pay 10% of that, so it cost me $15,000 all together for us to have our freedom again. Star got the money from me and Brew’s condo. It was hidden under my bed in a pair of old military boots. I hugged her and thanked her, and then I told her that I would talk to her later.

The first thing we tried to do was withdraw the money from our business account, but the account had a hold on it. We had over $700,000 in the account and we could not touch it. The police said that all the money was made illegally. Now I was really angry because I did not expect the police to freeze all of the assets of the Key Club.

A few days later, I called Brew and Ricardo to set up a meeting. I wanted to find out what in the hell was going on with the liquor license that we paid $50,000 to get. I decided to talk to a lawyer before I had the meeting so I could find out exactly where I stood. I explained to the lawyer that if the license was not real, I didn't know it. She explained that if I could get Brew to admit he bought the fake license without my knowledge, she would get me and Ricardo off the hook for the crime. She also said that the employees would not have to worry about a thing either, she would handle everything. She needed $25,000 cash to do that. I told her that I would get back to her after I talked to my partners.

I met with my partners at the club a couple of days later to talk about what happened. I did not want to talk business in the club because I did not know if it was bugged or not. So I decided that we should go to "Water Country", where they had all water rides. We took swimming trunks so we could talk while we were in the water. I could also make sure no one was wired. Before I got into the water I looked around in the park and all I saw was happiness on the faces of all the families. I thought to myself, this is how it is supposed to be, but not for me, I am going in the water to discuss how to stay out of prison.

I asked Brew what was the deal with the liquor license. He paused for a moment and then he started by saying how sorry he was for what he did. He told us that he found a guy who could get him a license for $5,000. He said the guy told him that it would look just like the real one so he purchased it. I asked him what he did with the $45,000 that he saved from not buying a real liquor license.

Brew told me that he had a gambling problem and he owed the money to his bookie. I asked him how long had he been gambling like that. Brew said, "I have been gambling for a long time. I just realized that I could not stop gambling about a year ago". I explained to him what he needed to do for the police to drop the cases against everyone else. Brew agreed to do it without hesitation. Not only was he a dope head, he also was addicted to gambling. Can I count on him being a stand up guy? He knows enough to send me and Ricardo to prison for a long time. The only thing the police have on him right now is that fake liquor license. If they get something else on him, I might have to consider killing him. I would rather be dead than to spend twenty years in prison.

A few weeks later all the charges were dismissed against everyone except Brew and he plea bargained out by paying a large fine and five years probation. My business with Ricardo and Brew had to change because of what Ricardo did when he helped move Star. I still was treating Ricardo the same way because I did not want to let him know that I knew what he did. When the time was right, I knew that I was going to quit dealing with Ricardo. I cannot deal with anyone that I cannot trust. Now Brew had a criminal record and was on probation. So I can't trust him anymore.

I had to be able to count on my partners in this life or death business. I felt like if I continued to deal drugs in Virginia, I would die or go to prison. I moved out of Brew's condo and moved into a hotel. I moved out without telling anyone. Brew just came home one day and I was gone. As far as I was concerned the business was over for me. They can continue on, I don't want anything to do with it or them. The Key Club is dead to me....

I had been so busy making money that I never had time to spend it. Now maybe I will have time to do something with the money. Maybe I can get my wife and kids back and then move out of Virginia to a quiet place. Put all this bullshit behind me and try to live a normal life. I had money buried all over Virginia, and I wanted to make sure the money was in a safer place. It took me a whole week to dig up all the money. But when I did, the money added up to $3,000,000.

I was the first millionaire to come from Jackson Street. I didn't even know it until I counted my money. I wanted to make sure that no matter what happened to me, I would always be a millionaire. I separated one million from the money. I drove for six and a half hours to bury the money somewhere that was part of what I have become. I promised myself that I would never touch that money again. As long as the money was there, I would always be a millionaire.

I had not seen or talked to Brew or Ricardo since we agreed that Brew would take the charge for the liquor license. I closed down all my clothing stores and was living at the Red Roof Inn in Hampton, Va. No one knew that I was staying at the hotel and that's the way I wanted it to be. I had been staying there for six months. I was working out at the gym that was at the hotel. I needed this time to figure out what I was going to do with the rest of my life. I decided to give Star a call and ask her could I come over to see her and the kids. She said okay. I was happy to hear her voice again. I'm hoping that I can find a happy ending to my journey….

I wanted to talk to her about her future plans with my kids and maybe me. When I got to her house and saw how she looked, I was shocked and disturbed about it. She was a crack addict and she looked like one. It was very upsetting for me to see her like that. She had lost a lot of weight and her face was beginning to look sunk in, like she was terminally ill. I asked her where the kids were and she said that they had been living with her mother in Brownsville for the last six months. She said that she and Robin lived together and Robin was at work right now.

I wondered if Mrs. Woods knew that Robin was living with all this drug activity going on here. It seemed like every five minutes Star kept going into her bedroom to get high. I could tell that she was getting high because of the way she was acting after she would come out the room. She smelled and talked funny when she came out of the bedroom. I asked her if she was getting high, and she denied it each time. I stayed for about one hour and I could not take it anymore. She asked me not to leave, but I told her that had to take care of some business.

When I left Star's apartment, I was planning on driving to Mrs. Wood's house and tell her about how Robin was living. I hoped Robin had enough sense to not try drugs. I knew that would kill Mrs. Woods if her baby got hooked on drugs. I started towards the door. Star grabbed hold of my arm and started to cry. She fell to her knees, holding on to my leg, saying please, please don't go.

I broke free and told her that I had to, but that I would be back soon. Star said that she was scared that if I went out that door, she would never see me again. She was really in bad shape, I felt sorry for her. I smiled and said I would see you tomorrow. I opened the door and stepped out on the porch. Star slammed the door behind me as if she didn't want to be seen. I looked back to see why she slammed the door shut so fast. Before I knew it, someone was firing bullets at me.

I dropped to the ground and started firing back towards the sounds of the gunfire as I was crawling towards my car. I could not see who or how many people were shooting at me because it was so dark outside. I knew it was more than one person because of how often I heard gunfire. The only thing that I could see was the red flashes coming from the barrels of the guns. I stayed low to the ground as the bullets were flying over my head. The bullets that were flying pass my head sounded like bees buzzing next to my ears.

While all this craziness was going on I did hear a familiar voice. It was the voice of Steady, Troy's cousin, shouting "kill that motherfucker before he gets to his car". I didn't want to waste any bullets because I only had fifteen rounds. I crawled up to a large tree and stayed there to evaluate the situation a little better. Bullets were striking the tree repeatedly. I couldn't get a clear shot at anyone. The shooting stopped and I could hear whispering about fifty feet away. I couldn't tell what they were saying. I was hoping that Star would have called the police by now. So far there was no sign of any help coming.

They started firing again, but this time the bullets seem to be coming from a different direction. They must have changed their locations. It would be bad news for me if I let them surround me. So I started crawling again towards my car. This seemed to be the only chance I had. I didn't shoot my gun because I didn't want to give my position away. Either they are bad shooters or there is an Angel watching over me. I finally made my way to my car and crawled into the driver's seat. Bullets were crashing through the windshield, throwing glass all over my face; I could hardly see to drive.

I got my car started and began racing down the highway, with my attackers following behind me in their car. They were hanging out the car windows shooting at my car. They didn't give a fuck who saw them. I couldn't shoot back and steer my car. This was like something out of the movies. Both our cars were doing over a hundred miles per hour and sometimes faster. I was crossing the Chesapeake Bay Bridge when one of the bullets shot out one of my tires. I began to lose control of the car. My car went across the median and started riding along the rail on the side of the highway. I could see sparks coming from the side of my car. The whole car started shaking real bad. I could smell burned metal and rubber.

Before I could do anything, the car flipped in the air over the rail towards the water. I closed my eyes because I did not want to see where I was heading. I braced myself for the pending impact. I put my arms around my head right before I was slammed up against the dashboard. I must have blacked out from the impact. When I opened my eyes again, half the car was in the ocean and sinking fast. I tried to get out the car, but I could not get the doors open for some reason. Water was up to my neck and there was nothing I could do to save myself from drowning. I made one last attempt to get out of the car, but the door would not budge.

I'm not sure how long I was in the water because everything seemed to be happening so fast to me. I didn't want to die from drowning. Since I was a kid I always had a fear of drowning. I rather kill myself then drown so I reached down to get my gun and put it to my head. Without thinking, I pulled the trigger, but the gun did not go off. I continued to pull the trigger, nothing happened. I guess the gun was too wet or I was just meant to drown like a fucking Jackson Street creek rat….

Reflecting back: after all those years of making it through all the floods on Jackson Street, finally the water was going to win and take my life. I remember how I used to taunt the flood waters by saying; "You will never get me no matter how hard you try". Only the one year on Jackson Street is when I really get scared. That was because the water came up to the second floor of our house. We had to be rescued by a boat that day, which was a close call for me:

Tears came to my eyes as the water started to cover my face. I took one last deep breath as sadness came over me that I had never felt before. There was so many people that I wanted to apologize to for bringing sadness and destruction into their lives. I wanted to say goodbye to Star and the kids, I wanted to say goodbye to Ann and my daughter. I wanted to see Mrs. Woods and the girls one last time. I wish I had a chance to do things differently in my life. I would like to be able to help other young people so that they do not make the same mistakes. I wished I could have at least donated the $2,000,000 to some organization that tries to help troubled youth. I wish that I had someone to help guide me when I was a kid. Maybe I would not be in this situation right now. Maybe if I would have tried harder to follow God's word. Maybe deep down inside I wanted to die. Maybe it is easier to die then it is to fight my demons. I guess it is time to find out….

I was beginning to feel like I was floating in the air towards a bright light in the sky. I heard voices coming from the light. I could not make out what the voices were saying to me. When I get closer to the light, I began to see who the voices were coming from. The voices were coming from some nuns who were sitting on the porch of my old house on Jackson Street. They were sitting there with my father, my brother Harry and my dog Tiger waving for me to come on. The three Nuns sitting there were dressed in white robes smiling at me passionately. I felt a wave of relaxation run through my body. I was slowly floating towards them. It was like I was being pulled by some unseen force. Everything about this whole situation felt right to me. I had no urge to resist any of this….

Before I knew it I was standing in front of my house on Jackson Street. One of the Nuns stood up and looked at my father and said, "Go now". He smiled at her and took Harry and Tiger inside the house. The Nun looked at me and said, "Hello Ron, we have been waiting on you to get here". She said, "We are here to help you so that you can devote your life to helping troubled youth". She said "We are going to guide you on this path of work that has been started by us, long before you were born". She said "When you get on this path of helping children you will not understand why or how. You will not be able to change your path, no matter how hard you try". She said, "Everything that you have been through in life was to get you ready for your true purpose. Your purpose is to help young people to believe in change". She said my final piece of advice is, "It is easier to teach when you have become an example of what you are teaching"….

I woke up three days later in a hospital at the Norfolk Naval Base; I thought that I was dead. The nurse told me that the coast guard found me lying on the shore hardly breathing, with a concussion. She said that the coast guard had to revive me three times, because my heart stopped beating while they were taking me to the hospital. The nurse said that now that I was recovering so well, the doctors said I could leave in about a week. She asked me if I remembered what happened to me that night. I told her that I had a tire blow out and I lost control of my car.

She said that the police were going to ask me some questions because they found bullet holes in my car. The nurse said that the police found over twenty bullet holes in my car. She said, "You must have had Angels looking over you. I told her I did not know about Angels, but I did have a feeling there might be some Nuns that were helping me. Maybe they weren't Nuns; maybe they were Angels who looked like Nuns. The police did come a few days later, but I told them that I did not know who was trying to kill me. I wanted to have the pleasure of getting my attackers myself.

Once I got out of the hospital, I called Robin and told her that I needed to see her. She met me at her mother's house the next day. Mrs. Woods wasn't home when we got there. We began to talk about what happened to me at Star's apartment. She said, "Everyone thought that you were dead because they didn't find your body in the car. She said it took the coast guard a couple days to figure out who you was". I did not know that everyone thought that I was dead until I heard that.

Robin told me that it was Star that told Steady that I was coming over to her house. Robin said, "Steady is the one who got Star hooked on drugs. She would do anything to get more drugs, even set you up to get killed". This was a fucked up feeling to know that Star tried to get me killed for some crack. As I think back, she did slam the door shut when I walked out. She was begging me not to go out the door. Maybe she had second thoughts about letting me be killed. I guess at the end, she was trying to fight that (Crack Demon)….

Robin said that when Brew and Ricardo heard about what Steady did to me, they had a big shoot out. Steady was dead and they arrested Brew and Ricardo. She also told me that Star got shot when a bullet went through the door and it struck her in the arm. I told Robin that was good for the bitch; she should have got shot in the head. She would be better off dead rather than to be a drug addict.

I knew that I had to get out of Virginia, but I just was not sure of where to go. I also knew that I did not want anything to do with the drug money that I made. I knew my life was spared for a reason. I believe that the reason was for me to help other young people who could be heading into destruction like I was. I decided to donate the drug money to an organization in Pittsburgh, Pa, that was created and run by Nuns. The organization is over 100 years old. The mission of the organization was to help troubled youth and their families. They did this by giving the children a place to live and putting love back into their lives. I wish that I could have known a place like that when I was a kid. Sounds like a wonderful place….

I wanted a fresh start so I decided to go to Philadelphia a few weeks later to work with my brother, Gary. He needed some help in his home improvement business. He lived a clean life and was a church going man so that is where I needed to be. When I left Virginia, the only things I took were seven suitcases full of clothes and a hundred dollars in my pocket. My brother picked me up at the Philadelphia Airport, and we stacked all the suitcases in his red van. He told me that he had to make a stop at his girlfriend's house to give her something.

I told him that I would wait in the van. I decided to get out the van to smoke a cigarette and that's when I saw this girl walking towards me. She had a red winter coat on and big hair rollers in her hair. She seemed to be walking in slow motion towards me. I could not stop staring at her for some reason. When she walked close to me, her eyes met mine. She said hello and I said hello to her as she moved pass me slowly. There was something very special about her. It was like I met her before….

That night in Philadelphia, on New Years Eve in (1988), was when I knew who was going to take me into my next chapter of my life. When the girl walked by me the visions of the Nuns came back to me. They told me that girl would be the one to take me where I was supposed to be. I believe that everything

I do is because that is what God wants me to do. Everything that I did in my past was to prepare me for what I am going to do next in my life. If I can change, then anyone can. My past creative my purpose for life….

If you read this story and you are able to figure out where I buried the million dollars, please do the right thing with the money. A lot of hearts were shattered because of this money, I believe the money is cursed with death, betrayal and broken dreams. I tried to find happiness with the money, and I couldn't. This leads me to believe that money has nothing to do with happiness. I have gone to the place where the money is buried for the last 15 years out of curiosity. So I know it is still there. There has been a few times when I thought about taking a few hundred thousand, but I fought the urges of the Devil. The story will tell you where the money is and if you decide to look for it, remember I told you the money is cursed…. More to come!!!

"Believe in Change and you will"

The End

About the Author

I have two degrees, one in "Child and Family Studies" and another in "Psychology". I' am now pursuing a master's degree in Developmental Psychology at the University of Pittsburgh. I also work with troubled youth as a primary youth counselor at a group home in Pittsburgh, Pa. I' am currently writing my second book titled "The heart of a panther"; based on the real life story of my daughter Latia Ronnelle Howard. She also was a student at the "University of Pittsburgh". She was a basketball star for the lady panthers until she had heart problems. She was not able to continue her love for basketball at the university. This book will be completed in the summer of 2007, so be ready for a great story. My third book will be about the troubled children who are put in placement. This book will be based on real stories from the children that I met while working as a Youth Counselor in Pittsburgh, Pa... At your request, there will be a sequel to the book "From the bottom to the Top, The Jackson Street Dreamer". Let me hear from you at jacksonstreetdreamer@yahoo.com "God Bless"

*Thank You for reading my book.... "**Believe in Change**"*
Ron Howard